THE
ARABIAN NIGHTS

THE
ARABIAN NIGHTS
THEIR BEST-KNOWN TALES

•

EDITED BY
KATE DOUGLAS WIGGIN AND NORA A. SMITH

ILLUSTRATED BY MAXFIELD PARRISH

INTRODUCTION BY MARK HELPRIN

QUALITY PAPERBACK BOOK CLUB

NEW YORK

CONTENTS

INTRODUCTION

THE RIVERS OF BABYLON, AND GULNARE OF THE SEA

✦

The book you hold in your hand may be more of a mystery than you think. The tales of *The Arabian Nights*, or *A Thousand Nights and A Night* (in Arabic, *Alf Laylah wa Laylah*), have been so well assimilated throughout the world that they are sometimes mistaken for part of the culture that receives them, or as a component of universal human memory passed from one generation to the next effortlessly and in a thousand mercurial forms. This despite the fact that, as everyone knows, they are the product of medieval Islamic civilization, from the Atlantic coast of Morocco to the Brahmaputra, from Socotra to Tashkent. Though heavily drawn from the hinterlands, from Persia, and India, they are most comfortably identified with Baghdad and the Arab Middle East. This is about as much as is certain of their origins, which is no more satisfying than knowing that *Hamlet*, for example, was written somewhere between the Mediterranean and the North Sea, in the middle of the second millennium, in English of course, a Scandinavian tale that nonetheless seems to have been associated with London.

But *Hamlet* is a part of the English written language, and however inexact its origins and editions they are a model of precision compared to those of *A Thousand Nights and A Night*, which, like the *Iliad* and the *Odyssey*, was carried upon the meandering currents of an oral tradition. The texts of the *Iliad* and the *Odyssey* were stabilized much more quickly than that of *A Thousand Nights and A Night*, the written word beginning to supplant the Greek oral tradition within a century or two of Homer, his epics recorded early enough to prevent them from becoming works in progress.

A Thousand Nights and A Night is still a work in progress, and is likely to remain so if only because, born in a tradition of scholarship entirely different from our own, it has no definitive text. It might have, but unlike the works of Homer it was not seen as a font of culture and legitimacy and thus worthy of careful and exact preservation, as in the case, for example, of the *Koran*.

This edition, the work of Kate Douglas Wiggin, is based on two previous English translations of two different Arabic texts. Both translators revised, rearranged, and abridged their versions, and one was just beginning his study of Arabic. Their disparate sources each consisted of varying overlays, composites, and alterations, and each was derived from multiple branches of an inexact oral tradition and written fragments that had been accumulating for a thousand years. The dozens of sources are enough to overwhelm any translator and force him to his own invention. Layered one upon the other, they sometimes jump from Arabic or Farsi into a European language and back, only to be retranslated into a European language and then from that one into another, all the while subject to alterations dictated by changing mores, theology, and politics.

Add to this the confusion of transliteration. The original in this case is born of multiple languages (Arabic, Farsi, and the languages of the Indian subcontinent), the Arabic expressed in numerous dialects each having its own particular slant on the classical literary language. Among all these languages and dialects are syntactical ambiguities and sounds that do not exist in the destination language. Translations were rendered into French, German, English, etc., and complicated by idiosyncratic systems of transliteration imported sometimes even from other languages. This is not to mention the literary difficulties and frumped-up prose style of many a translator: "Verily did Aladdin, seeking the girth of the wretched mule. . . ."

The only solution for these problems would be for every reader to learn classical literary Arabic so as to be able to study the mottled and inauthoritative Arabic texts with a modicum of linguistic coherence. Though to one acquainted with Arabic poor transliteration may be irritating, probably the best that can be hoped for are just plain consistency, and, not unimportantly, modesty, by which I mean accepting that some sounds in Arabic simply cannot be expressed in the Roman alphabet without entirely misleading everyone except the inventor of the transliteration. Unavoidably, the magnificent sound of the prose and poetry is lost, including even most of the names that so often find repetition. This is especially unfortunate in the case of *A Thousand Nights and A Night*, as part of its contemporary function was to serve as a kind of music. In those days (when music was rare if only because it required live musicians) language was much more like song than it is now, writing more like singing, and often it actually was singing.

What you have before you is a text that is as inexact as if you had heard it from a

INTRODUCTION

singer at the end of a chain of a thousand of his kind. It is a product that, echoing the culture it reflects, is ambiguous, enigmatic, and subject to authoritative interpretation no more than are the clouds. This is partly why, despite a thousand years of floating on whatever tide rose to take it, it has survived. As sometimes happens in the case of a powerless captive abducted to a far country, commanded to forget, dressed in strange clothes, and obliged to speak until the end in an alien language, the essence remains, and it is by this essence, which in man is the soul, that we know it.

Despite centuries of almost accidental transmission, *A Thousand Nights and A Night* still peerlessly represents a thousand years of the history of a place riven by countless variations in ethnicity, language, culture, and terrain. To understand these stories for what they are, however, it is necessary to distinguish between what they say about the milieu in which they were spawned and what they say about who wrote them. This is a distinction of particular subtlety because it is hard to know where the imprint of the civilization ends and the stress of the author begins. One clue may be found in the intense dream-like quality of *A Thousand Nights and A Night*, which is excessive even for a society that leans in that direction.

The Semite, T. E. Lawrence observes in *The Seven Pillars of Wisdom*, possessed "a universal clearness or hardness of belief, almost mathematical in its limitation, and repellent in its unsympathetic form. Semites [by which, in this case, Lawrence means Arabs] had no half-tones in their register of vision. They were a people of primary colors, or rather of black and white, who saw the world always in contour. They were a dogmatic people, despising doubt, our modern crown of thorns. They did not understand our metaphysical difficulties, our introspective questionings. They knew only truth and untruth, belief and unbelief, without our hesitating retinue of finer shades. . . ." They "showed a completeness of instinct, a reliance upon intuition, the unperceived foreknown, which left our centrifugal minds gasping."

Islam arose in the desert and will forever carry the stamp of the desert's utterly blue skies and arduous heat, of seemingly whole continents of silence, of cold black nights in which the stars burn like some sort of munition. The certainty of belief to which Lawrence refers is not only a reflection of the desert's absolute and even brutally clear definitions, but also a defense against its powers of disorientation. As if on the open sea, one needs a point of origin from which all movement may stem. With this (and a means to find it at any moment) you can go anywhere in any trackless waste, without fear that you will not return. Thus the tendency to dream in a society where all questions have been settled with passionate certainty, which mirrors the injunction to "live like a bourgeois, so that you may write like a wild man."

And if you have ever seen a line of camel-borne Bedouin suddenly appear in the desert's color-waving heat, robes as black as charcoal, rifles across their backs, you will understand that to live in such a place, indeed, to look back at it as the well of your legitimacy, you must be at ease with legends and dreams.

Western civilization has achieved its unparalleled power and depth because it is the battleground of contending principles: paganism and spirituality; reason and aesthetic; social order and individual freedom; North (as principle) and South (as principle); the Dionysian and the Apollonian; and so forth, with victories and near victories visiting one camp and then the other, sawing lazily back and forth across history in a grand equilibrium that, in a Hegelian sense, advances nonetheless. We have been engaged in these debates since the first days of the Israelites, and the terms are so constant that we sometimes forget we are debating. By the same token, we do not always realize that we view the products of other civilizations as auxiliaries to our own partisanship. This we do quite readily, just as we absorb words and ideas from other places, without second thought.

Islamic (and especially Arab) civilization prides itself not on its ability to change but upon its stability. It is not dynamic in the sense that it progresses, and as it weathers time its enduring energy is directed not to exploration, experimentation, or advancement, but to return to its origins, to seek out the pure, and to achieve stillness and perfection. Thus it has little need for half of the spectrum we take for granted in the West. Though Manichean in other senses, the civilization of the Arabs is unconcerned with a duality in which reason is one of the piers: reason is simply irrelevant. Though we tend to view Arabic literature as weighing against reason in our own debate, it simply isn't so: the terms are different.

And that they are affords us more of an opportunity than simply enlisting them in our struggles. It affords us the chance of escape. This generally is what is meant when *A Thousand Nights and A Night* is presented under the rubric of the exotic. At first blush the world of Islam may seem remarkably alien, but, with a second look, it can strike us as remarkably like our own. Conversely, it may at first seem inexplicably familiar, and then appear totally baffling. Just as the Near and Middle East have been the anteroom to the distant world of the Orient, the airlock between East and West, so its literature is a portal to a world of dreams. It is easier of access if only because we share with it many common references: our religions have sprung from the same well and in the same place, and we

INTRODUCTION

have been battling one another for so many centuries that our histories are tightly intertwined.

Still, *A Thousand Nights and A Night* is more fanciful, less contentious, and less deliberate than Arabic literature and discourse in general. It seems to have been isolated from any borrowing except from the East, to have been unaffected by the currents of rationalism that have been part of Middle Eastern history as a result of its inescapable contact with the West. Perhaps even more significantly, it is, apart from hollow ritual evocations of the name of God, an almost entirely secular work in a world of deeply felt and omnipresent spirituality. This cannot be explained away by citing Persia and India as influences, because on the whole the cloth from which these stories are cut is indisputably of the Near and Middle East. What, then, accounts for their unusual cast, their somewhat alien perspective? I believe it is their authorship, and that they are not quite what they seem.

As the centuries passed in the absence of a fixed text, virtually anything resembling the original stories was eligible for inclusion, but just as the collectors of the marginal tales could know what kind of story to include, we can discern representative attributes of the core. Running unavoidably throughout *A Thousand Nights and A Night* are the themes of captivity, escape, the restoration of a shattered past, and voyages in strange and frightening lands.

One story after another is about female slaves and their relations with their masters, told in such knowing and often erotic detail (though only in the Victorian sense and not in these selections) that they must have been written by someone who knew the Seraglio. They are frequently told with strikingly mechanical deference to the master's wishes and beliefs, though mainly with the idea of correcting them. More often than not they are couched in the kind of language that suggests a talent for maneuvering in a state of complete and hopeless submission. They are wistful and at times even heartbreaking in their evocations of the pain of being torn from a previous life.

A slave is by necessity the master of dreams. Much of imaginative literature springs from a condition of the mind and spirit seeking relief from inescapable oppression, whether it be approaching death, personal failure, grief, slavery, disease, or any of the endlessly inventive unpleasantries common to mankind. As a child I was always drawn to the lyric of the American slaves, "Swing low, sweet chariot, coming for to carry me home." Totally and acceptably within the context of an alien religion that had been adopted in captivity, justifiable to the masters as Christian piety, this was also a song about Africa and a past that only the first generations knew directly. I doubt that even now, so many years later and after the crossing of so many bridges, this spiritual can be sung in a Black church without the same ambiguity.

The anthem of the German concentration camps was the old Silesian song "*Die Gedanken Sind Frei* (Thoughts Are Free)," and for good reason, as the only escape from the grief and horror of these places was on the wings of the spirit and in the eye of the mind. So with the story of Moses, in which the sea opened for the captives of Egypt and a pillar of fire led them through the desert. No influence in literature has been more powerful than the longing for reconstitution, for regaining paradise, for the resurrection of life and love lost.

In the pages that follow is the story of "The Talking Bird, the Singing Tree, and the Golden Water." Here, it appears, are the disguised longings of a woman who was done a terrible injustice. Her remedies are found solely in dreaming, in impossible magic, in imagination spurred shamelessly by hope. Throughout, she remains bereft, and is saved only by preternatural intervention and the grace and luck afforded her children. It seems as much a cry for mercy as a wish for magic, an attempt to influence an unfeeling husband without offending him in the slightest, not only by means of ceaseless flattery but also, in the depiction of the two evil sisters, in letting him off the hook. In the end, a woman in cruel captivity is restored to her rightful place, her lost children found, the past resurrected.

Quite apart from a vigorous regional trade in slaves and the laments of daughters traded away in marriage, many a captive was brought to the heart of the Middle East from the Christian and pagan lands to the west and north. Military expeditions and merchants would return from the Danube and the Volga, from Africa and India, with boys for the army and girls for the *hareem*. Though the captives often rose to prominence, and sometimes to pre-eminence, they seldom returned to the world they had known.

In these selections is the story of "Gulnare of the Sea," which reads like a tale told by a captive woman from a different civilization—perhaps Slavic, European, or Chinese—who has lived for a long time in the court of a Muslim ruler. She knows the customs and requirements, is loyal and submissive, and has made peace with her fate, but a wonderful, jewel-like window remains open to her love of a distant past. And this she elevates into something much like a dream. Despite its imperfections and the inadequacy of the translation, the story is both remarkable and touching. Her lost family walks in the greater world of the sea. She cannot go back to them, but they come to her, summoned by the powers of her imagination.

The frame in which the tales of *A Thousand Nights and A Night* are set is the account of Shahrazad, who by means of storytelling (certainly the women of a *hareem* had call to

INTRODUCTION

invent entertainments for those whom they served and also to pass the time) saves her own life and those of the other women of the kingdom from the wrath of an omnipotent king. I would chance to believe that this is not merely a device, but the poetic expression of the historical truth of these stories, that they arose from the longing of captives, primarily but not solely women, whose only choice in life was to fashion a world of dreams.

The great value of the tales of A Thousand Nights and A Night, absent their original musicality in the language in which they were composed, lies in their capacity to lift the reader into another world, and indeed, their world is far different from our own. But that is not all. The principal stories have a strange resonance, which suggests a certain mystery, that they are not entirely what they seem, and that perhaps they can be read not as mere diversions but as a cri de coeur.

And if this is so, it would not be the first time, as we know from the beginning of Psalm 137:

> By the rivers of Babylon, there we sat down, yea,
> we wept, when we remembered Zion.
>
> We hanged our harps upon the willows in the midst
> thereof.
>
> For there they that carried us away captive
> required of us a song; and they that wasted
> of us required of us mirth. . . .

—Mark Helprin
New York, 1996

PREFACE

LITTLE excuse is needed, perhaps, for any fresh selection from the famous "Tales of a Thousand and One Nights," provided it be representative enough, and worthy enough, to enlist a new army of youthful readers.   Of the two hundred and sixty-four bewildering, unparalleled stories, the true lover can hardly spare one, yet there must always be favourites, even among these.   We have chosen some of the most delightful, in our opinion; some, too, that chanced to appeal particularly to the genius of the artist.   If, enticed by our choice and the beauty of the pictures, we manage to attract a few thousand more true lovers to the fountain-book, we shall have served our humble turn.   The only real danger lies in neglecting it, in rearing a child who does not know it and has never fallen under its spell.

You remember Maimoune, in the story of Prince Camaralzaman, and what she said to Danhasch, the genie who had just arrived from the farthest limits of China?   "Be sure thou tellest me nothing but what is true or I shall clip thy wings!"   This is what the modern child sometimes says to the genies of literature, and his own wings are too often clipped in consequence.

> "The Empire of the Fairies is no more.
> Reason has banished them from ev'ry shore;
> Steam has outstripped their dragons and their cars,
> Gas has eclipsed their glow-worms and their stars."

Edouard Laboulaye says in his introduction to Nouveaux Contes Bleus: "Mothers who love your children, do not set them too soon to the study of history; let them dream while they are young.   Do not close the soul to the first breath of poetry.   Noth-

ing affrights me so much as the reasonable, practical child who believes in nothing that he cannot touch. These sages of ten years are, at twenty, dullards, or what is still worse, egoists."

When a child has once read of Prince Agib, of Gulnare or Periezade, Sinbad or Codadad, in this or any other volume of its kind, the magic will have been instilled into the blood, for the Oriental flavour in the Arab tales is like nothing so much as magic. True enough they are a vast storehouse of information concerning the manners and the customs, the spirit and the life of the Moslem East (and the youthful reader does not have to study Lane's learned foot-notes to imbibe all this), but beyond and above the knowledge of history and geography thus gained, there comes something finer and subtler as well as something more vital. The scene is Indian, Egyptian, Arabian, Persian; but Bagdad and Balsora, Grand Cairo, the silver Tigris, and the blooming gardens of Damascus, though they can be found indeed on the map, live much more truly in that enchanted realm that rises o'er "the foam of perilous seas in faery lands forlorn." What craft can sail those perilous seas like the book that has been called a great three-decker to carry tired people to Islands of the Blest? "The immortal fragment," says Sir Richard Burton, who perhaps knew the Arabian Nights as did no other European, "will never be superseded in the infallible judgment of childhood. The marvellous imaginativeness of the Tales produces an insensible brightness of mind and an increase of fancy-power, making one dream that behind them lies the new and unseen, the strange and unexpected—in fact, all the glamour of the unknown."

It would be a delightful task to any boy or girl to begin at the beginning and read the first English version of these famous stories, made from the collection of M. Galland, Professor of Arabic in the Royal College of Paris. The fact that they had passed from

PREFACE

Arabic into French and from French into English did not prevent their instantaneous popularity. This was in 1704 or thereabouts, and the world was not so busy as it is nowadays, or young men would not have gathered in the middle of the night under M. Galland's window and cried: "O vous, qui savez de si jolis contes, et qui les racontez si bien, racontez nous en un!"

You can also read them in Scott's edition or in Lane's (both of which, but chiefly the former, we have used as the foundation of our text), while your elders—philologists or Orientalists—are studying the complete versions of John Payne or Sir Richard Burton. You may leave the wiseacres to wonder which were told in China or India, Arabia or Persia, and whether the first manuscript dates back to 1450 or earlier.

We, like many other editors, have shortened the stories here and there, omitting some of the tedious repetitions that crept in from time to time when Arabian story-tellers were adding to the text to suit their purposes.

Mr. Andrew Lang says amusingly that he has left out of his special versions "all the pieces that are suitable only for Arabs and old gentlemen," and we have done the same; but we have taken no undue liberties. We have removed no genies nor magicians, however terrible; have cut out no base deed of Vizier nor noble deed of Sultan; have diminished the size of no roc's egg, nor omitted any single allusion to the great and only Haroun Alraschid, Caliph of Bagdad, Commander of the Faithful, who must have been a great inspirer of good stories.

Enter into this "treasure house of pleasant things," then, and make yourself at home in the golden palaces, the gem-studded caves, the bewildering gardens. Sit by its mysterious fountains, hear the plash of its gleaming cascades, unearth its magic lamps and talismans, behold its ensorcelled princes and princesses.

PREFACE

Nowhere in the whole realm of literature will you find such a Marvel, such a Wonder, such a Nonesuch of a book; nowhere will you find impossibilities so real and so convincing; nowhere but in what Henley calls:

> " . . . *that blessèd brief*
>   *Of what is gallantest and best*
> *In all the full-shelved Libraries of Romance.*
>   *The Book of rocs,*
>   *Sandalwood, ivory, turbans, ambergris,*
> *Cream-tarts, and lettered apes, and Calenders,*
>   *And ghouls, and genies—O so huge*
> *They might have overed the tall Minster Tower,*
>   *Hands down, as schoolboys take a post;*
> *In truth the Book of Camaralzaman,*
> *Schemselnihar and Sinbad, Scheherezade*
>   *The peerless, Bedreddin, Badroulbadour,*
>   *Cairo and Serendib and Candahar,*
> *And Caspian, and the dim, terrific bulk—*
> *Ice-ribbed, fiend-visited, isled in spells and storms—*
>   *Of Kaf . . . That centre of miracles*
>   *The sole, unparalleled Arabian Nights.*"

KATE DOUGLAS WIGGIN.

August, 1909.

ILLUSTRATIONS

FROM DRAWINGS IN COLORS
BY MAXFIELD PARRISH

ILLUSTRATIONS

THE
ARABIAN NIGHTS

"When the breeze of a joyful dawn blew free
   In the silken sail of infancy,
   The tide of time flow'd back with me,
      The forward-flowing time of time;
   And many a sheeny summer morn,
   Adown the Tigris I was borne,
   By Bagdat's shrines of fretted gold,
   High-walled gardens green and old;
      True Mussulman was I and sworn,
         For it was in the golden prime
            Of good Haroun Alraschid.

"Anight my shallop, rustling thro'
      The low and bloomèd foliage, drove
      The fragrant, glistening deeps, and clove
   The citron-shadows in the blue:
      By garden porches on the brim,
   The costly doors flung open wide,
      Gold glittering thro' lamplight dim,
   And broider'd sofas on each side:
      In sooth it was a goodly time,
      For it was in the golden prime
         Of good Haroun Alraschid."

ALFRED, LORD TENNYSON.

THE TALKING BIRD, THE SINGING TREE, AND THE GOLDEN WATER

THERE was an emperor of Persia named Kosrouschah, who, when he first came to his crown, in order to obtain a knowledge of affairs, took great pleasure in night excursions, attended by a trusty minister. He often walked in disguise through the city, and met with many adventures, one of the most remarkable of which happened to him upon his first ramble, which was not long after his accession to the throne of his father.

After the ceremonies of his father's funeral rites and his own inauguration were over, the new sultan, as well from inclination as from duty, went out one evening attended by his grand vizier, disguised like himself, to observe what was transacting in the city. As he was passing through a street in that part of the town inhabited only by the meaner sort, he heard some people talking very loud; and going close to the house whence the noise proceeded, and looking through a crack in the door, perceived a light, and three sisters sitting on a sofa, conversing together after supper. By what the eldest said he presently understood the subject of their conversation was wishes: "for," said she, "since we are talking about wishes, mine shall be to have the sultan's baker for my husband, for then I shall eat my fill of that bread, which by way of excellence is called the sultan's; let us see if your tastes are as good as mine." "For my part," replied the second sister,

"I wish I was wife to the sultan's chief cook, for then I should eat of the most excellent dishes; and as I am persuaded that the sultan's bread is common in the palace, I should not want any of that; therefore you see," addressing herself to her eldest sister, "that I have a better taste than you." The youngest sister, who was very beautiful, and had more charms and wit than the two elder, spoke in her turn: "For my part, sisters," said she, "I shall not limit my desires to such trifles, but take a higher flight; and since we are upon wishing, I wish to be the emperor's queen-consort. I would make him father of a prince, whose hair should be gold on one side of his head, and silver on the other; when he cried, the tears from his eyes should be pearls; and when he smiled, his vermilion lips should look like a rosebud fresh-blown."

The three sisters' wishes, particularly that of the youngest, seemed so singular to the sultan, that he resolved to gratify them in their desires; but without communicating his design to his grand vizier, he charged him only to take notice of the house, and bring the three sisters before him the following day.

The grand vizier, in executing the emperor's orders, would but just give the sisters time to dress themselves to appear before his majesty, without telling them the reason. He brought them to the palace, and presented them to the emperor, who said to them, "Do you remember the wishes you expressed last night, when you were all in so pleasant a mood? Speak the truth; I must know what they were." At these unexpected words of the emperor, the three sisters were much confounded. They cast down their eyes and blushed, and the colour which rose in the cheeks of the youngest quite captivated the emperor's heart. Modesty, and fear lest they might have offended by their conversation, kept them silent. The emperor, perceiving their confusion, said to encourage them, "Fear nothing, I did not send for you to distress you; and since I see that without my intending it, this is the effect of the question I asked, as I know the wish of each, I will relieve you from your fears. You," added he, "who wished to be my wife, shall have your desire this day; and you," continued he, addressing himself to the two elder sisters, "shall also be married to my chief baker and cook."

As soon as the sultan had declared his pleasure, the youngest sister, setting her elders an example, threw herself at the emperor's feet to express her gratitude. "Sir," said she, "my wish, since it is come to your majesty's knowledge, was expressed only in the way of conversation and amusement. I am unworthy of the honour you do me, and supplicate your pardon for my presumption." The other two sisters would have excused themselves also, but the emperor, interrupting them, said, "No, no; it shall be as I have declared; the wishes of all shall be fulfilled." The nuptials were all celebrated that day, as the emperor had resolved, but in a different manner. The youngest sister's were solemnized with all the rejoicings usual at the marriages of the emperors of Persia; and those of the other two sisters according to the quality and distinction of their husbands; the one as the sultan's chief baker, and the other as head cook.

The two elder felt strongly the disproportion of their marriages to that of their younger sister. This consideration made them far from being content, though they were arrived at the utmost height of their late wishes, and much beyond their hopes. They gave themselves up to an excess of jealousy, which not only disturbed their joy, but was the cause of great trouble and affliction to the queen-consort, their younger sister. They had not an opportunity to communicate their thoughts to each other on the preference the emperor had given her, but were altogether employed in preparing themselves for the celebration of their marriages. Some days afterward, when they had an opportunity of seeing each other at the public baths, the eldest said to the other: "Well, what say you to our sister's great fortune? Is not she a fine person to be a queen!" "I must own," said the other sister, "I cannot conceive what charms the emperor could discover to be so bewitched by her. Was it a reason sufficient for him not to cast his eyes on you, because she was somewhat younger? You were as worthy of his throne, and in justice he ought to have preferred you."

"Sister," said the elder, "I should not have regretted if his majesty had but pitched upon you; but that he should choose that little simpleton really grieves me. But I will revenge myself; and you, I think, are as much concerned as I; therefore, I propose that we should contrive measures and act in concert: communicate to me what you think the likeliest way to mortify her, while I, on my side, will inform you what my desire of revenge shall suggest to me." After this wicked agreement, the two sisters saw each other frequently, and consulted how they might disturb and interrupt the happiness of the queen. They proposed a great many ways, but in deliberating about the manner of executing them, found so many difficulties that they durst not attempt them. In the meantime, with a detestable dissimulation, they often went together to make her visits, and every time showed her all the marks of affection they could devise, to persuade her how overjoyed they were to have a sister raised to so high a fortune. The queen, on her part, constantly received them with all the demonstrations of esteem they could expect from so near a relative. Some time after her marriage, the expected birth of an heir gave great joy to the queen and emperor, which was communicated to all the court, and spread throughout the empire.

THE TALKING BIRD

Upon this news the two sisters came to pay their compliments, and proffered their services, desiring her, if not provided with nurses, to accept of them.

The queen said to them most obligingly: "Sisters, I should desire nothing more, if it were in my power to make the choice. I am, however, obliged to you for your goodwill, but must submit to what the emperor shall order on this occasion. Let your husbands employ their friends to make interest, and get some courtier to ask this favour of his majesty, and if he speaks to me about it, be assured that I shall not only express the pleasure he does me but thank him for making choice of you."

The two husbands applied themselves to some courtiers, their patrons, and begged of them to use their interest to procure their wives the honour they aspired to. Those patrons exerted themselves so much in their behalf that the emperor promised them to consider of the matter, and was as good as his word; for in conversation with the queen he told her that he thought her sisters were the most proper persons to be about her, but would not name them before he had asked her consent. The queen, sensible of the deference the emperor so obligingly paid her, said to him, "Sir, I was prepared to do as your majesty might please to command. But since you have been so kind as to think of my sisters, I thank you for the regard you have shown them for my sake, and therefore I shall not dissemble that I had rather have them than strangers." The emperor therefore named the queen's two sisters to be her attendants; and from that time they went frequently to the palace, overjoyed at the opportunity they would have of executing the detestable wickedness they had meditated against the queen.

Shortly afterward a young prince, as bright as the day, was born to the queen; but neither his innocence nor beauty could move the cruel hearts of the merciless sisters. They wrapped him up carelessly in his cloths and put him into a basket, which they abandoned to the stream of a small canal that ran under the queen's apartment, and declared that she had given birth to a puppy. This dreadful intelligence was announced to the emperor, who became so angry at the circumstance, that he was likely to have occasioned the queen's death, if his grand vizier had not represented to him that he could not, without injustice, make her answerable for the misfortune.

In the meantime, the basket in which the little prince was exposed was carried by the stream beyond a wall which bounded the prospect of the queen's apartment, and from thence floated with the current down the gardens. By chance the intendant of the emperor's gardens, one of the principal officers of the kingdom, was walking in the garden by the side of this canal, and, perceiving a basket floating, called to a gardener who was not far off, to bring it to shore that he might see what it contained. The gardener, with a rake which he had in his hand, drew the basket to the side of the canal, took it up, and gave it to him. The intendant of the gardens was extremely surprised to see in the basket a child, which, though he knew it could be but just born, had very fine features. This officer had been married several years, but though he had always been desirous of having children, Heaven had never blessed him with any. This accident interrupted his walk: he made the gardener follow him with the child, and when he came to his own house, which was situated at the entrance to the gardens of the palace, went into his wife's apartment. "Wife," said he, "as we have no children of our own, God has sent us one. I recommend him to you; provide him a nurse, and take as much care of him as if he were our own son; for, from this moment, I acknowledge him as such." The intendant's wife received the child with great joy, and took particular pleasure in the care of him. The intendant himself would not inquire too narrowly whence the infant came. He saw plainly it came not far off from the queen's apartment, but it was not his business to examine too closely into what had passed, nor to create disturbances in a place where peace was so necessary.

The following year another prince was born, on whom the unnatural sisters had no more compassion than on his brother, but exposed him likewise in a basket and set him adrift in the canal, pretending, this time, that the sultana had given birth to a cat. It was happy also for this child that the intendant of the gardens was walking by the canal side, for he had it carried to his wife, and charged her to take as much care of it as of the former, which was as agreeable to her inclination as it was to his own.

The emperor of Persia was more enraged this time against the queen than before, and she had felt the effects of his anger if the grand vizier's remonstrances had not prevailed. The third year the queen gave birth to a princess, which innocent babe underwent the same fate as her brothers, for the two sisters, being determined not to desist from their detestable schemes till they had seen the queen cast off and humbled, claimed that a log of wood had been born and exposed this infant also on the canal. But the princess, as well as her brothers, was preserved from death by the compassion and charity of the intendant of the gardens.

Kosrouschah could no longer contain himself, when he was informed of the new misfortune. He pronounced sentence of death upon the wretched queen and ordered the grand vizier to see it executed.

The grand vizier and the courtiers who were present cast themselves at the emperor's feet, to beg of him to revoke the sentence. "Your majesty, I hope, will give me leave," said the grand vizier, "to represent to you, that the laws which condemn persons to death were made to punish crimes; the three extraordinary misfortunes of the queen are not crimes, for in what can she be said to have contributed toward them? Your majesty may abstain from seeing her, but let her live. The affliction in which she will spend the rest of her life, after the loss of your favour, will be a punishment sufficiently distressing."

The emperor of Persia considered with himself, and, reflecting that it was unjust to condemn the queen to death for what had happened, said: "Let her live then; I will spare her life, but it shall be on this condition: that she shall desire to die more than once every day. Let a wooden shed be built for her at the gate of the principal mosque, with iron bars to the windows, and let her be put into it, in the coarsest habit; and every Mussulman that shall go into the mosque to prayers shall heap scorn upon her. If any one fail, I will have him exposed to the same punishment; and that I may be punctually obeyed, I charge you, vizier, to appoint persons to see this done." The emperor pronounced his sentence in such a tone that the grand vizier durst not further remonstrate; and it was executed, to the great satisfaction of the two envious sisters. A shed was built, and the queen, truly worthy of compassion, was put into it and exposed ignominiously to the contempt of the people, which usage she bore with a patient resignation that excited the compassion of those who were discriminating and judged of things better than the vulgar.

The two princes and the princess were, in the meantime, nursed and brought up by the intendant of the gardens and his wife with the tenderness of a father and mother; and as they advanced in age, they all showed marks of superior dignity, which discovered itself every day by a certain air which could only belong to exalted birth. All this increased the affections of the intendant and his wife, who called the eldest prince Bahman, and the second Perviz, both of them names of the most ancient emperors of Persia, and the princess, Periezade, which name also had been borne by several queens and princesses of the kingdom.

As soon as the two princes were old enough, the intendant provided proper masters to teach them to read and write; and the princess, their sister, who was often with them, showing a great desire to learn, the intendant, pleased with her quickness, employed the same master to teach her also. Her vivacity and piercing wit made her, in a little time, as great a proficient as her brothers. From that time the brothers and sister had the same masters in geography, poetry, history, and even the secret sciences, and made so wonderful a progress that their tutors were amazed, and frankly owned that they could teach them nothing more. At the hours of recreation, the princess learned to sing and play upon all sorts of instruments; and when the princes were learning to ride she would not permit them to have that advantage over her, but went through all the exercises with them, learning to ride also, to bend the bow, and dart the reed or javelin, and oftentimes outdid them in the race and other contests of agility.

The intendant of the gardens was so overjoyed to find his adopted children so accomplished in all the perfections of body and mind, and that they so well requited the expense he had been at in their education, that he resolved to be at a still greater; for, as he had until then been content simply with his lodge at the entrance of the garden, and kept no country-house, he purchased a mansion at a short distance from the city, surrounded by a large tract of arable land, meadows, and woods. As the house was not sufficiently handsome nor convenient, he pulled it down, and spared no expense in building a more magnificent residence. He went every day to hasten, by his presence, the great number

of workmen he employed, and as soon as there was an apartment
ready to receive him, passed several days together there when his
presence was not necessary at court; and by the same exertions,
the interior was furnished in the richest manner, in consonance
with the magnificence of the edifice. Afterward he made gardens, according to a plan drawn by himself. He took in a large
extent of ground, which he walled around, and stocked with
fallow deer, that the princes and princess might divert themselves
with hunting when they chose.

When this country seat was finished and fit for habitation,
the intendant of the gardens went and cast himself at the emper-
or's feet, and, after representing how long he had served, and the
infirmities of age which he found growing upon him, begged that
he might be permitted to resign his charge into his majesty's
disposal and retire. The emperor gave him leave, with the more
pleasure, because he was satisfied with his long services, both in
his father's reign and his own, and when he granted it, asked what
he should do to recompense him. "Sir," replied the intendant of
the gardens, "I have received so many obligations from your
majesty and the late emperor, your father, of happy memory, that
I desire no more than the honour of dying in your favour." He
took his leave of the emperor and retired with the two princes and
the princess to the country retreat he had built. His wife had been
dead some years, and he himself had not lived above six months
with his charges before he was surprised by so sudden a death that
he had not time to give them the least account of the manner in
which he had discovered them. The Princes Bahman and Perviz,
and the Princess Periezade, who knew no other father than the
intendant of the emperor's gardens, regretted and bewailed him
as such, and paid all the honours in his funeral obsequies which
love and filial gratitude required of them. Satisfied with the

plentiful fortune he had left them, they lived together in perfect union, free from the ambition of distinguishing themselves at court, or aspiring to places of honour and dignity, which they might easily have obtained.

One day when the two princes were hunting, and the princess had remained at home, a religious old woman came to the gate, and desired leave to go in to say her prayers, it being then the hour. The servants asked the princess's permission, who ordered them to show her into the oratory, which the intendant of the emperor's gardens had taken care to fit up in his house, for want of a mosque in the neighbourhood. She bade them, also, after the good woman had finished her prayers, to show her the house and gardens and then bring her to the hall.

The old woman went into the oratory, said her prayers, and when she came out two of the princess's women invited her to see the residence, which civility she accepted, followed them from one apartment to another, and observed, like a person who understood what belonged to furniture, the nice arrangement of everything. They conducted her also into the garden, the disposition of which she found so well planned, that she admired it, observing that the person who had formed it must have been an excellent master of his art. Afterward she was brought before the princess, who waited for her in the great hall, which in beauty and richness exceeded all that she had admired in the other apartments.

As soon as the princess saw the devout woman, she said to her: "My good mother, come near and sit down by me. I am overjoyed at the happiness of having the opportunity of profiting for some moments by the example and conversation of such a person as you, who have taken the right way by dedicating yourself to the service of God. I wish every one were as wise."

The devout woman, instead of sitting on a sofa, would only sit upon the edge of one. The princess would not permit her to do so, but rising from her seat and taking her by the hand, obliged her to come and sit by her. The good woman, sensible of the civility, said: "Madam, I ought not to have so much respect shown me; but since you command, and are mistress of your own house, I will obey you." When she had seated herself, before they entered into any conversation, one of the princess's women brought a low stand of mother-of-pearl and ebony, with a china dish full of cakes upon it, and many others set round it full of fruits in season, and wet and dry sweetmeats.

The princess took up one of the cakes, and presenting her with it, said: "Eat, good mother, and make choice of what you like best; you had need to eat after coming so far." "Madam," replied the good woman, "I am not used to eat such delicacies, but will not refuse what God has sent me by so liberal a hand as yours."

While the devout woman was eating, the princess ate a little too, to bear her company, and asked her many questions upon the exercise of devotion which she practised and how she lived; all of which she answered with great modesty. Talking of various things, at last the princess asked her what she thought of the house, and how she liked it.

"Madam," answered the devout woman, "I must certainly have very bad taste to disapprove anything in it, since it is beautiful, regular, and magnificently furnished with exactness and judgment, and all its ornaments adjusted in the best manner. Its situation is an agreeable spot, and no garden can be more delightful; but yet, if you will give me leave to speak my mind freely, I will take the liberty to tell you that this house would be incomparable if it had three things which are wanting to complete it." "My good mother," replied the Princess Periezade, "what are those? I entreat you to tell me what they are; I will spare nothing to get them."

"Madam," replied the devout woman, "the first of these three things is the Talking Bird, so singular a creature, that it draws round it all the songsters of the neighbourhood which come to accompany its voice. The second is the Singing Tree, the leaves of which are so many mouths which form an harmonious concert of different voices and never cease. The third is the Golden Water, a single drop of which being poured into a vessel properly prepared, it increases so as to fill it immediately, and rises up in the middle like a fountain, which continually plays, and yet the basin never overflows."

"Ah! my good mother," cried the princess, "how much am I obliged to you for the knowledge of these curiosities! I never before heard there were such rarities in the world; but as I am persuaded that you know, I expect that you should do me the favour to inform me where they are to be found."

"Madam," replied the good woman, "I should be unworthy the hospitality you have shown me if I should refuse to satisfy your curiosity on that point, and am glad to have the honour to tell you that these curiosities are all to be met with in the same spot on the confines of this kingdom, toward India. The road lies before your house, and whoever you send needs but follow it for twenty days, and on the twentieth only let him ask the first person he meets where the Talking Bird, the Singing Tree, and the Golden Water are, and he will be informed." After saying this, she rose from her seat, took her leave, and went her way.

The Princess Periezade's thoughts were so taken up with the Talking Bird, Singing Tree, and Golden Water, that she never perceived the devout woman's departure, till she wanted to ask her some question for her better information; for she thought that what she had been told was not a sufficient reason for exposing herself by undertaking a long journey. However, she would not send after her visitor, but endeavoured to remember all the directions, and when she thought she had recollected every word, took real pleasure in thinking of the satisfaction she should have if she could get these curiosities into her possession; but the difficulties she apprehended and the fear of not succeeding made her very uneasy.

She was absorbed in these thoughts when her brothers returned from hunting, who, when they entered the great hall, instead of finding her lively and gay, as she was wont to be, were amazed to see her so pensive and hanging down her head as if something troubled her.

"Sister," said Prince Bahman, "what is become of all your mirth and gaiety? Are you not well? or has some misfortune befallen you? Tell us, that we may know how to act, and give you some relief. If any one has affronted you, we will resent his insolence."

The princess remained in the same posture some time without answering, but at last lifted up her eyes to look at her brothers, and then held them down again, telling them nothing disturbed her.

"Sister," said Prince Bahman, "you conceal the truth from us; there must be something of consequence. It is impossible we could observe so sudden a change if nothing was the matter with you. You would not have us satisfied with the evasive answer you have given; do not conceal anything, unless you would have us suspect that you renounce the strict union which has hitherto subsisted between us."

The princess, who had not the smallest intention to offend her brothers, would not suffer them to entertain such a thought, but said: "When I told you nothing disturbed me, I meant nothing that was of importance to you, but to me it is of some consequence; and since you press me to tell you by our strict union and friendship, which are so dear to me, I will. You think, and I always believed so too, that this house was so complete that nothing was wanting. But this day I have learned that it lacks three rarities which would render it so perfect that no country seat in the world could be compared with it. These three things are the Talking Bird, the Singing Tree, and the Golden Water." After she had informed them wherein consisted the excellency of these rarities, "A devout woman," added she, "has made this discovery to me, told me the place where they are to be found, and the way thither. Perhaps you may imagine these things of little consequence; that without these additions our house will always be thought sufficiently elegant, and that we can do without them. You may think as you please, but I cannot help telling you that I am persuaded they are absolutely necessary, and I shall not be easy without them. Therefore, whether you value them or not, I desire you to consider what person you may think proper for me to send in search of the curiosities I have mentioned."

"Sister," replied Prince Bahman, "nothing can concern you in which we have not an equal interest. It is enough that you desire these things to oblige us to take the same interest; but if you had not, we feel ourselves inclined of our own accord and for our own individual satisfaction. I am persuaded my brother is of the same opinion, and therefore we ought to undertake this conquest, for the importance and singularity of the undertaking deserve that name. I will take the charge upon myself; only tell me the place and the way to it, and I will defer my journey no longer than till to-morrow."

"Brother," said Prince Perviz, "it is not proper that you, who are the head of our family, should be absent. I desire my sister should join with me to oblige you to abandon your design, and allow me to undertake it. I hope to acquit myself as well as you, and it will be a more regular proceeding." "I am persuaded of your goodwill, brother," replied Prince Bahman, "and that you would succeed as well as myself in this journey; but I have resolved and will undertake it. You shall stay at home with our sister, and I need not recommend her to you."

The next morning Bahman mounted his horse, and Perviz and the princess embraced and wished him a good journey. But in the midst of their adieus, the princess recollected what she had not thought of before. "Brother," said she, "I had quite forgotten the accidents which attend travellers. Who knows whether I shall ever see you again? Alight, I beseech you, and give up this journey. I would rather be deprived of the sight and possession of the Talking Bird, the Singing Tree, and the Golden Water, than run the risk of never seeing you more."

"Sister," replied Bahman, smiling at her sudden fears, "my resolution is fixed. The accidents you speak of befall only those who are unfortunate; but there are more who are not so. However, as events are uncertain, and I may fail in this undertaking, all I can do is to leave you this knife."

Bahman pulling a knife from his vestband, and presenting it to the princess in the sheath, said: "Take this knife, sister, and give yourself the trouble sometimes to pull it out of the sheath; while you see it clean as it is now, it will be a sign that I am alive; but if you find it stained with blood, then you may believe me dead and indulge me with your prayers."

The princess could obtain nothing more of Bahman. He bade adieu to her and Prince Perviz for the last time and rode

away.   When he got into the road, he never turned to the right
hand nor to the left, but went directly forward toward India.
The twentieth day he perceived on the roadside a hideous old
man, who sat under a tree near a thatched house, which was his
retreat from the weather.

His eyebrows were as white as snow, as was also the hair of
his head; his whiskers covered his mouth, and his beard and
hair reached down to his feet.   The nails of his hands and
feet were grown to an extensive length, while a flat, broad um-
brella covered his head.   He had no clothes, but only a mat
thrown round his body.   This old man was a dervish for so
many years retired from the world to give himself up entirely to
the service of God that at last he had become what we have
described.

Prince Bahman, who had been all that morning very attentive,
to see if he could meet with anybody who could give him information of the place he was in search of, stopped when he came near
the dervish, alighted, in conformity to the directions which the
devout woman had given the Princess Periezade, and leading his
horse by the bridle, advanced toward him and saluting him,
said: "God prolong your days, good father, and grant you the
accomplishment of your desires."

The dervish returned the prince's salutation, but so unintelli-
gibly that he could not understand one word he said and Prince
Bahman, perceiving that this difficulty proceeded from the dervish's whiskers hanging over his mouth, and unwilling to go any
further without the instructions he wanted, pulled out a pair of
scissors he had about him, and having tied his horse to a branch
of the tree, said: "Good dervish, I want to have some talk with
you, but your whiskers prevent my understanding what you say;
and if you will consent, I will cut off some part of them and of

your eyebrows, which disfigure you so much that you look more like a bear than a man."

The dervish did not oppose the offer, and when the prince had cut off as much hair as he thought fit, he perceived that the dervish had a good complexion, and that he was not as old as he seemed. "Good dervish," said he, "if I had a glass I would show you how young you look: you are now a man, but before, nobody could tell what you were."

The kind behaviour of Prince Bahman made the dervish smile and return his compliment. "Sir," said he, "whoever you are, I am obliged by the good office you have performed, and am ready to show my gratitude by doing anything in my power for you. You must have alighted here upon some account or other. Tell me what it is, and I will endeavour to serve you."

"Good dervish," replied Prince Bahman, "I am in search of the Talking Bird, the Singing Tree, and the Golden Water; I know these three rarities are not far from hence, but cannot tell exactly the place where they are to be found; if you know, I conjure you to show me the way, that I may not lose my labour after so long a journey."

The prince, while he spoke, observed that the dervish changed countenance, held down his eyes, looked very serious, and remained silent, which obliged him to say to him again: "Good father, tell me whether you know what I ask you, that I may not lose my time, but inform myself somewhere else."

At last the dervish broke silence. "Sir," said he to Prince Bahman, "I know the way you ask of me; but the regard which I conceived for you the first moment I saw you, and which is grown stronger by the service you have done me, kept me in suspense as to whether I should give you the satisfaction you desire." "What motive can hinder you?" replied the prince; "and what difficulties do you find in so doing?"   "I will tell you," replied the dervish; "the danger to which you are going to expose yourself is greater than you may suppose.   A number of gentlemen of as much bravery as you can possibly possess have passed this way, and asked me the same question.   When I had used all my endeavours to persuade them to desist, they would not believe me; at last I yielded to their importunities; I was compelled to show them the way, and I can assure you they have all perished, for I have not seen one come back.   Therefore, if you have any regard for your life, take my advice, go no farther, but return home."

Prince Bahman persisted in his resolution.   "I will not suppose," said he to the dervish, "but that your advice is sincere. I am obliged to you for the friendship you express for me; but whatever may be the danger, nothing shall make me change my intention: whoever attacks me, I am well armed, and can say I am as brave as any one."   "But they who will attack you are not to be seen," replied the dervish; "how will you defend yourself against invisible persons?"   "It is no matter," answered the prince, "all you say shall not persuade me to do anything contrary to my duty.   Since you know the way, I conjure you once more to inform me."

When the dervish found he could not prevail upon Prince Bahman, and that he was obstinately bent to pursue his journey, notwithstanding his friendly remonstrance, he put his hand into a bag that lay by him and pulled out a bowl, which he presented to him.   "Since I cannot prevail on you to attend to my advice," said he, "take this bowl and when you are on horseback throw it before you, and follow it to the foot of a mountain, where it will stop.   As soon as the bowl stops, alight, leave your horse with the bridle over his neck, and he will stand in the same place till you return. As you ascend you will see on your right and left a great number of large black stones, and will hear on all sides a confusion of voices, which will utter a thousand abuses to discourage you, and prevent your reaching the summit of the mountain. Be not afraid; but, above all things, do not turn your head to look behind you, for in that instant you will be changed into such a black stone as those you see, which are all youths who have failed in this enterprise. If you escape the danger of which I give you but a faint idea, and get to the top of the mountain, you will see a cage, and in that cage is the bird you seek; ask him which are the Singing Tree and the Golden Water, and he will tell you. I have nothing more to say; this is what you have to do, and if you are prudent you will take my advice and not expose your life. Consider once more while you have time that the difficulties are almost insuperable."

"I am obliged to you for your advice," replied Prince Bahman, after he had received the bowl, "but cannot follow it. However, I will endeavour to conform myself to that part of it which bids me not to look behind me, and I hope to come and thank you when I have obtained what I am seeking." After these words, to which the dervish made no other answer than that he should be overjoyed to see him again, the prince mounted his horse, took leave of the dervish with a respectful salute, and threw the bowl before him.

The bowl rolled away with as much swiftness as when Prince Bahman first hurled it from his hand, which obliged him to put his horse to the same pace to avoid losing sight of it, and when it had reached the foot of the mountain it stopped. The prince alighted from his horse, laid the bridle on his neck, and having first surveyed the mountain and seen the black stones, began to ascend, but had not gone four steps before he heard the voices mentioned by the dervish, though he could see nobody. Some said: "Where is that fool going? Where is he going? What would he have? Do not let him pass." Others: "Stop him, catch him, kill him"; and others with a voice like thunder: "Thief! assassin! murderer!" while some in a gibing tone cried: "No, no, do not hurt him; let the pretty fellow pass, the cage and bird are kept for him."

Notwithstanding all these troublesome voices, Prince Bahman ascended with resolution for some time, but the voices redoubled with so loud a din, both behind and before, that at last he was seized with dread, his legs trembled under him, he staggered, and finding that his strength failed him, he forgot the dervish's advice, turned about to run down the hill, and was that instant changed into a black stone; a metamorphosis which had happened to many before him who had attempted the ascent. His horse, likewise, underwent the same change.

From the time of Prince Bahman's departure, the Princess Periezade always wore the knife and sheath in her girdle, and pulled it out several times in a day, to know whether her brother was alive. She had the consolation to understand he was in perfect health and to talk of him frequently with Prince Perviz. On the fatal day that Prince Bahman was transformed into a stone, as Prince Perviz and the princess were talking together in the evening, as usual, the prince desired his sister to pull out the knife to know how their brother did. The princess readily complied, and seeing the blood run down the point was seized with so much horror that she threw it down. "Ah! my dear brother," cried she, "I have been the cause of your death, and shall never see you more! Why did I tell you of the Talking Bird, Singing Tree, and Golden Water; or rather, of what importance was it to me to know whether the devout woman thought this house ugly or handsome, or complete or not? I wish to Heaven she had never addressed herself to me!"

Prince Perviz was as much afflicted at the death of Prince Bahman as the princess, but not to waste time in needless regret, as he knew that she still passionately desired possession of the marvellous treasures, he interrupted her, saying: "Sister, our regret for our brother is vain; our lamentations cannot restore him to life; it is the will of God; we must submit and adore the decrees of the Almighty without searching into them. Why should you now doubt of the truth of what the holy woman told you? Do you think she spoke to you of three things that were not in being, and that she invented them to deceive you who had received her with so much goodness and civility? Let us rather believe that our brother's death is owing to some error on his part, or some accident which we cannot conceive. It ought not therefore to prevent us from pursuing our object. I offered to go this journey, and am now more resolved than ever; his example has no effect upon my resolution; to-morrow I will depart."

The princess did all she could to dissuade Prince Perviz, conjuring him not to expose her to the danger of losing two brothers; but he was obstinate, and all the remonstrances she could urge had no effect upon him. Before he went, that she might know what success he had, he left her a string of a hundred pearls, telling her that if they would not run when she should count them upon the string, but remain fixed, that would be a certain sign he had undergone the same fate as his brother; but at the same time told her he hoped it would never happen, but that he should have the delight of seeing her again.

Prince Perviz, on the twentieth day after his departure, met the same dervish in the same place as his brother Bahman had done before him. He went directly up to him, and after he had saluted, asked him if he could tell him where to find the Talking Bird, the Singing Tree, and the Golden Water. The dervish urged the same remonstrances as he had done to Prince Bahman, telling him that a young gentleman, who very much resembled him, was with him a short time before; that, overcome by his importunity, he had shown him the way, given him a guide, and told him how he should act to succeed, but that he had not seen him since, and doubted not but he had shared the same fate as all other adventurers.

"Good dervish," answered Prince Perviz, "I know whom you speak of; he was my elder brother, and I am informed of the certainty of his death, but know not the cause." "I can tell you," replied the dervish; "he was changed into a black stone, as all I speak of have been; and you must expect the same transformation, unless you observe more exactly than he has done the advice I gave him, in case you persist in your resolution, which I once more entreat you to renounce."

"Dervish," said Prince Perviz, "I cannot sufficiently express how much I am obliged for the concern you take in my life, who am a stranger to you, and have done nothing to deserve your kindness; but I thoroughly considered this enterprise before I undertook it; therefore I beg of you to do me the same favour you have done my brother. Perhaps I may have better success in following your directions." "Since I cannot prevail with you," said the dervish, "to give up your obstinate resolution, if my age did not prevent me, and I could stand, I would get up to reach you a bowl I have here, which will show you the way."

Without giving the dervish time to say more, the prince alighted from his horse and went to the dervish, who had taken a bowl out of his bag, in which he had a great many, and gave it him, with the same directions he had given Prince Bahman; and after warning him not to be discouraged by the voices he should hear, however threatening they might be, but to continue his way up the hill till he saw the cage and bird, he let him depart.

Prince Perviz thanked the dervish, and when he had remounted and taken leave, threw the bowl before his horse, and spurring him at the same time, followed it. When the bowl came to the bottom of the hill it stopped, the prince alighted, and stood some time to recollect the dervish's directions. He encouraged himself, and began to walk up with a resolution to reach the summit; but before he had gone above six steps, he heard a voice, which seemed to be near, as of a man behind him, say in an insulting tone: "Stay, rash youth, that I may punish you for your presumption."

Upon this affront the prince, forgetting the dervish's advice, clapped his hand upon his sword, drew it, and turned about to revenge himself; but had scarcely time to see that nobody followed him before he and his horse were changed into black stones.

In the meantime the Princess Periezade, several times a day after her brother's departure, counted her chaplet. She did not omit it at night, but when she went to bed put it about her neck, and in the morning when she awoke counted over the pearls again to see if they would slide.

The day that Prince Perviz was transformed into a stone she was counting over the pearls as she used to do, when all at once they became immovably fixed, a certain token that the prince, her brother, was dead. As she had determined what to do in case it should so happen, she lost no time in outward demonstrations of grief, which she concealed as much as possible, but having disguised herself in man's apparel, she mounted her horse the next morning, armed and equipped, having told her servants she should return in two or three days, and took the same road that her brothers had done.

The princess, who had been used to ride on horseback in hunting, supported the fatigue of so long a journey better than most ladies could have done; and as she made the same stages as her brothers, she also met with the dervish on the twentieth day. When she came near him, she alighted from her horse, leading him by the bridle, went and sat down by the dervish, and after she had saluted him, said: "Good dervish, give me leave to rest myself; and do me the favour to tell me if you have not heard that there are somewhere in this neighbourhood a Talking Bird, a Singing Tree, and Golden Water.

"Princess," answered the dervish, "for so I must call you, since by your voice I know you to be a woman disguised in man's apparel, I know the place well where these things are to be found; but what makes you ask me this question?"

"Good dervish," replied the princess, "I have had such a flattering relation of them given me, that I have a great desire to possess them." "Madam," replied the dervish, "you have been told the truth. These curiosities are more singular than they have been represented, but you have not been made acquainted with the difficulties which must be surmounted in order to obtain them. If you had been fully informed of these, you would not have undertaken so dangerous an enterprise. Take my advice, return, and do not urge me to contribute toward your ruin."

"Good father," said the princess, "I have travelled a great way, and should be sorry to return without executing my design. You talk of difficulties and danger of life, but you do not tell me what those difficulties are, and wherein the danger consists. This is what I desire to know, that I may consider and judge whether I can trust my courage and strength to brave them."

The dervish repeated to the princess what he had said to the Princes Bahman and Perviz, exaggerating the difficulties of climbing up to the top of the mountain, where she was to make herself mistress of the Bird, which would inform her of the Singing Tree and Golden Water. He magnified the din of the terrible threatening voices which she would hear on all sides of her, and the great number of black stones alone sufficient to strike terror. He entreated her to reflect that those stones were so many brave gentlemen, so metamorphosed for having omitted to observe the principal condition of success in the perilous undertaking, which was not to look behind them before they had got possession of the cage.

When the dervish had done, the princess replied: "By what I comprehend from your discourse, the difficulties of succeeding in this affair are, first, the getting up to the cage without being frightened at the terrible din of voices I shall hear; and, secondly, not to look behind me. For this last, I hope I shall be mistress enough of myself to observe it; as to the first, I own that voices, such as you represent them to be, are capable of striking terror into the most undaunted; but as in all enterprises and dangers every one may use stratagem, I desire to know of you if I may use any in one of so great importance." "And what stratagem is it you would employ?" said the dervish. "To stop my ears with cotton," answered the princess, "that the voices, however terrible, may make the less impression upon my imagination, and my mind remain free from that disturbance which might cause me to lose the use of my reason."

"Princess," replied the dervish, "of all the persons who have addressed themselves to me for information, I do not know that ever one made use of the contrivance you propose. All I know is that they all perished. If you persist in your design, you may

It will be sufficient to break off a branch and carry it to plant in your garden.

make the experiment. You will be fortunate if it succeeds, **but** I would advise you not to expose yourself to the danger."

"My good father," replied the princess, "I am sure my precaution will succeed, and am resolved to try the experiment. Nothing remains for me but to know which way I must go, and I conjure you not to deny me that information." The dervish exhorted her again to consider well what she was going to do; but finding her resolute, he took out a bowl, and presenting it to her, said: "Take this bowl, mount your horse again, and when you have thrown it before you, follow it through all its windings, till it stops at the bottom of the mountain; there alight and ascend the hill. Go, you know the rest."

After the princess had thanked the dervish, and taken her leave of him, she mounted her horse, threw the bowl before her, and followed it till it stopped at the foot of the mountain.

She then alighted, stopped her ears with cotton, and after she had well examined the path leading to the summit began with a moderate pace and walked up with intrepidity. She heard the voices and perceived the great service the cotton was to her. The higher she went, the louder and more numerous the voices seemed, but they were not capable of making any impression upon her. She heard a great many affronting speeches and raillery very disagreeable to a woman, which she only laughed at. "I mind not," said she to herself, "all that can be said, were it worse; I only laugh at them and shall pursue my way." At last, she climbed so high that she could perceive the cage and the Bird which endeavoured, in company with the voices, to frighten her, crying in a thundering tone, notwithstanding the smallness of its size: "Retire, fool, and approach no nearer."

The princess, encouraged by this sight, redoubled her speed, and by effort gained the summit of the mountain, where the ground was level; then running directly to the cage and clapping her hand upon it, cried: "Bird, I have you, and you shall not escape me."

While Periezade was pulling the cotton out of her ears the Bird said to her: "Heroic princess, be not angry with me for joining with those who exerted themselves to preserve my liberty. Though in a cage, I was content with my condition; but since I am destined to be a slave, I would rather be yours than any other person's, since you have obtained me so courageously. From this instant, I swear entire submission to all your commands. I know who you are. You do not; but the time will come when I shall do you essential service, for which I hope you will think yourself obliged to me. As a proof of my sincerity, tell me what you desire and I am ready to obey you."

The princess's joy was the more inexpressible, because the conquest she had made had cost her the lives of two beloved brothers, and given her more trouble and danger than she could have imagined. "Bird," said she, "it was my intention to have told you that I wish for many things which are of importance, but I am overjoyed that you have shown your goodwill and prevented me. I have been told that there is not far off a Golden Water, the property of which is very wonderful; before all things, I ask you to tell me where it is." The Bird showed her the place, which was just by, and she went and filled a little silver flagon which she had brought with her. She returned at once and said: "Bird, this is not enough; I want also the Singing Tree; tell me where it is." "Turn about," said the Bird, "and you will see behind you a wood where you will find the tree." The princess went into the wood, and by the harmonious concert she heard, soon knew the tree among many others, but it was very large and high. She came back again and said: "Bird, I have found the

Singing Tree, but I can neither pull it up by the roots nor carry it." The Bird replied: "It is not necessary that you should take it up; it will be sufficient to break off a branch and carry it to plant in your garden; it will take root as soon as it is put into the earth, and in a little time will grow to as fine a tree as that you have seen."

When the princess had obtained possession of the three things for which she had conceived so great a desire, she said again: "Bird, what you have yet done for me is not sufficient. You have been the cause of the death of my two brothers, who must be among the black stones I saw as I ascended the mountain. I wish to take the princes home with me."

The Bird seemed reluctant to satisfy the princess in this point, and indeed made some difficulty to comply. "Bird," said the princess, "remember you told me that you were my slave. You are so; and your life is in my disposal." "That I cannot deny," answered the bird; "but although what you now ask is more difficult than all the rest, yet I will do it for you. Cast your eyes around," added he, "and look if you can see a little pitcher." "I see it already," said the princess. "Take it then," said he, "and as you descend the mountain, sprinkle a little of the water that is in it upon every black stone."

The princess took up the pitcher accordingly, carried with her the cage and Bird, the flagon of Golden Water, and the branch of the Singing Tree, and as she descended the mountain, threw a little of the water on every black stone, which was changed immediately into a man; and as she did not miss one stone, all the horses, both of her brothers and of the other gentlemen, resumed their natural forms also. She instantly recognised Bahman and Perviz, as they did her, and ran to embrace her. She returned their embraces and expressed her amazement. "What do you here, my dear brothers?" said she, and they told her they had been asleep. "Yes," replied she, "and if it had not been for me, perhaps you might have slept till the day of judgment. Do not you remember that you came to fetch the Talking Bird, the Singing Tree, and the Golden Water, and did not you see, as you came along, the place covered with black stones? Look and see if there be any now. The gentlemen and their horses who surround us, and you yourselves, were these black stones. If you desire to know how this wonder was performed," continued she, showing the pitcher, which she set down at the foot of the mountain, "it was done by virtue of the water which was in this pitcher, with which I sprinkled every stone. After I had made the Talking Bird (which you see in this cage) my slave, by his directions I found out the Singing Tree, a branch of which I have now in my hand; and the Golden Water, with which this flagon is filled; but being still unwilling to return without taking you with me, I constrained the Bird, by the power I had over him, to afford me the means. He told me where to find this pitcher, and the use I was to make of it."

The Princes Bahman and Perviz learned by this relation the obligation they had to their sister, as did all the other gentlemen, who expressed to her that, far from envying her happiness in the conquest she had made, and which they all had aspired to, they thought they could not better express their gratitude for restoring them to life again, than by declaring themselves her slaves, and that they were ready to obey her in whatever she should command.

"Gentlemen," replied the princess, "if you had given any attention to my words, you might have observed that I had no other intention in what I have done than to recover my brothers; therefore, if you have received any benefit, you owe me no obligation, and I have no further share in your compliment than your politeness toward me, for which I return you my thanks. In other respects, I regard each of you as quite as free as you were before your misfortunes, and I rejoice with you at the happiness which has accrued to you by my means. Let us, however, stay no longer in a place where we have nothing to detain us, but mount our horses and return to our respective homes."

The princess took her horse, which stood in the place where she had left him. Before she mounted, Prince Bahman desired her to give him the cage to carry. "Brother," replied the princess, "the Bird is my slave and I will carry him myself; if you will take the pains to carry the branch of the Singing Tree, there it is; only hold the cage while I get on horseback." When she had mounted her horse, and Prince Bahman had given her the cage, she turned about and said to Prince Perviz: "I leave the flagon of Golden Water to your care, if it will not be too much trouble for you to carry it," and Prince Perviz accordingly took charge of it with pleasure.

When Bahman, Perviz, and all the gentlemen had mounted their horses, the princess waited for some of them to lead the way. The two princes paid that compliment to the gentlemen, and they again to the princess, who, finding that none of them would accept the honour, but that it was reserved for her, addressed herself to them and said: "Gentlemen, I expect that some of you should lead the way"; to which one who was nearest to her, in the name of the rest, replied: "Madam, were we ignorant of the respect due to your sex, yet after what you have done for us there is no deference we would not willingly pay you, notwithstanding your modesty; we entreat you no longer to deprive us of the happiness of following you."

"Gentlemen," said the princess, "I do not deserve the honour you do me, and accept it only because you desire it." At the same time she led the way, and the two princes and the gentlemen followed.

This illustrious company called upon the dervish as they passed, to thank him for his reception and wholesome advice, which they had all found to be sincere. He was dead, however; whether of old age, or because he was no longer necessary to show the way to obtaining the three rarities, did not appear. They pursued their route, but lessened in their numbers every day. The gentlemen who, as we said before, had come from different countries, after severally repeating their obligations to the princess and her brothers, took leave of them one after another as they approached the road by which they had come.

As soon as the princess reached home, she placed the cage in the garden, and the Bird no sooner began to warble than he was surrounded by nightingales, chaffinches, larks, linnets, gold-finches, and every species of birds of the country. The branch of the Singing Tree was no sooner set in the midst of the parterre, a little distance from the house, than it took root and in a short time became a large tree, the leaves of which gave as harmonious a concert as those of the parent from which it was gathered. A large basin of beautiful marble was placed in the garden, and when it was finished, the princess poured into it all the Golden Water from the flagon, which instantly increased and swelled so much that it soon reached up to the edges of the basin, and after-ward formed in the middle a fountain twenty feet high, which fell again into the basin perpetually, without running over.

The report of these wonders was presently spread abroad, and as the gates of the house and those of the gardens were shut to nobody, a great number of people came to admire them.

THE TALKING BIRD

Some days after, when the Princes Bahman and Perviz had recovered from the fatigue of their journey, they resumed their former way of living; and as their usual diversion was hunting, they mounted their horses and went for the first time since their return, not to their own demesne, but two or three leagues from their house. As they pursued their sport, the emperor of Persia came in pursuit of game upon the same ground. When they perceived, by the number of horsemen in different places, that he would soon be up, they resolved to discontinue their chase, and retire to avoid encountering him; but in the very road they took they chanced to meet him in so narrow a way that they could not retreat without being seen. In their surprise they had only time to alight and prostrate themselves before the emperor, without lifting up their heads to look at him. The emperor, who saw they were as well mounted and dressed as if they had belonged to his court, had a curiosity to see their faces. He stopped and commanded them to rise. The princes rose up and stood before him with an easy and graceful air, accompanied with modest countenances. The emperor took some time to view them before he spoke, and after he had admired their good air and mien, asked them who they were and where they lived.

"Sir," said Prince Bahman, "we are the sons of the late intendant of your majesty's gardens, and live in a house which he built a little before he died, till we should be fit to serve your majesty and ask of you some employ when opportunity offered."

"By what I perceive," replied the emperor, "you love hunting." "Sir," replied Prince Bahman, "it is our common exercise, and what none of your majesty's subjects who intend to bear arms in your armies, ought, according to the ancient custom of the kingdom, to neglect." The emperor, charmed with so prudent an answer, said: "Since it is so, I should be glad to see your expertness in the chase; choose your own game."

The princes mounted their horses again and followed the emperor, but had not gone far before they saw many wild beasts together. Prince Bahman chose a lion and Prince Perviz a bear, and pursued them with so much intrepidity that the emperor was surprised. They came up with their game nearly at the same time, and darted their javelins with so much skill and address that they pierced the one the lion and the other the bear so effectually that the emperor saw them fall one after the other. Immediately afterward Prince Bahman pursued another bear, and Prince Perviz another lion, and killed them in a short time, and would have beaten out for fresh game, but the emperor would not let them, and sent to them to come to him. When they approached he said: "If I had given you leave, you would soon have destroyed all my game; but it is not that which I would preserve, but your persons; for I am so well assured your bravery may one time or other be serviceable to me, that from this moment your lives will be always dear to me."

The emperor, in short, conceived so great a kindness for the two princes, that he invited them immediately to make him a visit, to which Prince Bahman replied: "Your majesty does us an honour we do not deserve, and we beg you will excuse us."

The emperor, who could not comprehend what reason the princes could have to refuse this token of his favour, pressed them to tell him why they excused themselves. "Sir," said Prince Bahman, "we have a sister younger than ourselves, with whom we live in such perfect union, that we undertake nothing before we consult her, nor she anything without asking our advice." "I commend your brotherly affection," answered the emperor. "Consult your sister, meet me to-morrow, and give me an answer."

THE TALKING BIRD

The princes went home, but neglected to speak of their adventure in meeting the emperor and hunting with him, and also of the honour he had done them, yet did not the next morning fail to meet him at the place appointed. "Well," said the emperor, "have you spoken to your sister, and has she consented to the pleasure I expect of seeing you?" The two princes looked at each other and blushed. "Sir," said Prince Bahman, "we beg your majesty to excuse us, for both my brother and I forgot." "Then remember to-day," replied the emperor, "and be sure to bring me an answer to-morrow."

The princes were guilty of the same fault a second time, and the emperor was so good-natured as to forgive their negligence; but to prevent their forgetfulness the third time, he pulled three little golden balls out of a purse, and put them into Prince Bahman's bosom. "These balls," said he, smiling, "will prevent your forgetting a third time what I wish you to do for my sake; since the noise they will make by falling on the floor when you undress will remind you, if you do not recollect it before." The event happened just as the emperor foresaw; and without these balls the princes had not thought of speaking to their sister of this affair, for as Prince Bahman unloosed his girdle to go to bed the balls dropped on the floor, upon which he ran into Prince Perviz's chamber, when both went into the Princess Periezade's apartment, and after they had asked her pardon for coming at so unseasonable a time, they told her all the circumstances of their meeting the emperor.

The princess was somewhat surprised at this intelligence. "Your meeting with the emperor," said she, "is happy and honourable and may in the end be highly advantageous to you, but it places me in an awkward position. It was on my account, I know, you refused the emperor, and I am infinitely obliged

[37]

to you for doing so. I know by this that you would rather be guilty of incivility toward the emperor than violate the union we have sworn to each other. You judge right, for if you had once gone you would insensibly have been engaged to devote yourselves to him. But do you think it an easy matter absolutely to refuse the emperor what he seems so earnestly to desire? Monarchs will be obeyed in their desires, and it may be dangerous to oppose them; therefore, if to follow my inclination I should dissuade you from obeying him, it may expose you to his resentment, and may render myself and you miserable. These are my sentiments; but before we conclude upon anything let us consult the Talking Bird and hear what he says; he is penetrating, and has promised his assistance in all difficulties."

The princess sent for the cage, and after she had related the circumstances to the Bird in the presence of her brothers, asked him what they should do in this perplexity. The Bird answered: "The princes, your brothers, must conform to the emperor's pleasure, and in their turn invite him to come and see your house."

"But, Bird," replied the princess, "my brothers and I love one another, and our friendship is yet undisturbed. Will not this step be injurious to that friendship?" "Not at all," replied the Bird; "it will tend rather to cement it." "Then," answered the princess, "the emperor will see me." The Bird told her it was necessary he should, and that everything would go better afterward.

Next morning the princes met the emperor hunting, who asked them if they had remembered to speak to their sister. Prince Bahman approached and answered: "Sir, we are ready to obey you, for we have not only obtained our sister's consent with great ease, but she took it amiss that we should pay her that deference in a matter wherein our duty to your majesty was concerned. If we have offended, we hope you will pardon us." "Do not be uneasy," replied the emperor. "I highly approve of your conduct, and hope you will have the same deference and attachment to my person, if I have ever so little share in your friendship." The princes, confounded at the emperor's goodness, returned no other answer but a low obeisance.

The emperor, contrary to his usual custom, did not hunt long that day. Presuming that the princes possessed wit equal to their courage and bravery, he longed with impatience to converse with them more at liberty. He made them ride on each side of him, an honour which was envied by the grand vizier, who was much mortified to see them preferred before him.

When the emperor entered his capital, the eyes of the people, who stood in crowds in the streets, were fixed upon the two Princes Bahman and Perviz; and they were earnest to know who they might be.

All, however, agreed in wishing that the emperor had been blessed with two such handsome princes, and said that his children would have been about the same age, if the queen had not been so unfortunate as to lose them.

The first thing the emperor did when he arrived at his palace was to conduct the princes into the principal apartments, who praised without affectation the beauty and symmetry of the rooms, and the richness of the furniture and ornaments. Afterward a magnificent repast was served up, and the emperor made them sit with him, which they at first refused; but finding it was his pleasure, they obeyed.

The emperor, who had himself much learning, particularly in history, foresaw that the princes, out of modesty and respect, would not take the liberty of beginning any conversation. Therefore, to give them an opportunity, he furnished them with sub-

jects all dinner-time. But whatever subject he introduced, they
shewed so much wit, judgment, and discernment, that he was
struck with admiration. "Were these my own children," said
he to himself, "and I had improved their talents by suitable
education, they could not have been more accomplished or
better informed." In short, he took such great pleasure in their
conversation, that, after having sat longer than usual, he led them
into his closet, where he pursued his conversation with them, and
at last said: "I never supposed that there were among my subjects in the country youths so well brought up, so lively, so capable; and I never was better pleased with any conversation than
yours; but it is time now we should relax our minds with some
diversion; and as nothing is more capable of enlivening the mind
than music, you shall hear a vocal and instrumental concert
which may not be disagreeable to you."

The emperor had no sooner spoken than the musicians, who
had orders to attend, entered, and answered fully the expecta-
tions the princes had been led to entertain of their abilities.
After the concerts, an excellent farce was acted, and the entertainment was concluded by dancers of both sexes.

The two princes, seeing night approach, prostrated themselves
at the emperor's feet; and having first thanked him for the
favours and honours he had heaped upon them, asked his permission to retire; which was granted by the emperor, who, in
dismissing them, said: "I give you leave to go; but remember,
you will be always welcome, and the oftener you come the greater
pleasure you will do me."

Before they went out of the emperor's presence, Prince
Bahman said: "Sir, may we presume to request that your majesty
will do us and our sister the honour to pass by our house, and
refresh yourself after your fatigue, the first time you take the

diversion of hunting in that neighbourhood? It is not worthy of your presence; but monarchs sometimes have vouchsafed to take shelter in a cottage." "My children," replied the emperor, "your house cannot be otherwise than beautiful and worthy of its owners. I will call and see it with pleasure, which will be the greater for having for my hosts you and your sister, who is already dear to me from the account you give me of the rare qualities with which she is endowed: and this satisfaction I will defer no longer than to-morrow. Early in the morning I will be at the place where I shall never forget that I first saw you. Meet me, and you shall be my guides."

When the Princes Bahman and Perviz had returned home, they gave the princess an account of the distinguished reception the emperor had given them, and told her that they had invited him to do them the honour, as he passed by, to call at their house, and that he had appointed the next day.

"If it be so," replied the princess, "we must think of preparing a repast fit for his majesty; and for that purpose I think it would be proper we should consult the Talking Bird, who will tell us, perhaps, what meats the emperor likes best." The princes approved of her plan, and after they had retired she consulted the Bird alone. "Bird," said she, "the emperor will do us the honour to-morrow to come and see our house, and we are to entertain him; tell us what we shall do to acquit ourselves to his satisfaction."

"Good mistress," replied the Bird, "you have excellent cooks, let them do the best they can; but above all things, let them prepare a dish of cucumbers stuffed full of pearls, which must be set before the emperor in the first course before all the other dishes."

"Cucumbers stuffed full of pearls!" cried Princess Periezade with amazement; "surely, Bird, you do not know what you say; it is an unheard of dish. The emperor may admire it as a piece of magnificence, but he will sit down to eat, and not to admire pearls; besides, all the pearls I possess are not enough for such a dish."

"Mistress," said the Bird, "do what I say, and be not uneasy about what may happen. Nothing but good will follow. As for the pearls, go early to-morrow morning to the foot of the first tree on your right hand in the park, dig under it, and you will find more than you want."

That night the princess ordered a gardener to be ready to attend her, and the next morning early, led him to the tree which the Bird had told her of, and bade him dig at its foot. When the gardener came to a certain depth, he found some resistance to the spade, and presently discovered a gold box about a foot square, which he showed the princess. "This," said she, "is what I brought you for; take care not to injure it with the spade."

When the gardener took up the box, he gave it into the princess's hands, who, as it was only fastened with neat little hasps, soon opened it, and found it full of pearls of a moderate size, but equal and fit for the use that was to be made of them. Very well satisfied with having found this treasure, after she had shut the box again, she put it under her arm and went back to the house, while the gardener threw the earth into the hole at the foot of the tree as it had been before.

The Princes Bahman and Perviz, who, as they were dressing themselves in their own apartments, saw their sister in the garden earlier than usual, as soon as they could get out went to her, and met her as she was returning with a gold box under her arm, which much surprised them. "Sister," said Bahman, "you carried nothing with you when we saw you before with the gardener, and now we see you have a golden box; is this some treasure found by the gardener, and did he come and tell you of it?"

"No, brother," answered the princess, "I took the gardener to the place where this casket was concealed, and showed him where to dig; but you will be more amazed when you see what it contains."

The princess opened the box, and when the princes saw that it was full of pearls, which, though small, were of great value, they asked her how she came to the knowledge of this treasure. "Brothers," said she, "come with me and I will tell you." The princess, as they returned to the house, gave them an account of her having consulted the Bird, as they had agreed she should, and the answer he had given her; the objection she had raised to preparing a dish of cucumbers stuffed full of pearls, and how he had told her where to find this box. The sister and brothers formed many conjectures to penetrate into what the Bird could mean by ordering them to prepare such a dish; but after much conversation, they agreed to follow his advice exactly.

As soon as the princess entered the house, she called for the head cook; and after she had given him directions about the entertainment for the emperor, said to him: "Besides all this, you must dress an extraordinary dish for the emperor's own eating, which nobody else must have anything to do with besides yourself. This dish must be of cucumbers stuffed with these pearls"; and at the same time she opened him the box, and showed him the jewels.

The chief cook, who had never heard of such a dish, started back, and showed his thoughts by his looks; which the princess penetrating, said: "I see you take me to be mad to order such a dish, which one may say with certainty was never made. I know this as well as you; but I am not mad, and give you these orders with the most perfect recollection. You must invent and do the best you can, and bring me back what pearls are left." The cook could make no reply, but took the box and retired; and afterward the princess gave directions to all the domestics to have everything in order, both in the house and gardens, to receive the emperor.

Next day the two princes went to the place appointed, and as soon as the emperor of Persia arrived the chase began and lasted till the heat of the sun obliged him to leave off. While Prince Bahman stayed to conduct the emperor to their house, Prince Perviz rode before to show the way, and when he came in sight of the house, spurred his horse, to inform the princess that the emperor was approaching; but she had been told by some servants whom she had placed to give notice, and the prince found her waiting ready to receive him.

When the emperor had entered the court-yard and alighted at the portico, the princess came and threw herself at his feet, and the two princes informed him she was their sister, and besought him to accept her respects.

The emperor stooped to raise her, and after he had gazed some time on her beauty, struck with her fine person and dignified air, she said: "The brothers are worthy of the sister, and she worthy of them; since, if I may judge of her understanding by her person, I am not amazed that the brothers would do nothing without their sister's consent; but," added he, "I hope to be better acquainted with you, my daughter, after I have seen the house."

"Sir," said the princess, "it is only a plain country residence, fit for such people as we are, who live retired from the great world. It is not to be compared with the magnificent palaces of emperors." "I cannot perfectly agree with you in opinion," said the emperor very obligingly "for its first appearance makes me suspect you; however, I will not pass my judgment upon it till I have seen it all; therefore be pleased to conduct me through the apartments."

The princess led the emperor through all the rooms except the hall; and, after he had considered them very attentively, and admired their variety, "My daughter," said he to the princess, "do you call this a country house? The finest and largest cities would soon be deserted if all country houses were like yours. I am no longer surprised that you despise the town. Now let me see the garden, which I doubt not is answerable to the house."

The princess opened a door which led into the garden, and the first object which presented itself to the emperor's view was the golden fountain. Surprised at so rare an object, he asked from whence that wonderful water, which gave so much pleasure to behold, had been procured; where was its source, and by what art it was made to play so high. He said he would presently take a nearer view of it.

The princess then led him to the spot where the harmonious tree was planted; and there the emperor heard a concert, different from all he had ever heard before; and stopping to see where the musicians were, he could discern nobody far or near, but still distinctly heard the music which ravished his senses. "My daughter," said he to the princess, "where are the musicians whom I hear? Are they under ground, or invisible in the air? Such excellent performers will hazard nothing by being seen; on the contrary, they would please the more."

"Sir," answered the princess, smiling, "they are not musicians, but the leaves of the tree your majesty sees before you, which form this concert; and if you will give yourself the trouble to go a little nearer, you will be convinced, and the voices will be the more distinct."

The emperor went nearer and was so charmed with the sweet harmony that he would never have been tired with hearing it, but that his desire to have a nearer view of the fountain of golden water forced him away. "Daughter," said he, "tell me, I pray you, whether this wonderful tree was found in your garden by chance, or was a present made to you, or have you procured it from some foreign country? It must certainly have come from a great distance, otherwise curious as I am after natural rarities I should have heard of it. What name do you call it by?"

"Sir," replied the princess, "this tree has no other name than that of the Singing Tree, and is not a native of this country. It would at present take up too much time to tell your majesty by what adventures it came here; its history is connected with the Golden Water and the Talking Bird, which came to me at the same time, and which your majesty may presently see. But if it be agreeable to your majesty, after you have rested yourself and recovered the fatigue of hunting, which must be the greater because of the sun's intense heat, I will do myself the honour of relating it to you."

"My daughter," replied the emperor, "my fatigue is so well recompensed by the wonderful things you have shown me, that I do not feel it in the least. Let me see the Golden Water, for I am impatient to see and admire afterward the Talking Bird."

When the emperor came to the Golden Water, his eyes were fixed so steadfastly upon the fountain, that he could not take them off. At last, addressing himself to the princess, he said: "As you tell me, daughter, that this water has no spring or communication, I conclude that it is foreign, as well as the Singing Tree."

THE TALKING BIRD

"Sir," replied the princess, "it is as your majesty conjectures; and to let you know that this water has no communication with any spring, I must inform you that the basin is one entire stone, so that the water cannot come in at the sides or underneath. But what your majesty will think most wonderful is that all this water proceeded but from one small flagon, emptied into this basin, which increased to the quantity you see, by a property peculiar to itself, and formed this fountain." "Well," said the emperor, going from the fountain, "this is enough for one time. I promise myself the pleasure to come and visit it often; but now let us go and see the Talking Bird."

As he went toward the hall, the emperor perceived a prodigious number of singing birds in the trees around, filling the air with their songs and warblings, and asked why there were so many there and none on the other trees in the garden. "The reason, sir," answered the princess, "is because they come from all parts to accompany the song of the Talking Bird, which your majesty may see in a cage in one of the windows of the hall we are approaching; and if you attend, you will perceive that his notes are sweeter than those of any of the other birds, even the nightingale's."

The emperor went into the hall; and as the Bird continued singing, the princess raised her voice, and said, "My slave, here is the emperor, pay your compliments to him." The Bird left off singing that instant, when all the other birds ceased also, and said: "The emperor is welcome; God prosper him and prolong his life!" As the entertainment was served on the sofa near the window where the Bird was placed, the sultan replied, as he was taking his seat: "Bird, I thank you, and am overjoyed to find in you the sultan and king of birds."

As soon as the emperor saw the dish of cucumbers set before

him, thinking they were prepared in the best manner, he reached
out his hand and took one; but when he cut it, was in extreme
surprise to find it stuffed with pearls. "What novelty is this?"
said he; "and with what design were these cucumbers stuffed
thus with pearls, since pearls are not to be eaten?" He looked
at his hosts to ask them the meaning when the Bird interrupting him, said: "Can your majesty be in such great astonishment at cucumbers stuffed with pearls, which you see with your
own eyes, and yet so easily believe that the queen, your wife,
gave birth to a dog, a cat, and a piece of wood?" "I believed
those things," replied the emperor, "because the attendants assured me of the facts." "Those attendants, sir," replied the
Bird, "were the queen's two sisters, who, envious of her happiness
in being preferred by your majesty before them, to satisfy their
envy and revenge, have abused your majesty's credulity. If you
interrogate them, they will confess their crime. The two brothers
and the sister whom you see before you are your own children,
whom they exposed, and who were taken in by the intendant of
your gardens, who provided nurses for them, and took care of
their education."

This speech presently cleared up the emperor's understanding. "Bird," cried he, "I believe the truth which you discover to
me. The inclination which drew me to them told me plainly
they must be of my own blood. Come then, my sons, come, my
daughter, let me embrace you, and give you the first marks of a
father's love and tenderness." The emperor then rose, and after
having embraced the two princes and the princess, and mingled
his tears with theirs, said: "It is not enough, my children; you
must embrace each other, not as the children of the intendant of
my gardens, to whom I have been so much obliged for preserving
your lives, but as my own children, of the royal blood of the

monarchs of Persia, whose glory, I am persuaded you will maintain."

After the two princes and princess had embraced mutually with new satisfaction, the emperor sat down again with them, and finished his meal in haste; and when he had done, said: "My children, you see in me your father; to-morrow I will bring the queen, your mother, therefore prepare to receive her."

The emperor afterward mounted his horse, and returned with expedition to his capitol. The first thing he did, as soon as he had alighted and entered his palace, was to command the grand vizier to seize the queen's two sisters. They were taken from their houses separately, convicted, and condemned to death; which sentence was put in execution within an hour.

In the meantime, the Emperor Kosrouschah, followed by all the lords of his court who were then present, went on foot to the door of the great mosque; and after he had taken the queen out of the strict confinement she had languished under for so many years, embracing her in the miserable condition to which she was then reduced, said to her with tears in his eyes: "I come to entreat your pardon for the injustice I have done you, and to make you the reparation I ought; which I have begun, by punishing the unnatural wretches who put the abominable cheat upon me; and I hope you will look upon it as complete, when I present to you two accomplished princes and a lovely princess, our children. Come and resume your former rank, with all the honours which are your due." All this was done and said before great crowds of people who flocked from all parts at the first news of what was passing, and immediately spread the joyful intelligence through the city.

Next morning early the emperor and queen, whose mournful humiliating dress was changed for magnificent robes, went with all their court to the house built by the intendant of the gardens, where the emperor presented the Princes Bahman and Perviz, and the Princess Periezade to their enraptured mother. "These, much injured wife," said he, "are the two princes your sons, and the princess your daughter; embrace them with the same tenderness I have done, since they are worthy both of me and you." The tears flowed plentifully down their cheeks at these tender embraces, especially the queen's, from the comfort and joy of having two such princes for her sons, and such a princess for her daughter, on whose account she had so long endured the severest afflictions.

The two princes and the princess had prepared a magnificent repast for the emperor and queen and their court. As soon as that was over, the emperor led the queen into the garden, and shewed her the Harmonious Tree and the beautiful effect of the Golden Fountain. She had seen the Bird in his cage, and the emperor had spared no panegyric in his praise during the repast.

When there was nothing to detain the emperor any longer, he took horse, and with the Princes Bahman and Perviz on his right hand, and the queen consort and the princess at his left, preceded and followed by all the officers of his court, according to their rank, returned to his capital. Crowds of people came out to meet them, and with acclamations of joy ushered them into the city, where all eyes were fixed not only upon the queen, and her royal children, but also upon the Bird, which the princess carried before her in his cage, admiring his sweet notes, which had drawn all the other birds about him, and followed him flying from tree to tree in the country, and from one house top to another in the city. The Princes Bahman and Perviz and the Princess Periezade were at length brought to the palace with pomp, and nothing was to be seen or heard all that night but illuminations and rejoicings both in the palace and in the utmost parts of the city, which lasted many days, and were continued throughout the empire of Persia, as intelligence of the joyful event reached the several provinces.

THE STORY OF THE FISHERMAN
AND THE GENIE

THERE was once an aged fisherman who was so poor that he could scarcely earn as much as would maintain himself, his wife, and three children. He went every day to fish betimes in the morning, and imposed it as a law upon himself not to cast his nets above four times a day. He went one morning by moonlight, and coming to the seaside, undressed himself, and cast in his nets. As he drew them toward the shore, he found them very heavy, and thought he had a good draught of fish, at which he rejoiced; but a moment after, perceiving that instead of fish his net contained nothing but the carcass of an ass, he was much vexed.

When he had mended his nets, which the carcass of the ass had broken in several places, he threw them in a second time; and when he drew them, found a great deal of resistance, which made him think he had taken abundance of fish; but he found nothing except a basket full of gravel and slime, which grieved him extremely. "O Fortune!" cried he, with a lamentable tone, "be not angry with me, nor persecute a wretch who prays thee to spare him. I came hither from my house to seek for my livelihood, and thou pronouncest against me a sentence of death. I have no other trade but this to subsist by, and, notwithstanding all my care, I can scarcely provide what is necessary for my family. But I am to blame to complain of thee; thou takest pleasure to persecute honest people, and advancest those who have no virtue to recommend them."

Having finished this complaint, he fretfully threw away the basket, and, washing his nets from the slime, cast them a third time, but brought up nothing except stones, shells, and mud. No language can express his disappointment; he was almost distracted. However, when day began to appear, he did not forget to say his prayers like a good Mussulman, and he added to them this petition: "Lord, thou knowest that I cast my nets only four times a day; I have already drawn them three times, without the least reward for my labour: I am only to cast them once more; I pray thee to render the sea favourable to me, as thou didst to Moses."

The fisherman, having finished this prayer, cast his nets the fourth time; and when he thought it was proper, drew them as formerly with great difficulty; but instead of fish found nothing in them but a vessel of yellow copper, which, from its weight, seemed not to be empty; and he observed that it was fastened and closed with lead, having the impression of a seal upon it. This turn of fortune rejoiced him: "I will sell it," said he, "to the founder, and with the money buy a measure of corn." He examined the vessel on all sides, and shook it to see if its contents made any noise, but heard nothing. This circumstance, with the impression of the seal upon the cover, made him think it enclosed something precious. To try this, he took a knife and opened it with very little labour. He turned the mouth downward, but nothing came out, which surprised him extremely. He placed it before him, but while he viewed it attentively, there burst forth a very thick smoke, which obliged him to retire two or three paces back.

The smoke ascended to the clouds, and, extending itself along the sea and upon the shore, formed a great mist, which filled the fisherman with astonishment. When the smoke was all out of the vessel, it reunited, and became a solid body, of which was formed a genie twice as high as the greatest of giants. At the sight of such a monster the fisherman would fain have fled, but was so frightened that he could not move.

"Solomon," cried the genie immediately, "Solomon, the great prophet, pardon, pardon; I will never more oppose your will, I will obey all your commands."

The fisherman, when he heard these words of the genie, recovered his courage and said to him: "Thou proud spirit, what is it you say? It is above eighteen hundred years since the prophet Solomon died, and we are now at the end of time. Tell me your history, and how you came to be shut up in this vessel."

The genie, turning to the fisherman with a fierce look, said: "Thou must address me with more courtesy; thou art a presumptuous fellow to call me a proud spirit; speak to me more respectfully, or I will kill thee." "Ah!" replied the fisherman, "why should you kill me? Did I not just now set you at liberty, and have you already forgotten my services?"

"No, I remember it," said the genie, "but that shall not save thy life: I have only one favour to grant thee." "And what is that?" asked the fisherman. "It is," answered the genie, "to give thee thy choice in what manner thou wouldst have me put thee to death." "But wherein have I offended you?" demanded the fisherman. "Is that your reward for the service I have rendered you?" "I cannot treat thee otherwise," said the genie; "and that thou mayest know the reason, hearken to my story."

"I am one of those rebellious spirits that opposed the will of Solomon, the son of David, and to avenge himself, that monarch sent Asaph, the son of Barakhia, his chief minister, to apprehend me. Asaph seized my person, and brought me by force before his master's throne.

"Solomon commanded me to acknowledge his power, and to submit to his commands. I bravely refused, and told him I would rather expose myself to his resentment, than swear fealty as he required. To punish me, he shut me up in this copper vessel; and that I might not break my prison, he himself stamped upon this leaden cover his seal with the great name of God engraven upon it. He then gave the vessel to one of the genies who had submitted, with orders to throw me into the sea.

"During the first hundred years of my imprisonment, I swore that if any one should deliver me before the expiration of that period, I would make him rich, even after his death; but that century ran out, and nobody did me the good office. During the second, I made an oath that I would open all the treasures of the earth to any one that might set me at liberty; but with no better success. In the third, I promised to make my deliverer a potent monarch, and to grant him every day three requests, of what nature soever they might be; but this century passed as well as the two former, and I continued in prison. At last, being angry to find myself a prisoner so long, I swore that if afterward any one should deliver me, I would kill him without mercy, and grant him no favour but to choose the manner of his death; and, therefore, since thou hast delivered me to-day, I give thee that choice."

This discourse afflicted the fisherman extremely: "I am very unfortunate," cried he, "to come hither to do such a kindness to one that is so ungrateful. I beg you to consider your injustice, and revoke such an unreasonable oath; pardon me, and Heaven will pardon you; if you grant me my life, Heaven will protect you from all attempts against your own." "No, thy death is resolved on," said the genie, "only choose in what manner thou wilt die." The fisherman, perceiving the genie to be resolute, was extremely grieved, not so much for himself, as on account of his three children, and bewailed the misery they must be reduced to by his death. He endeavoured still to appease the genie, and said, "Alas! be pleased to take pity on me, in consideration of the service I have done you." "I have told thee already," replied the genie, "it is for that very reason I must kill thee." "That is strange," said the fisherman, "are you resolved to reward good with evil? The proverb truly says, 'He who does good to one who deserves it not, is always ill rewarded.'" "Do not lose time," interrupted the genie; "all thy chattering shall not divert me from my purpose; make haste, and tell me what kind of death thou preferrest?"

Necessity is the mother of invention. The fisherman bethought himself of a stratagem. "Since I must die then," said he to the genie, "I submit to the will of Heaven; but before I choose the manner of my death, I conjure you, by the great name which was engraven upon the seal of the prophet Solomon, to answer me truly the question I am going to ask you."

The genie finding himself obliged to a positive answer by this adjuration, trembled, and replied to the fisherman: "Ask what thou wilt, but make haste."

The genie having thus promised to speak the truth, the fisherman said to him: "I wish to know if you were actually in this vessel: dare you swear it by the name of the great God?" "Yes," replied the genie, "I do swear by His great name that I was." "In good faith," answered the fisherman, "I cannot believe you; the vessel is not capable of holding one of your size, and how should it be possible that your whole body could lie in it?" "I swear to thee, notwithstanding," replied the genie, "that

THE FISHERMAN AND THE GENIE

I was there just as you see me here. Is it possible that thou dost not believe me after the solemn oath I have taken ?" "Truly not I," said the fisherman; "nor will I believe you, unless you go into the vessel again."

Upon this the body of the genie dissolved and changed itself into smoke, extending as before upon the sea-shore; and at last being collected, it began to re-enter the vessel, which it continued to do by a slow and equal motion, till no part remained out; when immediately a voice came forth, which said to the fisherman: "Well, incredulous fellow, dost thou not believe me now ?"

The fisherman, instead of answering the genie, took the cover of lead, and having speedily replaced it on the vessel, "Genie," cried he, "now it is your turn to beg my favour, and to choose which way I shall put you to death; but it is better that I should throw you into the sea, whence I took you: and then I will build a house upon the shore, where I will reside and give notice to all fishermen who come to throw in their nets, to beware of such a wicked genie as you are, who have made an oath to kill him that shall set you at liberty."

The genie, enraged at these expressions, struggled to free himself; but it was impossible, for the impression of Solomon's seal prevented him. Perceiving that the fisherman had the advantage of him, he thought fit to dissemble his anger; "Fisherman," said he, "take heed you do not what you threaten; for what I spoke to you was only by way of jest." "O genie!" replied the fisherman, "thou who wast but a moment ago the greatest of all genies, and now art the least of them, thy crafty discourse will signify nothing, to the sea thou shalt return. If thou hast been there already so long as thou hast told me, thou mayest very well stay there till the day of judgment. I begged of thee, in

God's name, not to take away my life, and thou didst reject my prayers; I am obliged to treat thee in the same manner."

The genie omitted nothing that he thought likely to prevail with the fisherman: "Open the vessel," said he, "give me my liberty, and I promise to satisfy you to your own content." "Thou art a traitor," replied the fisherman, "I should deserve to lose my life, if I were such a fool as to trust thee."

"My good fisherman," replied the genie, "I conjure you once more not to be guilty of such cruelty; consider that it is not good to avenge one's self, and that, on the other hand, it is commendable to do good for evil; do not treat me as Imama formerly treated Ateca." "And what did Imama to Ateca?" inquired the fisherman. "Ho!" cried the genie, "if you have a mind to be informed, open the vessel: do you think that I can be in a humour to relate stories in so strait a prison? I will tell you as many as you please, when you have let me out." "No," said the fisherman, "I will not let thee out; it is in vain to talk of it; I am just going to throw thee into the bottom of the sea." "Hear me one word more," cried the genie; "I promise to do you no hurt; nay, far from that, I will show you a way to become exceedingly rich."

The hope of delivering himself from poverty prevailed with the fisherman. "I could listen to thee," said he, "were there any credit to be given to thy word; swear to me, by the great name of God, that thou wilt faithfully perform what thou promisest, and I will open the vessel; I do not believe thou wilt dare to break such an oath."

The genie swore to him, upon which the fisherman immediately took off the covering of the vessel. At that instant the smoke ascended, and the genie, having resumed his form, the first thing he did was to kick the vessel into the sea. This action alarmed the fisherman. "Genie," said he, "will not you keep the oath you just now made?"

The genie laughed at his fear, and answered: "Fisherman, be not afraid, I only did it to divert myself, and to see if you would be alarmed at it; but to convince you that I am in earnest, take your nets and follow me." As he spoke these words, he walked before the fisherman, who having taken up his nets, followed him, but with some distrust. They passed by the town, and came to the top of a mountain, from whence they descended into a vast plain, which brought them to a lake that lay betwixt four hills.

When they reached the side of the lake, the genie said to the fisherman: "Cast in your nets and catch fish." The fisherman did not doubt of taking some, because he saw a great number in the water; but he was extremely surprised when he found they were of four colours; white, red, blue, and yellow. He threw in his nets and brought out one of each colour. Having never seen the like before, he could not but admire them, and, judging that he might get a considerable sum for them, he was very joyful. "Carry those fish," said the genie to him, "and present them to your sultan; he will give you more money for them. You may come daily to fish in this lake; but I give you warning not to throw in your nets above once a day, otherwise you will repent." Having spoken thus, he struck his foot upon the ground, which opened, and after it had swallowed him up, closed again.

The fisherman, being resolved to follow the genie's advice, forbore casting in his nets a second time, and returned to the town very well satisfied, and making a thousand reflections upon his adventure. He went immediately to the sultan's palace to offer his fish, and his majesty was much surprised when he saw the wonders which the fisherman presented. He took them up one after another, and viewed them with attention; and after having admired them a long time, "Take those fish," said he to his vizier, "and carry them to the cook whom the emperor of the Greeks has sent me. I cannot imagine but that they must be as good as they are beautiful."

The vizier carried them as he was directed, and delivering them to the cook, said: "Here are four fish just brought to the sultan; he orders you to dress them." He then returned to the sultan, who commanded him to give the fisherman four hundred pieces of gold, which he did accordingly.

The fisherman, who had never seen so much money, could scarcely believe his good fortune, but thought the whole must be a dream, until he found it otherwise, by being able to provide necessaries for his family with the produce of his nets.

As soon as the sultan's cook had cleaned the fish, she put them upon the fire in a frying-pan, with oil, and when she thought them fried enough on one side, she turned them upon the other; but, O monstrous prodigy! scarcely were they turned, when the wall of the kitchen divided, and a young lady of wonderful beauty entered from the opening. She held a rod in her hand and was clad in flowered satin, with pendants in her ears, a necklace of large pearls, and bracelets of gold set with rubies. She moved toward the frying-pan, to the great amazement of the cook, and striking one of the fish with the end of the rod, said: "Fish, fish, are you in your duty?" The fish having answered nothing, she repeated these words, and then the four fish lifted up their heads, and replied: "Yes, yes: if you reckon, we reckon; if you pay your debts, we pay ours; if you fly, we overcome, and are content." As soon as they had finished these words, the lady overturned the frying-pan, and returned into the open part of the wall, which closed immediately, and became as it was before.

The smoke ascended to the clouds, and extending itself along
the sea and upon the shore formed a great mist.

THE FISHERMAN AND THE GENIE

The cook was greatly frightened at what had happened, and coming a little to herself went to take up the fish that had fallen on the hearth, but found them blacker than coal and not fit to be carried to the sultan. This grievously troubled her, and she fell to weeping most bitterly. "Alas!" said she, "what will become of me? If I tell the sultan what I have seen, I am sure he will not believe me, but will be enraged against me."

While she was thus bewailing herself, the grand vizier entered, and asked her if the fish were ready. She told him all that had occurred, which we may easily imagine astonished him; but without speaking a word of it to the sultan he invented an excuse that satisfied him, and sending immediately for the fisherman bid him bring four more such fish, for a misfortune had befallen the others, so that they were not fit to be carried to the royal table. The fisherman, without saying anything of what the genie had told him, told the vizier he had a great way to go for them, in order to excuse himself from bringing them that day, but said that he would certainly bring them on the morrow.

Accordingly the fisherman went away by night, and coming to the lake, threw in his nets betimes next morning, took four fish like the former, and brought them to the vizier at the hour appointed. The minister took them himself, carried them to the kitchen, and shutting himself up with the cook, she cleaned them and put them on the fire. When they were fried on one side, and she had turned them upon the other, the kitchen wall again opened, and the same lady came in with the rod in her hand, struck one of the fish, spoke to it as before, and all four gave her the same answer.

After they had spoken to the young lady, she overturned the frying-pan with her rod, and retired into the wall. The grand vizier being witness to what had passed, "This is too wonderful and extraordinary," said he, "to be concealed from the sultan; I will inform him of this prodigy."

The sultan, being much surprised, sent immediately for the fisherman, and said to him: "Friend, cannot you bring me four more such fish?" The fisherman replied: "If your majesty will be pleased to allow me three days, I will do it." Having obtained his time, he went to the lake immediately, and at the first throwing in of his net he caught four fish, and brought them directly to the sultan, who was so much the more rejoiced, as he did not expect them so soon, and ordered him four hundred pieces of gold. As soon as the sultan had the fish, he ordered them to be carried into his closet, with all that was necessary for frying them; and having shut himself up with the vizier, the minister cleaned them, put them into the pan, and when they were fried on one side, turned them upon the other; then the wall of the closet opened, but instead of the young lady, there came out a black, in the habit of a slave, and of a gigantic stature, with a great green staff in his hand. He advanced toward the pan, and touching one of the fish with his staff, said, with a terrible voice: "Fish, are you in your duty?" At these words the fish raised up their heads, and answered: "Yes, yes; we are; if you reckon, we reckon; if you pay your debts, we pay ours; if you fly, we overcome and are content."

The fish had no sooner finished these words, than the black threw the pan into the middle of the closet, and reduced them to a coal. Having done this, he retired fiercely, and entering again into the aperture, it closed, and the wall appeared just as it did before.

"After what I have seen," said the sultan to the vizier, "it will not be possible for me to be easy; these fish, without doubt, signify something extraordinary." He sent for the fisherman, and when he came, said to him: "Fisherman, the fish you have brought us make me very uneasy; where did you catch them?" "Sir," answered he, "I fished for them in a lake situated betwixt four hills, beyond the mountain that we see from hence." "Know'st thou not that lake?" said the sultan to the vizier. "No," replied the vizier, "I never so much as heard of it, although I have for sixty years hunted beyond that mountain." The sultan asked the fisherman how far the lake might be from the palace. The fisherman answered it was not above three hours' journey; upon this assurance the sultan commanded all his court to take horse, and the fisherman served them for a guide. They all ascended the mountain, and at the foot of it they saw, to their great surprise, a vast plain that nobody had observed till then, and at last they came to the lake, which they found to be situated betwixt four hills, as the fisherman had described. The water was so transparent that they observed all the fish to be like those which the fisherman had brought to the palace.

The sultan stood upon the bank of the lake, and after beholding the fish with admiration, demanded of his courtiers if it were possible they had never seen this lake which was within so short a distance of the town. They all answered that they had never so much as heard of it.

"Since you all agree that you never heard of it," said the sultan, "and as I am no less astonished than you are at this novelty, I am resolved not to return to my palace till I learn how this lake came here, and why all the fish in it are of four colours." Having spoken thus, he ordered his court to encamp; and immediately his pavilion and the tents of his household were planted upon the banks of the lake.

When night came the sultan retired under his pavilion, and spoke to the grand vizier thus: "Vizier, my mind is uneasy;

this lake transported hither, the black that appeared to us in my closet, and the fish that we heard speak; all these things so much excite my curiosity that I cannot resist my impatient desire to have it satisfied. To this end I am resolved to withdraw alone from the camp, and I order you to keep my absence secret: stay in my pavilion, and to-morrow morning, when the emirs and courtiers come to attend my levee, send them away and tell them that I am somewhat indisposed and wish to be alone; and the following days tell them the same thing, till I return."

The grand vizier endeavoured to divert the sultan from this design; he represented to him the danger to which he might be exposed, and that all his labour might perhaps be in vain; but it was to no purpose; the sultan was resolved. He put on a suit fit for walking and took his cimeter; and as soon as he found that all was quiet in the camp, went out alone, and passed over one of the hills without much difficulty; he found the descent still more easy, and when he came to the plain, walked on till the sun arose, and then he saw before him, at a considerable distance, a vast building. He rejoiced at the sight, in hopes of receiving there the information he sought. When he drew near, he found it was a magnificent palace, or rather a strong castle, of black polished marble, and covered with fine steel, as smooth as glass. Being highly pleased that he had so speedily met with something worthy his curiosity, he stopped before the front of the castle, and considered it with attention.

He then advanced toward the gate, which had two leaves, one of them open; though he might immediately have entered, yet he thought it best to knock. This he did at first softly, and waited for some time; but seeing no one, and supposing he had not been heard, he knocked harder the second time, and after that he knocked again and again, but no one yet appearing, he was exceedingly surprised; for he could not think that a castle in such repair was without inhabitants. "If there be no one in it," said he to himself, "I have nothing to fear; and if it be inhabited, I have wherewith to defend myself."

At last he entered, and when he came within the porch, he cried: "Is there no one here to receive a stranger who comes in for some refreshment as he passes by?" He repeated the same words two or three times; but though he spoke very loud, he was not answered. The silence increased his astonishment: he came into a spacious court, and looked on every side for inhabitants, but discovered none.

Perceiving nobody in the court, he entered the grand halls, which were hung with silk tapestry, the alcoves and sofas covered with stuffs of Mecca, and the porches with the richest stuffs of India. He came afterward into a superb saloon, in the middle of which was a fountain, with a lion of massy gold at each angle: water issued from the mouths of the four lions, and as it fell, formed diamonds and pearls resembling a jet d'eau, which, springing from the middle of the fountain, rose nearly to the top of a cupola painted in Arabesque.

The castle, on three sides, was encompassed by a garden, with parterres of flowers and shrubbery; and to complete the beauty of the place, an infinite number of birds filled the air with their harmonious notes, and always remained there, nets being spread over the garden, and fastened to the palace to confine them. The sultan walked from apartment to apartment, where he found everything rich and magnificent. Being tired with walking, he sat down in a veranda, which had a view over the garden, reflecting upon what he had seen, when suddenly he heard the voice of one complaining, in lamentable tones. He listened with attention, and heard distinctly these words: "O fortune! thou who wouldst not suffer me longer to enjoy a happy lot, forbear to persecute me, and by a speedy death put an end to my sorrows. Alas! is it possible that I am still alive, after so many torments as I have suffered!"

The sultan rose up, advanced toward the place whence he heard the voice, and coming to the door of a great hall, opened it, and saw a handsome young man, richly habited, seated upon a throne raised a little above the ground. Melancholy was painted on his countenance. The sultan drew near and saluted him; the young man returned his salutation, by an inclination of his head, not being able to rise, at the same time saying: "My lord, I should rise to receive you, but am hindered by sad necessity, and therefore hope you will not be offended." "My lord," replied the sultan, "I am much obliged to you for having so good an opinion of me: as to the reason of your not rising, whatever your apology be, I heartily accept it. Being drawn hither by your complaints, and afflicted by your grief, I come to offer you my help. I flatter myself that you will relate to me the history of your misfortunes; but inform me first of the meaning of the lake near the palace, where the fish are of four colours; whose castle is this; how you came to be here; and why you are alone."

Instead of answering these questions, the young man began to weep bitterly. "How inconstant is fortune!" cried he; "she takes pleasure to pull down those she has raised. Where are they who enjoy quietly the happiness which they hold of her, and whose day is always clear and serene?"

The sultan, moved with compassion to see him in such a condition, prayed him to relate the cause of his excessive grief. "Alas! my lord," replied the young man, "how is it possible but I should grieve, and my eyes be inexhaustible fountains of tears?"

THE YOUNG KING OF THE BLACK ISLES

At these words, lifting up his robe, he showed the sultan that he was a man only from the head to the girdle, and that the other half of his body was black marble.

The sultan was much surprised when he saw the deplorable condition of the young man. "That which you show me," said he, "while it fills me with horror, excites my curiosity, so that I am impatient to hear your history, which, no doubt, must be extraordinary, and I am persuaded that the lake and the fish make some part of it; therefore I conjure you to relate it. You will find some comfort in so doing, since it is certain that the unfortunate find relief in making known their distress." "I will not refuse your request," replied the young man, "though I cannot comply without renewing my grief. But I give you notice beforehand, to prepare your ears, your mind, and even your eyes, for things which surpass all that the imagination can conceive."

THE HISTORY OF THE YOUNG KING OF THE BLACK ISLES

"You must know, my lord," said the wretched prisoner, "that my father, named Mahmoud, was monarch of this country. This is the kingdom of the Black Isles, which takes its name from the four small neighbouring mountains; for those mountains were formerly isles, and the capital where the king, my father, resided was situated on the spot now occupied by the lake you have seen. The sequel of my history will inform you of the reason for those changes.

"The king, my father, died when he was seventy years of age; I had no sooner succeeded him than I married, and the lady I chose to share the royal dignity with me was my cousin. I had so much reason to be satisfied with her affection, and, on my part, loved her with so much tenderness, that nothing could surpass the harmony of our union. This lasted five years, at the end of which time I perceived the queen ceased to delight in my attentions.

"One day, after dinner, while she was at the bath, I found myself inclined to repose, and lay down upon a sofa. Two of her ladies, who were then in my chamber, came and sat down, one at my head and the other at my feet, with fans in their hands to moderate the heat, and to prevent the flies from disturbing me. They thought I was asleep, and spoke in whispers; but as I only closed my eyes, I heard all their conversation.

"One of them said to the other, 'Is not the queen wrong, not to love so amiable a prince?' 'Certainly,' replied her companion; 'I do not understand the reason, neither can I conceive why she goes out every night, and leaves him alone! Is it possible that he does not perceive it?' 'Alas!' said the first, 'how should he? She mixes every evening in his liquor the juice of a certain herb, which makes him sleep so sound all night that she has time to go where she pleases, and as day begins to appear she comes and wakes him by the smell of something she puts under his nostrils.'

"You may guess, my lord, how much I was surprised at this conversation, and with what sentiments it inspired me; yet whatever emotion it excited I had sufficient self-command to dissemble, and feigned to awake without having heard a word.

"The queen returned from the bath, we supped together, and she presented me with a cup full of such liquid as I was accustomed to drink; but instead of putting it to my mouth, I went to a window that was open, threw out the water so quickly that she did not perceive it, and returned.

THE YOUNG KING OF THE BLACK ISLES

"Soon after, believing that I was asleep, she arose with so little precaution, that she whispered loud enough for me to hear her distinctly, 'Sleep on, and may you never wake again!' and so saying, she dressed herself, and went out of the chamber.

"As soon as the queen, my wife, was gone, I arose in haste, took my cimeter, and followed her so quickly that I soon heard the sound of her feet before me, and then walked softly after her. She passed through several gates, which opened upon her pronouncing some magical words, and the last she opened was that of the garden, which she entered. I stopped at this gate, that she might not perceive me as she passed along a parterre; then looking after her as far as the darkness of the night permitted, I saw her enter a little wood, whose walks were guarded by thick palisadoes. I went thither by another way, and concealing myself, I saw her walking there with a man.

"I did not fail to lend the most attentive ear to their discourse, and heard her address herself thus to her gallant: 'I do not deserve,' she said, 'to be reproached by you for want of diligence. You well know the reason; but if all the proofs of affection I have already given you be not sufficient to convince you of my sincerity, I am ready to give you others more decisive: you need but command me, you know my power; I will, if you desire it, before sunrise convert this great city, and this superb palace, into frightful ruins, inhabited only by wolves, owls, and ravens. If you would have me transport all the stones of those walls so solidly built, beyond Mount Caucasus, the bounds of the habitable world, speak but the word, and all shall be changed.'

"As the queen finished this speech she and her companion came to the end of the walk, turned to enter another, and passed before me. I had already drawn my cimeter, and the man being next me, I struck him on the neck, and brought him to the ground. I concluded I had killed him, and therefore retired speedily without making myself known to the queen, whom I chose to spare, because she was my kinswoman.

"The wound I had given her companion was mortal; but by her enchantments she preserved him in an existence in which he could not be said to be either dead or alive. As I crossed the garden to return to the palace, I heard the queen loudly lamenting, and judging by her cries how much she was grieved, I was pleased that I had spared her life.

"As soon as I had reached my apartment, I went to bed, and being satisfied with having punished the villain who had injured me, fell asleep.

"Next morning I arose, went to my closet, and dressed myself. I afterward held my council. At my return, the queen, clad in mourning, her hair dishevelled, and part of it torn off, presented herself before me, and said: 'I come to beg your majesty not to be surprised to see me in this condition. My heavy affliction is occasioned by intelligence of three distressing events which I have just received.' 'Alas! what are they, madam?' said I. 'The death of the queen, my dear mother,' she replied, 'that of the king, my father, killed in battle, and of one of my brothers, who has fallen down a precipice.'

"I was not displeased that she used these pretexts to conceal the true cause of her grief. 'Madam,' said I, 'so far from blaming, I assure you I heartily commiserate your sorrow. I should feel surprise if you were insensible to such heavy calamities: weep on; your tears are so many proofs of your tenderness; but I hope that time and reflection will moderate your grief.'

"She retired into her apartment, where, giving herself wholly up to sorrow, she spent a whole year in mourning and lamentation. At the end of that period, she begged permission to erect a burying-place for herself, within the bounds of the palace, where she would continue, she told me, to the end of her days: I consented, and she built a stately edifice, and called it the Palace of Tears. When it was finished, she caused the object of her care to be conveyed thither; she had hitherto prevented his dying, by potions which she had administered to him; and she continued to convey them to him herself every day after he came to the Palace of Tears.

"Yet, with all her enchantments, she could not cure the wretch; he was not only unable to walk or support himself, but had also lost the use of his speech, and exhibited no sign of life except in his looks.

"Every day the queen made him two long visits. I was well apprised of this, but pretended ignorance. One day my curiosity induced me to go to the Palace of Tears, to observe how my consort employed herself, and from a place where she could not see me, I heard her thus address the wounded ruffian: 'I am afflicted to the highest degree to behold you in this condition,' she cried, 'I am as sensible as yourself of the tormenting pain you endure; but, dear soul, I am continually speaking to you, and you do not answer me: how long will you remain silent? Speak only one word: alas! the sweetest moments of my life are these I spend here in partaking of your grief.'

"At these words, which were several times interrupted by her sighs, I lost all patience: and discovering myself, came up to her, and said, 'Madam, you have wept enough, it is time to give over this sorrow, which dishonours us both; you have too much forgotten what you owe to me and to yourself.' 'Sire,' said she, 'if you have any kindness or compassion for me left, I beseech you to put no restraint upon me; allow me to indulge my grief, which it is impossible for time to assuage.'

"When I perceived that my remonstrance, instead of restoring her to a sense of duty, served only to increase her anguish, I ceased speaking and retired. She continued every day to visit her charge, and for two whole years abandoned herself to grief and despair.

"I went a second time to the Palace of Tears, while she was there. I concealed myself again, and heard her thus cry out: 'It is now three years since you spoke one word to me; you answer not the proofs I give you of my devotion by my sighs and lamentations. Is it from insensibility, or contempt? O tomb! tell me by what miracle thou becamest the depository of the rarest treasure the world ever contained.'

"I must confess, my lord, I was enraged at these expressions; for, in truth, this adored mortal was by no means what you would imagine him to have been. He was a black Indian, one of the original natives of this country. I was so enraged at the language addressed to him, that I discovered myself, and apostrophising the tomb in my turn, I cried, 'O tomb! why dost thou not swallow up that monster so revolting to human nature, or rather why dost thou not swallow up this pair of monsters?'

"I had scarcely uttered these words, when the queen, who sat by the black, rose up like a fury: 'Miscreant!' said she, 'thou art the cause of my grief; do not think I am ignorant of this, I have dissembled too long. It was thy barbarous hand that brought the object of my fondness into this lamentable condition; and thou hast the cruelty to come and insult me.' 'Yes,' said I, in a rage, 'it was I who chastised that monster, according to his desert; I ought to have treated thee in the same manner; I now repent that I did not; thou hast too long abused my goodness.' As I spoke these words, I drew out my cimeter, and lifted up my hand to punish her; but regarding me stead-

fastly, she said with a jeering smile, 'Moderate thine anger.'
At the same time she pronounced words I did not understand;
and afterward added, 'By virtue of my enchantments, I command thee to become half marble and half man.' Immediately,
my lord, I became what you see, a dead man among the living,
and a living man among the dead. After this cruel sorceress,
unworthy of the name of queen, had metamorphosed me thus,
and brought me into this hall, by another enchantment she
destroyed my capital, which was very flourishing and populous;
she annihilated the houses, the public places and markets, and
reduced the site of the whole to the lake and desert plain you have
seen; the fishes of four colours in the waters are the four kinds
of inhabitants, of different religions, which the city contained.
The white are the Mussulmans; the red, the Persians, who
worship fire; the blue, the Christians; and the yellow, the Jews.
The four little hills were the four islands that gave name to this
kingdom. I learned all this from the enchantress, who, to add to
my affliction, related to me these effects of her rage. But this
is not all; her revenge not being satisfied with the destruction of
my dominions, and the metamorphosis of my person, she comes
every day, and gives me over my naked shoulders a hundred
lashes with a whip until I am covered with blood. When she
has finished this part of my punishment, she throws over me a
coarse stuff of goat's hair, and over that this robe of brocade, not
to honour, but to mock me."

When he came to this part of his narrative, the young king
could not restrain his tears; and the sultan was himself so affected
by the relation, that he could not find utterance for any words
of consolation. Shortly after, the young king, lifting up his eyes
to heaven, exclaimed, "Mighty creator of all things, I submit
myself to Thy judgments, and to the decrees of Thy providence:

I endure my calamities with patience, since it is Thy will that things should be as they are; but I hope that Thy infinite goodness will ultimately reward me."

The sultan, greatly moved by the recital of this affecting story, and anxious to avenge the sufferings of the unfortunate prince, said to him: "Inform me whither this perfidious sorceress retires, and where may be found the vile wretch, who is entombed before his death." "My lord," replied the prince, "the Indian, as I have already told you, is lodged in the Palace of Tears, in a superb tomb constructed in the form of a dome: this palace joins the castle on the side in which the gate is placed. As to the queen, I cannot tell you precisely whither she retires, but every day at sunrise she goes to visit her charge, after having executed her bloody vengeance upon me; and you see I am not in a condition to defend myself. She carries to him the potion with which she has hitherto prevented his dying, and always complains of his never having spoken to her since he was wounded."

"Prince," said the sultan, "your condition can never be sufficiently deplored: no one can be more sensibly affected by your misfortune than I am. Never did anything so extraordinary befall any man! One thing only is wanting; the revenge to which you are entitled, and I will omit nothing in my power to effect it."

In his subsequent conversation with the young prince the sultan told him who he was, and for what purpose he had entered the castle; and afterward informed him of a mode of revenge which he had devised. They agreed upon the measures they were to take for accomplishing their design, but deferred the execution of it till the following day. In the meantime, the night being far spent, the sultan took some rest; but the young prince passed the night as usual, without sleep, never having slept since he was enchanted.

THE YOUNG KING OF THE BLACK ISLES

Next morning the sultan arose with the dawn, and prepared to execute his design, by proceeding to the Palace of Tears. He found it lighted up with an infinite number of flambeaux of white wax, and perfumed by a delicious scent issuing from several censers of fine gold of admirable workmanship. As soon as he perceived the bed where the Indian lay, he drew his cimeter and deprived him of his wretched life, dragged his corpse into the court of the castle, and threw it into a well. After this he went and lay down in the black's bed, placed his cimeter under the covering, and waited to complete his design.

The queen arrived shortly after. She first went into the chamber of her husband, the king of the Black Islands, stripped him, and with unexampled barbarity gave him a hundred stripes. The unfortunate prince filled the palace with his lamentations, and conjured her in the most affecting tone to take pity on him; but the cruel wretch ceased not till she had given the usual number of blows. "You had no compassion," said she, "and you are to expect none from me."

After the enchantress had given her husband a hundred blows with the whip, she put on again his covering of goat's hair, and his brocade gown over all; she went afterward to the Palace of Tears, and as she entered renewed her tears and lamentations; then approaching the bed, where she thought the Indian lay: "Alas!" said she, addressing herself to the sultan, conceiving him to be the black, "My sun, my life, will you always be silent? Are you resolved to let me die without affording me the comfort of hearing your voice?"

The sultan, as if he had awaked out of a deep sleep, and counterfeiting the pronunciation of the blacks, answered the queen with a grave tone: "There is no strength or power but in

God alone, who is almighty." At these words the enchantress, who did not expect them, uttered a loud exclamation of joy. "My dear lord," cried she, "do I not deceive myself; is it certain that I hear you, and that you speak to me?" "Unhappy woman," said the sultan, "art thou worthy that I should answer thee?" "Alas!" replied the queen, "why do you reproach me thus?" "The cries," returned the sultan, "the groans and tears of thy husband, whom thou treatest every day with so much indignity and barbarity, prevent my sleeping night or day. Hadst thou disenchanted him, I should long since have been cured, and have recovered the use of my speech. This is the cause of my silence, of which you complain." "Well," said the enchantress, "to pacify you, I am ready to execute your commands; would you have me restore him?" "Yes," replied the sultan; "make haste to set him at liberty, that I be no longer disturbed by his lamentations." The enchantress went immediately out of the Palace of Tears; she took a cup of water, and pronounced some words over it, which caused it to boil, as if it had been on the fire. She afterward proceeded to the young king, and threw the water upon him, saying: "If the Creator of all things did form thee as thou art at present, or if He be angry with thee, do not change; but if thou art in that condition merely by virtue of my enchantments, resume thy natural shape, and become what thou wast before." She had scarcely spoken these words when the prince, finding himself restored to his former condition, rose up and returned thanks to God. The enchantress then said to him, "Get thee from this castle, and never return on pain of death." The young king, yielding to necessity, went away without replying a word, and retired to a remote place, where he patiently awaited the event of the design which the sultan had so happily begun. Meanwhile the enchantress returned to the Palace of Tears, and

When he came to this part of his narrative the young king
could not restrain his tears.

supposing that she still spoke to the black, said, "Dear love, I have done what you required; nothing now prevents your rising and giving me the satisfaction of which I have so long been deprived."

The sultan, still counterfeiting the pronunciation of the black, said: "What you have now done is by no means sufficient for my cure; you have only removed a part of the evil; you must cut it up by the root." "My lovely black," resumed the queen, "what do you mean by the root?" "Wretched woman," replied the sultan, "understand you not that I allude to the town and its inhabitants, and the four islands, destroyed by thy enchantments? The fish every night at midnight raise their heads out of the lake, and cry for vengeance against thee and me. This is the true cause of the delay of my cure. Go speedily, restore things to their former state, and at thy return I will give thee my hand, and thou shalt help me to arise."

The enchantress, inspired with hope from these words, cried out in a transport of joy, "My heart, my soul, you shall soon be restored to your health, for I will immediately do as you command me." Accordingly she went that instant, and when she came to the brink of the lake she took a little water in her hand, and sprinkling it, she pronounced some words over the fish and the lake, and the city was immediately restored. The fish became men, women, and children; Mohammedans, Christians, Persians, or Jews; freemen or slaves, as they were before: every one having recovered his natural form. The houses and shops were immediately filled with their inhabitants, who found all things as they were before the enchantment. The sultan's numerous retinue, who found themselves encamped in the largest square, were astonished to see themselves in an instant in the middle of a large, handsome, well-peopled city.

To return to the enchantress: As soon as she had effected this wonderful change, she returned with all expedition to the Palace of Tears, that she might receive her reward. "My dear lord," cried she, as she entered, "I have done all that you required of me, then pray rise and give me your hand." "Come near," said the sultan, still counterfeiting the pronunciation of the black. She did so. "You are not near enough," he continued; "approach nearer." She obeyed. He then rose up, and seizing her by the arm so suddenly that she had not time to discover him, he with a blow of his cimeter cut her in two, so that one half fell one way and the other another. This done, he left the body on the spot, and going out of the Palace of Tears, went to seek the young king of the Black Isles, who waited for him with great impatience. When he found him, "Prince," said he, embracing him, "rejoice; you have now nothing to fear; your cruel enemy is dead."

The young prince returned thanks to the sultan in a manner that sufficiently evinced his gratitude, and in return wished him long life and happiness. "You may henceforward," said the sultan, "dwell peaceably in your capital, unless you will accompany me to mine, which is near: you shall there be welcome, and have as much honour shown you as if you were in your own kingdom." "Potent monarch, to whom I am so much indebted," replied the king, "you think, then, that you are near your capital." "Yes," said the sultan, "I know it is not above four or five hours' journey." "It will take you a whole year to return," said the prince. "I do indeed believe that you came hither from your capital in the time you mention, because mine was enchanted; but since the enchantment is taken off, things are changed: however, this shall not prevent my following you, were it to the utmost corners of the earth. You are my deliverer, and that I may give you proofs of my acknowledgment of this during my whole life, I am willing to accompany you, and to leave my kingdom without regret."

The sultan was extremely surprised to understand that he was so far from his dominions, and could not imagine how it could be, but the young king of the Black Islands convinced him beyond a possibility of doubt. Then the sultan replied: "It is no matter; the trouble of returning to my own country is sufficiently recompensed by the satisfaction of having obliged you, and by acquiring you for a son; for since you will do me the honour to accompany me, as I have no child, I look upon you as such, and from this moment appoint you my heir and successor."

The young prince then employed himself in making preparations for his journey, which were finished in three weeks, to the great regret of his court and subjects, who agreed to receive at his hands one of his nearest kindred for their monarch.

At length the sultan and the young prince began their journey, with a hundred camels laden with inestimable riches from the treasury, followed by fifty handsome gentlemen on horseback, perfectly well mounted and dressed. They had a pleasant journey; and when the sultan, who had sent couriers to give advice of his delay, and of the adventure which had occasioned it, approached his capital, the principal officers came to receive him, and to assure him that his long absence had occasioned no alteration in his empire. The inhabitants also came out in great crowds, received him with acclamations, and made public rejoicings for several days.

The day after his arrival the sultan acquainted his courtiers with his adoption of the king of the Four Black Islands, who was willing to leave a great kingdom to accompany and live with him; and in reward for their loyalty, he made each of them presents according to their rank.

As for the fisherman, as he was the first cause of the deliverance of the young prince, the sultan gave him a plentiful fortune, which made him and his family happy the rest of his days.

THE STORY OF GULNARE OF THE SEA

THERE was, in olden time, and in an ancient age and
period, in the land of the Persians, a king named
Shahzeman, and the place of his residence was Khoras-
san. He had not been blest, during his whole life, with a male
child nor a female; and he reflected upon this, one day, and
lamented that the greater portion of his life had passed, and he
had no heir to take the kingdom after him as he had inherited
it from his fathers and forefathers. So the utmost grief befell
him on this account.

Now while he was sitting one day, one of his mamelukes
came in to him, and said to him: "O my lord, at the door is a
slave-girl with a merchant: none more beautiful than she hath
been seen." And he replied: "Bring to me the merchant and
the slave-girl." The merchant and the slave-girl therefore came
to him; and when he saw her, he found her to resemble the
lance in straightness and slenderness. She was wrapped in
a garment of silk embroidered with gold, and the merchant uncovered her face, whereupon the place was illuminated by her
beauty, and there hung down from her forehead seven locks of
hair reaching to her anklets. The King, therefore, wondered
at the sight of her, and at her beauty, and her stature and justness of form; and he said to the merchant: "O sheikh, for how
much is this damsel to be sold?" The merchant answered:
"O my lord, I purchased her for two thousand pieces of gold of

[81]

the merchant who owned her before me, and I have been for three years travelling with her, and she hath cost, to the period of her arrival at this place, three thousand pieces of gold; and she is a present from me unto thee." Upon this, the king conferred upon him a magnificent robe of honour, and gave orders to present him with ten thousand pieces of gold. So he took them, and kissed the hands of the king, thanking him for his beneficence, and departed. Then the king committed the damsel to the tirewomen, saying to them: "Amend the state of this damsel, and deck her, and furnish for her a private chamber, and take her into it." He also gave orders to his chamberlains that everything which she required should be conveyed to her. The seat of government where he resided was on the shore of the sea, and his city was called the White City. And they conducted the damsel into a private chamber, which chamber had windows overlooking the sea; and the king commanded his chamberlains to close all the doors upon her after taking to her all that she required.

The king then went in to visit the damsel; but she rose not to him, nor took any notice of him. So the king said: "It seemeth that she hath been with people who have not taught her good manners." And looking at the damsel, he saw her to be a person surpassing in loveliness, her face was like the disk of the moon at the full, or the shining sun in the clear sky; and he wondered at her beauty, extolling the perfection of God, the Creator: then the king advanced to the damsel, and seated himself by her side, pressed her to his bosom, and kissed her lips, which he found to be sweeter than honey. After this, he gave orders to bring tables of the richest viands, comprising dishes of every kind; and he ate, and put morsels into her mouth until she was satisfied; but she spoke not a single word. The king talked to her, and inquired of her her name; but she was silent, not uttering a word, nor returning him an answer, ceasing not to hang down her head toward the ground; and what protected her from the anger of the king was her beauty, and her tenderness of manner. So the king said within himself: "Extolled be the perfection of God, the Creator of this damsel! How elegant is she, saving that she doth not speak!"—Then the king asked the female slaves whether she had spoken; and they answered him: "From the time of her arrival to the present moment she hath not spoken one word, and we have not heard her talk." The king therefore caused some of them to come, and sing to her, and make merry with her, thinking that then she might perhaps speak. Accordingly the female slaves played before her with all kinds of musical instruments, and enacted sports and other performances, and they sang so that every one who was present was moved with delight, except the damsel, who looked at them and was silent, neither laughing nor speaking. So the heart of the king was contracted. He however inclined to her entirely, paying no regard to others, but relinquishing all the rest of his favourites.

He remained with her a whole year, which seemed as one day, and still she spoke not; and he said to her one day, when his passion was excessive: "O desire of souls, verily the love that I have for thee is great, and I have relinquished for thy sake all my worldly portion, and been patient with thee a whole year. I beg God that He will, in His grace, soften thy heart toward me, and that thou mayest speak to me. Or, if thou be dumb, inform me by a sign, that I may give up hope of thy speaking. I also beg of God that He will bless thee with a son that may inherit my kingdom after me; for I am solitary, having none to be my heir, and my age hath become great. I conjure thee, then, by Allah, if thou love me, that thou return me a reply." And upon this, the damsel hung her head toward the ground, meditating. Then she raised her head, and smiled in the face of the king, whereat it appeared to the king that lightning filled the private chamber; and she said: "O magnanimous King, God hath answered thy prayer; for I am about to bring thee a child, and the time is almost come. And were it not that I knew this thing, I had not spoken to thee one word." And when the king heard what she said, his face brightened up with happiness, and he kissed her hands by reason of the violence of his joy, and said: "Praise be to God who hath favoured me with things that I desired; the first, thy speaking; and the second, thy information that thou art about to bring me a child." Then the king arose and went forth from her, and seated himself upon the throne of his kingdom in a state of exceeding happiness; and he ordered the vizier to give out to the poor and the needy a hundred thousand pieces of gold as a thank-offering to God. So the vizier did as the king had commanded him. And after that, the king went in to the damsel, and embraced her, saying to her: "O my mistress, wherefore hath been this silence, seeing that thou hast been with me a whole year, awake and asleep, yet hast not spoken to me, except on this day?"

The damsel answered: "Hear, O King of the age, and know that I am a poor person, a stranger, broken-hearted: I have become separated from my mother, and my family, and my brother." And when the king heard her words, he knew her desire, and he replied: "As to thy saying that thou art poor, there is no occasion for such an assertion; for all my kingdom and possessions are at thy service, and as to thy saying, 'I have become separated from my mother and my family and my brother' —inform me in what place they are, and I will send to them, and bring them to thee." So she said to him: "Know, O King, that my name is Gulnare (*Pomegranate Flower*) of the Sea. My father was one of the Kings of the Sea, and he died, and left to us the kingdom; but while we were enjoying it, another of the kings came upon us, and took the kingdom from our hands. I have also a brother named Saleh, and my mother is of the women of the sea; and I quarrelled with my brother, and swore that I would throw myself into the hands of a man of the inhabitants of the land. Accordingly I came forth from the sea, and sat upon the shore of an island in the moonlight, and there passed by a man who took me and sold me to this man from whom thou tookest me, and he was an excellent, virtuous man, a person of religion and fidelity and kindness. But had not thy heart loved me, and hadst thou not preferred me above all thy wives, I had not remained with thee one hour; for I should have cast myself into the sea from this window, and gone to my mother and my people. I was ashamed, however, to go to them; for they would imagine evil of me, and would not believe me, even though I should swear to them, were I to tell them that a king had purchased me with his money, and chosen me in preference to his other wives and all that his right hand possessed. This is my story, and peace be on thee!" And when he heard her words, he thanked her, and kissed her between the eyes, and said to her: "By Allah, O my mistress, and light of my eyes, I cannot endure separation from thee for one hour; and if thou quit me, I shall die instantly. How then shall the affair be?" She answered: "O my master, the time of the birth is near, and my family must come." "And how," said the king, "do they walk in the sea without being wetted?" She answered: "We walk in the sea as ye walk upon the land, through the influence of the names engraved upon the seal of Solomon, the son of David, upon both of whom be peace! But, O King, when my family and my brethren come, I will inform them that thou boughtest me with thy money, and hast treated me with beneficence, and it will be meet that thou confirm my assertion to them. They will also see thy state with their eyes, and will know that thou art a king, the son of a king." And thereupon the king said: "O my mistress, do what seemeth fit to thee, and what thou wishest; for I will comply with thy desire in all that thou wilt do." And the damsel said: "Know, O King of the age, that we walk in the sea with our eyes open, and see what is in it, and we see the sun, and the moon, and the stars, and the sky as on the face of the earth, and this hurteth us not. Know also, that in the sea are many peoples and various forms of all the kinds that are on the land; and know, moreover, that all that is on the land, in comparison with what is in the sea, is a very small matter." And the king wondered at her words.

Then the damsel took a bit of aloes-wood and, having lighted a fire in a perfuming-vessel, threw into it that bit, and she proceeded to speak words which no one understood; whereupon a great smoke arose, while the king looked on. After this, she said to the king: "O my lord, arise and conceal thyself in a closet, that I may shew thee my brother and my mother and my family without their seeing thee; for I desire to bring them, and thou shalt see in this place, at this time, a wonder, and shalt marvel at the various shapes and strange forms that God hath created." So the king arose immediately, and entered a closet, and looked to see what she would do. And she proceeded to burn perfume and repeat spells until the sea foamed and was agitated, and there came forth from it a young man of comely form, of beautiful countenance, like the moon at the full, with shining forehead, and red cheeks, and hair resembling pearls and jewels; he was, of all the creation, the most like to his sister, and the tongue of the case itself seemed to recite in his praise these verses:—

> The moon becometh perfect once in each month; but the loveliness of thy face is perfect every day.
> Its abode is in the heart of one sign at a time; but thine abode is in all hearts at once.

Afterward, there came forth from the sea a grizzly-haired old woman, and with her five damsels, resembling moons and bearing a likeness to the damsel whose name was Gulnare. Then the king saw the young man and the old woman and the damsels walk upon the surface of the water until they came to Gulnare; and when they drew near to the window, and she beheld them, she rose to them and met them with joy. On their seeing her, they knew her, and they went in to her and embraced her, weeping violently; and they said to her: "O Gulnare, how is it that thou leavest us for four years, and we know not the place in which thou art? By Allah, we had no delight in food nor in drink a single day, weeping night and day on account of the excess of our longing to see thee." Then the damsel began to kiss the hand of her brother, and the hand of her mother, and so also the hands of the daughters of her uncle, and they sat with her awhile, asking her respecting her state, and the things that had happened to her, and her present condition.

So she said to them: "Know ye, that when I quitted you, and came forth from the sea, I sat upon the shore of an island, and a man took me, and sold me to a merchant, and the merchant brought me to this city, and sold me to its king for ten thousand pieces of gold. Then he treated me with attention, and forsook all his favourites for my sake, and was diverted by his regard for me from everything that he possessed and what was in his city."

And when her brother heard her words, he said: "Praise be to God who hath reunited us! But it is my desire, O my sister, that thou wouldst arise and go with us to our country and our family." So when the king heard the words of her brother, his reason fled in consequence of his fear lest the damsel should accept the proposal of her kindred, and he could not prevent her, though he was inflamed with love of her; wherefore he became perplexed in violent fear of her separation. But as to the damsel Gulnare, on hearing the words of her brother she said: "By Allah, O my brother, the man who purchased me is the king of this city, and he is a great king, and a man of wisdom, generous, of the utmost liberality. He hath treated me with honour, and he is a person of kindness, and of great wealth, but hath no male child nor a female. He hath shewn me favour too, and acted well to me in every respect; and from the day when I came to him to the present time, I have not heard from him a word to grieve my heart; but he hath not ceased to treat me with courtesy, and I am living with him in the most perfect of enjoyments. Moreover, if I quitted him, he would perish: for he can never endure my separation even for a single hour. I also, if I quitted him, should die of my love for him in consequence of his kindness to me during the period of my residence with him; for if my father were living, my condition with him would not be like my condition with this great, glorious king. God (whose name be exalted!) afflicted me not, but compensated me well; and as the king hath not a male child nor a female, I beg God to bless me with a son that may inherit of this great king these palaces and possessions." And when her brother, and the daughters of her uncle, heard her words, their eyes became cheerful thereat, and they said to her: "O Gulnare, thou art acquainted with our affection for thee, and thou art assured that thou art the dearest of all persons to us, and art certain that we desire for thee comfort, without trouble or toil. Therefore if thou be not in a state of comfort, arise and accompany us to our country and our family; but if thou be comfortable here, in honour and happiness, this is our desire and wish." And Gulnare replied: "By Allah, I am in a state of the utmost enjoyment, in honour and desirable happiness." So when the king heard these words from her, he rejoiced, and he thanked her for them; his love for her penetrated to his heart's core, and he knew that she loved him as he loved her, and that she desired to remain with him to see his child which she was to bring to him.

Then the damsel Gulnare of the Sea gave orders to the female slaves to bring forward viands of all kinds; and Gulnare herself was the person who superintended the preparation of the viands in the kitchen. So the female slaves brought to them the viands, and the sweetmeats, and the fruits; and she ate with her family. But afterward they said to her: "O Gulnare, thy master is a man who is a stranger to us, and we have entered his abode without his permission, and thou praisest to us his excellence, and hast also brought to us his food, and we have eaten, but have not seen him, nor hath he seen us, nor come into our presence, nor eaten with us, that the bond of bread and salt might be established between us." And they all desisted from eating, and were enraged at her, and fire began to issue from their mouths as from cressets. So when the king beheld this, his reason fled, in consequence of the violence of his fear of them. Then Gulnare rose to them, and soothed their hearts; after which she walked along until she entered the closet in which was the king her master; and she said to him: "O my master, didst thou see, and didst thou hear my thanks to thee, and my praise of thee in the presence of my family; and didst thou hear what they said to me, that they desired to take me with them to our family and our country?" The king answered her: "I heard and saw. May God recompense thee! By Allah, I knew not the extent of the love that thou feelest for me until this blessed hour." She replied: "O my master, is the recompense of beneficence aught but beneficence? How then could my heart be happy to quit thee, and to depart from thee? Now I desire of thy goodness that thou come and salute my family, that they may see thee, and that pleasure and mutual friendship may ensue. For know, O King, that my brother and my mother and the daughters of my uncle have conceived a great love for thee in consequence of my praising thee to them, and they have said, 'We will not depart from thee to our country until we have an interview with the king, and salute him.'" And the king said to her: "I hear and obey; for this is what I desire." He then rose from his place, and went to them, and saluted them with the best salutation; and they hastened to rise to him; they met him in the most polite manner, and he sat with them in the pavilion, ate with them at the table, and remained with them for a period of thirty days. Then they desired to return to their country and abode. So they took leave of the king and Queen Gulnare of the Sea, and departed from them, after the king had treated them with the utmost honour.

After this, Gulnare gave birth to a boy, resembling the moon at the full, whereat the king experienced the utmost happiness, because he had not before been blessed with a son nor a daughter during his life. They continued the rejoicings, and the decoration of the city, for a period of seven days, in the utmost happiness and enjoyment; and on the seventh day, the mother of Gulnare, and her brother, and the daughters of her uncle, all came, when they knew that she had given birth to her child. The king met them, rejoicing at their arrival, and said to them: "I said that I would not name my son until ye should come, and that ye should name him according to your knowledge." And they named him Bedr Basim (*Smiling Full Moon*), all of them agreeing as to this name. They then presented the boy to his maternal uncle, Saleh, who took him upon his hands, and, rising with him from among them, walked about the palace to the right and left; after which he went forth with him from the palace, descended with him to the sea, and walked on until he became concealed from the eye of the king. So when the king saw that he had taken his son, and disappeared from him at the bottom of the sea, he despaired of him, and began to weep and wail. But Gulnare, seeing him in this state, said to him, "O King of the age, fear not nor grieve for thy son; for I love my child more than thou, and my child is with my brother; therefore fear not his being drowned. If my brother knew that any injury would betide the little one, he had not done what he hath done; and presently he will bring thee thy son safe, if it be the will of God, whose name be exalted!" And but a short time had elapsed when the sea was agitated, and the uncle of the little one came forth from it, having with him the king's son safe, and he flew from the sea until he came to them, with the little one in his arms, silent, and his face resembling the moon in the night of its fulness. Then the uncle of the little one looked toward the king, and said to him: "Perhaps thou fearedst some injury to thy son when I descended into the sea, having him with me." So he replied: "Yes, O my master, I feared for him, and I did not imagine that he would ever come forth from it safe." And Saleh said to him: "O King of the Land, we applied to his eyes a lotion that we know, and repeated over him the names engraved upon the seal of Solomon, the son of David; for when a

child is born among us, we do to him as I have told thee. Fear
not therefore, on his account, drowning, nor suffocation, nor all
the seas if he descend into them. Like as ye walk upon the
land, we walk in the sea."

He then took forth from his pocket a case, written upon, and
sealed; and he broke its seal, and scattered its contents, whereupon there fell from it strung jewels, consisting of all kinds of
jacinths and other gems, together with three hundred oblong
emeralds, and three hundred oblong large jewels, of the size of
the eggs of the ostrich, the light of which was more resplendent
than the light of the sun and the moon. And he said: "O King
of the age, these jewels and jacinths are a present from me unto
thee; for we never brought thee a present, because we knew not
the place of Gulnare's abode. So when we saw thee to have
become united to her, and that we all had become one, we
brought thee this present; and after every period of a few days,
we will bring thee the like of it. For these jewels and jacinths
with us are more plentiful than the gravel upon the land, and we
know the excellent among them, and the bad, and the places
where they are found, and they are easy of access to us."—And
when the king looked at those jewels, his reason was confounded
and his mind was bewildered, and he said: "By Allah, one of
these jewels is worth my kingdom!" Then the king thanked
Saleh of the Sea for his generosity, and looking toward the
Queen Gulnare said to her: "I am abashed at thy brother; for
he hath shewn favour to me, and presented me with this magnificent present, which the people of the earth would fail to procure."
So Gulnare thanked her brother for that which he had done;
but her brother said: "O King of the age, to thank thee hath
been incumbent on us; for thou hast treated my sister with beneficence, and we have entered thine abode, and eaten of thy pro-

*And she proceeded to burn perfume and repeat spells until the
sea foamed and was agitated.*

vision." Then Saleh said: "If we stood serving thee, O King of the age, a thousand years, regarding nothing else, we could not requite thee, and our doing so would be but a small thing in comparison with thy desert." And Saleh remained with the king, he and his mother and the daughters of his uncle, forty days; after which he arose and kissed the ground before the king, the husband of his sister. So the king said to him: "What dost thou desire, O Saleh?" And he answered: "O King of the age, we desire of thy goodness that thou wouldst give us permission to depart; for we have become desirous of seeing again our family and our country and our relations and our homes. We will not, however, relinquish the service of thee, nor that of my sister nor the son of my sister; and by Allah, O King of the age, to quit you is not pleasant to my heart; but how can we act, when we have been reared in the sea, and the land is not agreeable to us?" So when the king heard his words, he rose upon his feet, and bade farewell to Saleh of the Sea and his mother and the daughters of his uncle, and they wept together on account of the separation. Then they said to the king: "We will never relinquish you, but after every period of a few days we will visit you." And after this, they flew toward the sea, and descended into it, and disappeared.

The king treated Gulnare with beneficence, and honoured her exceedingly, and the little one grew up well; and his maternal uncle, with his grandmother and the daughters of his uncle, after every period of a few days used to come to the residence of the king, and to remain with him a month, and then return to their places. The boy ceased not to increase in beauty and loveliness until his age became fifteen years; and he was incomparable in his perfect beauty, and his stature and his justness of form. He had learned writing and reading, and history and grammar and philology, and archery; and he learned to play with the spear; and he also learned horsemanship, and all that the sons of the kings required. There was not one of the children of the inhabitants of the city, men and women, that talked not of the charms of that young man; for he was of surpassing loveliness and perfection; and the king loved him greatly. Then the king summoned the vizier and the emeers, and the lords of the empire, and the great men of the kingdom, and made them swear by binding oaths that they would make Bedr Basim king over them after his father; so they swore to him by binding oaths, and rejoiced thereat; and the king himself was beneficent to the people, courteous in speech and of auspicious aspect. And on the following day, the king mounted, together with the lords of the empire and all the emeers, and all the soldiers, and they ceased not to proceed until they arrived at the vestibule of the palace; the king's son riding. Thereupon he alighted, and his father embraced him, he and the emeers, and they seated him upon the throne of the kingdom, while his father stood, as also did the emeers, before him. Then Bedr Basim judged the people, displaced the tyrannical and invested the just, and continued to give judgment until near midday, when he rose from the throne of the kingdom, and went in to his mother, Gulnare of the Sea, having upon his head the crown, and resembling the moon. So when his mother saw him, and the king before him, she rose to him and kissed him, and congratulated him on his elevation to the dignity of sultan; and she offered up a prayer in favour of him and his father for length of life, and victory over their enemies. He then sat with his mother and rested; and when the time of afternoon-prayers arrived, he rode with the emeers before him until he came to the horse-course, where he played with arms till the time of nightfall, together with his father and the lords of his empire; after which he returned to the palace, with all the people before him. Every day he used to ride to the horse-course; and when he returned, he sat to judge the people, and administered justice between the emeer and the poor man. He ceased not to do thus for a whole year; and after that, he used to ride to the chase, and go about through the cities and provinces that were under his rule making proclamation of safety and security, and doing as do the kings; and he was incomparable among the people of his age in glory and courage, and in justice to the people.

Now it came to pass that the old king, the father of Bedr Basim, fell sick one day, whereupon his heart throbbed, and he felt that he was about to be removed to the mansion of eternity. Then his malady increased so that he was at the point of death. He therefore summoned his son, and charged him to take care of his subjects and his mother and all the lords of his empire and all the dependants. He also made them swear, and covenanted with them a second time, that they would obey his son; and he confided in their oaths. And after this he remained a few days, and was admitted to the mercy of God, whose name be exalted! His son Bedr Basim, and his wife Gulnare and the emeers and viziers and the lords of the empire, mourned over him; and they made for him a tomb, and buried him in it, and continued the ceremonies of mourning for him a whole month. Saleh, the brother of Gulnare, and her mother, and the daughters of her uncle, also came, and consoled them for the loss of the king; and they said: "O Gulnare, if the king hath died, he hath left this ingenuous youth, and he who hath left such as he is hath not died. This is he who hath not an equal, the crushing lion, and the splendid moon." Then the lords of the empire, and the grandees, went in to the King Bedr Basim, and said to him: "O

King, there is no harm in mourning for the king; but mourning becometh not any save women; therefore trouble not thy heart and ours by mourning for thy father; for he hath died and left thee, and he who hath left such as thou art hath not died." They proceeded to address him with soft words, and to console him, and after that they conducted him into the bath; and when he came forth from the bath, he put on a magnificent suit woven of gold, adorned with jewels and jacinths, and he put the royal crown upon his head, seated himself upon the throne of his kingdom, and performed the affairs of the people, deciding equitably between the strong and the weak, and exacting for the poor man his due from the emeer; wherefore the people loved him exceedingly. Thus he continued to do for the space of a whole year; and after every short period, his family of the sea visited him; so his life was pleasant, and his eye was cheerful: and he ceased not to live in this state until he was visited by the terminator of delights and the separator of companions. This is the end of their story. The mercy of God be on them all!

THE STORY OF ALADDIN; OR, THE WONDERFUL LAMP

IN the capital of one of the large and rich provinces of the kingdom of China there lived a tailor, named Mustapha, who was so poor that he could hardly, by his daily labour, maintain himself and his family, which consisted of a wife and son.

His son, who was called Aladdin, had been brought up in a very careless and idle manner, and by that means had contracted many vicious habits. He was obstinate, and disobedient to his father and mother, who, when he grew up, could not keep him within doors. He was in the habit of going out early in the morning, and would stay out all day, playing in the streets with idle children of his own age.

When he was old enough to learn a trade, his father, not being able to put him out to any other, took him into his own shop, and taught him how to use his needle: but neither fair words nor the fear of chastisement were capable of fixing his lively genius. All his father's endeavours to keep him to his work were in vain; for no sooner was his back turned, than he was gone for that day. Mustapha chastised him, but Aladdin was incorrigible, and his father, to his great grief, was forced to abandon him to his idleness: and was so much troubled at not being able to reclaim him, that it threw him into a fit of sickness, of which he died in a few months.

The mother, finding that her son would not follow his father's business, shut up the shop, sold off the implements of trade, and with the money she received for them, and what she could get by spinning cotton, thought to maintain herself and her son.

Aladdin, who was now no longer restrained by the fear of a father, and who cared so little for his mother that whenever she chid him he would abuse her, gave himself entirely over to his idle habits, and was never out of the streets from his companions. This course he followed till he was fifteen years old, without giving his mind to any useful pursuit, or the least reflection on what would become of him. In this situation, as he was one day playing with his vagabond associates, a stranger passing by stood to observe him.

This stranger was a sorcerer, called the African magician; as he was a native of Africa, and had been but two days arrived from thence.

The African magician, who was a good physiognomist, observing in Aladdin's countenance something absolutely necessary for the execution of the design he was engaged in, inquired artfully about his family, who he was, and what were his inclinations; and when he had learned all he desired to know, went up to him, and taking him aside from his comrades, said: "Child, was not your father called Mustapha, the tailor?" "Yes, sir," answered the boy; "but he has been dead a long time."

At these words, the African magician threw his arms about Aladdin's neck, and kissed him several times with tears in his eyes. Aladdin, who observed his tears, asked him what made him weep. "Alas! my son," cried the African magician with a sigh, "how can I forbear? I am your uncle; your worthy father was my own brother. I have been many years abroad, and now I am come home with the hopes of seeing him, you tell me he is dead. But it is some relief to my affliction, that I knew you at first sight, you are so like him." Then he asked Aladdin, putting his hand into his purse, where his mother lived, and as soon as he had informed him, gave him a handful of small money, saying: "Go, my son, to your mother, give my love to her, and tell her that I will visit her to-morrow, that I may have the satisfaction of seeing where my good brother lived so long."

As soon as the African magician left his newly-adopted nephew, Aladdin ran to his mother, overjoyed at the money his uncle had given him. "Mother," said he, "have I an uncle?" "No, child," replied his mother, "you have no uncle by your father's side, or mine." "I am just now come," said Aladdin, "from a man who says he is my uncle on my father's side. He cried and kissed me when I told him my father was dead; and to show you that what I tell you is truth," added he, pulling out the money, "see what he has given me; he charged me to give his love to you, and to tell you that to-morrow he will come and pay you a visit, that he may see the house my father lived and died in." "Indeed, child," replied the mother, "your father had a brother, but he has been dead a long time, and I never heard of another."

The mother and son talked no more then of the African magician; but the next day Aladdin's uncle found him playing in another part of the town with other youths, and embracing him as before, put two pieces of gold into his hand, and said to him: "Carry this, child, to your mother, tell her that I will come and see her to-night, and bid her get us something for supper; but first show me the house where you live."

After Aladdin had showed the African magician the house, he carried the two pieces of gold to his mother, and when he had told her of his uncle's intention, she went out and bought provisions. She spent the whole day in preparing the supper; and at night, when it was ready, said to her son: "Perhaps your uncle knows not how to find our house; go and bring him if you meet with him."

Though Aladdin had showed the magician the house, he was ready to go, when somebody knocked at the door, which he immediately opened; and the magician came in loaded with wine, and all sorts of fruits, which he brought for a dessert.

After the African magician had given what he brought into Aladdin's hands, he saluted his mother, and desired her to shew him the place where his brother Mustapha used to sit on the sofa; and when she had so done, he fell down and kissed it several times, crying out with tears in his eyes: "My poor brother! how unhappy am I, not to have come soon enough to give you one last embrace." Aladdin's mother desired him to sit down in the same place, but he declined. "No," said he, "but give me leave to sit opposite, that although I am deprived of the satisfaction of seeing one so dear to me, I may at least have the pleasure of beholding the place where he used to sit."

When the magician had sat down, he began to enter into discourse with Aladdin's mother: "My good sister," said he, "do not be surprised at your never having seen me all the time you were married to my brother Mustapha. I have been forty years absent from this country, which is my native place, as well as my late brother's; and during that time have travelled into the Indies, Persia, Arabia, Syria, and Egypt; have resided in the finest towns of those countries; and afterward crossed over into Africa, where I made a longer stay. At last, as it is natural for a man to remember his native country, I was desirous to see mine again, and to embrace my dear brother; and finding I had strength enough to undertake so long a journey, I immediately made the necessary preparations, and set out. I will not tell you the length of time it took me, all the obstacles I met with, and what fatigues I have endured to come hither; but nothing ever afflicted me so much, as hearing of my brother's death. I observed his features in the face of my nephew, your son, and distinguished him among a number of lads with whom he was at play; he can tell you how I received the most melancholy news that ever reached my ears. But God be praised for all things! it is a comfort for me to find, as it were, my brother in a son, who has his most remarkable features."

The African magician, perceiving that the widow began to weep at the remembrance of her husband, changed the conversation, and turning toward her son, asked him his name. "I am called Aladdin," said he. "Well, Aladdin," replied the magician, "what business do you follow? Are you of any trade?"

At this question the youth hung down his head, and was not a little abashed when his mother answered: "Aladdin is an idle fellow; his father, when alive, strove all he could to teach him his trade, but could not succeed; and since his death he does nothing but idle away his time in the streets, as you saw him, without considering he is no longer a child; and if you do not make him ashamed of it, I despair of his ever coming to any good. He knows that his father left him no fortune, and sees me endeavour to get bread by spinning cotton; for my part, I am resolved one of these days to turn him out of doors, and let him provide for himself."

After these words, Aladdin's mother burst into tears; and the magician said: "This is not well, nephew; you must think of getting your livelihood. There are many sorts of trades, consider if you have not an inclination to some of them; perhaps you did not like your father's and would prefer another; come, do not disguise your sentiments from me; I will endeavour to help you."

But finding that Aladdin returned no answer, "If you have no mind," continued he, "to learn any handicraft, I will take a shop for you, furnish it with all sorts of fine stuffs and linens; and with the money you make of them lay in fresh goods, and then you will live in an honourable way. Consult your inclination, and tell me freely what you think of my proposal."

This plan greatly flattered Aladdin, who hated work but had sense enough to know that such shops were much frequented and the owners respected. He told the magician he had a greater inclination to that business than to any other, and that he should be much obliged to him for his kindness. "Since this profession is agreeable to you," said the African magician, "I will carry you with me to-morrow, clothe you as handsomely as the best merchants in the city, and afterward we will think of opening a shop as I mentioned."

The widow, who never till then could believe that the magician was her husband's brother, no longer doubted after his promises of kindness to her son. She thanked him for his good intentions; and after having exhorted Aladdin to render himself worthy of his uncle's favour by good behaviour, served up supper, at which they talked of several indifferent matters; and then the magician, who saw that the night was pretty far advanced, took his leave, and retired.

He came again the next day, as he had promised, and took Aladdin with him to a merchant, who sold all sorts of clothes for different ages and ranks ready made, and a variety of fine stuffs. He asked to see some that suited Aladdin in size; and Aladdin, charmed with the liberality of his new uncle, made choice of one, and the magician immediately paid for it.

When the boy found himself so handsomely equipped, he returned his uncle thanks; who promised never to forsake him, but always to take him along with him; which he did to the most frequented places in the city, and particularly where the principal merchants kept their shops. When he brought him into the street where they sold the richest stuffs and finest linens, he said to Aladdin: "As you are soon to be a merchant, it is proper you should frequent these shops, and be acquainted with them." He then showed him the largest and finest mosques, carried him to the khans or inns where the merchants and travellers lodged, and afterward to the sultan's palace, where he had free access; and at last brought him to his own khan, where, meeting with some merchants he had become acquainted with since his arrival, he gave them a treat, to bring them and his pretended nephew acquainted.

This entertainment lasted till night, when Aladdin would have taken leave of his uncle to go home, but the magician would not let him go by himself, but conducted him to his mother, who, as soon as she saw him so well dressed, was transported with joy, and bestowed a thousand blessings upon the magician, for being at so great an expense for her child. "Generous relation!" said she, "I know not how to thank you for your liberality! I wish you may live long enough to witness my son's gratitude, which he cannot better shew than by regulating his conduct by your good advice."

"Aladdin," replied the magician, "is a good boy, and I believe we shall do very well; but I am sorry for one thing, which is, that I cannot perform to-morrow what I promised, because, as it is Friday, the shops will be shut up, and therefore we cannot hire or furnish one till Saturday. I will, however, call on him to-morrow and take him to walk in the gardens, where people of the best fashion generally resort. Perhaps he has never seen these amusements, he has only hitherto been among children;

but now he must see men." The African magician then took his leave of the mother and the son, and retired.

Aladdin rose early the next morning, dressed himself to be ready, and after he had waited some time began to be impatient and stood watching at the door; but as soon as he perceived his uncle coming, he told his mother, took his leave of her, and ran to meet him.

The magician caressed Aladdin, and said: "Come, my dear child, and I will shew you fine things." He then led him out at one of the gates of the city, to some magnificent palaces, to each of which belonged beautiful gardens, into which anybody might enter. At every building he came to, he asked Aladdin if he did not think it fine; and the youth was ready to answer when any one presented itself, crying out: "Here is a finer house, uncle, than any we have seen yet." By this artifice, the cunning magician led Aladdin some way into the country; and as he meant to carry him farther, pretending to be tired, he took an opportunity to sit down in one of the gardens on the brink of a fountain of clear water, which discharged itself by a lion's mouth of bronze into a basin: "Come, nephew," said he, "you must be weary as well as I; let us rest ourselves, and we shall be better able to pursue our walk."

After they had sat down, the magician pulled from his girdle a handkerchief with cakes and fruit, which he had provided, and laid them on the edge of the basin. He broke a cake in two, gave one half to Aladdin and ate the other himself; and in regard to the fruit, left him at liberty to take which sort he liked best. During this short repast, he exhorted his nephew to leave off keeping company with vagabonds, and seek that of wise and prudent men, to improve by their conversation; "For," said he, "you will soon be at man's estate, and you cannot too early begin to imitate their example." When they had eaten as much as they liked, they pursued their walk through gardens separated from one another only by small ditches, which marked out the limits without interrupting the communication; so great was the confidence the inhabitants reposed in each other. By this means, the African magician drew Aladdin insensibly beyond the gardens, and crossed the country, till they nearly reached the mountains.

Aladdin, who had never been so far before, began to find himself much tired, and said to the magician: "Where are we going, uncle? We have left the gardens a great way behind us, and I see nothing but mountains; if we go much farther, I do not know whether I shall be able to reach the town again!" "Never fear, nephew," said the false uncle; "I will shew you another garden which surpasses all we have yet seen; and when we come there, you will say that you would have been sorry to have been so nigh, and not seen it." Aladdin was soon persuaded; and the magician, to make the way seem shorter and less fatiguing, told him a great many stories.

At last they arrived between two mountains of moderate height, and equal size, divided by a narrow valley, which was the place where the magician intended to execute the design that had brought him from Africa to China. "We will go no farther now," said he to Aladdin: "I will shew you here some extraordinary things, which, when you have seen, you will thank me for: but while I strike a light, gather up all the loose dry sticks you can see, to kindle a fire with."

Aladdin collected a great heap and the magician presently set them on fire, and when they were in a blaze, threw in some incense which raised a cloud of smoke. This he dispersed on each side, by pronouncing several magical words which the lad did not understand.

At the same time the earth, trembling, opened just before the magician, and uncovered a stone, laid horizontally, with a brass ring fixed into the middle. Aladdin was so frightened at what he saw, that he would have run away; but the magician caught hold of him, abused him, and gave him such a box on the ear that he knocked him down. Aladdin got up trembling, and with tears in his eyes, said to the magician: "What have I done, uncle, to be treated in this severe manner?" "I have my reasons," answered the magician; "I am your uncle, I supply the place of your father, and you ought to make no reply. But, child," added he, softening, "do not be afraid; for I shall not ask anything of you, but that you obey me punctually, if you would reap the advantages which I intend you." These fair promises calmed Aladdin's fears and resentment; and when the magician saw that he was appeased, he said to him: "You see what I have done by virtue of my incense, and the words I pronounced. Know then, that under this stone there is hidden a treasure, destined to be yours, and which will make you richer than the greatest monarch in the world: no person but yourself is permitted to lift this stone, or enter the cave; so you must punctually execute what I may command, for it is a matter of great consequence both to you and me."

Aladdin, amazed at all he saw and heard the magician say of the treasure which was to make him happy forevermore, forgot what was past, and rising, said: "Well, uncle, what is to be done? Command me, I am ready to obey." "I am overjoyed, child," said the African magician, embracing him; "take hold of the ring, and lift up that stone." "Indeed, uncle," replied Aladdin, "I am not strong enough; you must help me." "You have no occasion for my assistance," answered the magician; "if I help you, we shall be able to do nothing; take hold of the ring, pronounce the names of your father and grandfather, then lift it up, and you will find it will come easily." Aladdin did as the magician bade him, raised the stone with ease, and laid it on one side.

When the stone was pulled up, there appeared a cavity of about three or four feet deep, with a little door, and steps to go down lower. "Observe, my son," said the African magician, "what I direct. Descend into the cave, and when you are at the bottom of those steps you will find a door which will lead you into a spacious vault, divided into three great halls, in each of which you will see four large brass cisterns placed on each side, full of gold and silver; but take care you do not meddle with them. Before you enter the first hall, be sure to tuck up your vest, wrap it about you, and then pass through the second into the third without stopping. Above all, have a care that you do not touch the walls; for if you do, you will die instantly. At the end of the third hall, you will find a door which opens into a garden planted with fine trees loaded with fruit; walk directly across the garden by a path which will lead you to five steps that will bring you upon a terrace, where you will see a niche before you, and in that niche a lighted lamp. Take the lamp down, and extinguish it: when you have thrown away the wick, and poured out the liquor, put it in your vestband and bring it to me. Do not be afraid that the liquor will spoil your clothes, for it is not oil; and the lamp will be dry as soon as it is thrown out. If you should wish for any of the fruit of the garden, you may gather as much as you please."

After these words, the magician drew a ring off his finger, and put it on one of Aladdin's, telling him that it was a preservative against all evil, while he should observe what he had prescribed to him. After this instruction he said: "Go down boldly, child, and we shall both be rich all our lives."

Aladdin jumped into the cave, descended the steps, and found the three halls just as the African magician had described. He went through them with all the precaution the fear of death could inspire; crossed the garden without stopping, took down the lamp from the niche, threw out the wick and the liquor, and, as the magician had desired, put it in his vestband. But as he came down from the terrace, he stopped in the garden to observe the fruit, which he only had a glimpse of in crossing it. All the trees were loaded with extraordinary fruit, of different colours on each tree. Some bore fruit entirely white, and some clear and transparent as crystal; some pale red, and others deeper; some green, blue, and purple, and others yellow: in short, there was fruit of all colours. The white were pearls; the clear and transparent, diamonds; the deep red, rubies; the green, emeralds; the blue, turquoises; the purple, amethysts; and those that were of yellow cast, sapphires. Aladdin was altogether ignorant of their worth, and would have preferred figs and grapes, or any other fruits. But though he took them only for coloured glass of little value, yet he was so pleased with the variety of the colours, and the beauty and extraordinary size of the seeming fruit, that he resolved to gather some of every sort; and accordingly filled the two new purses his uncle had bought for him with his clothes. Some he wrapped up in the skirts of his vest, which was of silk, large and full, and he crammed his bosom as full as it could hold.

Aladdin, having thus loaded himself with riches, returned through the three halls with the same precaution, made all the haste he could, that he might not make his uncle wait, and soon arrived at the mouth of the cave, where the African magician expected him with the utmost impatience. As soon as Aladdin saw him, he cried out: "Pray, uncle, lend me your hand, to help me out." "Give me the lamp first," replied the magician; "it

At the same time the earth, trembling, opened just before the
magician, and uncovered a stone, laid horizontally,
with a brass ring fixed into the middle.

will be troublesome to you." "Indeed, uncle," answered Aladdin, "I cannot now; it is not troublesome to me: but I will as soon as I am up." The African magician was so obstinate, that he would have the lamp before he would help him up; and Aladdin, who had encumbered himself so much with his fruit that he could not well get at it, refused to give it to him till he was out of the cave. The African magician, provoked at this obstinate refusal, flew into a passion, threw a little of his incense into the fire, which he had taken care to keep in, and no sooner pronounced two magical words, than the stone which had closed the mouth of the cave moved into its place, with the earth over it in the same manner as it lay at the arrival of the magician and Aladdin.

This action of the African magician's plainly shewed him to be neither Aladdin's uncle, nor Mustapha the tailor's brother; but a true African. Africa is a country whose inhabitants delight most in magic of any in the whole world, and he had applied himself to it from his youth. After forty years' experience in enchantments and reading of magic books, he had found out that there was in the world a wonderful lamp, the possession of which would render him more powerful than any monarch; and by a late operation of geomancy, he had discovered that this lamp lay concealed in a subterranean place in the midst of China. Fully persuaded of the truth of this discovery, he set out from the farthest part of Africa; and after a long and fatiguing journey came to the town nearest to this treasure. But though he had a certain knowledge of the place where the lamp was, he was not permitted to take it himself, nor to enter the subterranean place, but must receive it from the hands of another person. For this reason he had addressed himself to Aladdin, whom he looked upon as a lad fit to serve his purpose, resolving, as soon as he should get the lamp into his hands, to sacrifice him to his avarice and wickedness, by making the fumigation mentioned before, and repeating two magical words, the effect of which would remove the stone into its place, so that no witness would remain of the transaction.

The blow he had given Aladdin was intended to make him obey the more readily, and give him the lamp as soon as he should ask for it. But his too great precipitation, and his fear lest somebody should come that way and discover what he wished to keep secret, produced an effect quite contrary to what he had proposed.

When the African magician saw that all his hopes were frustrated forever, he returned the same day for Africa; but went quite round the town, and at some distance from it, lest some persons who had observed him walk out with the boy, on seeing him come back without him, should entertain suspicions, and stop him.

According to all appearances, there was no prospect of Aladdin being heard of any more. But the magician, when he had contrived his death, forgot the ring he had put upon his finger, which preserved him, though he knew not its virtue. It may seem astonishing that the loss of that, together with the lamp, did not drive the magician to despair; but magicians are so much used to misfortunes that they do not lay them to heart, but still feed themselves, to the end of life, with unsubstantial notions and chimeras.

The surprise of Aladdin, who had never suspected this treachery from his pretended uncle, is more easily to be imagined than expressed. When he found himself buried alive, he cried, and called out to his uncle, to tell him he was ready to give him the lamp; but in vain, since his cries could not be heard. He descended to the bottom of the steps, with a design to get into the garden, but the door, which was opened before by enchantment, was now shut by the same means. He then redoubled his cries, sat down on the steps, without any hopes of ever seeing light again, and in a melancholy certainty of passing from the present darkness into that of a speedy death.

Aladdin remained in this state two days, without eating or drinking, and on the third looked upon death as inevitable. Clasping his hands with resignation to the will of God, he said: "There is no strength or power but in the great and high God." In joining his hands he rubbed the ring which the magician had put on his finger, and of which he knew not yet the virtue. Immediately a genie of enormous size and frightful aspect rose out of the earth, his head reaching the roof of the vault, and said to him: "What wouldst thou have? I am ready to obey thee as the slave of all who may possess the ring on thy finger; I, and the other slaves of that ring."

At another time, Aladdin, who had not been used to such appearances, would have been so frightened at the sight of so extraordinary a figure that he would not have been able to speak; but the danger he was in made him answer without hesitation: "Whoever thou art, deliver me from this place, if thou art able." He had no sooner spoken these words, than he found himself on the very spot where the magician had caused the earth to open.

It was some time before his eyes could bear the light, after being so long in total darkness: but after he had endeavoured by degrees to support it, and began to look about him, he was much surprised not to find the earth open, and could not comprehend how he had got so soon out of its bowels. There was nothing to be seen but the place where the fire had been, by which he could nearly judge the situation of the cave. Then turning himself toward the town, he perceived it at a distance in the midst of the gardens that surrounded it, and saw the way by which the magician had brought him. Returning God thanks to find himself once more in the world, he made the best of his way home. When he got within his mother's door, the joy of seeing her and his weakness for want of food for three days made him faint, and he remained for a long time as dead. His mother, who had given him over for lost, seeing him in this condition, omitted nothing to bring him to himself. As soon as he recovered, the first words he spoke were: "Pray, mother, give me something to eat, for I have not put a morsel of anything into my mouth these three days." His mother brought what she had, and set it before him. "My son," said she, "be not too eager, for it is dangerous; eat but little at a time, and take care of yourself. Besides, I would not have you talk; you will have time enough to tell me what has happened to you when you are recovered. It is a great comfort to me to see you again, after the affliction I have been in since Friday, and the pains I have taken to learn what was become of you."

Aladdin took his mother's advice, and ate and drank moderately. When he had done, "Mother," said he to her, "I cannot help complaining of you, for abandoning me so easily to the discretion of a man who had a design to kill me, and who at this very moment thinks my death certain. You believed he was my uncle, as well as I; and what other thoughts could we entertain of a man who was so kind to me? but I must tell you, mother, he is a rogue and a cheat, and only made me those promises to accomplish my death; but for what reason neither you nor I can guess. You shall judge yourself, when you have heard all that passed from the time I left you, till he came to the execution of his wicked design."

Aladdin then related to his mother all that had happened to him, from the Friday when the magician took him to see the

palaces and gardens about the town, till they came to the place
between the two mountains where the great deed was to be
performed; how, with incense which the magician threw into
the fire, and some magical words which he pronounced, the earth
opened, and discovered a cave, which led to an inestimable
treasure. He did not forget the blow the magician had given
him, and in what manner he softened again, and engaged him
by great promises, and putting a ring on his finger, to go
down into the cave. He did not omit the least circumstance of
what he saw in crossing the three halls and the garden, and his
taking the lamp, which he pulled out of his bosom and shewed
to his mother: as well as the transparent fruit of different colours,
which he had gathered in the garden as he returned. But,
though these fruits were precious stones, brilliant as the sun, she
was as ignorant of their worth as her son. She had been bred
in a low rank of life, and her husband's poverty prevented his
being possessed of jewels, nor had she, her relations, or neighbours
ever seen any; so that we must not wonder that she regarded
them as things of no value.

Aladdin put them behind one of the cushions of the sofa, and
continued his story. When he had come to an end, Aladdin said
to his mother: "I need say no more! this is my adventure, and
the dangers I have been exposed to since you saw me."

His mother heard with much interest this surprising relation,
notwithstanding it could be no small affliction to a mother who
loved her son tenderly; but yet in the most moving part, which
discovered the perfidy of the African magician, she could not help
showing, by marks of the greatest indignation, how much she
detested him; and when her son had finished his story, she broke
out into a thousand reproaches against that vile impostor. She
called him perfidious traitor, barbarian, assassin, deceiver,

magician, and an enemy and destroyer of mankind. "Without doubt, child," added she, "he is a magician, and they are plagues to the world, and by their enchantments and sorceries have commerce with the devil. Bless God for preserving you from his wicked designs; for your death would have been inevitable, if you had not called upon Him, and implored His assistance." She said a great deal more against the magician's treachery; but finding that whilst she talked, Aladdin began to doze, she left him to his repose, and retired.

Aladdin, who had not closed his eyes while he was in the subterranean abode, slept very soundly till late the next morning; when the first thing he said to his mother was, that he wanted something to eat, and that she could not do him a greater kindness than to give him his breakfast. "Alas! child," said she, "I have not a bit of bread to give you, you ate up all the provisions I had in the house yesterday; but have a little patience, and it shall not be long before I will bring you some: I have a little cotton, which I have spun; I will go and sell it, buy bread, and something for our dinner." "Mother," replied Aladdin, "keep your cotton for another time, and give me the lamp I brought home with me yesterday; I will go and sell it, and the money I shall get for it will serve both for breakfast and dinner, and perhaps supper too."

Aladdin's mother took the lamp, and said to her son: "Here it is, but it is very dirty; if it was a little cleaner I believe it would bring something more." She took some fine sand and water to clean it; but had no sooner begun to rub it, than in an instant a hideous genie of gigantic size appeared before her, and said to her in a voice like thunder: "What wouldst thou have? I am ready to obey thee as thy slave, and the slave of all those who have that lamp in their hands; I and the other slaves of the lamp."

ALADDIN

Aladdin's mother, terrified at the sight of the genie, fainted; when the lad, who had seen such another phantom in the cavern, snatched the lamp out of his mother's hand, and said to the genie boldly: "I am hungry, bring me something to eat." The genie disappeared immediately, and in an instant returned with a large silver tray, holding twelve covered dishes of the same metal, which contained the most delicious viands; six large white bread-cakes on two plates, two flagons of wine, and two silver cups. All these he placed upon a carpet, and disappeared: this was done before Aladdin's mother recovered from her swoon.

Aladdin fetched some water, and sprinkled it in her face, to recover her: whether that or the smell of the meat brought her to life again, it was not long before she came to herself. "Mother," said Aladdin, "do not mind this; here is what will put you in heart, and at the same time satisfy my extreme hunger: do not let such delicious meat get cold."

His mother was much surprised to see the great tray, twelve dishes, six loaves, the two flagons and cups, and to smell the savoury odour which exhaled from the dishes. "Child," said she, "to whom are we obliged for this great plenty and liberality; has the sultan been made acquainted with our poverty, and had compassion on us?" "It is no matter, mother," said Aladdin; "let us sit down and eat, for you have almost as much need of breakfast as myself; when we have done, I will tell you." Accordingly, both mother and son sat down, and ate with the better relish as the table was so well furnished. But all the time Aladdin's mother could not forbear looking at and admiring the dishes, though she could not judge whether they were silver or any other metal, and the novelty more than the value attracted her attention.

The mother and son sat at breakfast till it was dinner-time, and then they thought it would be best to put the two meals together; yet after this they found they should have enough left for supper, and two meals for the next day.

When Aladdin's mother had taken away what was left, she went and sat by her son on the sofa, saying: "I expect now that you should satisfy my impatience, and tell me exactly what passed between the genie and you while I was in a swoon;" which he readily complied with.

She was in as great amazement at what her son told her, as at the appearance of the genie; and said to him: "But, son, what have we to do with genies? I never heard that any of my acquaintance had ever seen one. How came that vile genie to address himself to me, and not to you, to whom he had appeared before in the cave?" "Mother," answered Aladdin, "the genie you saw is not the one who appeared to me, though he resembles him in size; no, they had quite different persons and habits; they belong to different masters. If you remember, he that I first saw called himself the slave of the ring on my finger; and this you saw, called himself the slave of the lamp you had in your hand: but I believe you did not hear him, for I think you fainted as soon as he began to speak."

"What!" cried the mother, "was your lamp then the occasion of that cursed genie's addressing himself rather to me than to you? Ah! my son, take it out of my sight, and put it where you please. I will never touch it. I had rather you would sell it, than run the hazard of being frightened to death again by touching it: and if you would take my advice, you would part also with the ring, and not have anything to do with genies, who, as our prophet has told us, are only devils."

"With your leave, mother," replied Aladdin, "I shall take care how I sell a lamp which may be so serviceable both to you and me. Have you not been an eye-witness of what it has procured us? and it shall still continue to furnish us with subsistence. My false and wicked uncle would not have taken so much pains, and undertaken so long a journey, if it had not been to get into his possession this wonderful lamp, which he preferred before all the gold and silver which he knew was in the halls. He knew too well the worth of this lamp, not to prefer it to so great a treasure; and since chance hath discovered the virtue of it to us, let us make a profitable use of it, without making any great show, and exciting the envy and jealousy of our neighbours. However, since the genies frighten you so much, I will take it out of your sight, and put it where I may find it when I want it. The ring I cannot resolve to part with; for without that you had never seen me again; and though I am alive now, perhaps, if it was gone, I might not be so some moments hence; therefore I hope you will give me leave to keep it, and to wear it always on my finger. Who knows what dangers you and I may be exposed to, which neither of us can foresee, and from which it may deliver us?" As Aladdin's arguments were just, his mother had nothing to say against them; she only replied, that he might do what he pleased; for her part, she would have nothing to do with genies, but would wash her hands of them.

By the next night they had eaten all the provisions the genie had brought: and the next day Aladdin, who could not bear the thought of hunger, putting one of the silver dishes under his vest, went out early to sell it, and addressing himself to a Jew whom he met in the streets, took him aside, and pulling out the plate, asked him if he would buy it. The cunning Jew took the dish, examined it, and as soon as he found that it was good silver, asked Aladdin at how much he valued it. Aladdin, who knew not its value, and never had been used to such traffic, told him he would trust to his judgment and honour. The Jew was somewhat confounded at this plain dealing; and doubting whether Aladdin understood the material or the full value of what he offered to sell, took a piece of gold out of his purse and gave it to him, though it was but the sixtieth part of the worth of the plate. Aladdin, taking the money very eagerly, retired with so much haste, that the Jew, not content with the exorbitancy of his profit, was vexed he had not penetrated into his ignorance, and was going to run after him, to endeavour to get some change out of the piece of gold; but the lad ran so fast, and had got so far, that it would have been impossible for him to overtake him.

Before Aladdin went home, he called at a baker's, bought some cakes of bread, changed his money, and on his return gave the rest to his mother, who went and purchased provisions enough to last them some time. After this manner they lived, till Aladdin had sold the twelve dishes singly, as necessity pressed, to the Jew, for the same money; who, after the first time, durst not offer him less, for fear of losing so good a bargain. When he had sold the last dish, he had recourse to the tray, which weighed ten times as much as the dishes, and would have carried it to his old purchaser, but that it was too large and cumbersome; therefore he was obliged to bring him home with him to his mother's, where, after the Jew had examined the weight of the tray, he laid down ten pieces of gold, with which Aladdin was very well satisfied.

They lived on these ten pieces in a frugal manner, for Aladdin, though formerly used to an idle life, had left off playing with young lads of his own age ever since his adventure with the African magician. He spent his time in walking about, and conversing with decent people, with whom he gradually got acquainted. Sometimes he would stop at the principal merchants' shops, where people of distinction met, and listen to their discourse, by which he gained some little knowledge of the world.

ALADDIN

When all the money was spent, Aladdin had recourse again to the lamp. He took it in his hand, looked for the part where his mother had rubbed it with the sand, and rubbed it also, when the genie immediately appeared, and said: "What wouldst thou have? I am ready to obey thee as thy slave, and the slave of all those who have that lamp in their hands; I, and the other slaves of the lamp." "I am hungry," said Aladdin; "bring me something to eat." The genie disappeared, and presently returned with a tray, and the same number of covered dishes as before, set them down, and vanished.

Aladdin's mother, knowing what her son was going to do, went out about some business, on purpose to avoid being in the way when the genie came; and when she returned, was almost as much surprised as before at the prodigious effect of the lamp. However, she sat down with her son, and when they had eaten as much as they liked, she set enough by to last them two or three days.

As soon as Aladdin found that their provisions were expended, he took one of the dishes, and went to look for his Jew again; but passing by the shop of a goldsmith, who had the character of a very fair and honest man, the goldsmith perceiving him, called to him, and said: "My lad, I have often observed you go by, loaded as you are at present, and talk with such a Jew, and then come back again empty-handed. I imagine that you carry something which you sell to him; but perhaps you do not know that he is the greatest rogue even among the Jews, and that nobody of prudence will have anything to do with him. If you will shew me what you now carry, and it is to be sold, I will give you the full worth of it; or I will direct you to other merchants who will not cheat you."

The hopes of getting more money for his plate induced Aladdin to pull it from under his vest, and shew it to the goldsmith, who at first sight saw that it was made of the finest silver and asked him if he had sold such as that to the Jew, when Aladdin told him that he had sold him twelve such, for a piece of gold each. "What a villain!" cried the goldsmith; "but," added he, "my son, what is past cannot be recalled. By shewing you the value of this plate, which is of the finest silver we use in our shops, I will let you see how much the Jew has cheated you."

The goldsmith took a pair of scales, weighed the dish, and after he had mentioned how much an ounce of fine silver was worth, assured him that his plate would fetch by weight sixty pieces of gold, which he offered to pay down immediately. "If you dispute my honesty," said he, "you may go to any other of our trade, and if he gives you more, I will be bound to forfeit twice as much!"

Aladdin thanked him for his fair dealing, so greatly to his advantage, took the gold, and never after went to any other person, but sold him all his dishes and the tray.

Though Aladdin and his mother had an inexhaustible treasure in their lamp, and might have had whatever they wished for, yet they lived with the same frugality as before, except that Aladdin dressed better; as for his mother, she wore no clothes but what she earned by spinning cotton. After their manner of living, it may easily be supposed that the money for which Aladdin had sold the dishes and tray was sufficient to maintain them for some time.

During this interval, Aladdin frequented the shops of the principal merchants, where they sold cloth of gold and silver, linens, silk stuffs, and jewelry, and oftentimes joining in their conversation, acquired a knowledge of the world, and respectable demeanour. By his acquaintance among the jewellers, he came to know that the fruits which he had gathered when he took the lamp were, instead of coloured glass, stones of inestimable value; but he had the prudence not to mention this to any one, not even to his mother.

One day as Aladdin was walking about the town, he heard an order proclaimed, commanding the people to shut up their shops and houses, and keep within doors, while the Princess Badroulboudour, the sultan's daughter, went to the baths and returned.

This proclamation inspired Aladdin with eager curiosity to see the princess's face, which he could not do without admission into the house of some acquaintance, and then only through a window; but to gratify his curiosity, he presently thought of a scheme, which succeeded; it was to place himself behind the door of the bath, which was so situated that he could not fail of seeing her face.

Aladdin had not waited long before the princess came, and he could see her plainly through a chink of the door without being discovered. She was attended by a great crowd of ladies, slaves, and eunuchs, who walked on each side, and behind her. When she came within three or four paces of the door of the baths, she took off her veil, and gave Aladdin an opportunity of a full view.

As soon as Aladdin had seen the princess, his heart could not withstand those inclinations so charming an object always inspires. She was the most beautiful brunette in the world; her eyes were large, lively, and sparkling; her looks sweet and modest; her nose was of a just proportion and without a fault, her mouth small, her lips of a vermilion red; in a word, all the features of her face were perfectly regular. It is not therefore surprising that Aladdin, who had never before seen such a blaze of charms, was dazzled, and his senses ravished by such an assemblage. With all these perfections the princess had so majestic an air, that the sight of her was sufficient to inspire love and admiration.

After the princess had passed by, and entered the baths, Aladdin remained some time astonished and in a kind of ecstasy, retracing and imprinting the idea of so charming an object deeply in his mind, but at last, he resolved to quit his hiding-place and go home. He could not so far conceal his uneasiness but that his mother perceived it, was surprised to see him so much more thoughtful than usual; and asked if he were ill? He returned her no answer, but sat carelessly down on the sofa, and remained silently musing on the image of the charming Badroulboudour.

After supper, his mother asked him again why he was so melancholy, but could get no information, and he determined to go to bed rather than give her the least satisfaction. As he sat next day on the sofa, opposite his mother, however, as she was spinning cotton, he spoke to her in these words: "I perceive, mother, that my silence yesterday has much troubled you; I was not, nor am I ill; but I assure you, that what I felt then, and now endure, is worse than any disease.

"It was not proclaimed in this quarter of the town, and therefore you could know nothing of it, that the sultan's daughter was yesterday to go to the baths. I had a great curiosity to see her face; and as it occurred to me that when she came nigh the bath, she would pull her veil off, I resolved to conceal myself behind the door. She did so and I had the happiness of seeing her lovely face with the greatest security. This, mother, was the cause of my silence yesterday; I love the princess with more violence than I can express; and as my passion increases every moment, I am resolved to ask her in marriage of the sultan, her father."

ALADDIN

Aladdin's mother listened with interest to what her son told her; but when he talked of asking the princess in marriage, she could not help bursting out into a loud laugh. He would have gone on with his rhapsody, but she interrupted him: "Alas! child," said she, "what are you thinking of? you must be mad to talk thus."

"I assure you, mother," replied Aladdin, "that I am not mad, but in my right senses; I foresaw that you would reproach me with folly and extravagance; but I must tell you once more, that I am resolved to demand the princess in marriage!"

"Indeed, son," replied the mother seriously, "I cannot help telling you that you have forgotten yourself, and I do not see who will venture to make the proposal for you." "You yourself," replied he immediately. "I go to the sultan!" answered the mother, amazed. "I shall be cautious how I engage in such an errand. Why, who are you, son," continued she, "that you can have the assurance to think of your sultan's daughter? Have you forgotten that your father was one of the poorest tailors in the capital, and that I am of no better extraction; and do not you know that sultans never marry their daughters but to sons of sovereigns like themselves?"

"Mother," answered Aladdin, "I foresaw all that you have said, or can say: and tell you that neither your discourse nor your remonstrances shall make me change my mind. I have told you that you must ask the princess in marriage for me. I beg of you not to refuse, unless you would rather see me in my grave, than by your compliance give me new life."

The good old woman was much embarrassed, when she found Aladdin persisting in so wild a design. "My son," said she again, "I am your mother, and there is nothing that is reasonable but I would readily do for you. If I were to go and treat about your marriage with some neighbour's daughter, I would do it with all my heart; and even then they would expect you should have some little estate, or be of some trade. When such poor folks as we are wish to marry, the first thing they ought to think of, is how to live. But without reflecting on the meanness of your birth, and the little fortune you have to recommend you, you aim at the highest pitch of exaltation; and your pretensions are no less than to demand in marriage the daughter of your sovereign, who with one single word can crush you to pieces. How could so extraordinary a thought come into your head, as that I should go to the sultan and ask him to give his daughter in marriage to you? Suppose I had the impudence to present myself before the sultan, to whom should I address myself to be introduced to his majesty? Do you not think the first person I should speak to would take me for a mad woman, and chastise me as I should deserve? I know there is no difficulty to those who go to petition for justice, which the sultan distributes equally among his subjects; I know, too, that to those who ask a favour he grants it with pleasure when he sees it is deserved. But do you think you have merited the honour you would have me ask? What have you done to claim such a favour, either for your prince or country? How can I open my mouth to make the proposal to the sultan? His majestic presence and the lustre of his court would absolutely confound me. There is another reason, my son, which you do not think of, which is that nobody ever goes to ask a favour of the sultan without a present. But what presents have you to make? and what proportion could they bear to the favour you would ask? Therefore, reflect well, and consider that you aspire to an object which it is impossible for you to obtain."

Aladdin heard very calmly all that his mother could say to dissuade him from his design, and after he had weighed her representations replied: "I own, mother, it is great rashness in me to presume to carry my pretensions so far; and a great want of consideration to ask you to go and make the proposal to the sultan, without first taking proper measures to procure a favourable reception, and I therefore beg your pardon. But be not surprised that I did not at first see every measure necessary to procure me the happiness I seek. I love the princess, and shall always persevere in my design of marrying her. I am obliged to you for the hint you have given me, and look upon it as the first step I ought to take to procure the happy issue I promise myself.

"You say it is not customary to go to the sultan without a present, and that I have nothing worthy of his acceptance. Do not you think, mother, that what I brought home with me the day on which I was delivered from death may be an acceptable present? I mean those things that you and I both took for coloured glass: but now I can tell you that they are jewels of inestimable value. I know the worth of them by frequenting the shops; and you may take my word that all the precious stones which I saw in the jewellers' shops were not to be compared to those we have, either for size or beauty; I am persuaded that they will be received very favourably by the sultan: you have a large porcelain dish fit to hold them; fetch it, and let us see how they will look, when we have arranged them according to their different colours."

Aladdin's mother brought the china dish, when he took the jewels out of the two purses in which he had kept them, and placed them in order according to his fancy. But the brightness and lustre they emitted in the daytime so dazzled the eyes both of mother and son, that they were astonished beyond measure; for they had only seen them by the light of a lamp; and though the latter had beheld them pendent on the trees like fruit beautiful to the eye, yet as he was then but a boy, he looked on them only as glittering playthings.

After they had admired the beauty of the jewels some time, Aladdin said to his mother: "Now you cannot excuse yourself from going to the sultan, under pretext of not having a present to make him, since here is one which will gain you a favourable reception."

Though the good widow did not believe the precious stones so valuable as her son estimated them, she thought such a present might nevertheless be agreeable to the sultan, but she still hesitated. "My son," said she, "I cannot conceive that the sultan will look upon me with a favourable eye; I am sure, that if I attempt to deliver your strange message, I shall have no power to open my mouth; therefore I shall not only lose my labour, but the present, which you say is so valuable, and shall return home again in confusion, to tell you that your hopes are frustrated. But," added she, "I will do my best to please you, though certainly the sultan will either laugh at me, or be in so great a rage, as to make us both the victims of his fury."

She used many other arguments to endeavour to make Aladdin change his mind; but he persisted in importuning his mother to execute his resolution, and she, out of tenderness, complied with his request.

As it was now late, and the time for admission to the palace was passed, the visit was put off till the next day. The mother and son talked of different matters the remaining hours; and Aladdin strove to encourage her in the task she had undertaken; while she could not persuade herself she should succeed; and it must be confessed she had reason enough to doubt. "Child," said she to Aladdin, "if the sultan should hear my proposal with calmness, and after this should think of asking me where lie your riches and your estate, what answer would you have me return him?"

"Let us not be uneasy, mother," replied Aladdin, "about what may never happen. First, let us see how the sultan receives, and what answer he gives you. If he desires to be informed of what you mention, I am confident that the lamp will not fail me in time of need."

The tailor's widow reflected that the lamp might be capable of doing greater wonders than just providing victuals for them, and this removed all the difficulties which might have prevented her from undertaking the service she had promised. Aladdin, who penetrated into his mother's thoughts, said to her: "Above all things, mother, be sure to keep secret our possession of the lamp, for thereon depends the success we have to expect;" and after this caution they parted to go to rest. Aladdin rose before daybreak, awakened his mother, pressing her to get herself dressed to go to the sultan's palace, and to get admittance, if possible, before the great officers of state went in to take their seats in the divan, where the sultan always assisted in person.

Aladdin's mother took the china dish, in which they had put the jewels the day before, wrapped in two napkins, one finer than the other, which was tied at the four corners for more easy carriage, and set out for the palace. When she came to the gates, the grand vizier, the other viziers, and most distinguished lords of the court, were just gone in; but, notwithstanding the great crowd of people who had business there, she got into the divan, a spacious hall, the entrance into which was very magnificent. She placed herself just before the sultan, grand vizier, and the great lords, who sat in council, on his right and left hand.

Several causes were called, according to their order, pleaded and adjudged, until the time the divan generally broke up, when the sultan rising, returned to his apartment, attended by the grand vizier; the other viziers and ministers of state then retired, as also did all those whose business had called them thither; some pleased with gaining their causes, others dissatisfied at the sentences pronounced against them, and some in expectation of being heard the next sitting.

Aladdin's mother, seeing the sultan retire, and all the people depart, judged rightly that he would not sit again that day, and resolved to go home. When Aladdin saw her return with the present, he knew not what to think, and in fear lest she should bring him some ill news, had not courage to ask her any questions; but she, who had never set foot into the sultan's palace before, and knew not what was every day practised there, freed him from his embarrassment, and said to him: "Son, I have seen the sultan, and am very well persuaded he has seen me too; for I placed myself just before him; but he was so much taken up with those who attended on all sides of him, that I pitied him, and wondered at his patience. At last I believe he was heartily tired, for he rose up suddenly, and would not hear a great many who were ready prepared to speak to him, but went away, at which I was well pleased, for indeed I began to lose all patience, and was extremely fatigued with staying so long. But there is no harm done; I will go again to-morrow; perhaps the sultan may not be so busy."

Though his passion was very violent, Aladdin was forced to be satisfied, and to fortify himself with patience. He had at least the satisfaction to find that his mother had got over the greatest difficulty, which was to procure access to the sultan, and hoped that the example of those she saw speak to him would embolden her to acquit herself better of her commission when a favourable opportunity might offer.

The next morning she repaired to the sultan's palace with the present, as early as the day before, but when she came there, she found the gates of the divan shut, and understood that the council sat but every other day, therefore she must come again the next. This news she carried to her son, whose only relief was to guard himself with patience. She went six times afterward on the days appointed and placed herself always directly before the sultan, but with as little success as the first morning, and might have perhaps come a thousand times to as little purpose, if luckily the sultan himself had not taken particular notice of her.

On the sixth day, after the divan was broken up, when the sultan returned to his own apartment, he said to his grand vizier: "I have for some time observed a certain woman, who attends constantly every day that I give audience, with something wrapped up in a napkin: she always stands up from the beginning to the breaking up of the audience, and affects to place herself just before me. Do you know what she wants?"

"Sir," replied the grand vizier, who knew no more than the sultan what she wanted, but did not wish to seem uninformed, "your majesty knows that women often make complaints on trifles; perhaps she may come to complain that somebody has sold her some bad flour, or some such trifling matter." The sultan was not satisfied with this answer, but replied: "If this woman comes to our next audience, do not fail to call her, that I may hear what she has to say." The grand vizier made answer by lowering his hand, and then lifting it up above his head, signifying his willingness to lose it if he failed.

By this time, the tailor's widow was so much used to go to audience, and stand before the sultan, that she did not think it any trouble, if she could but satisfy her son that she neglected nothing that lay in her power to please him: so the next audience-day she went to the divan and placed herself in front of the sultan as usual; and before the grand vizier had made his report of business, the sultan perceived her, and compassionating her for having waited so long, said to the vizier: "Before you enter upon any business, remember the woman I spoke to you about; bid her come near, and let us despatch her business first." The grand vizier immediately called the chief of the macebearers, and pointing to her, bade him tell her to come before the sultan.

The chief of the officers went to Aladdin's mother, and at a sign he gave her, she followed him to the foot of the sultan's throne, where he left her, and retired to his place by the grand vizier. The old woman bowed her head down to the carpet, which covered the platform of the throne, and remained in that posture till the sultan bade her rise, when he said to her: "Good woman, I have observed you to stand from the beginning to the rising of the divan; what business brings you here?"

After these words, Aladdin's mother prostrated herself a second time; and when she arose, said: "Monarch of monarchs, before I tell your majesty the extraordinary and incredible business which brings me before your high throne, I beg of you to pardon the boldness of the demand I am going to make, which is so uncommon, that I tremble, and am ashamed to propose it to my sovereign." In order to give her the more freedom to explain herself, the sultan ordered all to quit the divan but the grand vizier, and then told her she might speak without restraint.

Aladdin's mother, not content with this favour of the sultan's to save her the confusion of speaking before so many people, was, notwithstanding, a little apprehensive; therefore, resuming her discourse, she said: "I beg of your majesty, if you should think my demand the least offensive, to assure me first of your forgiveness." "Well," replied the sultan, "I will forgive you, be it what it may, and no hurt shall come to you: speak boldly."

When Aladdin's mother had taken all these precautions, she told him faithfully how Aladdin had seen the Princess Badroulboudour, the violent love that fatal sight had inspired him with, the declaration he had made to her when he came home, and what she had said to dissuade him. "But," continued she, "my son, instead of taking my advice and reflecting on his presumption, was so obstinate as to persevere, and to threaten me with some desperate act, if I refused to come and ask the princess in marriage of your majesty; and it was not without the greatest reluctance that I was led to accede to his request, for which I beg your majesty once more to pardon not only me, but also Aladdin my son, for entertaining so rash a project."

The sultan hearkened to this discourse without shewing the least anger; but before he gave her any answer, asked her what she had brought tied up in the napkin? She took the china dish, which she had set down at the foot of the throne before she prostrated herself before him, untied it, and presented it to the sultan.

The monarch's amazement and surprise were inexpressible, when he saw so many large, beautiful, and valuable jewels collected in the dish. He remained for some time motionless with admiration. At last, when he had recovered himself, he received the present, crying out in a transport of joy: "How rich, how beautiful!" After he had admired and handled all the jewels, one after another, he turned to his grand vizier, and shewing him the dish, said: "Behold, admire, wonder, and confess that your eyes never beheld jewels so rich and beautiful before." The vizier was charmed. "Well," continued the sultan, "what sayest thou to such a present? Is it not worthy of the princess, my daughter? And ought I not to bestow her on one who values her at so great price?"

These words put the grand vizier into extreme agitation. The sultan had some time before signified to him his intention of bestowing the princess on a son of his; therefore he was afraid, and not without grounds, that the present might change his majesty's mind. Therefore going to him, and whispering him in the ear, he said: "I cannot but own that the present is worthy of the princess; but I beg of your majesty to grant me three months before you come to a final resolution. I hope, before that time, my son, on whom you have had the goodness to look with a favourable eye, will be able to make a nobler present than Aladdin, who is an entire stranger to your majesty."

The sultan, though he was fully persuaded that it was not possible for the vizier to provide so considerable a present for his son, yet hearkened to him, and granted his request. Turning therefore to the old widow, he said to her: "Good woman, go home, and tell your son that I agree to the proposal you have made me; but I cannot marry the princess, my daughter, till the paraphernalia I design for her be got ready, which cannot be finished these three months; but at the expiration of that time, come again."

The widow returned home much more gratified than she had expected, since she had met with a favourable answer.

Aladdin thought himself the most happy of all men at hearing this news, and thanked his mother for the pains she had taken in the affair, the good success of which was of so great importance to his peace.

When two of the three months were passed, his mother one evening going to light the lamp, and finding no oil in the house, went out to buy some, and when she came into the city, found a general rejoicing. The shops were open, dressed with foliage, silks, and carpeting, every one striving to shew their zeal in the most distinguished manner according to their ability. The streets were crowded with officers in habits of ceremony, mounted on horses richly caparisoned, each attended by a great many foot-men. Aladdin's mother asked the oil-merchant what was the meaning of all this preparation of public festivity? "Whence come you, good woman," said he, "that you do not know that the grand vizier's son is to marry the Princess Badroulboudour, the sultan's daughter, to-night? She will presently return from the baths; and these officers whom you see are to assist at the cavalcade to the palace, where the ceremony is to be solemnised."

This was news enough for Aladdin's mother. She ran till she was quite out of breath home to her son, who little suspected any such event. "Child," cried she, "you are undone! you depend upon the sultan's fine promises, but they will come to nothing." Aladdin was alarmed at these words. "Mother," replied he, "how do you know the sultan has been guilty of a breach of promise?" "This night," answered the mother, "the grand vizier's son is to marry the Princess Badroulboudour." She then related how she had heard it; so that he had no reason to doubt the truth of what she said.

At this account, Aladdin was thunderstruck. Any other man would have sunk under the shock; but a sudden hope of disap-pointing his rival soon roused his spirits, and he bethought him-self of the lamp, which had in every emergency been so useful to him; and without venting his rage in empty words against the sultan, the vizier, or his son, he only said: "Perhaps, mother, the vizier's son may not be so happy to-night as he promises himself: while I go into my chamber a moment, do you get supper ready." She accordingly went about it, but guessed that her son was going to make use of the lamp, to prevent, if possible, the consummation of the marriage.

When Aladdin had got into his chamber, he took the lamp, rubbed it in the same place as before, when immediately the genie appeared, and said to him: "What wouldst thou have? I am ready to obey thee as thy slave, and the slave of all those who have that lamp in their possession; I and the other slaves of the lamp." "Hear me," said Aladdin; "thou hast hitherto brought me whatever I wanted as to provisions; but now I have business of the greatest importance for thee to execute. I have demanded the Princess Badroulboudour in marriage of the sultan, her father; he promised her to me, only requiring three months' delay; but instead of keeping that promise, has this night planned to marry her to the grand vizier's son. What I ask of you is, that as soon as the two are made one, you bring them both hither to me." "Master," replied the genie, "I will obey you. Have you any other commands?" "None at present," answered Aladdin, and then the genie disappeared.

Aladdin having left his chamber, supped with his mother, with the same tranquillity of mind as usual; and after supper talked of the princess's marriage as of an affair wherein he had not the least concern; he then retired to his own chamber again, but sat up waiting the execution of his orders to the genie.

In the meantime, everything was prepared with the greatest magnificence in the sultan's palace to celebrate the princess's nuptials; and the evening was spent with all the usual ceremonies and great rejoicings.

No sooner had the bride and bridegroom slipped away from the company, however, than the genie, as the faithful slave of the lamp, and punctual in executing the command of those who possessed it, to the great amazement of them both, took them up and transported them in an instant to Aladdin's chamber, where he set them down.

Aladdin had waited impatiently for this moment. "Take this new-married man," said he to the genie, "shut him up in the house of office, and come again to-morrow morning before daybreak." The genie instantly carried the vizier's son whither Aladdin had commanded him; and after he had breathed upon him, which prevented his stirring, left him there.

Passionate as was Aladdin's love for the princess, he did not talk much to her when they were alone; but only said with a respectful air: "Fear nothing, adorable princess; you are here in safety. If I have been forced to come to this extremity, it is to prevent an unjust rival's possessing you, contrary to your father's promise in favour of myself."

The princess, who knew nothing of these particulars, gave very little attention to what Aladdin could say. The fright and amazement of so surprising an adventure had alarmed her so much that he could not get one word from her. Badroulboudour never passed a night so ill in her life; and if we consider the condition in which the genie left the grand vizier's son, we may imagine that the new bridegroom spent it much worse.

Aladdin had no occasion the next morning to rub the lamp to call the genie; who appeared at the hour appointed, and said to him: "I am here, master; what are your commands?" "Go," said Aladdin, "fetch the vizier's son out of the place where you left him, and carry the pair to the sultan's palace, from whence you brought them." The genie presently returned with the vizier's son, and in an instant they were transported into the same chamber of the palace from whence they had been brought. But we must observe, that all this time the genie never was visible either to the princess or the grand vizier's son. His hideous form would have made them die with fear. Neither did they hear anything of the discourse between Aladdin and him; they only perceived the motion through the air, and their transportation from one place to another; which we may well imagine was enough to alarm them.

The sultan went to the room of the princess next morning and kissed her between the eyes, according to custom, wishing her a good morrow, but was extremely surprised to see her so melancholy. She only cast at him a sorrowful look, expressive of great affliction. He said a few words to her; but finding that he could not get an answer, was forced to retire. Nevertheless, he suspected that there was something extraordinary in this silence, and thereupon went immediately to the sultaness's apartment, told her in what a state he had found the princess, and how she had received him. "Sir," said the sultaness, "I will go and see her; I am much deceived if she receives me in the same manner."

As soon as the sultaness was dressed, she went to the princess's apartment, who was still in bed. She undrew the curtain, wished her good morrow, and kissed her. But how great was her surprise when she returned no answer; and looking more attentively at her, she perceived her to be much dejected, which made her judge that something had happened, which she did not understand. "How comes it, child," said the sultaness, "that you do not return my caresses? Ought you to treat your mother after this manner? I am induced to believe something extraordinary has happened; come, tell me freely, and leave me no longer in a painful suspense."

At last the princess broke silence with a deep sigh, and said: "Alas! most honoured mother, forgive me if I have failed in the respect I owe you. My mind is so full of the extraordinary circumstances which have befallen me that I have not yet recovered from my amazement and alarm." She then related her surprising adventures, which the sultaness heard very patiently, but could scarcely believe. "You did well, child," said she, "not to speak of this to your father: take care not to mention it to anybody; for you will certainly be thought mad if you talk in this manner." "Madam," replied the princess, "I can assure you I am in my right senses; ask my husband and he will tell you the same circumstances." "I will," said the sultaness; "but if he should talk in the same manner, I shall not be better persuaded of the truth. Come, rise, and throw off this idle fancy; it will be strange if all the feasts and rejoicings in the kingdom should be interrupted by such a vision. Do not you hear the trumpets of congratulation, and concerts of the finest music? Cannot these inspire you with joy and make you forget the fancies of a dream?" At the same time the sultaness called the princess's women, and after she had seen her get up, went to the sultan's apartment, told him that her daughter had got some odd notions in her head, but that there was nothing in them but idle phantasy.

She then sent for the vizier's son, to know of him something of what the princess had told her; but he, thinking himself highly honoured to be allied to the sultan, and not willing to lose the princess, denied what had happened. "That is enough," answered the sultaness; "I ask no more. I see you are wiser than my daughter."

The rejoicings lasted all that day in the palace, and the sultaness, who never left the princess, forgot nothing to divert her, and induce her to take part in the various diversions and shows; but she was so struck with the idea of what had happened to her in the night, that it was easy to see her thoughts were entirely taken up with it. Neither was the grand vizier's son in less tribulation, though his ambition made him disguise his feelings so well, that nobody doubted of his being a happy bridegroom.

Aladdin, who was well acquainted with what passed in the palace, was resolved that the troublesome adventure of the night before should again disturb the unhappy pair, and therefore had recourse to his lamp, and when the genie appeared and offered his service, he said to him: "Bring the grand vizier's son and the Princess Badroulboudour hither to-night, as thou didst yesterday."

The genie obeyed as faithfully and exactly as the day before; the grand vizier's son passed the night as coldly and disagreeably, and the princess had the same alarm and mortification. The genie, according to orders, came the next morning, and returned the new-married couple again to the palace.

The sultan, after the reception the princess had given him, was very anxious to know how she had passed the second night, and therefore went into her chamber as early as the morning before. After the same caresses he had given her the former morning, he bade her good-morrow. "Well, daughter," said he, "are you in a better humour than yesterday?" Still the princess was silent, and the sultan, perceiving her to be in greater confusion than before, doubted not that something very extraordinary was the cause; but provoked that his daughter should conceal it, he said to her in a rage, with his sabre in his hand: "Daughter, tell me what is the matter, or I will cut off your head immediately."

The princess, more frightened at the tone of the enraged sultan than at the sight of the drawn sabre, at last broke silence, and said with tears in her eyes: "My dear father and sultan, I ask your majesty's pardon if I have offended you, and hope that out of your goodness you will have compassion on me."

After this preamble, which appeased the sultan, she told him what had happened to her in so moving a manner, that he, who loved her tenderly, was most sensibly grieved. She added: "If your majesty doubts the truth of this account, you may inform yourself from my husband, who will tell you the same thing."

The sultan immediately felt all the uneasiness so surprising an adventure must have given the princess. "Daughter," said he, "you are much to blame for not telling me this yesterday, since it concerns me as much as yourself. I did not marry you to make you miserable, but that you might enjoy all the happiness you might hope for from a husband, who to me seemed agreeable to you. Efface all these troublesome ideas from your memory; I will take care that you shall have no more such disagreeable experiences."

As soon as the sultan had returned to his own apartment, he sent for the grand vizier: "Vizier," said he, "have you seen your son, and has he told you anything?" The vizier replied: "No." The sultan related all the circumstances of which the princess had informed him, and afterward said: "I do not doubt but that my daughter has told me the truth; but nevertheless I should be glad to have it confirmed by your son, therefore go and ask him how it was."

The grand vizier went immediately to his son, communicated what the sultan had told him, and enjoined him to conceal nothing, but to relate the whole truth. "I will disguise nothing from you, father," replied the son, "for indeed all that the princess has stated is true. Yet I must tell you, that all these experiences do not in the least lessen those sentiments of love and gratitude I entertain for her; but I must confess, that notwithstanding all the honour that attends marrying my sovereign's daughter, I would much rather die than continue in so exalted an alliance, if

I must undergo much longer what I have already endured. I do not doubt but that the princess entertains the same sentiments, and that she will readily agree to a separation which is so necessary both for her repose and mine. Therefore, father, I beg, by the same tenderness which led you to procure me so great an honour, to obtain the sultan's consent that our marriage may be declared null and void."

Notwithstanding the grand vizier's ambition to have his son allied to the sultan, the firm resolution he saw he had formed to be separated from the princess caused the father to give his majesty a full account of what had passed, begging him finally to give his son leave to retire from the palace, alleging it was not just that the princess should be a moment longer exposed to so terrible a persecution upon his son's account.

The grand vizier found no great difficulty to obtain what he asked, as the sultan had determined upon it already; orders were given to put a stop to all rejoicings in the palace and town, and expresses despatched to all parts of his dominions to countermand his first orders; and in a short time, all merry-making ceased.

This sudden change gave rise both in the city and kingdom to various speculations and inquiries; but no other account could be given of it, except that both the vizier and his son went out of the palace much dejected. Nobody but Aladdin knew the secret, who rejoiced at the happy success procured by his lamp. Neither the sultan nor the grand vizier, who had forgotten Aladdin and his request, had the least thought that he had any concern in the enchantment which caused the dissolution of the marriage.

Aladdin waited till the three months were completed, which the sultan had appointed for the consummation of the marriage between the Princess Badroulboudour and himself; and the next day sent his mother to the palace, to remind the sultan of his promise.

The widow went to the palace, and stood in the same place as before in the hall of audience. The sultan no sooner cast his eyes upon her than he knew her again, remembered her business, and how long he had put her off: therefore, when the grand vizier was beginning to make his report, the sultan interrupted him, and said: "Vizier, I see the good woman who made me the present of jewels some months ago; forbear your report, till I have heard what she has to say." The vizier, looking about the divan, perceived the tailor's widow, and sent the chief of the mace-bearers to conduct her to the sultan.

Aladdin's mother came to the foot of the throne, prostrated herself as usual, and when she rose, the sultan asked her what she would have. "Sir," said she, "I come to represent to your majesty, in the name of my son, Aladdin, that the three months, at the end of which you ordered me to come again, are expired; and to beg you to remember your promise."

The sultan, when he had fixed a time to answer the request of this good woman, little thought of hearing any more of a marriage, which he imagined would be very disagreeable to the princess; so this summons for him to fulfil his promise was somewhat embarrassing; he declined giving an answer till he had consulted his vizier, and signified to him the little inclination he had to conclude a match for his daughter with a stranger, whose rank he supposed to be very mean.

The grand vizier freely told the sultan his thoughts, and said to him: "In my opinion, sir, there is an infallible way for your majesty to avoid a match so disproportionate, without giving Aladdin, were he known to your majesty, any cause of complaint; which is, to set so high a price upon the princess that, however rich he may be, he cannot comply with it. This is the only way to make him desist from so bold an undertaking."

The sultan, approving of the grand vizier's advice, turned to the tailor's widow and said to her: "Good woman, it is true sultans ought to abide by their words, and I am ready to keep mine, by making your son happy in marriage with the princess, my daughter. But as I cannot marry her without some further valuable consideration from your son, you may tell him, I will fulfil my promise as soon as he shall send me forty trays of massy gold, full of the same sort of jewels you have already made me a present of, and carried by the like number of black slaves, who shall be led by as many young and handsome white slaves, all dressed magnificently. On these conditions I am ready to bestow the princess, my daughter, upon him; therefore, good woman, go and tell him so, and I will wait till you bring me his answer."

Aladdin's mother prostrated herself a second time before the sultan's throne, and retired. On her way home, she laughed within herself at her son's foolish imagination. "Where," said she, "can he get so many large gold trays, and such precious stones to fill them? Must he go again to that subterranean abode and gather them off the trees? and where will he get so many such slaves as the sultan requires? It is altogether out of his power, and I believe he will not be much pleased with my embassy this time." When she came home, full of these thoughts, she said to her son: "Indeed, child, I would not have you think any farther of your marriage with the princess. The sultan received me very kindly, and I believe he was well inclined to you; but if I am not much deceived the grand vizier has made him change his mind." She then gave her son an exact account of what the sultan had said to her, and the conditions on which he consented to the match. Afterward she said to him: "The sultan expects your answer immediately; but," continued she, laughing, "I believe he may wait long enough."

"Not so long, mother, as you imagine," replied Aladdin; "the sultan is mistaken, if he thinks by this exorbitant demand to prevent my entertaining thoughts of the princess. I expected that he would have set a higher price upon her incomparable charms. His demand is but a trifle to what I could have done for her. But while I think of satisfying his request, go and get something for our dinner, and leave the rest to me."

As soon as his mother was gone out, Aladdin took the lamp, and rubbing it, the genie appeared, and offered his service as usual. "The sultan," said Aladdin to him, "gives me the princess his daughter in marriage; but demands first, forty large trays of massy gold, full of the fruits of the garden from whence I took this lamp; and these he expects to have carried by as many black slaves, each preceded by a young handsome white slave, richly clothed. Go, and fetch me this present as soon as possible, that I may send it to him before the divan breaks up." The genie told him his command should be immediately obeyed, and disappeared.

In a little time afterward the genie returned with forty black slaves, each bearing on his head a heavy tray of pure gold, full of pearls, diamonds, rubies, emeralds, and every sort of precious stones, all larger and more beautiful than those formerly presented to the sultan. Each tray was covered with silver tissue, embroidered with flowers of gold: these, together with the white slaves, quite filled the house, which was but a small one, the little court before it, and a small garden behind. The genie asked if he had any other commands, and Aladdin telling him that he wanted nothing further, he disappeared.

When Aladdin's mother came from market, she was much surprised to see so many people and such vast riches. As soon as she had laid down her provisions, she was going to pull off her veil; but her son prevented her, and said: "Mother, let us lose no time; before the sultan and the divan rise, I would have you return to the palace with this present as the dowry demanded for the princess, that he may judge by my diligence of the ardent desire I have to procure myself the honour of this alliance." Without waiting for his mother's reply, Aladdin opened the street-door, and made the slaves walk out; each white slave followed by a black with a tray upon his head. When they were all out, the mother followed the last black slave; he shut the door, and then retired to his chamber, full of hopes that the sultan, after this present, which was such as he required, would receive him as his son-in-law.

The first white slave who went out made all the people who were going by stop; and before they were all clear of the house, the streets were crowded with spectators, who ran to see so extraordinary and magnificent a procession. The dress of each slave was so rich, both for the stuff and the jewels, that those who were dealers in them valued each at no less than a million of money; besides, the neatness and propriety of the dress, the noble air, fine shape and proportion of each slave were unparalleled; their grave walk at an equal distance from each other, the lustre of the jewels, curiously set in their girdles of gold, and the egrets of precious stones in their turbans, put the spectators into such great admiration, that they could not avoid following them with their eyes as far as possible. As soon as the first of these slaves arrived at the palace gate, the porters formed themselves into order, taking him for a prince from the magnificence of his habit, and were going to kiss the hem of his garment; but the slave, who was instructed by the genie, prevented them, and said: "We are only slaves, our master will appear at a proper time."

The first slave, followed by the rest, advanced into the second court, which was very spacious, and in which the sultan's household was ranged during the sitting of the divan. The magnificence of the officers, who stood at the head of their troops, was considerably eclipsed by the slaves who bore Aladdin's present, of which they themselves made a part.

As the sultan, who had been informed of their approach to the palace, had given orders for them to be admitted, they went into the divan in regular order, one part filing to the right, and the other to the left. After they were all entered, and had formed a semicircle before the sultan's throne, the black slaves laid the golden trays on the carpet, prostrating themselves, and at the same time the white slaves did the same. When they rose, the black slaves uncovered the trays, and then all stood with their arms crossed over their breasts.

In the meantime Aladdin's mother advanced to the foot of the throne, and having paid her respects, said to the sultan: "Sir, my son is sensible that this present, which he has sent your majesty, is much below the Princess Badroulboudour's worth; but hopes, nevertheless, that your majesty will accept of it."

The sultan was not able to give the least attention to this compliment. The moment he cast his eyes on the forty trays, full of the most precious and beautiful jewels he had ever seen, and the fourscore slaves, who appeared by the elegance of their persons, and the magnificence of their dress, like so many princes, he was overwhelmed. Instead of answering the compliment of Aladdin's mother, he addressed himself to the grand vizier, who could not any more than the sultan comprehend from whence such a profusion of richness could come. "Well, vizier," said he aloud, "who do you think it can be that has sent me so extraordinary a present? Do you think him worthy of the Princess Badroulboudour, my daughter?"

The vizier, notwithstanding his envy and grief at seeing a stranger preferred to his son, durst not disguise his sentiments. It was too visible that Aladdin's present was more than sufficient to merit his being received into royal alliance; therefore, consulting his master's feelings, he returned this answer: "I am so far from having any thoughts that the person who has made your majesty so noble a present is unworthy of the honour you would do him, that I should say he deserved much more, if I were not persuaded that the greatest treasure in the world ought not to be put in competition with the princess, your majesty's daughter."

The sultan made no longer hesitation, nor thought of informing himself whether Aladdin was endowed with all the qualifications requisite in one who aspired to be his son-in-law. The sight alone of such immense riches, and Aladdin's quickness in satisfying his demand, without starting the least difficulty at the exorbitant conditions he had imposed, easily persuaded him that he could want nothing to render him accomplished, and such as he desired. Therefore, to send Aladdin's mother back with all the satisfaction she could desire, he said to her: "My good lady, go and tell your son that I wait with open arms to embrace him, and the more haste he makes to come and receive the princess, my daughter, from my hands, the greater pleasure he will do me."

As soon as the tailor's widow had retired, overjoyed to see her son raised to such exalted fortune, the sultan put an end to the audience; and rising from his throne, ordered that the princess's eunuchs should come and carry the trays into their mistress's apartment, whither he went himself to examine them with her at his leisure. The fourscore slaves were conducted into the palace; and the sultan, telling the princess of their magnificent appearance, ordered them to be brought before her apartment, that she might see through the lattices that he had not exaggerated in his account of them.

In the meantime, Aladdin's mother got home, and shewed in her countenance the good news she brought her son. "My son," said she to him, "you have now all the reason in the world to be pleased. The sultan, with the approbation of the whole court, has declared that you are worthy to possess the Princess Badroulboudour, and waits to embrace you, and conclude your marriage; therefore, you must think of making preparations for your interview, which may answer the high opinion he has formed of your person."

Aladdin, enraptured with this news, made little reply, but retired to his chamber. There, after he had rubbed the lamp, which had never failed him, the obedient genie appeared. "Genie," said Aladdin, "I want to bathe immediately, and you must afterward provide me the richest and most magnificent habit ever worn by a monarch." No sooner were the words out of his mouth than the genie rendered him invisible, and transported him into a bath of the finest marble, where he was undressed, without seeing by whom, in a magnificent and spacious hall. From the hall he was led to the bath, which was of a moderate heat, and he was there rubbed with various scented waters. After he had passed through several degrees of heat, he came out quite a different man from what he was before. His skin was clear white and red, his body lightsome and free; and when he returned into the hall, he found, instead of his own, a suit the magnificence of which astonished him. The genie helped him to dress, and when he had done, transported him back to his own chamber, where he asked him if he had any other commands? "Yes," answered Aladdin, "I expect you to bring me as soon as possible a charger that surpasses in beauty and goodness the best in the sultan's stables, with a saddle, bridle, and other caparisons worth a million of money. I want also twenty slaves, as richly clothed as those who carried the present to the sultan, to walk by my side, and twenty more to go before me in two ranks. Besides these, bring my mother six women slaves to attend her, as richly dressed at least as any of the Princess Badroulboudour's, each carrying a complete dress fit for any sultaness. I want also ten thousand pieces of gold in ten purses; go, and make haste."

As soon as Aladdin had given these orders, the genie disappeared, but presently returned with the horse, the forty slaves, ten of whom carried each a purse containing ten thousand pieces of gold, and six women slaves, each carrying on her head a different dress for Aladdin's mother, wrapped up in a piece of silver tissue.

Of the ten purses Aladdin took four, which he gave to his mother, telling her, those were to supply her with necessaries; the other six he left in the hands of the slaves who brought them, with an order to throw them by handfuls among the people as they went to the sultan's palace. The six slaves who carried the purses he ordered likewise to march before him, three on the right hand and three on the left. Afterward he presented the six women slaves to his mother, telling her that they were her slaves, and that the dresses they had brought were for her use.

When Aladdin had thus settled matters, he told the genie he would call for him when he wanted him, and thereupon the

genie disappeared. Aladdin's thoughts now were only upon
answering, as soon as possible, the desire the sultan had shewn
to see him. He despatched one of the forty slaves to the palace,
with an order to address himself to the chief of the porters, to
know when he might have the honour to come and throw himself
at the sultan's feet. The slave soon acquitted himself of his
commission, and brought for answer that the sultan waited for
him with impatience.

Aladdin immediately mounted his charger, and though he
never was on horseback before, appeared with such extraordinary
grace, that the most experienced horseman would not have taken
him for a novice. The streets through which he was to pass
were almost instantly filled with an innumerable concourse of
people, who made the air echo with their acclamations, especially
every time the six slaves who carried the purses threw handfuls
of gold among the populace. Neither did these shouts of joy
come from those alone who scrambled for the money, but from
a superior rank of people, who could not forbear applauding
Aladdin's generosity. Not only those who knew him when he
played in the streets like a vagabond did not recollect him, but
those who saw him but a little while before hardly recognised
him, so much were his features altered: such were the effects of
the lamp, as to procure by degrees to those who possessed it
perfections suitable to the rank to which the right use of it advanced them. Much more attention was paid to Aladdin's
person than to the pomp and magnificence of his attendants, as
a similar show had been seen the day before, when the slaves
walked in procession with the present to the sultan. Nevertheless, the horse was much admired by good judges, who knew how
to discern his beauties, without being dazzled by the jewels and
richness of his furniture. When the report was everywhere

spread that the sultan was going to give the princess in marriage to Aladdin, nobody regarded his birth, nor envied his good fortune, so worthy he seemed of it in the public opinion.

When he arrived at the palace, everything was prepared for his reception; and when he came to the gate of the second court, he would have alighted from his horse, agreeably to the custom observed by the grand vizier, the commander-in-chief of the empire, and governors of provinces of the first rank; but the chief of the mace-bearers, who waited on him by the sultan's order, prevented him, and attended him to the grand hall of audience, where he helped him to dismount. The officers formed themselves into two ranks at the entrance of the hall. The chief put Aladdin on his right hand, and through the midst of them led him to the sultan's throne.

As soon as the sultan perceived Aladdin, he was no less surprised to see him more richly and magnificently habited than ever he had been himself, than struck at his good mien, fine shape, and a certain air of unexpected dignity, very different from the meanness of his mother's late appearance.

But, notwithstanding, his amazement and surprise did not hinder him from rising off his throne, and descending two or three steps, quickly enough to prevent Aladdin's throwing himself at his feet. He embraced him with all possible demonstrations of joy at his arrival. After this civility Aladdin would have thrown himself at his feet again; but he held him fast by the hand, and obliged him to sit close to the throne.

Aladdin then addressed the sultan, saying: "I receive the honour which your majesty out of your great condescension is pleased to confer; but permit me to assure you that I know the greatness of your power, and that I am not insensible how much my birth is below the lustre of the high rank to which I am raised.

I ask your majesty's pardon for my rashness, but I cannot dissemble that I should die with grief were I to lose my hopes of seeing myself united to the divine princess who is the object of my wishes."

"My son," answered the sultan, embracing him a second time, "you would wrong me to doubt for a moment of my sincerity: your life from this moment is too dear to me not to preserve it, by presenting you with the remedy which is at my disposal."

After these words, the sultan gave a signal, and immediately the air echoed with the sound of trumpets, hautboys, and other musical instruments: and at the same time he led Aladdin into a magnificent hall, where was laid out a most splendid collation. The sultan and Aladdin ate by themselves, while the grand vizier and the great lords of the court, according to their dignity and rank, sat at different tables. The conversation turned on different subjects; but all the while the sultan took so much pleasure in looking at his intended son-in-law, that he hardly ever took his eyes off him; and throughout the whole of their conversation Aladdin shewed so much good sense, as confirmed the sultan in the high opinion he had formed of him.

After the feast, the sultan sent for the chief judge of his capital, and ordered him to draw up immediately a contract of marriage between the Princess Badroulboudour, his daughter, and Aladdin.

When the judge had drawn up the contract in all the requisite forms, the sultan asked Aladdin if he would stay in the palace, and solemnise the ceremonies of marriage that day; to which he answered: "Sir, though great is my impatience to enjoy your majesty's goodness, yet I beg of you to give me leave to defer it till I have built a palace fit to receive the princess; therefore I petition you to grant me a convenient spot of ground near your abode, that I may the more frequently pay my respects, and I will take care to have it finished with all diligence." "Son," said the sultan, "take what ground you think proper, there is space enough on every quarter round my palace; but consider, I cannot see you too soon united with my daughter, which alone is wanting to complete my happiness." After these words he embraced Aladdin again, who took his leave with as much politeness as if he had been bred up and had always lived at court.

Aladdin returned home in the order he had come, amidst the acclamations of the people, who wished him all happiness and prosperity. As soon as he dismounted, he retired to his own chamber, took the lamp, and called the genie as before, who in the usual manner made him a tender of his service. "Genie," said Aladdin, "I have every reason to commend your exactness in executing hitherto punctually whatever I have demanded; but now, if you have any regard for the lamp, your protector, you must shew, if possible, more zeal and diligence than ever. I would have you build me, as soon as you can, a palace opposite, but at a proper distance from, the sultan's, fit to receive my spouse, the Princess Badroulboudour. I leave the choice of the materials to you, that is to say, porphyry, jasper, agate, lapis lazuli, or the finest marble of various colours, and also the architecture of the building. But I expect that on the terraced roof of this palace you will build me a large hall crowned with a dome, and having four equal fronts; and that instead of layers of bricks, the walls be formed of massy gold and silver, laid alternately: that each front shall contain six windows, the lattices of all of which (except one, which must be left unfinished) shall be so enriched in the most tasteful workmanship, with diamonds, rubies, and emeralds, that they shall exceed anything of the kind ever seen in the world. I would have an inner and outer court in front of the palace, and a spacious garden; but above all things, take care that there be laid in a place which you shall point out to me, a treasure of gold and silver coin. Besides, the edifice must be well provided with kitchens and offices, storehouses, and rooms to keep choice furniture in, for every season of the year. I must have stables full of the finest horses, with their equerries and grooms, and hunting equipage. There must be officers to attend the kitchens and offices, and women slaves to wait on the princess. You understand what I mean; therefore go about it, and come and tell me when all is finished."

By the time Aladdin had instructed the genie respecting the building of his palace, the sun was set. The next morning, before break of day, our bridegroom, whose love for the princess would not let him sleep, was up, when the genie presented himself and said: "Sir, your palace is finished; come and see how you like it." Aladdin had no sooner signified his consent, than the genie transported him thither in an instant, and he found it so much beyond his expectation, that he could not enough admire it. The genie led him through all the apartments, where he met with nothing but what was rich and magnificent, with officers and slaves all habited according to their rank and the services to which they were appointed. The genie then shewed him the treasury, which was opened by a treasurer, where Aladdin saw heaps of purses, of different sizes, piled up to the top of the ceiling, and disposed in most excellent order. The genie assured him of the treasurer's fidelity, and thence led him to the stables, where he shewed him some of the finest horses in the world, and the grooms busy in dressing them; from thence they went to the storehouses, which were filled with all things necessary, both for food and ornament.

When Aladdin had examined the palace from top to bottom, and particularly the hall with the four and twenty windows, and found it much beyond whatever he could have imagined, he said: "Genie, no one can be better satisfied than I am; and indeed I should be much to blame if I found any fault. There is only one thing wanting which I forgot to mention; that is, to lay from the sultan's palace to the door of the apartment designed for the princess, a carpet of fine velvet for her to walk upon." The genie immediately disappeared, and Aladdin saw what he desired executed in an instant. The genie then returned, and carried him home before the gates of the sultan's palace were opened.

When the porters, who had always been used to an open prospect, came to open the gates, they were amazed to find it obstructed, and to see a carpet of velvet spread from the grand entrance. They did not immediately look how far it extended, but when they could discern Aladdin's palace distinctly, their surprise was increased. The news of so extraordinary a wonder was presently spread through the palace. The grand vizier, who arrived soon after the gates were open, being no less amazed than others at this novelty, ran and acquainted the sultan, but endeavoured to make him believe it to be all enchantment. "Vizier," replied the sultan, "why will you have it to be enchantment? You know as well as I that it must be Aladdin's palace, which I gave him leave to build, for the reception of my daughter. After the proof we have had of his riches, can we think it strange that he should raise a palace in so short a time? He wished to surprise us, and let us see what wonders are to be done with money in only one night. Confess sincerely that the enchantment you talk of proceeds from a little envy on account of your son's disappointment."

ALADDIN

When Aladdin had been conveyed home, and had dismissed the genie, he found his mother up, and dressing herself in one of those suits which had been brought her. By the time the sultan rose from the council, Aladdin had prepared his mother to go to the palace with her slaves, and desired her, if she saw the sultan, to tell him she should do herself the honour toward evening to attend the princess to her palace. Accordingly she went; but though she and the women slaves who followed her were all dressed like sultanesses, yet the crowd was not near so great as the preceding day, because they were all veiled, and each had on an upper garment agreeable to the richness and magnificence of their habits. Aladdin, taking care not to forget his wonderful lamp, mounted his horse, left his paternal home forever, and went to the palace in the same pomp as the day before.

As soon as the porters of the sultan's palace saw Aladdin's mother, they went and informed the sultan, who immediately ordered the bands of trumpets, cymbals, drums, fifes, and hautboys, placed in different parts of the palace, to play, so that the air resounded with concerts which inspired the whole city with joy: the merchants began to adorn their shops and houses with fine carpets and silks, and to prepare illuminations against night. The artisans of every description left their work, and the populace repaired to the great space between the royal palace and that of Aladdin; which last drew all their attention, not only because it was new to them, but because there was no comparison between the two buildings. But their amazement was to comprehend by what unheard-of miracle so magnificent a palace could have been so soon erected, it being apparent to all that there were no prepared materials, or any foundations laid the day before.

Aladdin's mother was received in the palace with honour, and introduced into the Princess Badroulboudour's apartment by the chief of the eunuchs. As soon as the princess saw her, she rose, saluted, and desired her to sit down on a sofa; and while her women finished dressing, and adorning her with the jewels which Aladdin had presented to her, a collation was served up. At the same time the sultan, who wished to be as much with his daughter as possible before he parted with her, came in and paid the old lady great respect. Aladdin's mother had talked to the sultan in public, but he had never seen her with her veil off, as she was then; and though she was somewhat advanced in years, she had the remains of a good face, which showed what she had been in her youth. The sultan, who had always seen her dressed very meanly, not to say poorly, was surprised to find her as richly and magnificently attired as the princess, his daughter. This made him think Aladdin equally prudent and wise in whatever he undertook.

When it was night, the princess left her own apartment for Aladdin's palace, with his mother on her left hand carried in a superb litter, followed by a hundred women slaves, dressed with surprising magnificence. All the bands of music, which had played from the time Aladdin's mother arrived, being joined together, led the procession, followed by a hundred state ushers, and the like number of black eunuchs, in two files, with their officers at their head. Four hundred of the sultan's young pages carried flambeaux on each side, which, together with the illuminations of the sultan's and Aladdin's palaces, made it as light as day.

At length the princess arrived at the new palace and Aladdin ran with all imaginable joy to receive her at the grand entrance. His mother had taken care to point him out to the princess, in the midst of the officers who surrounded him, and she was charmed with his person. "Adorable princess," said Aladdin, accosting her, and saluting her respectfully, as soon as she had entered her apartment, "if I have the misfortune to have displeased you by my boldness in aspiring to the possession of so lovely a creature, I must tell you, that you ought to blame your bright eyes and charms, not me." "Prince," answered the princess, "I am obedient to the will of my father; and it is enough for me to have seen you, to tell you that I obey without reluctance."

Aladdin, charmed with so agreeable an answer, would not keep the princess standing; but took her by the hand, which he kissed with the greatest demonstration of joy, and led her into a large hall, illuminated with an infinite number of wax candles; where, by the care of the genie, a noble feast was served up. The dishes were of massy gold, and contained the most delicate viands, and all the other ornaments and embellishments of the hall were answerable to this display. The princess, dazzled to see so much riches, said to Aladdin: "I thought, prince, that nothing in the world was so beautiful as the sultan my father's palace, but the sight of this hall alone is sufficient to shew I was deceived."

Then Aladdin led the princess to the place appointed for her, and as soon as she and his mother were seated, a band of the most harmonious instruments, accompanied with the voices of beautiful ladies, began a concert, which lasted without intermission to the end of the repast. The princess was so charmed, that she declared she had never heard anything like it in the sultan her father's court; but she knew not that these musicians were fairies chosen by the genie, the slave of the lamp.

When the supper was ended, there entered a company of female dancers, who performed, according to the custom of the country, several figure dances, singing at the same time verses in praise of the bride and bridegroom. About midnight the happy pair retired to their apartments and the nuptial ceremonies were at an end.

The next morning, when Aladdin arose, his attendants presented themselves to dress him, and brought him another habit as magnificent as that worn the day before. He then ordered one of the horses appointed for his use to be got ready, mounted him, and went in the midst of a large troop of slaves to the sultan's palace. The sultan received him with the same honours as before, embraced him, placed him on the throne near him, and ordered a collation. Aladdin said: "I beg your majesty will dispense with my eating with you to-day; I came to entreat you to take a repast in the princess's palace, attended by your grand vizier, and all the lords of your court." The sultan consented with pleasure, rose up immediately, and, preceded by the principal officers of his palace, and followed by all the great lords of his court, accompanied Aladdin.

The nearer the sultan approached Aladdin's palace, the more he was struck with its beauty, but was much more amazed when he entered it; and could not forbear breaking out into exclamations of approbation. But when he came into the hall, and cast his eyes on the windows, enriched with diamonds, rubies, emeralds, all large perfect stones, he was so much surprised, that he remained some time motionless. After he recovered himself, he said to his vizier: "Is it possible that there should be such a stately palace so near my own, and I be an utter stranger to it till now?" "Sir," replied the grand vizier, "your majesty may remember that the day before yesterday you gave Aladdin, whom you accepted for a son-in-law, leave to build a palace opposite your own, and that very day at sunset there was no palace on this spot, but yesterday I had the honour first to tell you that the palace was built and finished." "I remember," replied the sultan, "but never imagined that the palace was one of the wonders of the world; for where in all the world besides shall we find walls built of massy gold and silver, instead of brick, stone, or marble; and diamonds, rubies, and emeralds composing the windows!"

The sultan would examine and admire the beauty of all the windows, and counting them, found that there were but three and twenty so richly adorned, and he was greatly astonished that the twenty-fourth was left imperfect. "Vizier," said he, for that minister made a point of never leaving him, "I am surprised that a hall of this magnificence should be left thus imperfect." "Sir," replied the grand vizier, "without doubt Aladdin only wanted time to finish this window like the rest; for it is not to be supposed but that he has sufficient jewels for the purpose, or that he will not complete it at the first opportunity."

Aladdin, who had left the sultan to go and give some orders, returned just as the vizier had finished his remark. "Son," said the sultan to him, "this hall is the most worthy of admiration of any in the world; there is only one thing that surprises me, which is, to find one of the windows unfinished. Is it from the forgetfulness or negligence of the workmen, or want of time, that they have not put the finishing stroke to so beautiful a piece of architecture?" "Sir," answered Aladdin, "it was for none of these reasons that your majesty sees it in this state. The omission was by design; it was by my orders that the workmen left it thus, since I wished that your majesty should have the glory of finishing this hall." "If you did it with this intention," replied the sultan, "I take it kindly, and will give orders about it immediately." He accordingly sent for the most considerable jewellers and goldsmiths in his capital.

Aladdin then conducted the sultan into the saloon where he had regaled his bride the preceding night. The princess entered immediately afterward, and received her father with an air that shewed how much she was satisfied with her marriage. Two tables were immediately spread with the most delicious meats, all served up in gold dishes. The sultan was much pleased with the cookery, and owned he had never eaten anything more excellent. He said the same of the wines, which were delicious; but what he most of all admired were four large buffets, profusely furnished with large flagons, basins, and cups, all of massy gold, set with jewels.

When the sultan rose from table, he was informed that the jewellers and goldsmiths attended; upon which he returned to the hall, and shewed them the window which was unfinished: "I sent for you," said he, "to fit up this window in as great perfection as the rest; examine well, and make all the despatch you can."

The jewellers and goldsmiths examined the three and twenty windows with great attention, and after they had consulted together they returned and presented themselves before the sultan, when the principal jeweller, undertaking to speak for the rest, said: "Sir, we are all willing to exert our utmost care and industry to obey your majesty; but among us all we cannot furnish jewels enough for so great a work." "I have more than are necessary," said the sultan; "come to my palace, and you shall choose what may answer your purpose."

When the sultan returned to his palace, he ordered his jewels to be brought out, and the jewellers took a great quantity, particularly those Aladdin had made him a present of, which they soon used, without making any great advance in their work. They came again several times for more, and in a month's time had not finished half their work. In short, they used all the jewels the sultan had, and borrowed of the vizier, but yet the work was not half done.

Aladdin, who knew that all the sultan's endeavours to make this window like the rest were in vain, sent for the jewellers and goldsmiths, and not only commanded them to desist from their work, but ordered them to undo what they had begun, and to carry all their jewels back to the sultan and to the vizier. They undid in a few hours what they had been six weeks about, and retired, leaving Aladdin alone in the hall. He took the lamp, which he carried about him, rubbed it, and presently the genie appeared. "Genie," said Aladdin, "I ordered thee to leave one of the four and twenty windows of this hall imperfect and thou hast executed my commands punctually; now I would have thee make it like the rest." The genie immediately disappeared. Aladdin went out of the hall, and returning soon after, found the window like the others.

In the meantime, the jewellers and goldsmiths repaired to the palace, and were introduced into the sultan's presence; where the chief jeweller, presenting the precious stones which he had brought back, said, in the name of all the rest: "Your majesty knows how long we have been upon the work you were pleased to set us about, in which we used all imaginable industry. It was far advanced, when Prince Aladdin commanded us not only to leave off, but to undo what we had already begun, and bring your majesty your jewels back." The sultan asked them if Aladdin had given them any reason for so doing, and they answering that he had given them none, he ordered a horse to be brought, which he mounted, and rode to his son-in-law's palace, with some few attendants on foot. When he came there, he alighted at the staircase, which led to the hall with the twenty-four windows, and went directly up to it, without giving previous notice to Aladdin; but it happened that at that very juncture Aladdin was opportunely there, and had just time to receive him at the door.

The sultan, without giving Aladdin time to complain obligingly of his not having given notice, that he might have acquitted himself with the more becoming respect, said to him: "Son, I come myself to know the reason why you commanded the jewellers to desist from work, and take to pieces what they had done."

Aladdin disguised the true reason, which was, that the sultan was not rich enough in jewels to be at so great an expense, but said: "I beg of you now to see if anything is wanting."

The sultan went directly to the window which was left imperfect, and when he found it like the rest, fancied that he was mistaken, examined the two windows on each side, and afterward all the four and twenty; but when he was convinced that the window which several workmen had been so long about was finished in so short a time, he embraced Aladdin, and kissed him between his eyes. "My son," said he, "what a man you are to do such surprising things always in the twinkling of an eye: there is not your fellow in the world; the more I know, the more I admire you."

Aladdin received these praises from the sultan with modesty, and replied in these words: "Sir, it is a great honour to me to deserve your majesty's good-will and approbation, and I assure you, I shall study to deserve them more."

The sultan returned to his palace, but would not let Aladdin attend him. When he came there, he found his grand vizier waiting, to whom he related the wonder he had witnessed with the utmost admiration, and in such terms as left the minister no room to doubt but that the fact was as the sultan related it;

though he was the more confirmed in his belief that Aladdin's palace was the effect of enchantment, as he had told the sultan the first moment he saw it. He was going to repeat the observation, but the sultan interrupted him, and said: "You told me so once before; I see, vizier, you have not forgotten your son's espousals to my daughter." The grand vizier plainly saw how much the sultan was prepossessed, therefore avoided disputes, and let him remain in his own opinion. The sultan as soon as he rose every morning went into the closet, to look at Aladdin's palace, and would go many times in a day to contemplate and admire it.

Aladdin did not confine himself in his palace; but took care to show himself once or twice a week in the town, by going sometimes to one mosque, and sometimes to another, to prayers; or to visit the grand vizier, who affected to pay his court to him on certain days; or to do the principal lords of the court the honour to return their visits after he had regaled them at his palace. Every time he went out, he caused two slaves, who walked by the side of his horse, to throw handfuls of money among the people as he passed through the streets and squares, which were generally on these occasions crowded. Besides, no one came to his palace gates to ask alms but returned satisfied with his liberality. In short, he so divided his time, that not a week passed but he went either once or twice a-hunting, sometimes in the environs of the city, sometimes farther off; at which time the villages through which he passed felt the effects of his generosity, which gained him the love and blessings of the people; and it was common for them to swear by his head. With all these good qualities he showed a zeal for the public good which could not be sufficiently applauded. He gave sufficient proofs of both in a revolt on the borders of the kingdom; for he no sooner understood that the sultan was levying an army to disperse the rebels than he begged the command of it, which he found not difficult to obtain. As soon as he was empowered, he marched with so much expedition, that the sultan heard of the defeat of the rebels before he had received an account of his son-in-law's arrival in the army.

Aladdin had conducted himself in this manner several years, when the African magician, who undesignedly had been the instrument of raising him to so high a pitch of prosperity, recalled him to his recollection in Africa, whither, after his expedition, he had returned. And though he was almost persuaded that Aladdin must have died miserably in the subterranean abode where he had left him, yet he had the curiosity to inform himself about his end with certainty; and as he was a great geomancer, he took out of a cupboard a square, covered box, which he used in his geomantic observations. After he had prepared and levelled the sand which was in it with an intention to discover whether or not Aladdin had died, he cast the points, drew the figures, and formed a horoscope, by which, when he came to examine it, he found that instead of dying in the cave, his victim had made his escape, lived splendidly, was in possession of the wonderful lamp, had married a princess, and was much honoured and respected.

The magician no sooner understood, by the rules of his diabolical art, that Aladdin had arrived to this height of good fortune, than his face became inflamed with anger, and he cried out in a rage: "This sorry tailor's son has discovered the secret and virtue of the lamp! I believed his death to be certain; but find that he enjoys the fruit of my labour and study! I will, however, prevent his enjoying it long, or perish in the attempt." He was not a great while deliberating on what he should do, but the next morning mounted a barb, set forward, and never stopped but to refresh himself and his horse, till he arrived at the capital of China. He alighted, took up his lodging in a khan, and stayed there the remainder of the day and the night.

The next day, his first object was to inquire what people said of Aladdin; and, taking a walk through the town, he went to the most public and frequented places, where persons of the best distinction met to drink a certain warm liquor, which he had drunk often during his former visit. As soon as he had seated himself, he was presented with a cup of it, which he took; but listening at the same time to the discourse of the company on each side of him, he heard them talking of Aladdin's palace. When he had drunk off his liquor, he joined them, and taking this opportunity, inquired particularly of what palace they spoke with so much commendation. "From whence come you?" said the person to whom he addressed himself; "you must certainly be a stranger not to have seen or heard talk of Prince Aladdin's palace. I do not say," continued the man, "that it is one of the wonders of the world, but that it is the only wonder of the world; since nothing so grand, rich, and magnificent was ever beheld. Go and see it, and then judge whether I have told you more than the truth." "Forgive my ignorance," replied the African magician; "I arrived here but yesterday from the farthest part of Africa, where the fame of this palace had not reached when I came away. The business which brought me hither was so urgent, that my sole object was to arrive as soon as I could, without stopping anywhere, or making any acquaintance. But I will not fail to go and see it, if you will do me the favour to show me the way thither."

The person to whom the African magician addressed himself took a pleasure in showing him the way to Aladdin's palace, and he got up and went thither instantly. When he came to the palace, and had examined it on all sides, he doubted not but that Aladdin had made use of the lamp to build it. Without attending to the inability of a poor tailor's son, he knew that none but the genies, the slaves of the lamp, could have performed such wonders; and piqued to the quick at Aladdin's happiness and splendour, he returned to the khan where he lodged.

The next point was to ascertain where the lamp was; whether Aladdin carried it about with him, or where he kept it; and this he was to discover by an operation of geomancy. As soon as he entered his lodging, he took his square box of sand, which he always carried with him when he travelled, and after he had performed some operations, he found that the lamp was in Aladdin's palace, and so great was his joy at the discovery that he could hardly contain himself. "Well," said he, "I shall have the lamp, and I defy Aladdin to prevent my carrying it off, thus making him sink to his original meanness, from which he has taken so high a flight."

It was Aladdin's misfortune at that time to be absent in the chase for eight days, and only three were expired, which the magician came to know. After he had performed the magical operation he went to the superintendent of the khan, entered into conversation with him on indifferent subjects, and among the rest, told him he had been to see Aladdin's palace; and after exaggerating on all that he had seen most worthy of observation, added: "But my curiosity leads me further, and I shall not be satisfied till I have seen the person to whom this wonderful edifice belongs." "That will be no difficult matter," replied the master of the khan; "there is not a day passes but he gives an opportunity when he is in town, but at present he has been gone these three days on a hunting-match, which will last eight."

ALADDIN

The magician wanted to know no more; he took his leave of the superintendent of the khan, and returning to his own chamber, said to himself: "This is an opportunity I ought by no means to neglect." To that end, he went to a coppersmith and asked for a dozen copper lamps: the master of the shop told him he had not so many by him, but if he would have patience till the next day, he would have them ready. The magician appointed his time, and desired him to take care that they should be handsome and well polished. After promising to pay him well, he returned to his inn.

The next day the magician called for the twelve lamps, paid the man his full price, put them into a basket which he bought on purpose, and with the basket hanging on his arm, went directly to Aladdin's palace; as he approached beginning to cry: "Who will change old lamps for new ones?" As he went along, a crowd of children collected, who hooted, and thought him, as did all who chanced to be passing by, a madman or a fool.

The African magician regarded not their scoffs, hootings, or all they could say to him, but still continued crying: "Who will change old lamps for new?" He repeated this so often, walking backward and forward in front of the palace, that the princess, who was then in the hall with the four and twenty windows, hearing a man cry something and not being able to distinguish his words, owing to the hooting of the children, and increasing mob about him, sent one of her women slaves to know what he cried.

The slave was not long before she returned, and ran into the hall, laughing so heartily that the princess could not forbear herself. "Well, giggler," said the princess, "will you tell me what you laugh at?" "Madam," answered the slave, laughing still, "who can forbear laughing, to see a fool with a basket on his arm, full of fine new lamps, ask to change them for old ones?"

Another female slave hearing this, said: "Now you speak of lamps, I know not whether the princess may have observed it, but there is an old one upon a shelf of the prince's robing-room. If the princess chooses, she may have the pleasure of trying if this fool is so silly as to give a new lamp for an old one, without taking anything for the exchange."

The lamp this slave spoke of was the wonderful lamp, which Aladdin had laid upon the shelf before he departed for the chase: this he had done several times before; but neither the princess, the slaves, nor the eunuchs had ever taken notice of it. At all other times except when hunting he carried it about his person.

The princess, who knew not the value of this lamp, and the interest that Aladdin, not to mention herself, had to keep it safe, entered into the pleasantry, and commanded a eunuch to take it and make the exchange. The eunuch obeyed, went out of the hall, and no sooner got to the palace gates than he saw the African magician, called to him, and showing him the old lamp, said: "Give me a new lamp for this?"

The magician never doubted but this was the lamp he wanted. There could be no other such in the palace, where every utensil was gold or silver. He snatched it eagerly out of the eunuch's hand, and thrusting it as far as he could into his breast, offered him his basket, and bade him choose which he liked best. The eunuch picked out one, and carried it to the princess; but the exchange was no sooner made than the place rang with the shouts of the children, deriding the magician's folly.

The African magician gave everybody leave to laugh as much as they pleased; he stayed not long near the palace, but made the best of his way, without crying any longer: "New lamps for old ones." His end was answered, and by his silence he got rid of the children and the mob.

As soon as he was out of the square between the two palaces, he hastened down the streets which were the least frequented; and having no more occasion for his lamps or basket, set all down in an alley where nobody saw him: then going down another street or two, he walked till he came to one of the city gates, and pursuing his way through the suburbs, which were very extensive, at length reached a lonely spot, where he stopped for a time to execute the design he had in contemplation, never caring for his horse which he had left at the khan; but thinking himself perfectly compensated by the treasure he had acquired.

In this place the African magician passed the remainder of the day, till the darkest time of night, when he pulled the lamp out of his breast and rubbed it. At that summons the genie appeared, and said: "What wouldst thou have? I am ready to obey thee as thy slave, and the slave of all those who have that lamp in their hands; both I and the other slaves of the lamp." "I command thee," replied the magician, "to transport me immediately and the palace which thou and the other slaves of the lamp have built in this city, with all the people in it, to Africa." The genie made no reply, but with the assistance of the other genies, the slaves of the lamp immediately transported him, and the palace entire, to the spot whither he was desired to convey it.

As soon as the sultan rose the next morning, according to custom, he went into his closet, to have the pleasure of contemplating and admiring Aladdin's palace; but when he first looked that way, and instead of a palace saw an empty space such as it was before the palace was built, he thought he was mistaken, and rubbed his eyes; but when he looked again, he still saw nothing more the second time than the first, though the weather was fine, the sky clear, and the dawn advancing had made all objects very distinct. He looked again in front, to the right and left, but beheld nothing more than he had formerly been used to see from his window. His amazement was so great, that he stood for some time turning his eyes to the spot where the palace had stood, but where it was no longer to be seen. He could not comprehend how so large a palace as Aladdin's, which he had seen plainly every day for some years, and but the day before, should vanish so soon, and not leave the least remains behind.

"Certainly," said he to himself, "I am not mistaken; it stood there: if it had fallen, the materials would have lain in heaps; and if it had been swallowed up by an earthquake, there would be some mark left." At last he retired to his apartment, not without looking behind him before he quitted the spot, ordered the grand vizier to be sent for with expedition, and in the meantime sat down, his mind agitated by so many different conjectures that he knew not what to resolve.

The grand vizier did not make the sultan wait long for him, but came with so much precipitation, that neither he nor his attendants, as they passed, missed Aladdin's palace; neither did the porters, when they opened the palace gates, observe any alteration.

When he came into the sultan's presence, he said to him: "The haste in which your majesty sent for me makes me believe something extraordinary has happened, since you know this is a day of public audience, and I should not have failed of attending at the usual time." "Indeed," said the sultan, "it is something very extraordinary, as you say, and you will allow it to be so: tell me what is become of Aladdin's palace?" "His palace!" replied the grand vizier in amazement; "I thought as I passed it stood in its usual place." "Go into my closet," said the sultan, "and tell me if you can see it."

The grand vizier went into the closet, where he was struck with no less amazement than the sultan had been. When he was well assured that there was not the least appearance of the palace, he returned to the sultan. "Well," said the sultan, "have you seen Aladdin's palace?" "No," answered the vizier, "but your majesty may remember, that I had the honour to tell you, that the edifice, which was the subject of your admiration, was only the work of magic and a magician; but your majesty would not pay the least attention to what I said." The sultan, who could not deny what the grand vizier had represented to him, flew into the greater passion: "Where is that impostor, that wicked wretch," said he, "that I may have his head taken off immediately?" "Sir," replied the grand vizier, "it is some days since he came to take his leave of your majesty, on pretence of hunting; he ought to be sent for, to know what is become of his palace, since he cannot be ignorant of what has been transacted." "To send for him would be too great an indulgence," replied the sultan: "command a detachment of horse to bring him to me loaded with chains." The grand vizier gave orders for a detachment, and instructed the officer who commanded the men how they were to act, that Aladdin might not escape. The detachment pursued its orders; and about five or six leagues from the town met him returning from the chase. The officer advanced respectfully, and informed him the sultan was so impatient to see him, that he had sent his party to accompany him home.

Aladdin had not the least suspicion of the true reason of their meeting him; but when he came within half a league of the city, the detachment surrounded him, when the officer addressed himself to him, and said: "Prince, it is with great regret that I declare to you the sultan's order to arrest you, and to carry you before him as a criminal: I beg of you not to take it ill that we acquit ourselves of our duty, and to forgive us." Aladdin, who felt himself innocent, was much surprised at this declaration, and asked the officer if he knew what crime he was accused of; who replied, he did not. Then Aladdin, finding that his retinue was much inferior to this detachment, alighted from his horse, and said to the officers: "Execute your orders; I am not conscious that I have committed any offence against the sultan's person or government." A heavy chain was immediately put about his neck, and fastened round his body, so that both his arms were pinioned down; the officer then put himself at the head of the detachment, and one of the troopers taking hold of the end of the chain and proceeding after the officer, led Aladdin, who was obliged to follow him on foot, into the city.

When this detachment entered the suburbs, the people, who saw Aladdin thus led as a state criminal, never doubted but that his head was to be cut off; and as he was generally beloved, some took sabres and other arms; and those who had none gathered stones, and followed the escort. Their numbers presently increased so much, that the soldiery began to think it would be well if they could get into the sultan's palace before Aladdin was rescued; to prevent which, according to the different extent of the streets, they took care to cover the ground by extending or closing. In this manner they with much difficulty arrived at the palace square, and there drew up in a line, till their officer and troopers with Aladdin had got within the gates, which were immediately shut.

Aladdin was carried before the sultan, who waited for him, attended by the grand vizier; and as soon as he saw him he ordered the executioner, who waited there for the purpose, to strike off his head without hearing him, or giving him leave to clear himself. As soon as the executioner had taken off the chain that was fastened about Aladdin's neck and body, he made the supposed criminal kneel down, and tied a bandage over his eyes. Then drawing his sabre, he took his aim by flourishing it three times in the air, waiting for the sultan's giving the signal to strike.

At that instant the grand vizier perceiving that the populace had crowded the great square before the palace, and were scaling the walls in several places, said to the sultan, before he gave the signal: "I beg of your majesty to consider what you are going to do, since you will hazard your palace being destroyed; and who knows what fatal consequence may follow?" "My palace forced!" replied the sultan; "who can have that audacity?" "Sir," answered the grand vizier, "if your majesty will but cast your eyes toward the great square, and on the palace walls, you will perceive the truth of what I say."

The sultan was so much alarmed when he saw so great a crowd, and how enraged they were, that he ordered the executioner to put his sabre immediately into the scabbard, to unbind Aladdin, and at the same time commanded the porters to declare to the people that the sultan had pardoned him, and that they might retire. Those who had already got upon the walls abandoned their design and got quickly down, overjoyed that they had saved the life of a man they dearly loved, and published the news amongst the rest, which was presently confirmed by the mace-bearers from the top of the terraces. The justice which the sultan had done to Aladdin soon disarmed the populace of their rage; the tumult abated and the mob dispersed.

When Aladdin found himself at liberty, he turned toward the balcony, and perceiving the sultan, raised his voice, and said to him in a moving manner: "I beg of your majesty to add one favour more to that which I have already received, which is, to let me know my crime?" "Your crime," answered the sultan; "perfidious wretch! Do you not know it? Come hither, and I will show it you." Aladdin went up, when the sultan, going before him without looking at him, said: "Follow me"; and then led him into his closet. When he came to the door, he said: "Go in; you ought to know whereabouts your palace stood: look round and tell me what is become of it?"

Aladdin looked, but saw nothing. He perceived the spot upon which his palace had stood; but not being able to divine how it had disappeared, was thrown into such great confusion and amazement that he could not return one word of answer. The sultan, growing impatient, demanded of him again: "Where is your palace, and what is become of my daughter?" Aladdin, breaking silence, replied: "Sir, I perceive and own that the palace which I have built is not in its place, but is vanished; neither can I tell your majesty where it may be, but can assure you I had no concern in its removal."

"I am not so much concerned about your palace," replied the sultan; "I value my daughter ten thousand times more, and would have you find her out, otherwise I will cause your head to be struck off, and no consideration shall divert me from my purpose."

"I beg of your majesty," answered Aladdin, "to grant me forty days to make my inquiries; and if in that time I have not the success I wish, I will offer my head at the foot of your throne, to be disposed of at your pleasure." "I give you the forty days you ask, "said the sultan; "but think not to escape my resentment if you fail; for I will find you out in whatsoever part of the world you may conceal yourself."

Aladdin went out of the sultan's presence with great humiliation, and in a condition worthy of pity. He crossed the courts

of the palace, hanging down his head, and in such great confusion
that he durst not lift up his eyes. The principal officers of the
court, who had all professed themselves his friends, instead of
going up to him to comfort him, turned their backs to avoid
seeing him. But had they accosted him with an offer of service,
they would have no more known Aladdin. He did not know
himself, and was no longer in his senses, as plainly appeared by
his asking everybody he met, and at every house, if they had seen
his palace, or could tell him any news of it. These questions
made the generality believe that Aladdin was mad. Some
laughed at him, but people of sense and humanity, particularly
those who had had any connection of business or friendship with
him, really pitied him. For three days he rambled about the
city in this manner, without coming to any resolution or eating
anything but what some compassionate people forced him to take
out of charity. At last he took the road to the country; and
after he had traversed several fields in wild uncertainty, at the
approach of night came to the bank of a river. There, possessed
by his despair, he said to himself: "Where shall I seek my palace?
In what province, country, or part of the world, shall I find that
and my dear princess? I shall never succeed; I would better free
myself at once from fruitless endeavours, and such bitter grief
as preys upon me." He was just going to throw himself into the
river, but, as a good Mussulman, true to his religion, he thought
he should not do it without first saying his prayers. Going to
prepare himself, he went to the river's brink, in order to perform
the usual ablutions. The place being steep and slippery, he slid
down, and had certainly fallen into the river, but for a little rock,
which projected about two feet out of the earth. Happily also
for him, he still had on the ring which the African magician had
put on his finger before he went down into the subterranean abode

to fetch the precious lamp. In slipping down the bank he rubbed the ring so hard by holding on the rock, that immediately the same genie appeared whom he had seen in the cave where the magician had left him. "What wouldst thou have?" said the genie. "I am ready to obey thee as thy slave, and the slave of all those that have that ring on their finger; both I and the other slaves of the ring."

Aladdin, agreeably surprised at an apparition he so little expected in his present calamity, replied: "Save my life, genie, a second time, either by showing me to the place where the palace I caused to be built now stands, or immediately transporting it back where it first stood." "What you command me," answered the genie, "is not wholly in my power; I am only the slave of the ring; you must address yourself to the slave of the lamp." "If that be the case," replied Aladdin, "I command thee, by the power of the ring, to transport me to the spot where my palace stands, in what part of the world soever it may be, and set me down under the window of the Princess Badroulboudour." These words were no sooner out of his mouth than the genie transported him into Africa, to the midst of a large plain, where his palace stood, and placing him exactly under the window of the princess's apartment, left him. All this was done almost in an instant. Aladdin, notwithstanding the darkness of the night, knew his palace again; but as the night was far advanced and all was quiet, he retired to some distance, and sat down at the foot of a large tree. There, full of hopes, and reflecting on his happiness, for which he was indebted to chance, he found himself in a much more comfortable situation than when he was arrested and carried before the sultan, being now delivered from the immediate danger of losing his life. He amused himself for some time with these agreeable thoughts; but not having slept for two days, was unable to resist the drowsiness which came upon him, but fell fast asleep.

The next morning, as soon as day appeared, Aladdin was agreeably awakened by the singing not only of the birds which had roosted in the tree under which he had passed the night, but also of those which frequented the thick groves of the palace garden. When he cast his eyes on that wonderful edifice, he felt inexpressible joy at thinking he might soon be master of it again, and once more greet his dear Princess Badroulboudour. Pleased with these hopes, he immediately arose, went toward the princess's apartment, and walked some time under her window in expectation of her rising, that he might see her. During this expectation, he began to consider with himself whence the cause of his misfortune had proceeded; and after mature reflection, no longer doubted that it was owing to having trusted the lamp out of his sight. He accused himself of negligence in letting it be a moment away from him. But what puzzled him most was, that he could not imagine who had been so envious of his happiness. He would soon have guessed this, if he had known that both he and his palace were now in Africa, the very name of which would soon have made him remember the magician, his declared enemy; but the genie, the slave of the ring, had not made mention of the name of the country, nor had Aladdin inquired.

The princess rose earlier that morning than she had done since her transportation into Africa by the magician, whose presence she was forced to support once a day, because he was master of the palace; though she had always treated him so harshly that he dared not reside in it. As she was dressing, one of the women looking through the window perceived Aladdin, and instantly told her mistress. The princess, who could not believe the joyful tidings, hastened herself to the window, and seeing Aladdin, immediately opened it. The noise of opening the window made Aladdin turn his head that way, and perceiving the princess he saluted her with joy. "To lose no time," said she to him, "I have sent to have the private door opened for you; enter, and come up." The private door, which was just under the princess's apartment, was soon opened, and Aladdin conducted up into the chamber. It is impossible to express the joy of both at seeing each other, after so cruel a separation. After embracing and shedding tears of joy, they sat down, and Aladdin said: "I beg of you, princess, in Heaven's name, before we talk of anything else, to tell me, both for your own sake, the sultan your father's, and mine, what is become of an old lamp which I left upon a shelf in my robing-chamber, when I departed for the chase."

"Alas! dear husband," answered the princess, "I was afraid our misfortune might be owing to that lamp: and what grieves me most is, that I have been the cause of it." "Princess," replied Aladdin, "do not blame yourself, for I ought to have taken more care of it. But let us now think only of repairing the loss; tell me what has happened, and into whose hands it has fallen." The princess then related how she had changed the old lamp for a new one, and how the next morning she found herself in the unknown country they were then in, which she was told was Africa, by the traitor who had transported her thither by his magic art.

"Princess," said Aladdin, interrupting her, "you have informed me who the traitor is, by telling me we are in Africa. He is the most perfidious of men; but this is neither a time nor place to give you a full account of his villainies. I desire you only to tell me what he has done with the lamp, and where he has put it." "He carries it carefully wrapt up in his bosom," said the princess; "and this I can assure you, because he pulled it out before me, and showed it to me in triumph."

"Princess," said Aladdin, "do not be displeased that I trouble you with so many questions, since they are equally important to us both. But to come to what most particularly concerns me: tell me, I conjure you, how so wicked and perfidious a man treats you?" "Since I have been here," replied the princess, "he repairs once every day to see me; and I am persuaded the little satisfaction he receives from his visits makes him come no oftener. All his addresses tend to persuade me to break that faith I have pledged to you, and to take him for my husband; giving me to understand I need not entertain hopes of ever seeing you again, for that you were dead, having had your head struck off by my father's order. He added, to justify himself, that you were an ungrateful wretch; that your good fortune was owing to him, and a great many other things of that nature which I forbear to repeat: but as he received no other answer from me but grievous complaints and tears, he was always forced to retire with as little satisfaction as he came. I doubt not his intention is to allow me time to overcome my grief, in hopes that afterward I may change my sentiments. But my dear husband's presence removes all my apprehensions."

"I am confident my attempts to punish the magician will not be in vain," replied Aladdin, "since my princess's fears are removed, and I think I have found the means to deliver you from both your enemy and mine; to execute this design, it is necessary for me to go to the town. I shall return by noon, will then communicate my design, and what must be done by you to ensure success. But that you may not be surprised, I think it proper to acquaint you that I shall change my apparel, and beg of you to give orders that I may not wait long at the private door, but that it may be opened at the first knock."

When Aladdin was out of the palace, he looked round him on all sides, and perceiving a peasant going into the country, hastened after him; and when he had overtaken him, made a proposal to him to change habits, which the man agreed to. When they had made the exchange, the countryman went about his business, and Aladdin to the city. After traversing several streets, he came to that part of the town where all descriptions of merchants had their particular streets, according to their trades. He went into that of the druggists; and going into one of the largest and best-furnished shops, asked the druggist if he had a certain powder which he named. The druggist, judging Aladdin by his habit to be very poor, and that he had not money enough to pay for it, told him he had it, but that it was very dear; upon which Aladdin penetrating his thoughts, pulled out his purse, and showing him some gold, asked for half a drachm of the powder; which the druggist weighed, wrapped up in paper, and gave him, telling him the price was a piece of gold. Aladdin put the money into his hand, and returned to the palace, where he waited not long at the private door. When he came into the princess's apartment, he said to her: "Princess, perhaps the aversion you tell me you have for your captor may be an objection to your executing what I am going to propose; but permit me to say it is proper that you should dissemble a little, and do violence to your inclinations, if you would deliver yourself from him.

"If you will take my advice," continued he, "dress yourself this moment in one of your richest habits, and when the African magician comes, make no difficulty to give him the best reception; so that he may imagine time has removed your disgust at his addresses. In your conversation let him understand that you strive to forget me; and that he may be the more fully convinced, invite him to sup with you, and tell him you should be glad to taste of some of the best wines of his country. He will presently go to fetch you some. During his absence, put into one of the cups which you are accustomed to drink of, this powder, and setting it by, charge the slave you may order that night to attend you, on a signal you shall agree upon, to bring that cup to you. When the magician and you have eaten and drunk as much as you choose, let her bring you the cup, and then change cups with him. He will esteem it so great a favour that he will not refuse, but eagerly quaff it off; but no sooner will he have drunk, than you will see him fall backward."

When Aladdin had finished, "I own," answered the princess, "I shall do myself violence in consenting to make the magician such advances; but what cannot one resolve to do against a cruel enemy? I will therefore follow your advice, since both my repose and yours depend upon it." After the princess had agreed to the measures proposed by Aladdin, he took his leave and went and spent the rest of the day in the neighbourhood of the palace till it was night, and he might safely return to the private door.

The princess, who had remained inconsolable at being parted from her husband, had, ever since their cruel separation, lived in great neglect of her person. She had almost forgotten the neatness so becoming persons of her sex and quality, particularly after the first time the magician paid her a visit and she had understood by some of the women, who knew him again, that it was he who had taken the old lamp in exchange for a new one. However, the opportunity of taking the revenge he deserved made her resolve to gratify Aladdin. As soon, therefore, as he was gone, she sat down to dress, and was attired by her women to the best advantage in the richest habit of her wardrobe. Her girdle was of the finest and largest diamonds set in gold, her necklace of pearls, six on a side, so well proportioned to that in the middle, which was the largest ever seen, that the greatest sultanesses would have been proud to have been adorned with only two of the smallest. Her bracelets, which were of diamonds and rubies intermixed, corresponded admirably to the richness of the girdle and necklace.

When the Princess Badroulboudour was completely dressed, she consulted her glass and women upon her adjustment; and when she found she wanted no charms to flatter the foolish passion of the African magician, she sat down on a sofa expecting his arrival. The magician came at the usual hour, and as soon as he entered the great hall where the princess waited to receive him, she rose with an enchanting grace and smile, and pointed with her hand to the most honourable place, waiting till he sat down, that she might sit at the same time, which was a civility she had never shown him before.

The African magician, dazzled more with the lustre of the princess's eyes than the glittering of her jewels, was much surprised. The smiling air with which she received him, so opposite to her former behaviour, quite fascinated his heart. When he was seated, the princess, to free him from his embarrassment, broke silence first, looking at him all the time in such a manner as to make him believe that he was not so odious to her as she had given him to understand hitherto, and said: "You are doubtless amazed to find me so much altered to-day; but your surprise will not be so great when I acquaint you, that I am naturally of a disposition so opposite to melancholy and grief, that I always strive to put them as far away as possible when I find the subject of them is past. I have reflected on what you told me of Aladdin's fate, and know my father's temper so well that I am persuaded, with you, he could not escape the terrible effects of the sultan's rage: therefore, should I continue to lament him all my life, my tears cannot recall him. For this reason, since I have paid all the duties decency requires of me to his memory, now he is in the grave I think I ought to endeavour to comfort myself. These are the motives of the change you see in me; I am resolved to banish melancholy entirely; and persuaded that you will bear me company to-night, I have ordered a supper to be prepared; but as I have no wines but those of China, I have a great desire to taste of the produce of Africa, and doubt not your procuring some of the best."

The African magician, who had looked upon the happiness of getting so soon and so easily into the Princess Badroulboudour's good graces as impossible, could not think of words expressive enough to testify how sensible he was of her favours: but to put an end the sooner to a conversation which would have embarrassed him, if he had engaged farther in it, he turned it upon the wines of Africa, and said: "Of all the advantages Africa can boast, that of producing the most excellent wines is one of the principal. I have a vessel of seven years old, which has never been broached; and it is indeed not praising it too much to say it is the finest wine in the world. If my princess," added he, "will give me leave, I will go and fetch two bottles, and return again immediately." "I should be sorry to give you that trouble," replied the princess; "you had better send for them." "It is necessary I should go myself," answered the African magician, "for nobody but myself knows where the key of the cellar is laid, or has the secret to unlock the door." "If it be so," said the princess, "make haste back; for the longer you stay the greater will be my impatience, and we shall sit down to supper as soon as you return." The

African magician, full of hopes of his expected happiness, rather flew than ran, and returned quickly with the wine. The princess, not doubting but he would make haste, put with her own hand the powder Aladdin had given her into the cup set apart for that purpose. They sat down at the table opposite to each other, the magician's back toward the buffet. The princess presented him with the best at the table, and said to him: "If you please, I will entertain you with a concert of vocal and instrumental music; but as we are only two, I think conversation may be more agreeable." This the magician took as a new favour. After they had eaten some time, the princess called for some wine, drank the magician's health, and afterward said to him: "Indeed you had a full right to commend your wine, since I never tasted any so delicious." "Charming princess," said he, holding in his hand the cup which had been presented to him, "my wine becomes more exquisite by your approbation." "Then drink my health," replied the princess: "you will find I understand wines." He drank the princess's health, and returning the cup said; "I think myself fortunate, princess, that I reserved this wine for so happy an occasion; and own I never before drank any in every respect so excellent." When they had each drunk two or three cups more, the princess, who had completely charmed the African magician by her obliging behaviour, gave the signal to the slave who served them with wine, bidding her bring the cup which had been filled for herself, and at the same time bring the magician a full goblet. When they both had their cups in their hands, she said to him: "I know not how you express your loves in these parts when drinking together." With us in China lovers reciprocally exchange cups, and drink each other's health": at the same time she presented to him the cup which was in her hand, and held out her hand to receive his. He hastened to make the exchange with the more pleasure, because he looked upon this favour as a token of conquest over the princess, which raised his rapture to the highest pitch. Before he drank, he said to her, with the cup in his hand: "Indeed, princess, we Africans are not so refined in the art of love as you Chinese: and your instructing me in a lesson I was ignorant of, informs me how sensible I ought to be of the favour done me. I shall never, lovely princess, forget my recovering, by drinking out of your cup, that life, which your cruelty, had it continued, must have made me despair of."

The princess, who began to be tired with his declarations, interrupted him and said: "Let us drink first, and then say what you will afterward"; at the same time she set the cup to her lips, while the African magician, who was eager to get his wine off first, drank up the very last drop. In finishing it, he leaned his head back to show his eagerness, and remained some time in that state. The princess kept the cup at her lips till she saw his eyes turn in his head, when he fell backward lifeless on the sofa. The princess had no occasion to order the private door to be opened to Aladdin; for her women were so disposed from the great hall to the foot of the staircase, that the word was no sooner given that the magician was fallen, than the door was immediately opened. As soon as Aladdin entered the hall, he saw the magician stretched backward on the sofa. The princess rose from her seat, and ran overjoyed to embrace him; but he stopped her and said: "Princess, it is not yet time; let me be left alone a moment, while I endeavour to transport you back to China as speedily as you were brought from thence." When the princess, her women and eunuchs, were gone out of the hall, Aladdin shut the door, and, going directly to the dead body of the magician, opened his vest, took out the lamp which was carefully wrapped up, as the princess had told him, and unfolding and rubbing it, the genie immediately appeared. "Genie," said Aladdin, "I have called to command thee, on the part of thy good mistress, this lamp, to transport this palace instantly into China, to the place from whence it was brought hither." The genie bowed his head in token of obedience, and disappeared. Immediately the palace was transported into China, and its removal was only felt by two little shocks, the one when it was lifted up, the other when it was set down, and both in a very short interval of time.

From the time of the transportation of Aladdin's palace, the princess's father had been inconsolable for the loss of her. Before the disaster he used to go every morning into his closet to please himself with viewing the palace; he went now many times in the day to renew his tears, and plunge himself into the deepest melancholy, by reflecting how he had lost what was most dear to him in this world.

The very morning of the return to the palace, the sultan went into his closet to indulge his sorrows. Absorbed in himself, and in a pensive mood, he cast his eyes toward the spot, expecting only to see an open space; but perceiving the vacancy filled up, he at first imagined the appearance to be the effect of a fog; looking more attentively, he was convinced beyond the power of doubt that it was his son-in-law's palace. Joy and gladness succeeded to sorrow and grief. He returned immediately into his apartment, and ordered a horse to be saddled and brought to him without delay, which he mounted that instant, thinking he could not make haste enough to the palace.

Aladdin, who foresaw what would happen, rose that morning by daybreak, put on one of the most magnificent habits his wardrobe afforded, and went up into the hall of twenty-four windows,

ALADDIN

from whence he perceived the sultan approaching, and got down soon enough to receive him at the foot of the great staircase. "Aladdin," said the sultan, "I cannot speak to you till I have seen and embraced my daughter." The happy father was then led to the princess's apartment and embraced her with his face bathed in tears of joy. The sultan was some time before he could open his lips, so great was his surprise and joy to find his daughter again, after he had given her up for lost; and the princess, upon seeing her father, let fall tears of rapture and affection.

At last the sultan broke silence, and said: "I would believe, daughter, your joy to see me makes you seem as little changed as if no misfortune had befallen you; yet I cannot be persuaded but that you have suffered much alarm; for a large palace cannot be so suddenly transported as yours has been, without causing great fright and apprehension. I would have you tell me all that has happened, and conceal nothing from me."

The princess, who took great pleasure in giving the sultan the satisfaction he demanded, said: "If I appear so little altered, I beg of your majesty to consider that I received new life yesterday morning by the presence of my dear husband and deliverer, Aladdin, whom I looked upon and bewailed as lost to me. My greatest suffering was to find myself forced not only from your majesty, but from my dear husband; not only from the love I bore him, but from the uneasiness I laboured under through fear that he, though innocent, might feel the effects of your anger. As to what relates to my transportation, I was myself the innocent cause of it." To persuade the sultan of the truth of what she said, she gave him a full account of how the African magician had disguised himself, and offered to change new lamps for old ones; how she had amused herself in making that exchange; how the palace and herself were carried away and transported into Africa, with the magician, who was recognised by two of her women and the eunuch who made the exchange of the lamp, when he had the audacity, after the success of his daring enterprise, to propose himself for her husband; how he persecuted her till Aladdin's arrival; how they had concerted measures to get the lamp from him again, and the success they had fortunately met with by her dissimulation in inviting him to supper, and giving him the cup with the powder prepared for him. "For the rest," added she, "I leave it to Aladdin to recount."

Aladdin had not much to tell the sultan, but only said: "When the private door was opened I went up into the great hall, where I found the magician lying dead on the sofa; and as I thought it not proper for the princess to stay there any longer, I desired her to go down into her own apartment, with her women and eunuchs. As soon as I was alone, and had taken the lamp out of the magician's breast, I made use of the same secret he had done, to remove the palace, and carry off the princess; and by that means the palace was reconveyed to the place where it stood before; and I have the happiness to restore the princess to your majesty. But that your majesty may not think that I impose upon you, if you will give yourself the trouble to go up into the hall, you may see the magician punished as he deserved."

The sultan rose instantly and went into the hall, where, when he saw the African magician dead, and his face already livid by the strength of the poison, he embraced Aladdin with great tenderness, and said: "My son, be not displeased at my proceedings against you; they arose from my paternal love; and therefore you ought to forgive the excesses to which it hurried me." "Sir," replied Aladdin, "I have not the least reason to complain of your majesty's conduct, since you did nothing but what your duty required. This infamous magician, the basest of men, was the sole cause of my misfortune. When your majesty has leisure, I will give you an account of another villainous action he was guilty of toward me, which was no less black and base than this." "I will take an opportunity, and that very shortly," replied the sultan, "to hear it; but in the meantime let us think only of rejoicing."

The sultan then commanded the drums, trumpets, cymbals, and other instruments of music to announce his joy to the public, and a festival of ten days to be proclaimed for the return of the princess and Aladdin.

Within a few years afterward, the sultan died in a good old age, and as he left no male children, the Princess Badroulboudour, as lawful heir of the throne, succeeded him, and communicating the power to Aladdin, they reigned together many years, and left a numerous and illustrious progeny.

THE STORY OF PRINCE AGIB

I WAS a king, and the son of a king; and when my father died, I succeeded to his throne, and governed my subjects with justice and beneficence. I took pleasure in sea-voyages; and my capital was on the shore of an extensive sea, interspersed with fortified and garrisoned islands, which I desired, for my amusement, to visit; I therefore embarked with a fleet of ten ships, and took with me provisions sufficient for a whole month. I proceeded twenty days, after which there arose against us a contrary wind; but at daybreak it ceased, and the sea became calm, and we arrived at an island, where we landed, and cooked some provisions and ate; after which we remained there two days. We then continued our voyage; and when twenty days more had passed, we found ourselves in strange waters, unknown to the captain, and desired the watch to look out from the mast head: so he went aloft, and when he had come down he said to the captain: "I saw, on my right hand, fish floating upon the surface of the water; and looking toward the midst of the sea, I perceived something looming in the distance, sometimes black, and sometimes white."

When the captain heard this report of the watch, he threw his turban on the deck, and plucked his beard, and said to those who were with him: "Receive warning of our destruction, which will befall all of us: not one will escape!" So saying, he began to weep; and all of us in like manner bewailed our lot. I desired him to inform us of that which the watch had seen. "O my lord," he replied, "know that we have wandered from our course

[190]

since the commencement of the contrary wind that was followed in the morning by a calm, in consequence of which we remained stationary two days: from that period we have deviated from our course for twenty-one days, and we have no wind to carry us back from the fate which awaits us after this day. To-morrow we shall arrive at a mountain of black stone, called loadstone: the current is now bearing us violently toward it, and the ships will fall in pieces, and every nail in them will fly to the mountain, and adhere to it; for God hath given to the loadstone a secret property by virtue of which everything of iron is attracted toward it. On that mountain is such a quantity of iron as no one knoweth but God, whose name be exalted; for from times of old great numbers of ships have been destroyed by the influence of that mountain. There is, upon the summit of the mountain, a cupola of brass supported by ten columns, and upon the top of this is a horseman upon a horse of brass, having in his hand a brazen spear, and upon his breast suspended a tablet of lead, upon which are engraved mysterious names and talismans: and as long, O King, as this horseman remains upon the horse, so long will every ship that approaches be destroyed, with every person on board, and all the iron contained in it will cleave to the mountain: no one will be safe until the horseman shall have fallen from the horse." The captain then wept bitterly; and we felt assured that our destruction was inevitable, and every one of us bade adieu to his friend.

On the following morning we drew near to the mountain; the current carried us toward it with violence, and when the ships were almost close to it, they fell asunder, and all the nails, and everything else that was of iron, flew from them toward the loadstone. It was near the close of day when the ships fell in pieces. Some of us were drowned, and some escaped; but the greater number were drowned, and of those who saved their lives none know what became of the others, so stupefied were they by the waves and the boisterous wind. As for myself, God, whose name be exalted, spared me on account of the trouble and torment and affliction that He had predestined to befall me. I placed myself upon a plank, and the wind and waves cast it upon the mountain; and when I had landed, I found a practicable way to the summit, resembling steps cut in the rock: so I exclaimed: "In the name of God!" and offered up a prayer, and attempted the ascent, holding fast by the notches; and presently God stilled the wind, so that I arrived in safety at the summit. Rejoicing greatly in my escape, I immediately entered the cupola, and performed prayers in gratitude to God for my preservation; after which I slept beneath the cupola, and heard a voice saying to me: "O son of Khasib, when thou awakest, dig beneath thy feet, and thou wilt find a bow of brass, and three arrows of lead, whereon are engraved talismans: then take the bow and arrows and shoot at the horseman that is upon the top of the cupola, and relieve mankind from this great affliction; for when thou hast shot at the horseman he will fall into the sea; the bow will also fall, and do thou bury it in its place; and as soon as thou hast done this, the sea will swell and rise until it attains the summit of the mountain; and there will appear upon it a boat bearing a man, different from him whom thou shalt have cast down, and he will come to thee, having an oar in his hand: then do thou embark with him; but utter not the name of God; and he will convey thee in ten days to a safe sea, where, on thy arrival, thou wilt find one who will take thee to thy city. All this shall be done if thou utter not the name of God."

Awaking from my sleep, I sprang up, and did as the voice had directed. I shot at the horseman, and he fell into the sea;

and the bow having fallen from my hand, I buried it: the sea then became troubled, and rose to the summit of the mountain, and when I had stood waiting there a little while, I beheld a boat in the midst of the sea, approaching me. I praised God, whose name be exalted, and when the boat came to me, I found in it a man of brass, with a tablet of lead upon his breast, engraven with names and talismans. Without uttering a word, I embarked in the boat, and the man rowed me ten successive days, after which I beheld the islands of security, whereupon, in the excess of my joy, I exclaimed: "There is no deity but God! God is most great!"—and as soon as I had done this, the man cast me out of the boat, and sank in the sea.

Being able to swim, I swam until night, when my arms and shoulders were tired, and, in this perilous situation, I repeated the profession of the faith, and gave myself up as lost; but the sea rose with the violence of the wind, and a wave like a vast castle threw me upon the land, in order to the accomplishment of the purpose of God. I ascended the shore, and after I had wrung out my clothes, and spread them upon the ground to dry, I slept; and in the morning I put on my clothes again, and, looking about to see which way I should go, I found a tract covered with trees; and when I had walked round it, I found that I was upon a small island in the midst of the sea; upon which I said within myself: "Every time that I escape from one calamity I fall into another that is worse:" but while I was reflecting upon my unfortunate case, and wishing for death, I beheld a vessel bearing a number of men. I arose immediately, and climbed into a tree; and lo, the vessel came to the shore, and there landed from it ten black slaves bearing axes. They proceeded to the middle of the island, and, digging up the earth, uncovered and lifted up a trap-door, after which they returned to the vessel, and brought from it bread and flour, and clarified butter and honey, and sheep and everything that the wants of an inhabitant would require, continuing to pass backward and forward between the vessel and the trap-door, bringing loads from the former, and entering the latter, until they had removed all the stores from the ship. They then came out of the vessel with various clothes of the most beautiful description, and in the midst of them was an old sheikh, enfeebled and wasted by extreme age, leading by the hand a young man cast in the mould of graceful symmetry, and invested with such perfect beauty as deserved to be a subject for proverbs. He was like a fresh and slender twig, enchanting and captivating every heart by his elegant form. The party proceeded to the trap-door, and, entering it, became concealed from my eyes.

They remained beneath about two hours, or more; after which, the sheikh and the slaves came out; but the youth came not with them; and they replaced the earth, and embarked and set sail. Soon after, I descended from the tree, and went to the excavation. I removed the earth, and, entering the aperture, saw a flight of wooden steps, which I descended; and, at the bottom, I beheld a handsome dwelling-place, furnished with a variety of silken carpets; and there was the youth, sitting upon a high mattress, with sweet-smelling flowers and fruits placed before him. On seeing me, his countenance became pale; but I saluted him, and said: "Let thy mind be composed, O my master: thou hast nothing to fear; for I am a man, and the son of a king, like thyself: fate hath impelled me to thee, that I may cheer thee in thy solitude." The youth, when he heard me thus address him, and was convinced that I was one of his own species, rejoiced exceedingly at my arrival, his colour returned, and, desiring me to approach him, he said: "O my brother, my story is wonderful: my father is a jeweller: he had slaves who made voyages by his orders, for the purposes of commerce, and he had dealings with kings; but he had never been blest with a son; and he dreamt that he was soon to have a son, but one whose life would be short; and he awoke sorrowful. Shortly after, in accordance with the decrees of God, my mother gave birth to me; and my father was greatly rejoiced: the astrologers, however, came to him, and said: "Thy son will live fifteen years: his fate is intimated by the fact that there is in the sea a mountain called the Mountain of Loadstone, whereon is a horseman on a horse of brass, on the former of which is a tablet of lead suspended to his neck; and when the horseman shall be thrown down from his horse, thy son will be slain: the person who is to slay him is he who will throw down the horseman, and his name is King Agib, the son of King Khasib. My father was greatly afflicted at this announcement; and when he had reared me until I had nearly attained the age of fifteen years, the astrologers came again, and informed him that the horseman had fallen into the sea, and that it had been thrown down by King Agib, the son of King Khasib; on hearing which, he prepared for me this dwelling, and here left me to remain until the completion of the term, of which there now remain ten days. All this he did from fear lest King Agib should kill me."

When I heard this, I was filled with wonder, and said within myself: "I am King Agib, the son of King Khasib, and it was I who threw down the horseman; but, by Allah, I will neither kill him nor do him any injury." Then said I to the youth: "Far from thee be both destruction and harm, if it be the will of God: thou hast nothing to fear: I will remain with thee to serve thee, and will go forth with thee to thy father, and beg of him to send me back to my country, for the which he will obtain a reward." The youth rejoiced at my words, and I sat and conversed with him until night, when I spread his bed for him, and covered him, and slept near to his side. And in the morning I brought him water, and he washed his face, and said to me: "May God requite thee for me with every blessing. If I escape from King Agib, I will make my father reward thee with abundant favours." "Never," I replied, "may the day arrive that would bring thee misfortune!" I then placed before him some refreshments, and after we had eaten together, we passed the day conversing with the utmost cheerfulness.

I continued to serve him for nine days; and on the tenth day the youth rejoiced at finding himself in safety, and said to me: "O my brother, I wish that thou wouldst in thy kindness warm for me some water, that I may wash myself and change my clothes; for I have smelt the odour of escape from death, in consequence of thy assistance." "With pleasure," I replied; and I arose, and warmed the water; after which, he entered a place concealed from my view, and, having washed himself and changed his clothes, laid himself upon the mattress to rest after his bath. He then said to me: "Cut up for me, O my brother, a water-melon, and mix its juice with some sugar: so I arose, and, taking a melon, brought it upon a plate, and said to him: "Knowest thou, O my master, where is the knife?" "See, here it is," he answered, "upon the shelf over my head." I sprang up hastily, and took it from its sheath, and as I was drawing back, my foot slipped, as God had decreed, and I fell upon the youth, grasping in my hand the knife, which entered his body, and he died instantly. When I perceived that he was dead, and that I had killed him, I uttered a loud shriek, and beat my face, and rent my clothes: saying: "This is, indeed, a calamity! O my Lord, I implore thy pardon, and declare to Thee my innocence of his death! Would that I had died before him!"

And when the boat came to me I found in it a man of brass,
with a tablet of lead upon his breast, engraven with names and talismans.

With these reflections I ascended the steps, and, having replaced the trap-door, returned to my first station, and looked over the sea, where I saw the vessel that had come before, approaching, and cleaving the waves in its rapid course. Upon this I said within myself: "Now will the men come forth from the vessel, and find the youth slain, and they will slay me also:" so I climbed into a tree, and concealed myself among its leaves, and sat there till the vessel arrived and cast anchor, when the slaves landed with the old sheikh, the father of the youth, and went to the place, and removed the earth. They were surprised at finding it moist, and, when they had descended the steps, they discovered the youth lying on his back, exhibiting a face beaming with beauty, though dead, and clad in white and clean clothing, with the knife remaining in his body. They all wept at the sight, and the father fell down in a swoon, which lasted so long that the slaves thought he was dead. At length, however, he recovered, and came out with the slaves, who had wrapped the body of the youth in his clothes. They then took back all that was in the subterranean dwelling to the vessel, and departed.

I remained, by day hiding myself in a tree, and at night walking about the open part of the island. Thus I continued for the space of two months; and I perceived that, on the western side of the island, the water of the sea every day retired, until, after three months, the land that had been beneath it became dry. Rejoicing at this, and feeling confident now in my escape, I traversed this dry tract, and arrived at an expanse of sand; whereupon I emboldened myself, and crossed it. I then saw in the distance an appearance of fire, and, advancing toward it, found it to be a palace, overlaid with plates of red copper. which, reflecting the rays of the sun, seemed from a distance to be fire: and when I drew near to it, reflecting upon this sight, there approached me an old sheikh, accompanied by ten young men who were all blind of one eye, at which I was extremely surprised. As soon as they saw me, they saluted me, and asked me my story, which I related to them from first to last; and they were filled with wonder. They then conducted me into the palace, where I saw ten benches, upon each of which was a mattress covered with a blue stuff; and each of the young men seated himself upon one of these benches, while the sheikh took his place upon a smaller one; after which they said to me: "Sit down, O young man, and ask no question respecting our condition, nor respecting our being blind of one eye." Then the sheikh arose, and brought to each of them some food, and the same to me also; and next he brought to each of us some wine: and after we had eaten, we sat drinking together until the time for sleep, when the young men said to the sheikh: "Bring to us our accustomed supply"—upon which the sheikh arose, and entered a closet, from which he brought, upon his head, ten covered trays. Placing these upon the floor, he lighted ten candles, and stuck one of them upon each tray; and, having done this, he removed the covers, and there appeared beneath them ashes mixed with pounded charcoal. The young men then tucked up their sleeves above the elbow, and blackened their faces, and slapped their cheeks, exclaiming: "We were reposing at our ease, and our impertinent curiosity suffered us not to remain so!" Thus they did until the morning, when the sheikh brought them some hot water, and they washed their faces, and put on other clothes.

On witnessing this conduct, my reason was confounded, my heart was so troubled that I forgot my own misfortunes, and I asked them the cause of their strange behaviour; upon which they looked toward me, and said: "O young man, ask not respecting that which doth not concern thee; but be silent; for

in silence is security from error." I remained with them a whole
month, during which, every night they did the same, and at
length I said to them: "I conjure you by Allah to remove this
disquiet from my mind, and to inform me of the cause of your
acting in this manner, and of your exclaiming: 'We were reposing
at our ease, and our impertinent curiosity suffered us not to
remain so!' if ye inform me not, I will leave you, and go my
way." On hearing these words, they replied: "We have not
concealed this affair from thee but in our concern for thy welfare,
lest thou shouldst become like us, and the same affliction that
hath befallen us happen also to thee." I said, however: "Ye
must positively inform me of this matter." "We give thee good
advice," said they, "and do thou receive it, and ask us not
respecting our case; otherwise thou wilt become blind of one
eye, like us"—but I still persisted in my request; whereupon
they said: "O young man, if this befall thee, know that thou wilt
be banished from our company." They then all arose, and, taking a ram, slaughtered and skinned it, and said to me: "Take
this knife with thee, and introduce thyself into the skin of the
ram, and we will sew thee up in it, and go away; whereupon a
bird called the roc will come to thee, and, taking thee up by its
talons, will fly away with thee, and set thee down upon a mountain: then cut open the skin with this knife, and get out, and the
bird will fly away. Thou must arise, as soon as it hath gone,
and journey for half a day, and thou wilt see before thee a lofty
palace, encased with red gold, set with various precious stones
such as emeralds and rubies; and if thou enter it thy case will
be as ours; for our entrance into that palace was the cause of our
being blind of one eye; and if one of us would relate to thee all
that hath befallen him, his story would be too long for thee to
hear."

They then sewed me up in the skin, and entered their palace; and soon after, there came an enormous white bird, which seized me, and flew away with me, and set me down upon the mountain; whereupon I cut open the skin, and got out; and the bird, as soon as it saw me, flew away. I rose up quickly, and proceeded toward the palace, which I found to be as they had described it to me; and when I had entered it, I beheld, at the upper end of a saloon, forty young damsels, beautiful as so many moons, and magnificently attired, who, as soon as they saw me, exclaimed: "Welcome! Welcome! O our master and our lord! We have been for a month expecting thee. Praise be to God who hath blessed us with one who is worthy of us, and one of whom we are worthy!" After having thus greeted me, they seated me upon a mattress, and said: "Thou art from this day our master and prince, and we are thy handmaids, and entirely under thy authority." They then brought to me some refreshments, and, when I had eaten and drunk, they sat and conversed with me, full of joy and happiness. So lovely were these ladies, that even a devotee, if he saw them, would gladly consent to be their servant, and to comply with all that they would desire. At the approach of night they all assembled around me, and placed before me a table of fresh and dried fruits, with other delicacies that the tongue cannot describe, and wine; and one began to sing, while another played upon the lute. The wine-cups circulated among us, and joy overcame me to such a degree as to obliterate from my mind every earthly care, and make me exclaim: "This is indeed a delightful life!" I passed a night of such enjoyment as I had never before experienced; and on the morrow I entered the bath; and, after I had washed myself, they brought me a suit of the richest clothing, and we again sat down to a repast.

In this manner I lived with them a whole year; but on the

first day of the new year, they seated themselves around me, and began to weep, and bade me farewell, clinging to my skirts. "What calamity hath befallen you?" said I. "Ye are breaking my heart." They answered: "Would that we had never known thee; for we have associated with many men, but have seen none like thee. May God, therefore, not deprive us of thy company." And they wept afresh. I said to them: "I wish that you would acquaint me with the cause of this weeping." "Thou," they replied, "art the cause; yet now, if thou wilt attend to what we tell thee, we shall never be parted; but if thou act contrary to it, we are separated from this time; and our hearts whisper to us that thou wilt not regard our warning." "Inform me," said I, "and I will attend to your directions." And they replied: "If then thou wouldst inquire respecting our history, know that we are the daughters of kings: for many years it hath been our custom to assemble here, and every year we absent ourselves during a period of forty days; then returning, we indulge ourselves for a year in feasting and drinking. This is our usual practice; and now we fear that thou wilt disregard our directions when we are absent from thee. We deliver to thee the keys of the palace, which are a hundred in number, belonging to a hundred closets. Open each of these, and amuse thyself, and eat and drink, and refresh thyself, excepting the closet that hath a door of red gold; for if thou open this, the consequence will be a separation between us and thee. We conjure thee, therefore, to observe our direction, and to be patient during this period." Upon hearing this, I swore to them that I would never open the closet to which they alluded; and they departed, urging me to be faithful to my promise.

I remained alone in the palace, and at the approach of evening I opened the first closet, and, entering it, found a mansion like paradise, with a garden containing green trees loaded with ripe fruits, abounding with singing birds, and watered by copious streams. My heart was soothed by the sight, and I wandered among the trees, scenting the fragrance of the flowers, and listening to the warbling of the birds as they sang the praises of the One, the Almighty. After admiring the mingled colours of the apple resembling the hue upon the cheek of the beloved maid and the sallow countenance of the perplexed and timid lover, the sweet-smelling quince diffusing an odour like musk and ambergris, and the plum shining as the ruby, I retired from this place, and, having locked the door, opened that of the next closet, within which I beheld a spacious tract planted with numerous palm-trees, and watered by a river flowing among rose-trees, and jasmine, and marjoram, and eglantine, and narcissus, and gilliflower, the odours of which, diffused in every direction by the wind, inspired me with the utmost delight. I locked again the door of the second closet, and opened that of the third. Within this I found a large saloon, paved with marbles of various colours, and with costly minerals and precious gems, and containing cages constructed of sandal and aloes-wood with singing birds within them, and others upon the branches of trees which were planted there. My heart was charmed, my trouble was dissipated, and I slept there until the morning. I then opened the door of the fourth closet, and within this door I found a great building in which were forty closets with open doors; and entering these, I beheld pearls, and rubies, and chrysolites, and emeralds, and other precious jewels such as the tongue cannot describe. I was astonished at the sight, and said: "Such things as these, I imagine, are not found in the treasury of any king. I am now the King of my age, and all these treasures, through the goodness of God, are mine."

PRINCE AGIB

Thus I continued to amuse myself, passing from one place to another, until thirty-nine days had elapsed, and I had opened the doors of all the closets excepting that which they had forbidden me to open. My heart was then disturbed by curiosity respecting this hundredth closet, and the Devil, in order to plunge me into misery, induced me to open it. I had not patience to abstain, though there remained of the appointed period only one day: so I approached the closet, and opened the door; and when I had entered, I perceived a fragrant odour, such as I had never before smelt, which intoxicated me so that I fell down insensible, and remained some time in this state: but at length recovering, I fortified my heart, and proceeded. I found the floor overspread with saffron, and the place illuminated by golden lamps and by candles, which diffused the odours of musk and ambergris. I saw also a black horse, of the hue of the darkest night, before which was a manger of white crystal filled with cleansed sesame, and another, similar to it, containing rose-water infused with musk: he was saddled and bridled, and his saddle was of red gold. Wondering at the sight of him, I said within myself: "This must be an animal of extraordinary qualities;" and, seduced by the Devil, I led him out, and mounted him; but he moved not from his place. I kicked him with my heel; but still he moved not: so I took a switch and struck him with it; and as soon as he felt the blow he uttered a sound like thunder, and, expanding a pair of wings, soared with me to an immense height through the air, and then alighted upon the roof of another palace, where he threw me from his back, and, by a violent blow with his tail upon my face, struck out my eye, and left me.

Thus it was I became blind of one eye. I then recollected the predictions of the ten young men. The horse again took wing, and soon disappeared. I got up much vexed at the misfortune I had brought upon myself. I walked upon the terrace, covering my eye with one of my hands, for it pained me exceedingly, and then descended, and entered into a hall. I soon discovered by the ten benches in a circle, and the eleventh in the middle, smaller than the rest, that I was in the castle whence I had been carried by the roc.

The ten young men were not in the hall when I entered; but came in soon after, attended by the sheikh. They seemed not at all surprised to see me, nor at the loss of my eye; but said: "We are sorry that we cannot congratulate you on your return, as we could wish; but we are not the cause of your misfortune." "I should do you wrong," I replied, "to lay it to your charge; I have only myself to accuse." "If," said they, "it be a subject of consolation to the afflicted to know that others share their sufferings, you have in us this alleviation of your misfortune. All that has happened to you we have also endured; we each of us tasted the same pleasures during a year; and we had still continued to enjoy them, had we not opened the golden door, when the princesses were absent. You have been no wiser than we, and have incurred the same punishment. We would gladly receive you into our company, to join with us in the penance to which we are bound, and the duration of which we know not. But we have already stated to you the reasons that render this impossible: depart, therefore, and proceed to the court of Bagdad, where you will meet with the person who is to decide your destiny." After they had explained to me the road I was to travel, I departed from them, with mournful heart and weeping eye, and, God having decreed me a safe journey hither, I arrived at Bagdad, after I had shaved my beard, and become a mendicant. Praise be to God, whose name be exalted, and whose purposes concerning me are as yet hid in darkness.

At the approach of evening I opened the first closet and,
entering it, found a mansion like paradise.

THE STORY OF THE CITY OF BRASS

THERE was, in olden time, in Damascus of Syria, a king, named Abd-El-Melik the son of Marwan; and he was sitting, one day, having with him the great men of his empire, consisting of kings and sultans, when a discussion took place among them, respecting the traditions of former nations. They called to mind the stories of Solomon, son of David, and the dominion which God had bestowed upon him over mankind, and the genies, and the birds, and the wild beasts, and they said: "We have heard from those who were before us, that God bestowed not upon any one the power which He bestowed upon Solomon, so that he used to imprison the genies and the devils in bottles of brass, and pour molten lead over them, and seal a cover over them with his signet."

Then Talib, one of the sultans, related, that a man once embarked in a ship with a company of others, and they voyaged to the island of Sicily and ceased not in their course until there arose against them a wind which bore them away to an unknown land. This happened during the black darkness of night, and when the day shone forth, there came out to them, from caves in that land, people of black complexion and with naked bodies, like wild beasts, not understanding speech. They had a king of their own race, and none of them knew Arabic save their king. So when they saw the ship and those who were in her, he came forth to them attended by a party of his companions, and saluted them and welcomed them: They acquainted him with their state; and he said to them, "No harm shall befall you; there

hath not come to us any one of the sons of Adam before you."
And he entertained them with a banquet of the flesh of birds and
of wild beasts and of fish. And after this, the people of the ship
went down to divert themselves in the city, and they found one
of the fishermen who had cast his net in the sea to catch fish, and
he drew it up, and, lo, in it was a bottle of brass stopped with
lead, which was sealed with the signet of Solomon the son of
David. And the fisherman came forth and broke it; whereupon
there proceeded from it a blue smoke, which united with the
clouds of heaven; and they heard a horrible voice, saying: "Repentance! repentance! O Prophet of God!" Then, of that
smoke there was formed a person of terrible aspect, of terrific
make, whose head would reach as high as a mountain; and he
disappeared from before their eyes. As to the people of the
ship, their hearts were almost eradicated; but the blacks thought
nothing of the event. And a man returned to the king, and
asked him respecting this; and the king answered him: "Know
that this is one of the genies whom Solomon, the son of David,
when he was incensed against them, imprisoned in these bottles,
and he poured lead over them, and threw them into the sea.
When the fisherman casteth his net, it generally bringeth up
these bottles; and when they are broken, there cometh forth
from them a genie, who imagineth that Solomon is still living;
wherefore he repenteth, and saith: 'Repentance! O Prophet of
God!'"

And the Prince of the Faithful, Abd-El-Melik, wondered at
these words, and said: "By Allah, I desire to see some of these
bottles!" So Talib replied: "O Prince of the Faithful, thou art
able to do so, and yet remain in thy country. Send to thy brother
Abd-El-Azeez, that he may write orders to the Emeer Moosa to
journey from the Western Country to this mountain which we

have mentioned, and to bring thee what thou desirest of these bottles; for the furthest tract of his province is adjacent to this mountain." And the Prince of the Faithful approved of his advice, and said: "O Talib, thou hast spoken truth and I desire that thou be my messenger to Moosa for this purpose." To this, Talib replied: "Most willingly, O Prince of the Faithful." And the king said to him: "Go in dependence on the blessing of God, and his aid." Then he gave orders that they should write for him a letter to his brother Abd-El-Azeez, his viceroy in Egypt, and another letter to Moosa, his viceroy in the Western Country, commanding him to journey, himself, in search of the bottles of Solomon. He sealed the two letters, and delivered them to Talib, commanding him to hasten, and he gave him riches and riders and footmen to aid him in his way.

So Talib went forth on his way to Egypt, and when the Emeer Moosa knew of his approach, he went forth to him and met him, and rejoiced at his arrival; and Talib handed to him the letter. So he took it and read it, and understood its meaning; and he put it upon his head, saying: "I hear and obey the command of the Prince of the Faithful." He determined to summon his great men; and they presented themselves; and he inquired of them respecting that which had been made known to him by the letter; whereupon they said: "O Emeer, if thou desire him who will guide thee to that place, have recourse to the Sheikh Abd-Es-Samad; for he is a knowing man, and hath travelled much, and he is acquainted with the deserts and wastes and the seas, and their inhabitants and their wonders, and the countries and their districts. Have recourse therefore to him, and he will direct thee to the object of thy desire." Accordingly he gave orders to bring him, and he came before him; and, lo, he was a very old man, whom the vicissitudes of years and times had rendered decrepit. The Emeer Moosa saluted him, and said to him: "O Sheikh Abd-Es-Samad, our lord, the Prince of the Faithful, hath commanded us thus and thus, and I possess little knowledge of that land, and it hath been told me that thou art acquainted with that country and the routes. Hast thou then a wish to accomplish the affair of the Prince of the Faithful?" The sheikh replied: "Know, O Emeer, that this route is difficult, far extending, with few tracks." The emeer said to him: "How long a period doth it require?" He answered: "It is a journey of two years and some months going, and the like returning; and on the way are difficulties and horrors, and extraordinary and wonderful things. But," he said, "God will assuredly make this affair easy to us through the blessing attendant upon thee, O Viceroy of the Prince of the Faithful."

After this they departed, and they continued their journey until they arrived at a palace; whereupon the sheikh said: "Advance with us to this palace, which presenteth a lesson to him who will be admonished." So the Emeer Moosa advanced thither, together with the Sheikh Abd-Es-Samad and his chief companions, till they came to its entrance. And they found it open, and having lofty angles, and steps, among which were two wide steps of coloured marbles, the like of which hath not been seen: the ceilings and walls were decorated with gold and silver and minerals, and over the entrance was a slab, whereon was an inscription in ancient Greek; and the Sheikh Abd-Es-Samad said: "Shall I read it, O Emeer?" The emeer answered: "Advance and read." So he read it; and, lo, it was poetry; and it was this:

Here was a people whom, after their works, thou shalt see wept over for their lost
    dominion;
And in this palace is the last information respecting lords collected in the dust.

THE CITY OF BRASS

Death hath destroyed them and disunited them, and in the dust they have lost what
    they amassed;
As though they had only put down their loads to rest a while: quickly have they
    departed!

And the Emeer Moosa wept and said: "There is no deity but
God, the Living, the Enduring without failure!"

Then they attentively viewed the palace; and, lo, it was devoid
of inhabitants, destitute of household and occupants: its courts
were desolate, and its apartments were deserted; and in the
midst of it was a chamber covered with a lofty dome, rising high
into the air, around which were four hundred tombs.

And the Emeer Moosa drew near to the dome-crowned
chamber, and, lo, it had eight doors of sandal-wood, with nails
of gold, ornamented with stars of silver set with various jewels,
and he beheld in it a long tomb, of terrible appearance, whereon
was a tablet of iron of China; and the Sheikh Abd-Es-Samad
drew near to it, and read its inscription; and, lo, on it was
written:

Shouldst thou think upon me after the length of my age, and the vicissitudes of days
    and circumstances,
I am the son of Sheddad, who held dominion over mankind and each tract of the
    whole earth.
All the stubborn troops became abject unto me, and Esh-Sham from Misr unto Adnan.
In glory I reigned, abasing their kings, the people of the earth fearing my dominion;
And I beheld the tribes and armies in my power, and saw the countries and their
    inhabitants dread me.
When I mounted, I beheld my army comprising a million bridles upon neighing steeds;
And I possessed wealth that could not be calculated, which I treasured up against
    misfortunes,
Determining to devote the whole of my property for the purpose of extending the term
    of my life.

But the Deity would nought save the execution of his purpose; and thus I became
    separated from my brethren.
Death, the disuniter of mankind, came to me, and I was removed from grandeur
    to the mansion of contempt;

And I found the recompense of all my past actions, for which I am pledged: for I
was sinful!

Then raise thyself, lest thou be upon a brink; and beware of calamities! Mayest
thou be led aright!

And again the Emeer Moosa wept, in considering the fates of the
people; after which, as they were going about through the different apartments of the palace, and viewing attentively its chambers
and its places of diversion, they came to a table upon four legs
of alabaster, whereon was inscribed:

Upon this table have eaten a thousand one-eyed kings, and a thousand kings each
sound in both eyes. All of them have quitted the world, and taken up their abode in
the burial-grounds and the graves.

And the Emeer Moosa wrote down all this. Then he went forth,
and took not with him from the palace aught save the table.

The soldiers proceeded, with the Sheikh Abd-Es-Samad before
them shewing them the way, until all the first day had passed, and
the second, and the third. They then came to a high hill, at
which they looked, and, lo, upon it was a horseman of brass, on
the top of whose spear was a wide and glistening head that almost
deprived the beholder of sight, and on it was inscribed:

O thou who comest unto me, if thou know not the way that leadeth to the City of
Brass, rub the hand of the horseman, and he will turn, and then will stop, and in
whatsoever direction he stoppeth, thither proceed, without fear and without difficulty;
for it will lead thee to the City of Brass.

And when the Emeer Moosa had rubbed the hand of the
horseman, it turned like the blinding lightning, and faced a
different direction from that in which they were travelling.

The party therefore turned thither and journeyed on, and it
was the right way. They took that route, and continued their
course the same day and the next night until they had traversed
a wide tract of country. And as they were proceeding, one day,
they came to a pillar of black stone, wherein was a person sunk

to his arm-pits, and he had two huge wings, and four arms; two of them like those of the sons of Adam, and two like the fore-legs of lions, with claws. He had hair upon his head like the tails of horses, and two eyes like two burning coals, and he had a third eye, in his forehead, like the eye of the lynx, from which there appeared sparks of fire. He was black and tall; and he was crying out: "Extolled be the perfection of my Lord, who hath appointed me this severe affliction and painful torture until the day of resurrection!" When the party beheld him, their reason fled from them, and they were stupefied at the sight of his form, and retreated in flight; and the Emeer Moosa said to the Sheikh Abd-Es-Samad: "What is this?" He answered: "I know not what he is." And the emeer said: "Draw near to him, and investigate his case: perhaps he will discover it, and perhaps thou wilt learn his history." So the Sheikh Abd-Es-Samad drew near to him, and said to him: "O thou person, what is thy name, and what is thy nature, and what hath placed thee here in this manner?" And the person answered him: "As to me, I am an efreet of the genies, and my name is Dahish, and I am restrained here by the majesty of God." Then the Emeer Moosa said: "O Sheikh Abd-Es-Samad, ask him what is the cause of his confinement in this pillar." He therefore asked respecting that, and the efreet answered him: "Verily my story is wonderful; and it is this:

"There belonged to one of the sons of Iblees an idol of red carnelian, of which I was made guardian; and there used to worship it one of the Kings of the Sea, of great glory, leading, among his troops of the genies, a million warriors who smote with swords before him, and who answered his prayer in cases of difficulty. These genies who obeyed him were under my command and authority, following my words when I ordered them: all of them were in rebellion against Solomon, the son of David; and I used to enter the body of the idol, and command them and forbid them. Now the daughter of that king was a frequent adorer of the idol, assiduous in the worship of it, and she was the handsomest of the people of her age, endowed with beauty and loveliness, and elegance and perfection; and I described her to Solomon, on whom be peace! So he sent to her father, saying to him: 'Marry to me thy daughter, and break thy carnelian-idol, and bear witness that there is no deity but God, and that Solomon is the Prophet of God. But if thou refuse, I will come to thee with forces that shall leave thee like yesterday that hath passed.' And when the messenger of Solomon came to him, the King of the Sea was insolent, and magnified himself and was proud. Then he said to his viziers: 'What say ye respecting the affair of Solomon? For he hath sent demanding my daughter, and commanding me to break my carnelian-idol, and to adopt his faith.' And they replied: 'O great King, can Solomon do aught unto thee, when thou art in the midst of this vast sea? He cannot prevail against thee; since the genies will fight on thy side; and thou shalt seek aid against him of thine idol that thou worshippest. The right opinion is, that thou consult thy red carnelian-idol, and hear what will be his reply: if he counsel thee to fight him, fight him; but otherwise, do not.' And upon this the king went immediately, and, going in to his idol, after he had offered a sacrifice and slain victims, fell down before it prostrate, and began to weep, and to seek counsel.

"Thereupon I entered the body of the idol, by reason of my ignorance, and my solicitude respecting the affair of Solomon, and recited this couplet:

'As for me, I am not in fear of him; for I am acquainted with everything.
If he wish to wage war with me, I will go forth, and I will snatch his soul from him.'

So when the king heard my reply to him, his heart was strength-
ened, and he determined to wage war with Solomon the Prophet
of God and to fight against him. Accordingly, when the messenger of Solomon came, he inflicted upon him a painful beating,
and returned him a shameful reply; and he sent to threaten
Solomon, saying to him, by the messenger: 'Dost thou threaten
me with false words? Either come thou to me, or I will go to
thee.'

"Then the messenger returned to Solomon, and acquainted
him with all that had occurred. And when the Prophet of God
heard that, his resolution was roused, and he prepared his forces,
consisting of genies and men, and wild beasts, and birds and
reptiles. He commanded his vizier, Ed-Dimiryat, the king of the
genies, to collect them from every place: so he collected for him,
of the devils, six hundred millions. He also commanded Asaf,
his vizier of men, to collect his soldiers of mankind; and their
number was one million, or more. He made ready the accoutre-
ments and weapons, and mounted, with his forces, upon the magic
carpet, with the birds flying over his head, and the wild beasts
beneath the carpet marching, until he alighted upon his enemy's
coast, and surrounded his island, having filled the land with the
forces. He then sent to our king, saying to him: 'Behold, I have
arrived: therefore submit thyself to my authority, and acknowledge my mission, and break thine idol, and worship the One, the
Adored God, and marry to me thy daughter according to law,
and say thou, and those who are with thee, I testify that there is
no deity but God, and I testify that Solomon is the Prophet of
God. If thou say that, peace and safety shall be thy lot. But
if thou refuse, thy defending thyself from me in this island shall
not prevent thee: for God hath commanded the wind to obey
me, and I will order it to convey me unto thee on the carpet, and

will make thee an example to restrain others.' So the messenger came to him, and communicated to him the message of the Prophet! But the king said to him: 'There is no way for the accomplishment of this thing that he requireth: therefore inform him that I am coming forth unto him.' Accordingly the messenger returned to Solomon, and gave him the reply. The king then sent to the people of his country, and collected for himself, of the genies that were under his authority, a million; and to these he added others, of the devils that were in the islands and on the mountains; after which he made ready his forces, and opened the armouries, and distributed to them the weapons. And as to the Prophet of God, he disposed his troops, commanding the wild beasts to form themselves into two divisions, on the right of the people and on their left, and commanding the birds to be upon the islands. He ordered them also when the assault should be made, to tear out the eyes of their antagonists with their beaks, and to beat their faces with their wings; and he ordered the wild beasts to tear in pieces their horses; and they replied: 'We hear and obey God and thee, O Prophet of God!' Then Solomon set for himself a couch of alabaster adorned with jewels, and plated with plates of red gold, and he placed his vizier Asaf on the right side, and his vizier, Ed-Dimiryat, on the left side, and the kings of mankind on his right, and the kings of the genies on his left, and the wild beasts and the vipers and serpents before him.

"After this, they came upon us all together, and we contended with him in a wide tract for a period of two days; and calamity befell us on the third day, and the decree of God was executed among us. The first who charged upon Solomon were I and my troops; and I said to my companions: 'Keep in your places in the battle-field while I go forth to them and challenge Ed-Dimiryat.' And, lo, he came forth, like a great mountain, his fires flaming, and his smoke ascending; and he approached, and smote me with a flaming fire; and his arrow prevailed over my fire. He cried out at me with a prodigious cry, so that I imagined the heaven had fallen, and the mountains shook at his voice. Then he commanded his companions, and they charged upon us all together: we also charged upon them: the fires rose and the smoke ascended, the hearts of the combatants were almost cleft asunder, and the battle raged. The birds fought in the air; and the wild beasts in the dust; and I contended with Ed-Dimiryat until he wearied me and I wearied him; after which my companions and troops were enervated, and my tribes were routed. I flew from before Ed-Dimiryat; but he followed me a journey of three months, until he overtook me. I had fallen down through fatigue, and he rushed upon me, and made me a prisoner. So I said to him: 'By Him who hath exalted thee and abased me, pity me, and take me before Solomon.' But when I came before Solomon, he met me in a most evil manner: he caused this pillar to be brought, and hollowed it, and put me in it, and sealed me with his signet; after which, he chained me, and Ed-Dimiryat conveyed me to this place, where he set me down as thou seest me; and this pillar is my prison until the day of resurrection."

The party therefore wondered at him, and at the horrible nature of his form; and the Emeer Moosa said: "There is no deity but God!" And the Sheikh Abd-Es-Samad said to the efreet: "O thou, I ask thee concerning a thing of which do thou inform us." The efreet replied: "Ask concerning what thou wilt." And the sheikh said: "Are there in this place any of the efreets confined in bottles of brass from the time of Solomon?" He answered: "Yes, in the Sea of El-Karkar, where are a people of the descendants of Noah, whose country the deluge reached

not, and they are separated there from the rest of the sons of
Adam." "And where," said the sheikh, "is the way to the City
of Brass, and the place wherein are the bottles? What distance
is there between us and it?" The efreet answered: "It is near."
So the party left him, and proceeded; and there appeared to them
in the distance a great black object, with two fires corresponding
with each other in position; whereupon the Emeer Moosa said
to the sheikh: "What is this great black object, and these two
corresponding fires?" The guide answered him: "Be rejoiced,
O Emeer; for this is the City of Brass, and this is the appearance
of it that I find described in the Book of Hidden Treasures;
that its wall is of black stones, and it hath two towers of brass,
which the beholder seeth resembling two corresponding fires;
and thence it is named the City of Brass." They ceased not to
proceed until they arrived at it; and, lo, it was lofty, strongly
fortified, rising high into the air, impenetrable: the height of its
walls was eighty cubits, and it had five and twenty gates, none
of which would open but by means of some artifice. They
stopped before it, and endeavoured to discover one of its gates;
but they could not; and the Emeer Moosa said to the Sheikh
Abd-Es-Samad: "O sheikh, I see not to this city any gate."
The sheikh replied: "O Emeer, thus do I find it described in
the Book of Hidden Treasures; that it hath five and twenty
gates, and that none of its gates may be opened but from
within the city." "And how," said the emeer, "can we
contrive to enter it, and divert ourselves with a view of its
wonders?"

Then the Emeer Moosa ordered one of his young men to
mount a camel, and ride round the city, in the hope that he might
discover a trace of a gate. So one of his young men mounted,
and proceeded around it for two days with their nights, prose-

cuting his journey with diligence, and not resting; and when the third day arrived, he came in sight of his companions, and he was astounded at that which he beheld of the extent of the city, and its height. Then he said: "O Emeer, the easiest place in it is this place at which ye have alighted." And thereupon the Emeer Moosa took Talib and the Sheikh Abd-Es-Samad, and they ascended a mountain opposite the city, and overlooking it; and when they had ascended that mountain, they saw a city than which eyes had not beheld any greater. Its pavilions were lofty, and its domes were shining; its rivers were running, its trees were fruitful, and its gardens bore ripe produce. It was a city with impenetrable gates, empty, still, without a voice but the owl hooting in its quarters, and the raven croaking in its thoroughfare-streets, and bewailing those who had been in it.

And the Emeer Moosa fainted with sorrow; his tears ran down upon his cheeks, and he said: "By Allah, indifference to the world is the most appropriate and the most sure course!"

And when they came back to the troops, they passed the day devising means of entering the city; and the Emeer Moosa said to those of his chief officers who were around him: "How shall we contrive to enter the city, that we may see its wonders? Perhaps we shall find in it something by which we may ingratiate ourselves with the Prince of the Faithful." Talib replied: "Let us make a ladder, and mount upon it, and perhaps we shall gain access to the gate from within." And the emeer said: "This is what occurred to my mind, and excellent is the advice." Then he called to the carpenters and blacksmiths, and ordered them to make straight some pieces of wood, and to construct a ladder covered with plates of iron. And they did so, and made it strong. They employed themselves in constructing it a whole month, and many men were occupied in making it. And they

set it up and fixed it against the wall, and it proved to be equal
to the wall in height, as though it had been made for it before
that day. So the Emeer Moosa wondered at it, and said: "God
bless you! It seemeth, from the excellence of your work, as
though ye had adapted it by measurement to the wall." He then
said to the people: "Which of you will ascend this ladder, and
mount upon the wall, and walk along it, and contrive means of
descending into the city, that he may see how the case is, and then
inform us of the mode of opening the gate?" And one of them
answered: "I will ascend it, O Emeer, and descend and open
the gate." The emeer therefore replied: "Mount. God bless
thee!" Accordingly, the man ascended the ladder until he
reached the top of it; when he stood, and fixed his eyes toward
the city, clapped his hands, and cried out with his loudest voice,
saying: "Thou art beautiful!" Then he cast himself down into
the city, and was destroyed. So the Emeer Moosa said: "If
we do thus with all our companions, there will not remain of them
one; and we shall be unable to accomplish our affair, and the
affair of the Prince of the Faithful. Depart ye; for we have no
concern with this city." But one of them said: "Perhaps another
than this may be more steady than he." And a second ascended,
and a third, and a fourth, and a fifth; and they ceased not to
ascend by that ladder to the top of the wall, one after another,
until twelve men of them had gone, acting as acted the first.
Therefore the Sheikh Abd-Es-Samad said: "There is none for
this affair but myself, and the experienced is not like the inex-
perienced." But the Emeer Moosa said to him: "Thou shalt
not do that, nor will I allow thee to ascend to the top of this
wall; for shouldst thou die, thou wouldst be the cause of the
death of us all, and there would not remain of us one; since thou
art the guide of the party." The sheikh, however, replied:

"Perhaps the object will be accomplished by my means, through the will of God, whose name be exalted!" And thereupon all the people agreed to his ascending.

Then Abd-Es-Samad arose, and, having said: "In the name of God, the Compassionate, the Merciful!"—he ascended the ladder, repeating the praises of God, and reciting the Verses of Safety, until he reached the top of the wall; when he clapped his hands, and fixed his eyes. The people therefore all called out to him, and said: "O Sheikh Abd-Es-Samad, do not cast thyself down! If Abd-Es-Samad fall, we all perish!" Then Abd-Es-Samad sat a long time repeating the praises of God, and reciting the Verses of Safety; after which he rose with energy, and called out with his loudest voice: "O Emeer, no harm shall befall you; for God hath averted from me the effect of the artifice of the Devil." So the emeer said to him: "What hast thou seen, O Sheikh?" He answered: "When I reached the top of the wall I beheld ten damsels, like moons, who made a sign with their hands, as though they would say: 'Come to us!' And it seemed to me that beneath me was a sea of water; whereupon I desired to cast myself down, as our companions did: but I beheld them dead; so I withheld myself from them, and recited some words of the book of God, whereupon He averted from me the influence of those damsels, and they departed; therefore I cast not myself down. There is no doubt that this is an enchantment which the people of this city contrived in order to repel from it every one who should wish to obtain access to it."

He then walked along the wall till he came to the two towers of brass, when he saw that they had gates of gold, without any sign of the means of opening them. Therefore the sheikh, looking attentively, saw in the middle of one of the gates a figure of a horseman of brass, having one hand extended, as though he were pointing with it, and on it was an inscription, which the sheikh read, and, lo, it contained these words:

Turn the pin that is in the middle of the front of the horseman's body twelve times, and then the gate will open.

So he turned the pin twelve times; whereupon the gate opened immediately, with a noise like thunder; and the sheikh entered. He was a learned man, acquainted with all languages and characters. And he walked on until he entered a long passage, whence he descended some steps, and he found a place with handsome wooden benches, on which were people dead, and over their heads were elegant shields, and keen swords, and strung bows, and notched arrows. And behind the next gate were a bar of iron, and barricades of wood, and locks of delicate fabric, and strong apparatus. Upon this, the sheikh said within himself: "Perhaps the keys are with these people." Then he looked, and, lo, there was a sheikh who appeared to be the oldest of them, and he was upon a high wooden bench among the dead men. So Abd-Es-Samad said: "May not the keys of the city be with this sheikh! Perhaps he was the gate-keeper of the city, and these were under his authority." He therefore drew near to him, and lifted up his garments, and, lo, the keys were hung to his waist. At the sight of them, Abd-Es-Samad rejoiced exceedingly; and he took the keys, opened the locks, and pulled the gate and the barricades and other apparatus, which opened and the gate also opened, with a noise like thunder. Upon this the sheikh exclaimed: "God is most great!" and the people made the same exclamation with him, rejoicing at the event. The Emeer Moosa also rejoiced at the safety of Abd-Es-Samad, and at the opening of the gate of the city; the people thanked him for that which he had done, and all the troops hastened to

And when they had ascended that mountain they saw a city
than which eyes had not beheld any greater.

enter the gate.   But the Emeer Moosa cried out to them, saying
to them: "O people, if all of us enter, we shall not be secure from
accident.   Half shall enter, and half shall remain behind."

The Emeer Moosa then entered the gate, and with him half
of the people, who bore their weapons of war.   And the party
saw their companions lying dead: so they buried them.   They
saw also the gate-keepers and servants and chamberlains and
lieutenants lying upon beds of silk, all of them dead.   And they
entered the market of the city, and beheld that the shops were
open, and the scales hung up, and the utensils of brass ranged
in order, and the stores were full of all kinds of goods.   And they
saw the merchants dead in their shops: their skins were dried,
and they had become examples to him who would be admonished.
And they left this place, and passed on to the silk-market, in
which were silks and brocades interwoven with red gold and
white silver upon various colours, and the owners were dead,
lying upon skins, and appearing almost as though they would
speak.   Leaving these, they went on to the market of jewels
and pearls and jacinths; and they left it, and passed on to the
market of the money-changers, whom they found dead, with
varieties of silks beneath them, and their shops were filled with
gold and silver.   These they left, and they proceeded to the
markets of the perfumers; and, lo, their shops were filled with
varieties of perfumes, and bags of musk, and ambergris, and
aloes-wood, and camphor; and the owners were all dead, not
having with them any food.   And when they went forth from the
market of the perfumers, they found near unto it a palace, decorated, and strongly constructed; and they entered it, and found
banners unfurled, and drawn swords, and strung bows and
shields hung up by chains of gold and silver, and helmets gilded
with red gold.   And in the passages of that palace were benches

of ivory, ornamented with plates of brilliant gold, and with silk, on which were men whose skins had dried upon the bones; the ignorant would imagine them to be sleeping; but, from the want of food, they had died, and tasted mortality.

And the Emeer Moosa went on into the interior of the palace. There he beheld a great hall, and four large and lofty chambers, each one fronting another, wide, decorated with gold and silver and with various colours. In the midst of the hall was a great fountain of alabaster, over which was a canopy of brocade; and in those chambers were fountains lined with marble; and channels of water flowed along the floors of those chambers, the four streams meeting in a great tank lined with marbles of various colours. The Emeer Moosa then said to the Sheikh Abd-Es-Samad: "Enter these chambers with us." So they entered the first chamber; and they found it filled with gold and with white silver, and pearls and jewels, and jacinths and precious minerals. They found in it also chests full of red and yellow and white brocades. And they went thence to the second chamber, and opened a closet in it, and, lo, it was filled with arms and weapons of war, consisting of gilded helmets, and coats of mail, and swords, and lances, and maces, and other instruments of war and battle. Then they passed thence to the third chamber, in which they found closets having upon their doors closed locks, and over them were curtains worked with various kinds of embroidery. They opened one of these closets, and found it filled with weapons decorated with varieties of gold and silver and jewels. And they went thence to the fourth chamber, where also they found closets, one of which they opened, and they found it full of utensils for food and drink, consisting of various vessels of gold and silver, and saucers of crystal, and cups set with brilliant pearls and cups of carnelian, and other things. So they began to take what suited them of those things, and each of the soldiers carried off what he could. And when they determined to go forth from those chambers, they saw there a door inlaid with ivory and ebony, and adorned with plates of brilliant gold. Over it was hung a curtain of silk worked with various kinds of embroidery, and upon it were locks of white silver, to be opened by artifice, without a key. The Sheikh Abd-Es-Samad therefore advanced to those locks, and he opened them by his knowledge and excellent skill. And the party entered a passage paved with marble, upon the sides of which were curtains whereon were figured various wild beasts and birds, all these being worked with red gold and white silver, and their eyes were of pearls and jacinths: whosoever beheld them was confounded.

They then passed on, and found a saloon constructed of polished marble adorned with jewels. The beholder imagined that upon its floor was running water, and if any one walked upon it he would slip. The Emeer Moosa therefore ordered the Sheikh Abd-Es-Samad to throw upon it something that they might be enabled to walk on it; and he did this, and contrived so that they passed on. And they found in it a great dome constructed of stones gilded with red gold. The party had not beheld, in all that they had seen, anything more beautiful than it. And in the midst of that dome was a great dome-crowned structure of alabaster, around which were lattice windows, decorated, and adorned with oblong emeralds, such as none of the kings could procure. In it was a pavilion of brocade, raised upon columns of red gold, and within this were birds, the feet of which were of emeralds; beneath each bird was a net of brilliant pearls, spread over a fountain; and by the brink of the fountain was placed a couch adorned with pearls and jewels and jacinths, whereon was a damsel resembling the shining sun.

Eyes had not beheld one more beautiful. Upon her was a garment of brilliant pearls, on her head was a crown of red gold, with a fillet of jewels, on her neck was a necklace of jewels in the middle of which were refulgent gems, and upon her forehead were two jewels the light of which was like that of the sun; and she seemed as though she were looking at the people, and observing them to the right and left. When the Emeer Moosa beheld this damsel, he wondered extremely at her loveliness, and was confounded by her beauty and the redness of her cheeks and the blackness of her hair. Any beholder would imagine that she was alive, and not dead. And they said to her: "Peace be on thee, O damsel!" But Talib said to the emeer: "May God amend thy state! Know that this damsel is dead. There is no life in her. How then can she return the salutation?" And he added: "O Emeer, she is skilfully embalmed; and her eyes have been taken out after her death, and quicksilver hath been put beneath them, after which they have been restored to their places; so they gleam; and whenever the air putteth them in motion, the beholder imagineth that she twinkleth her eyes, though she is dead."

And as to the couch upon which was the damsel, it had steps, and upon the steps were two slaves, one of them white and the other black; and in the hand of one of them was a weapon of steel, and in the hand of the other a jewelled sword that blinded the eyes; and before the two slaves was a tablet of gold, whereon was read an inscription, which was this:

In the name of God, the Compassionate, the Merciful. Praise be to God, the Creator of Man; and He is the Lord of lords, and the Cause of causes. O thou, if thou know me not, I will acquaint thee with my name and my descent. I am Tedmur, the daughter of the King of the Amalekites. I possessed what none of the kings possessed, and ruled with justice, and acted impartially toward my subjects: I gave and bestowed, and I lived a long time in the enjoyment of happiness and an easy life, and possessing emancipated female and male slaves. Thus I did until the summoner of death came to my abode, and disasters occurred before me. And the case was this: Seven years in succession came upon us, during which no water descended on us from heaven, nor did any grass grow for us on the face of the earth. So we ate what food we had in our dwellings, and after that we fell upon the beasts and ate them, and there remained nothing. Upon this, therefore, I caused the wealth to be brought, and meted it with a measure, and sent it by trusty men, who went about with it through all the districts, not leaving unvisited a single large city, to seek for some food. But they found it not; and they returned to us with the wealth, after a long absence. So thereupon we exposed to view our riches and our treasures, locked the gates of the fortresses in our city, and submitted ourselves to the decree of our Lord, committing our case to our Master; and thus we all died, as thou beholdest, and left what we had built and what we had treasured. This is our story: Whoso arriveth at our city, and entereth it, let him take of the wealth what he can, but not touch anything that is on my body; for it is the covering of my person. Therefore let him fear God, and not seize aught of it; for he would destroy himself. Peace be on you! I beg God, moreover, to save you from the evil of trials and sickness

The Emeer Moosa, when he heard these words, again wept and was admonished by what he witnessed. He then said to his companions: "Bring the sacks, and fill them with part of these riches and these vessels and rarities and jewels." And thereupon, Talib, the son of Sahl, said to the Emeer Moosa: "O Emeer, shall we leave this damsel with the things that are upon her? They are things that have no equal, nor is the like of them at any time found, and they are more than the riches thou hast taken, and will be the best present by which thou mayest ingratiate thyself with the Prince of the Faithful." But the emeer replied: "Heardest thou not that which the damsel hath given as a charge, in the inscription upon this tablet? Moreover, and especially, she hath given it as a charge offered in confidence, and we are not of the people of treachery." The Vizier Talib, however, said: "And on account of these words wilt thou leave these riches and these jewels, when she is dead? What then should she do with these things, which are the ornaments of the world, and the decoration of the living? With a garment of cotton might this damsel be covered, and we are more worthy of the things than she." Then he drew near to the steps, and ascended them until he reached the spot between the two slaves, when, lo, one of these two smote him upon his back, and the other smote him with the sword that was in his hand, and struck off his head, and he fell down dead. So the Emeer Moosa said: "May God not regard with mercy thy resting-place! There was, in these riches, a sufficiency; and covetousness doth dishonour the person in whom it existeth!" He thereupon gave orders for the entry of the troops, who accordingly entered, and they loaded the camels with part of those riches and minerals; after which the Emeer Moosa commanded them to close the gate as it was before.

They then proceeded along the sea-coast until they came in sight of a high mountain overlooking the sea. In it were many caves, and, lo, in these was a people of the blacks, clad in hides, and with burnouses of hides upon their heads, whose language was not known. And when they saw the troops, they ran away from them, and fled, while their women and their children stood at the entrances of the caves. So the Emeer Moosa said: "O Sheikh Abd-Es-Samad, what are these people?" And he answered: "These are the objects of the inquiry of the Prince of the Faithful." They therefore alighted, and the tents were pitched, and the riches were put down; and they had not rested when the king of the blacks came down from the mountain, and drew near to the troops. He was acquainted with the Arabic language; wherefore, when he came to the Emeer Moosa, he saluted him; and the emeer returned his salutation, and treated him with honour. Then the king of the blacks said to the emeer: "Are ye of mankind, or of the genies?" The emeer answered: "As to us, we are of mankind; and as to you, there is

no doubt but that ye are of the genies, because of your seclusion
in this mountain that is separated from the world, and because
of the greatness of your make." But the king of the blacks
replied: "Nay, we are a people of the race of Adam, of the sons
of Ham, the son of Noah, on whom be peace! And as to this
sea, it is known by the name of El-Karkar."

The Emeer Moosa then said to him: "We are the associates
of the King of El-Islam, Abd-El-Melik the son of Marwan; and
we have come on account of the bottles of brass that are here in
your sea, and wherein are the devils imprisoned from the time
of Solomon, the son of David. He hath commanded us to bring
him some of them, that he may see them, and divert himself
by the view of them." And the king of the blacks replied: "Most
willingly." Then he feasted him with fish, and ordered the
divers to bring up from the sea some of the bottles of Solomon;
and they brought up for them twelve bottles; wherewith the
Emeer Moosa was delighted, and the Sheikh Abd-Es-Samad
also, and the soldiers, on account of the accomplishment of the
affair of the Prince of the Faithful. The Emeer Moosa thereupon
presented to the king of the blacks many presents, and gave him
large gifts. In like manner, too, the king of the blacks gave to
the Emeer Moosa a present consisting of wonders of the sea.

Then they bade him farewell, and they journeyed back until
they came to the land of Syria, and went in to the Prince of the
Faithful; whereupon the Emeer Moosa acquainted him with all
that he had seen, and all that had occurred to him with respect
to the verses and histories and admonitions, and told him of the
case of Talib the son of Sahl. And the Prince of the Faithful
said to him: "Would that I had been with you, that I might
have beheld what ye beheld!" He then took the bottles, and
proceeded to open one after another, and the devils came forth

from them, saying: "Repentance, O Prophet of God! We will not return to the like conduct ever!" And Abd-El-Melik the son of Marwan wondered at this. After this, the Prince of the Faithful caused the riches to be brought before him, and divided them among the people. And he said: "God hath not bestowed upon any one the like of what He bestowed upon Solomon the son of David."

This is the end of that which hath come down to us, of the history of the City of Brass, entire. And God is all-knowing.

THE STORY OF ALI BABA AND THE FORTY THIEVES

IN a town in Persia, there lived two brothers, one named Cassim, the other Ali Baba. Their father left them scarcely anything; but as he had divided his little property equally between them, it would seem that their fortune ought to have been equal; but chance determined otherwise.

Cassim married a wife, who soon after became heiress to a large sum, and to a warehouse full of rich goods; so that he all at once became one of the richest and most considerable merchants, and lived at his ease. Ali Baba, on the other hand, who had married a woman as poor as himself, lived in a very wretched habitation, and had no other means to maintain his wife and children but his daily labour of cutting wood, and bringing it to town to sell, upon three asses, which were his whole substance.

One day, when Ali Baba was in the forest, and had just cut wood enough to load his asses, he saw at a distance a great cloud of dust, which seemed to be driven toward him: he observed it very attentively, and distinguished soon after a body of horse. Though there had been no rumour of robbers in that country, Ali Baba began to think that they might prove such, and without considering what might become of his asses, was resolved to save himself. He climbed up a large, thick tree, whose branches, at a little distance from the ground, were so close to one another that there was but little space between them. He placed himself in the middle, from whence he could see all that passed without being discovered; and the tree stood at the base of a single rock, so steep and craggy that nobody could climb up it.

The troop, who were all well mounted and armed, came to the foot of this rock, and there dismounted. Ali Baba counted forty of them, and, from their looks and equipage, was assured that they were robbers. Nor was he mistaken in his opinion; for they were a troop of banditti, who, without doing any harm to the neighbourhood, robbed at a distance, and made that place their rendezvous; but what confirmed him in his opinion was, that every man unbridled his horse, tied him to some shrub, and hung about his neck a bag of corn which they brought behind them. Then each of them took his saddle wallet, which seemed to Ali Baba to be full of gold and silver from its weight. One, who was the most personable amongst them, and whom he took to be their captain, came with his wallet on his back under the tree in which Ali Baba was concealed, and making his way through some shrubs, pronounced these words so distinctly: "*Open, Sesame,*" that Ali Baba heard him. As soon as the captain of the robbers had uttered these words, a door opened in the rock; and after he had made all his troop enter before him, he followed them, when the door shut again of itself. The robbers stayed some time within the rock, and Ali Baba, who feared that some one, or all of them together, might come out and catch him, if he should endeavour to make his escape, was obliged to sit patiently in the tree. He was nevertheless tempted to get down, mount one of their horses, and lead another, driving his asses before him with all the haste he could to town; but the uncertainty of the event made him choose the safest course.

At last the door opened again, and the forty robbers came out. As the captain went in last, he came out first, and stood to see them all pass by him, when Ali Baba heard him make the door close by pronouncing these words: "*Shut, Sesame.*" Every man went and bridled his horse, fastened his wallet, and mounted again; and when the captain saw them all ready, he put himself at their head, and they returned the way they had come. Ali Baba did not immediately quit his tree; for, said he to himself, they may have forgotten something and may come back again, and then I shall be taken. He followed them with his eyes as far as he could see them; and afterward stayed a considerable time before he descended. Remembering the words the captain of the robbers used to cause the door to open and shut, he had the curiosity to try if his pronouncing them would have the same effect. Accordingly, he went among the shrubs, and perceiving the door concealed behind them, stood before it, and said: "*Open, Sesame!*" The door instantly flew wide open. Ali Baba, who expected a dark dismal cavern, was surprised to see it well lighted and spacious, in the form of a vault, which received the light from an opening at the top of the rock. He saw all sorts of provisions, rich bales of silk stuff, brocade, and valuable carpeting, piled upon one another; gold and silver ingots in great heaps, and money in bags. The sight of all these riches made him suppose that this cave must have been occupied for ages by robbers, who had succeeded one another. Ali Baba did not stand long to consider what he should do, but went immediately into the cave, and as soon as he had entered, the door shut of itself, but this did not disturb him, because he knew the secret to open it again. He never regarded the silver, but made the best use of his time in carrying out as much of the gold coin as he thought his three asses could carry. He collected his asses, which were dispersed, and when he had loaded them with the bags, laid wood over in such a manner that they could not be seen. When he had done he stood before the door, and pronouncing the words: "*Shut, Sesame !*" the door closed after him, for it had shut of itself while he was within, but remained open while he was out. He then made the best of his way to town.

When Ali Baba got home, he drove his asses into a little yard, shut the gates very carefully, threw off the wood that covered the bags, carried them into his house, and ranged them in order before his wife, who sat on a sofa. His wife handled the bags, and finding them full of money, suspected that her husband had been robbing, insomuch that she could not help saying: "Ali Baba, have you been so unhappy as to——" "Be quiet, wife," interrupted Ali Baba, "do not frighten yourself; I am no robber, unless he may be one who steals from robbers. You will no longer entertain an ill opinion of me, when I shall tell you my good fortune." He then emptied the bags, which raised such a great heap of gold as dazzled his wife's eyes; and when he had done, told her the whole adventure from beginning to end; and, above all, recommended her to keep it secret. The wife, cured of her fears, rejoiced with her husband at their good fortune, and would count all the gold piece by piece. "Wife," replied Ali Baba, "you do not know what you undertake, when you pretend to count the money; you will never have done. I will dig a hole, and bury it; there is no time to be lost." "You are in the right, husband," replied she; "but let us know, as nigh as possible, how much we have. I will borrow a small measure in the neighbourhood, and measure it, while you dig the hole." "What you are going to do is to no purpose, wife," said Ali Baba; "if you would take my advice, you had better let it alone; but keep the secret, and do what you please." Away the wife ran to her brother-in-law Cassim, who lived just by, but was not then at home; and addressing herself to his wife, desired her to lend her a measure for a little while. Her sister-in-law asked her, whether she would have a great or a small one. The wife asked for a small one. The sister-in-law agreed to lend one, but as she knew Ali Baba's poverty, she was curious to know what sort of grain his wife wanted to measure, and artfully putting some suet at the bottom of the measure, brought it to her with an excuse, that she was sorry that she had made her stay so long, but that she could not find it sooner. Ali Baba's wife went home, set the measure upon the heap of gold, filled it and emptied it often upon the sofa, till she had done: when she was very well satisfied to find the number of measures amounted to so many as they did, and went to tell her husband, who had almost finished digging the hole. While Ali Baba was burying the gold, his wife, to show her exactness and diligence to her sister-in-law, carried the measure back again, but without taking notice that a piece of gold had stuck to the bottom. "Sister," said she, giving it to her again, "you see that I have not kept your measure long; I am obliged to you for it, and return it with thanks."

As soon as her sister-in-law was gone, Cassim's wife looked at the bottom of the measure, and was inexpressibly surprised to find a piece of gold stuck to it. Envy immediately possessed her breast. "What!" said she, "has Ali Baba gold so plentiful as to measure it? Where has that poor wretch got all this wealth?" Cassim, her husband, was not at home, but at his counting-house, which he left always in the evening. His wife waited for him, and thought the time an age; so great was her impatience to tell him the circumstance, at which she guessed he would be as much surprised as herself.

When Cassim came home, his wife said to him: "Cassim, I know you think yourself rich, but you are much mistaken; Ali Baba is infinitely richer than you; he does not count his money, but measures it." Cassim desired her to explain the riddle, which she did, by telling him the stratagem she had used to make the discovery, and showed him the piece of money, which was so old that they could not tell in what prince's reign it was coined. Cassim, instead of being pleased, conceived a base envy at his brother's prosperity; he could not sleep all that night, and went to him in the morning before sunrise, although after he had married the rich widow, he had never treated him as a brother, but neglected him. "Ali Baba," said he, accosting him, "you are very reserved in your affairs; you pretend to be miserably poor, and yet you measure gold." "How, brother?" replied Ali Baba; "I do not know what you mean: explain yourself." "Do not pretend ignorance," replied Cassim, showing him the piece of gold his wife had given him. "How many of these pieces," added he, "have you? My wife found this at the bottom of the measure you borrowed yesterday."

By this discourse, Ali Baba perceived that Cassim and his wife, through his own wife's folly, knew what they had so much reason to conceal; but what was done could not be recalled; therefore, without shewing the least surprise or trouble, he confessed all, told his brother by what chance he had discovered this retreat of the thieves, in what place it was; and offered him part of his treasure to keep the secret. "I expect as much," replied Cassim haughtily; "but I must know exactly where this treasure is, and how I may visit it myself when I choose; otherwise I will go and inform against you, and then you will not only get no more, but will lose all you have, and I shall have a share for my information."

Ali Baba, more out of his natural good temper, than frightened by the menaces of his unnatural brother, told him all he desired, and even the very words he was to use to gain admission into the cave.

ALI BABA AND THE FORTY THIEVES

Cassim, who wanted no more of Ali Baba, left him, resolving to be beforehand with him, and hoping to get all the treasure to himself. He rose the next morning long before the sun, and set out for the forest with ten mules bearing great chests, which he designed to fill; and followed the road which Ali Baba had pointed out to him. He was not long before he reached the rock, and found out the place by the tree, and other marks, which his brother had given him. When he reached the entrance of the cavern, he pronounced the words: *"Open, Sesame!"* and the door immediately opened, and when he was in, closed upon him. In examining the cave, he was in great admiration to find much more riches than he had apprehended from Ali Baba's account. He was so covetous, and greedy of wealth, that he could have spent the whole day in feasting his eyes with so much treasure, if the thought that he came to carry some away had not hindered him. He laid as many bags of gold as he could carry at the door of the cavern, but his thoughts were so full of the great riches he should possess, that he could not think of the necessary word to make it open, but instead of *"Sesame,"* said: *"Open, Barley!"* and was much amazed to find that the door remained fast shut. He named several sorts of grain, but still the door would not open. Cassim had never expected such an incident, and was so alarmed at the danger he was in, that the more he endeavoured to remember the word *"Sesame,"* the more his memory was confounded, and he had as much forgotten it as if he had never heard it mentioned. He threw down the bags he had loaded himself with and walked distractedly up and down the cave, without having the least regard to the riches that were round him. About noon the robbers chanced to visit their cave, and at some distance from it saw Cassim's mules straggling about the rock, with great chests on their backs. Alarmed at this novelty, they galloped full speed to the cave. They drove away the mules, which Cassim had neglected to fasten, and they strayed through the forest so far, that they were soon out of sight. The robbers never gave themselves the trouble to pursue them, being more concerned to know to whom they belonged, and while some of them searched about the rock, the captain and the rest went directly to the door, with their naked sabres in their hands, and pronouncing the proper words, it opened.

Cassim, who heard the noise of the horses' feet from the middle of the cave, never doubted of the arrival of the robbers, and his approaching death; but was resolved to make one effort to escape from them. To this end he rushed to the door, and no sooner heard the word *Sesame*, which he had forgotten, and saw the door open, than he ran out and threw the leader down, but could not escape the other robbers, who with their sabres soon deprived him of life. The first care of the robbers after this was to examine the cave. They found all the bags which Cassim had brought to the door, to be ready to load his mules, and carried them again to their places, without missing what Ali Baba had taken away before. Then holding a council, and deliberating upon this occurrence, they guessed that Cassim, when he was in, could not get out again; but could not imagine how he had entered. It came into their heads that he might have got down by the top of the cave; but the aperture by which it received light was so high, and the rocks so inaccessible without, that they gave up this conjecture. That he came in at the door they could not believe, however, unless he had the secret of making it open. In short, none of them could imagine which way he had entered; for they were all persuaded nobody knew their secret, little imagining that Ali Baba had watched them. It was a matter of the greatest importance to them to secure their

Cassim . . . was so alarmed at the danger he was in that the
more he endeavoured to remember the word Sesame the
more his memory was confounded.

riches.   They agreed therefore to cut Cassim's body into quarters,
to hang two on one side and two on the other, within the door of
the cave, to terrify any person who should attempt again to enter.
They had no sooner taken this resolution than they put it in
execution, and when they had nothing more to detain them, left
the place of their hoards well closed.   They then mounted their
horses, went to beat the roads again, and to attack the caravans
they might meet.

In the meantime, Cassim's wife was very uneasy when night
came, and her husband was not returned.   She ran to Ali Baba
in alarm, and said: "I believe, brother-in-law, that you know
Cassim, your brother, is gone to the forest, and upon what account; it is now night, and he is not returned; I am afraid some
misfortune has happened to him."   Ali Baba, who had expected
that his brother, after what he had said, would go to the forest,
had declined going himself that day, for fear of giving him any
umbrage; therefore told her, without any reflection upon her
husband's unhandsome behaviour, that she need not frighten
herself, for that certainly Cassim would not think it proper to
come into the town till the night should be pretty far advanced.

Cassim's wife, considering how much it concerned her husband to keep the business secret, was the more easily persuaded
to believe her brother-in-law.   She went home again, and waited
patiently till midnight.   She repented of her foolish curiosity,
and cursed her desire of penetrating into the affairs of her
brother and sister-in-law.   She spent all the night in weeping;
and as soon as it was day, went to them, telling them, by her tears,
the cause of her coming.   Ali Baba did not wait for his sister-in-
law to desire him to go and see what was become of Cassim, but
departed immediately with his three asses, begging of her first
to moderate her affliction.   He went to the forest, and when he

came near the rock, having seen neither his brother nor the mules in his way, was seriously alarmed at finding some blood spilt near the door, which he took for an ill omen; but when he had pronounced the word, and the door had opened, he was struck with horror at the dismal sight of his brother's body. Without adverting to the little fraternal affection his brother had shewn for him, Ali Baba went into the cave to find something to enshroud his remains, and having loaded one of his asses with them, covered them over with wood. The other two asses he loaded with bags of gold, covering them with wood also as before; and then bidding the door shut, came away; but was so cautious as to stop some time at the end of the forest, that he might not go into the town before night. When he came home, he drove the two asses loaded with gold into his little yard, and left the care of unloading them to his wife, while he led the other to his sister-in-law's house.

Ali Baba knocked at the door, which was opened by Morgiana, an intelligent slave, fruitful in inventions to insure success in the most difficult undertakings: and Ali Baba knew her to be such. When he came into the court, he unloaded the ass, and taking Morgiana aside, said to her: "The first thing I ask of you is an inviolable secrecy, both for your mistress's sake and mine. Your master's body is contained in these two bundles, and our business is, to bury him as if he had died a natural death. Go, tell your mistress I want to speak with her; and mind what I have said to you."

Morgiana went to her mistress, and Ali Baba followed her. "Well, brother," said she, with impatience, "what news do you bring me of my husband? I perceive no comfort in your countenance." "Sister," answered Ali Baba, "I cannot satisfy your inquiries unless you hear my story without speaking a word;

for it is of as great importance to you as to me to keep what has happened secret." "Alas!" said she, "this preamble lets me know that my husband is not to be found; but at the same time I know the necessity of secrecy, and I must constrain myself: say on, I will hear you."

Ali Baba then detailed the incidents of his journey, till he came to the finding of Cassim's body. "Now," said he, "sister, I have something to relate which will afflict you the more, because it is what you so little expect; but it cannot now be remedied; if my endeavours can comfort you, I offer to put that which God hath sent me to what you have, and marry you: assuring you that my wife will not be jealous, and that we shall live happily together. If this proposal is agreeable to you, we must think of acting so that my brother should appear to have died a natural death. I think you may leave the management of the business to Morgiana, and I will contribute all that lies in my power to your consolation." What could Cassim's widow do better than accept of this proposal? for though her first husband had left behind him a plentiful substance, his brother was now much richer, and by the discovery of this treasure might be still more so. Instead, therefore, of rejecting the offer, she regarded it as the sure means of comfort; and drying up her tears, which had begun to flow abundantly, and suppressing the outcries usual with women who have lost their husbands, showed Ali Baba that she approved of his proposal. Ali Baba left the widow, recommended to Morgiana to act her part well, and then returned home with his ass.

Morgiana went out at the same time to an apothecary, and asked for a sort of lozenges which he prepared, and were very efficacious in the most dangerous disorders. The apothecary inquired who was ill at her master's? She replied with a sigh, her good master Cassim himself: that they knew not what his disorder was, but that he could neither eat nor speak. After these words, Morgiana carried the lozenges home with her, and the next morning went to the same apothecary's again, and with tears in her eyes, asked for an essence which they used to give to sick people only when at the last extremity. "Alas!" said she, taking it from the apothecary, "I am afraid that this remedy will have no better effect than the lozenges; and that I shall lose my good master." On the other hand, as Ali Baba and his wife were often seen to go between Cassim's and their own house all that day, and to seem melancholy, nobody was surprised in the evening to hear the lamentable shrieks and cries of Cassim's wife and Morgiana, who gave out everywhere that her master was dead. The next morning, soon after day appeared, Morgiana, who knew a certain old cobbler that opened his stall early, before other people, went to him, and bidding him good morrow, put a piece of gold into his hand. "Well," said Baba Mustapha, which was his name, and who was a merry old fellow, looking at the gold, "this is good hansel: what must I do for it? I am ready."

"Baba Mustapha," said Morgiana, "you must take with you your sewing tackle, and go with me; but I must tell you, I shall blindfold you when you come to such a place." Baba Mustapha seemed to hesitate a little at these words. "Oh! oh!" replied he, "you would have me do something against my conscience or against my honour?" "God forbid!" said Morgiana, putting another piece of gold into his hand, "that I should ask anything that is contrary to your honour; only come along with me, and fear nothing."

Baba Mustapha went with Morgiana, who, after she had bound his eyes with a handkerchief, conveyed him to her deceased master's house, and never unloosed his eyes till he had entered the room where she had put the corpse together. "Baba Mustapha," said she, "you must make haste and sew these quarters together; and when you have done, I will give you another piece of gold." After Baba Mustapha had finished his task, she blindfolded him again, gave him the third piece of gold as she had promised, and recommending secrecy to him, carried him back to the place where she first bound his eyes, pulled off the bandage, and let him go home, but watched him that he returned toward his stall, till he was quite out of sight, for fear he should have the curiosity to return and track her.

By the time Morgiana had warmed some water to wash the body, Ali Baba came with incense to embalm it, after which it was sewn up in a winding-sheet. Not long after, the joiner, according to Ali Baba's orders, brought the bier, which Morgiana received at the door, and helped Ali Baba to put the body into it; when she went to the mosque to inform the imaum that they were ready. The people of the mosque, whose business it was to wash the dead, offered to perform their duty, but she told them that it was done already. Morgiana had scarcely got home before the imaum and the other ministers of the mosque arrived. Four neighbours carried the corpse on their shoulders to the burying-ground, following the imaum, who recited some prayers. Morgiana, as a slave to the deceased, followed the corpse, weeping, beating her breast, and tearing her hair; and Ali Baba came after with some neighbours, who often relieved the others in carrying the corpse to the burying-ground. Cassim's wife stayed at home mourning, uttering lamentable cries with the women of the neighbourhood, who came according to custom during the funeral, and joining their lamentations with hers, filled the quarter far and near with sorrow. In this manner Cassim's melancholy death was concealed and hushed up between Ali Baba, his wife, Cassim's widow, and Morgiana, with so much contrivance, that nobody in the city had the least knowledge or suspicion of the cause of it.

Three or four days after the funeral, Ali Baba removed his few goods openly to the widow's house; but the money he had taken from the robbers he conveyed thither by night: soon after the marriage with his sister-in-law was published, and as these marriages are common in the Mussulman religion, nobody was surprised. As for Cassim's warehouse, Ali Baba gave it to his own eldest son, promising that if he managed it well, he would soon give him a fortune to marry very advantageously according to his situation.

Let us now leave Ali Baba to enjoy the beginning of his good fortune, and return to the forty robbers. They came again at the appointed time to visit their retreat in the forest; but great was their surprise to find Cassim's body taken away, with some of their bags of gold. "We are certainly discovered," said the captain, "and if we do not speedily apply some remedy, shall gradually lose all the riches which we have, with so much pains and danger, been so many years amassing together. All that we can think of the loss which we have sustained is, that the thief whom we surprised had the secret of opening the door, and we arrived luckily as he was coming out: but his body being removed, and with it some of our money, plainly shows that he had an accomplice; and as it is likely that there were but two who had discovered our secret, and one has been caught, we must look narrowly after the other. What say you, my lads?" All the robbers thought the captain's proposal so advisable, that they unanimously approved of it, and agreed that they must lay all other enterprises aside, to follow this closely, and not give it up till they had succeeded.

ALI BABA AND THE FORTY THIEVES

"I expected no less," said the captain, "from your fidelity: but, first of all, one of you who is artful, and enterprising, must go into the town disguised as a traveller, to try if he can hear any talk of the strange death of the man whom we have killed, as he deserved; and endeavour to find out who he was, and where he lived. This is a matter of the first importance for us to ascertain, that we may do nothing which we may have reason to repent of, by discovering ourselves in a country where we have lived so long unknown. But to warn him who shall take upon himself this commission, and to prevent our being deceived by his giving us a false report, I ask you all, if you do not think that in case of treachery, or even error of judgment, he should suffer death?" Without waiting for the suffrages of his companions, one of the robbers started up, and said: "I submit to this condition, and think it an honour to expose my life, by taking the commission upon me; but remember, at least, if I do not succeed. that I neither wanted courage nor good will to serve the troop." After this robber had received great commendations from the captain, he disguised himself, and taking his leave of the troop that night, went into the town just at daybreak; and walked up and down, till accidentally he came to Baba Mustapha's stall, which was always open before any of the shops.

Baba Mustapha was seated with an awl in his hand, just going to work. The robber saluted him, bidding him good morrow; and perceiving that he was old, said: "Honest man, you begin to work very early: is it possible that one of your age can see so well? I question, even if it were somewhat lighter, whether you could see to stitch."

"Certainly," replied Baba Mustapha, "you must be a stranger, and do not know me; for old as I am, I have extraordinarily good eyes; and you will not doubt it when I tell you that I sewed a dead body together in a place where I had not so much light as I have now." The robber was overjoyed to think that he had addressed himself, at his first coming into the town, to a man who in all probability could give him the intelligence he wanted. "A dead body!" replied he with affected amazement. "What could you sew up a dead body for? You mean you sewed up his winding-sheet." "No, no," answered Baba Mustapha, "I perceive your meaning; you want to have me speak out, but you shall know no more." The robber wanted no farther assurance to be persuaded that he had discovered what he sought. He pulled out a piece of gold, and putting it into Baba Mustapha's hand, said to him: "I do not want to learn your secret, though I can assure you I would not divulge it, if you trusted me with it; the only thing which I desire of you is, to do me the favour to shew me the house where you stitched up the dead body."

"If I were disposed to do you that favour," replied Baba Mustapha, holding the money in his hand, ready to return it, "I assure you I cannot. I was taken to a certain place, where I was blinded, I was then led to the house, and afterward brought back again in the same manner; you see, therefore, the impossibility of my doing what you desire."

"Well," replied the robber, "you may, however, remember a little of the way that you were led blindfolded. Come, let me blind your eyes at the same place. We will walk together; perhaps you may recognise some part; and as everybody ought to be paid for his trouble, there is another piece of gold for you; gratify me in what I ask you." So saying, he put another piece of gold into his hand.

The two pieces of gold were great temptations to Baba Mustapha. He looked at them a long time in his hand, without saying a word, thinking with himself what he should do; but at last he pulled out his purse, and put them in. "I cannot assure you," said he to the robber, "that I can remember the way exactly; but since you desire, I will try what I can do." At these words Baba Mustapha rose up, to the great joy of the robber, and without shutting his shop, where he had nothing valuable to lose, he led the robber to the place where Morgiana had bound his eyes. "It was here," said Baba Mustapha, "I was blindfolded; and I turned as you see me." The robber, who had his handkerchief ready, tied it over his eyes, walked by him till he stopped, partly leading, and partly guided by him. "I think," said Baba Mustapha, "I went no farther," and he had now stopped directly at Cassim's house, where Ali Baba then lived. The thief, before he pulled off the band, marked the door with a piece of chalk, which he had ready in his hand; and then asked him if he knew whose house that was; to which Baba Mustapha replied, that as he did not live in that neighbourhood he could not tell. The robber, finding he could discover no more from Baba Mustapha, thanked him for the trouble he had taken, and left him to go back to his stall, while he returned to the forest, persuaded that he should be very well received. A little after the robber and Baba Mustapha had parted, Morgiana went out of Ali Baba's house upon some errand, and upon her return, seeing the mark the robber had made, stopped to observe it. "What can be the meaning of this mark?" said she to herself. "Somebody intends my master no good: however, with whatever intention it was done, it is advisable to guard against the worst." Accordingly, she fetched a piece of chalk, and marked two or three doors on each side in the same manner, without saying a word to her master or mistress.

In the meantime the thief rejoined his troop in the forest, and recounted to them his success. All the robbers listened to him with the utmost satisfaction; when the captain, after commending his diligence, addressing himself to them all, said: "Comrades, we have no time to lose: let us set off well armed; but that we may not excite any suspicion, let only one or two go into the town together, and join at our rendezvous, which shall be the great square. In the meantime, our comrade who brought us the good news, and I, will go and find out the house, that we may consult what had best be done."

This plan was approved of by all, and they were soon ready. They filed off in parties of two each, and got into the town without being in the least suspected. The captain, and he who had visited the town in the morning as spy, came in the last. He led the captain into the street where he had marked Ali Baba's residence; and when they came to the first of the houses which Morgiana had marked, he pointed it out. But the captain observed that the next door was chalked in the same manner; and shewing it to his guide, asked him which house it was, that, or the first? The guide was so confounded, that he knew not what answer to make; but still more puzzled, when he saw five or six houses similarly marked. He assured the captain, with an oath, that he had marked but one, and could not tell who had chalked the rest so that he could not distinguish the house which the cobbler had stopped at.

The captain, finding that their design had proved abortive, went directly to the place of rendezvous, and told the first of his troop whom he met that they had lost their labour, and must return to their cave. When the troop was all got together, the captain told them the reason of their returning; and presently the conductor was declared by all worthy of death. He condemned himself, acknowledging that he ought to have taken better precaution, and prepared to receive the stroke from him who was appointed to cut off his head. Another of the gang, who promised himself that he should succeed better, immediately presented himself, and his offer being accepted, he went and corrupted Baba Mustapha, as the other had done; and being shewn the house, marked it in a place more remote from sight, with red chalk.

Not long after, Morgiana, whose eyes nothing could escape, went out, and seeing the red chalk, and arguing with herself as she had done before, marked the other neighbours' houses in the same place and manner. The robber, at his return to his company, valued himself much on the precaution he had taken, which he looked upon as an infallible way of distinguishing Ali Baba's house from the others; and the captain and all of them thought it must succeed. They conveyed themselves into the town with the same precaution as before; but when the robber and his captain came to the street, they found the same difficulty: at which the captain was enraged, and the robber in as great confusion as his predecessor. Thus the captain and his troop were forced to retire a second time, and much more dissatisfied; while the unfortunate robber, who had been the author of the mistake, underwent the same punishment; which he willingly submitted to.

The captain, having lost two brave fellows of his troop, was afraid of diminishing it too much by pursuing this plan to get information of the residence of their plunderer. He found by their example that their heads were not so good as their hands on such occasions; and therefore resolved to take upon himself the important commission. Accordingly, he went and addressed himself to Baba Mustapha, who did him the same service he had done to the other robbers. He did not set any particular mark on the house, but examined and observed it so carefully, by passing often by it, that it was impossible for him to mistake it.

The captain, well satisfied with his attempt, and informed of what he wanted to know, returned to the forest; and when he came into the cave, where the troop waited for him, said: "Now, comrades, nothing can prevent our full revenge, as I am certain of the house, and in my way hither I have thought how to put it into execution, but if any one can form a better expedient, let him communicate it." He then told them his contrivance; and as they approved of it, ordered them to go into the villages about, and buy nineteen mules, with thirty-eight large leather jars, one full of oil, and the others empty. In two or three days' time the robbers had purchased the mules and jars, and as the mouths of the jars were rather too narrow for his purpose, the captain caused them to be widened; and after having put one of his men into each, with the weapons which he thought fit, leaving open the seam which had been undone to leave them room to breathe, he rubbed the jars on the outside with oil from the full vessel. Things being thus prepared, when the nineteen mules were loaded with thirty-seven robbers in jars, and the jar of oil, the captain, as their driver, set out with them, and reached the town by the dusk of the evening, as he had intended. He led them through the streets till he came to Ali Baba's, at whose door he designed to have knocked; but was prevented by his sitting there after supper to take a little fresh air. He stopped his mules, addressed himself to him, and said: "I have brought some oil a great way, to sell at to-morrow's market; and it is now so late that I do not know where to lodge. If I should not be troublesome to you, do me the favour to let me pass the night with you, and I shall be very much obliged by your hospitality."

ALI BABA AND THE FORTY THIEVES

Though Ali Baba had seen the captain of the robbers in the forest, and had heard him speak, it was hardly possible to know him in the disguise of an oil-merchant. He told him he should be welcome, and immediately opened his gates for the mules to go into the yard. At the same time he called to a slave, and ordered him, when the mules were unloaded, to put them into the stable, and give them fodder; and then went to Morgiana, to bid her get a good supper. He did more. When he saw the captain had unloaded his mules, and that they were put into the stables as he had ordered, and he was looking for a place to pass the night in the air, he brought him into the hall where he received his company, telling him he would not suffer him to be in the court. The captain excused himself on pretence of not being troublesome; but really to have room to execute his design, and it was not till after the most pressing importunity that he yielded. Ali Baba, not content to keep company, till supper was ready, with the man who had a design on his life, continued talking with him till it was ended, and repeating his offer of service. The captain rose up at the same time with his host; and while Ali Baba went to speak to Morgiana he withdrew into the yard, under pretence of looking at his mules. Ali Baba, after charging Morgiana afresh to take care of his guest, said to her: "To-morrow morning I design to go to the bath before day; take care my bathing linens be ready, give them to Abdoollah," which was the slave's name, "and make me some good broth against I return." After this he went to bed.

In the meantime, the captain went from the stable to give his people orders what to do; and beginning at the first jar, and so on to the last, said to each man: "As soon as I throw some stones out of the chamber window where I lie, do not fail to cut the jar open with the knife you have about you for the purpose, and come out, and I will immediately join you." After this he returned into the house, when Morgiana, taking up a light, conducted him to his chamber, where she left him; and he, to avoid any suspicion, put the light out soon after, and laid himself down in his clothes, that he might be the more ready to rise.

Morgiana, remembering Ali Baba's orders, got his bathing linens ready, and ordered Abdoollah to set on the pot for the broth; but while she was preparing it, the lamp went out, and there was no more oil in the house, nor any candles. What to do she did not know, for the broth must be made. Abdoollah seeing her very uneasy, said: "Do not fret and tease yourself, but go into the yard, and take some oil out of one of the jars." Morgiana thanked Abdoollah for his advice, took the oil-pot, and went into the yard; when as she came nigh the first jar, the robber within said softly: "Is it time?" Though the robber spoke low, Morgiana was struck with the voice the more, because the captain, when he unloaded the mules, had taken the lids off this and all the other jars to give air to his men, who were ill enough at their ease, almost wanting room to breathe. As much surprised as Morgiana naturally was at finding a man in a jar, instead of the oil she wanted, many would have made such an outcry as to have given an alarm; whereas Morgiana comprehending immediately the importance of keeping silence, and the necessity of applying a speedy remedy without noise, conceived at once the means, and collecting herself without shewing the least emotion, answered: "Not yet, but presently." She went in this manner to all the jars, giving the same answer, till she came to the jar of oil.

By this means, Morgiana found that her master Ali Baba, who thought that he had entertained an oil merchant, had admitted thirty-eight robbers into his house, regarding this pretended merchant as their captain. She made what haste she could to fill her oil-pot, and returned into her kitchen; where, as soon as she had lighted her lamp, she took a great kettle, went again to the oil-jar, filled the kettle, set it on a large wood-fire, and as soon as it boiled went and poured enough into every jar to stifle and destroy the robber within.

When this action, worthy of the courage of Morgiana, was executed without any noise, she returned into the kitchen with the empty kettle; and having put out the great fire she had made to boil the oil, and leaving just enough to make the broth, put out the lamp also, and remained silent; resolving not to go to rest till she had observed what might follow through a window of the kitchen, which opened into the yard.

She had not waited long before the captain of the robbers got up, opened the window, and finding no light, and hearing no noise, or any one stirring in the house, gave the appointed signal, by throwing little stones, several of which hit the jars, as he doubted not by the sound they gave. He then listened, but not hearing or perceiving anything whereby he could judge that his companions stirred, he began to grow very uneasy, threw stones again a second and also a third time, and could not comprehend the reason that none of them should answer his signal. Much alarmed, he went softly down into the yard, and going to the first jar, whilst asking the robber, whom he thought alive, if he was in readiness, smelt the hot boiled oil, which sent forth a steam out of the jar. Hence he suspected that his plot to murder Ali Baba and plunder his house was discovered. Examining all the jars one after another, he found that all the members of his gang were dead; and by the oil he missed out of the last jar guessed the means and manner of their death. Enraged to despair at having failed in his design, he forced the lock of a door that led from the yard to the garden, and climbing over the walls, made his escape.

When Morgiana heard no noise, and found, after waiting some time, that the captain did not return, she concluded that he had chosen rather to make his escape by the garden than the street door, which was double-locked. Satisfied and pleased to have succeeded so well, in saving her master and family, she went to bed.

Ali Baba rose before day, and, followed by his slave, went to the baths, entirely ignorant of the important event which had happened at home; for Morgiana had not thought it safe to wake him before, for fear of losing her opportunity; and after her successful exploit she thought it needless to disturb him.

When he returned from the baths, the sun was risen; he was very much surprised to see the oil jars and that the merchant was not gone with the mules. He asked Morgiana, who opened the door, and had let all things stand as they were, that he might see them, the reason of it. "My good master," answered she, "God preserve you and all your family; you will be better informed of what you wish to know when you have seen what I have to show you, if you will but give yourself the trouble to follow me."

As soon as Morgiana had shut the door, Ali Baba followed her; when she requested him to look into the first jar and see if there was any oil. Ali Baba did so, and seeing a man, started back in alarm, and cried out. "Do not be afraid," said Morgiana; "the man you see there can neither do you nor anybody else any harm. He is dead." "Ah, Morgiana!" said Ali Baba, "what is it you show me? Explain yourself." "I will," replied Morgiana; "moderate your astonishment, and do not excite the curiosity of your neighbours. Look into all the other jars."

ALI BABA AND THE FORTY THIEVES

Ali Baba examined all the other jars, and when he came to that which had the oil in, found it prodigiously sunk, and stood for some time motionless, sometimes looking at the jars, and sometimes at Morgiana, without saying a word, so great was his surprise: at last, when he had recovered himself, he said: "And what is become of the merchant?"

"Merchant!" answered she, "he is as much one as I am; I will tell you who he is, and what is become of him: but you had better hear the story in your own chamber; for it is time for your health that you had your broth after your bathing."

While Ali Baba retired to his chamber, Morgiana went into the kitchen to fetch the broth, but before he would drink it, he first entreated her to satisfy his impatience, and tell him what had happened, with all the circumstances; and she obeyed him.

"This," she said, when she had completed her story, "is the account you asked of me; and I am convinced it is the consequence of what I observed some days ago, but did not think fit to acquaint you with; for when I came in one morning early I found our street door marked with white chalk, and the next morning with red; upon which, both times without knowing what was the intention of those chalks, I marked two or three neighbours' doors on each side in the same manner. If you reflect on this, and what has since happened, you will find it to be a plot of the robbers of the forest, of whose gang there are two wanting, and now they are reduced to three: all this shows that they had sworn your destruction, and it is proper you should be upon your guard, while there is one of them alive: for my part, I shall neglect nothing necessary to your preservation, as I am in duty bound."

When Morgiana had left off speaking, Ali Baba was so sensible of the great service she had done him, that he said to her: "I will not die without rewarding you as you deserve; I owe my life to you, and for the first token of my acknowledgment, give you your liberty from this moment, till I can complete your recompense as I intend. I am persuaded with you, that the forty robbers have laid snares for my destruction. God, by your means, has delivered me from them as yet, and I hope will continue to preserve me from their wicked designs, and deliver the world from their persecution. All that we have to do is to bury the bodies of these pests of mankind immediately, and with all the secrecy imaginable, that nobody may suspect what is become of them. But that labour Abdoollah and I will undertake."

Ali Baba's garden was very long, and shaded at the farther end by a great number of large trees. Under these he and the slave dug a trench, long and wide enough to hold all the robbers. Afterward they lifted the bodies out of the jars, took away their weapons, carried them to the end of the garden, laid them in the trench, and levelled the ground again. When this was done, Ali Baba hid the jars and weapons; and as he had no occasion for the mules, he sent them at different times to be sold in the market by his slave.

While Ali Baba took these measures to prevent the public from knowing how he came by his riches in so short a time, the captain of the forty robbers returned to the forest with inconceivable mortification; and in his confusion at his ill success, so contrary to what he had promised himself, entered the cave, not being able, all the way from the town, to come to any resolution how to revenge himself of Ali Baba.

The loneliness of the gloomy cavern became frightful to him. "Where are you, my brave lads," cried he, "old companions of my watchings, inroads, and labour? What can I do without you? Did I collect you only to lose you by so base a fate, and so unworthy of your courage! Had you died with your sabres in your hands, like brave men, my regret had been less! When shall I enlist so gallant a troop again? And if I could, can I undertake it without exposing so much gold and treasure to him who hath already enriched himself out of it? I cannot, I ought not to think of it, before I have taken away his life. I will undertake that alone, which I could not accomplish with your powerful assistance; and when I have taken measures to secure this treasure from being pillaged, I will provide for it new masters and successors after me, who shall preserve and augment it to all posterity." This resolution being taken, he was not at a loss how to execute his purpose; but full of hopes, slept all that night very quietly.

When he awoke early next morning, he dressed himself, agreeably to the project he had formed, went to the town, and took a lodging in a khan. As he expected what had happened at Ali Baba's might make a great noise, he asked his host what news there was in the city? Upon which the innkeeper told him a great many circumstances, which did not concern him in the least. He judged by this, that the reason why Ali Baba kept his affairs so secret, was for fear people should know where the treasure lay; and because he knew his life would be sought on account of it. This urged him the more to neglect nothing to rid himself of so cautious an enemy.

The captain now assumed the character of a merchant, and conveyed gradually a great many sorts of rich stuffs and fine linen to his lodging from the cavern, but with all the necessary precautions imaginable to conceal the place whence he brought them. In order to dispose of the merchandise, when he had amassed them together, he took a warehouse, which happened to be opposite to Cassim's, which Ali Baba's son had occupied since the death of his uncle.

He took the name of Khaujeh Houssain, and as a new-comer, was, according to custom, extremely civil and complaisant to all the merchants his neighbours. Ali Baba's son was from his vicinity one of the first to converse with Khaujeh Houssain, who strove to cultivate his friendship more particularly when, two or three days after he was settled, he recognised Ali Baba, who came to see his son, and stopped to talk with him as he was accustomed to do. When he was gone, the impostor learnt from his son who he was. He increased his assiduities, caressed him in the most engaging manner, made him some small presents, and often asked him to dine and sup with him.

Ali Baba's son did not choose to lie under such obligation to Khaujeh Houssain, without making the like return; but was so much straitened for want of room in his house, that he could not entertain him so well as he wished; he therefore acquainted his father Ali Baba with his intention, and told him that it did not look well for him to receive such favours from Khaujeh Houssain without inviting him in return.

Ali Baba, with great pleasure, took the treat upon himself. "Son," said he, "to-morrow being Friday, which is a day that the shops of such great merchants as Khaujeh Houssain and yourself are shut, get him to take a walk with you, and as you come back, pass by my door and call in. It will look better to have it happen accidentally, than if you gave him a formal invitation. I will go and order Morgiana to provide a supper."

The next day Ali Baba's son and Khaujeh Houssain met by appointment, took their walk, and as they returned, Ali Baba's son led Khaujeh Houssain through the street where his father lived; and when they came to the house, stopped and knocked at the door. "This, sir," said he, "is my father's house; who, from the account I have given him of your friendship, charged me to procure him the honour of your acquaintance."

Though it was the sole aim of Khaujeh Houssain to introduce himself into Ali Baba's house, that he might kill him without hazarding his own life or making any noise; yet he excused himself, and offered to take his leave. But a slave having opened the door, Ali Baba's son took him obligingly by the hand, and in a manner forced him in.

Ali Baba received Khaujeh Houssain with a smiling countenance, and in the most obliging manner. He thanked him for all the favours he had done his son; adding withal, the obligation was the greater, as he was a young man not much acquainted with the world.

Khaujeh Houssain returned the compliment, by assuring Ali Baba, that though his son might not have acquired the experience of older men, he had good sense equal to the knowledge of many others. After a little more conversation on different subjects, he offered again to take his leave; when Ali Baba, stopping him, said: "Where are you going, sir, in so much haste? I beg you would do me the honour to sup with me, though what I have to give you is not worth your acceptance; but such as it is, I hope you will accept it as heartily as I give it." "Sir," replied Khaujeh Houssain, "I am thoroughly persuaded of your good will; and if I ask the favour of you not to take it ill that I do not accept your obliging invitation, I beg of you to believe that it does not proceed from any slight or intention to affront, but from a reason which you would approve if you knew it.

"And what may that reason be, sir," replied Ali Baba, "if I may be so bold as to ask you?" "It is," answered Khaujeh Houssain, "that I can eat no victuals that have any salt in them; therefore judge how I should feel at your table." "If that is the only reason," said Ali Baba, "it ought not to deprive me of the honour of your company at supper; for, in the first place, there is no salt ever put into my bread, and as to the meat we shall have to-night, I promise you there shall be none in that. Therefore you must do me the favour to stay. I will return immediately."

Ali Baba went into the kitchen, and ordered Morgiana to put no salt to the meat that was to be dressed that night; and to make quickly two or three ragouts besides what he had ordered, but be sure to put no salt in them.

Morgiana, who was always ready to obey her master, could not help seeming somewhat dissatisfied at his strange order. "Who is this difficult man," said she, "who eats no salt with his meat? Your supper will be spoiled, if I keep it back so long." "Do not be angry, Morgiana," replied Ali Baba; "he is an honest man; therefore do as I bid you."

Morgiana obeyed, though with no little reluctance, and had a curiosity to see this man who ate no salt. To this end, when she had finished what she had to do in the kitchen, she helped Abdoollah to carry up the dishes; and looking at Khaujeh Houssain, knew him at first sight, notwithstanding his disguise, to be the captain of the robbers, and examining him very carefully, perceived that he had a dagger under his garment. "I am not in the least amazed," said she to herself, "that this wicked wretch, who is my master's greatest enemy, would eat no salt with him, since he intends to assassinate him; but I will prevent him."

Morgiana, while they were eating, made the necessary preparations for executing one of the boldest acts ever meditated, and had just determined, when Abdoollah came for the dessert of fruit, which she carried up, and as soon as he had taken the meat away, set upon the table; after that, she placed three glasses

ALI BABA AND THE FORTY THIEVES

by Ali Baba, and going out, took Abdoollah with her to sup, and to give Ali Baba the more liberty of conversation with his guest.

Khaujeh Houssain, or rather the captain of the robbers, thought he had now a favourable opportunity of being revenged on Ali Baba. "I will," said he to himself, "make the father and son both drunk: the son, whose life I intend to spare, will not be able to prevent my stabbing his father to the heart; and while the slaves are at supper, or asleep in the kitchen, I can make my escape over the gardens as before."

Instead of going to supper, Morgiana, who had penetrated the intentions of the counterfeit Khaujeh Houssain, would not give him time to put his villainous design into execution, but dressed herself neatly with a suitable head-dress like a dancer, girded her waist with a silver-gilt girdle, to which there hung a poniard with a hilt and guard of the same metal, and put a handsome mask on her face. When she had thus disguised herself, she said to Abdoollah: "Take your tabor, and let us go and divert our master and his son's guest, as we do sometimes when he is alone."

Abdoollah took his tabor and played all the way into the hall before Morgiana, who when she came to the door made a low obeisance, with a deliberate air, in order to draw attention, and by way of asking leave to exhibit her skill. Abdoollah, seeing that his master had a mind to say something, left off playing. "Come in, Morgiana," said Ali Baba, "and let Khaujeh Houssain see what you can do, that he may tell us what he thinks of you. But, sir," said he, turning toward his guest, "do not think that I put myself to any expense to give you this diversion, since these are my slave and my cook and housekeeper; and I hope you will not find the entertainment they give us disagreeable."

Khaujeh Houssain, who did not expect this diversion after supper, began to fear he should not be able to improve the opportunity he thought he had found: but hoped, if he now missed his aim, to secure it another time, by keeping up a friendly correspondence with the father and son; therefore, though he could have wished Ali Baba would have declined the dance, he had the complaisance to express his satisfaction at what he saw pleased his host.

As soon as Abdoollah saw that Ali Baba and Khaujeh Houssain had done talking, he began to play on the tabor, and accompanied it with an air; to which Morgiana, who was an excellent performer, danced in such a manner as would have created admiration in any other company besides that before which she now exhibited, among whom, perhaps, none but the false Khaujeh Houssain was in the least attentive to her, the rest having seen her so frequently.

After she had danced several dances with equal propriety and grace, she drew the poniard, and holding it in her hand, began a dance, in which she outdid herself, by the many different figures, light movements, and the surprising leaps and wonderful exertions with which she accompanied it. Sometimes she presented the poniard to one person's breast, sometimes to another's, and oftentimes seemed to strike her own. At last, as if she was out of breath, she snatched the tabor from Abdoollah with her left hand, and holding the dagger in her right, presented the other side of the tabor, after the manner of those who get a livelihood by dancing, and solicit the liberality of the spectators.

Ali Baba put a piece of gold into the tabor, as did also his son: and Khaujeh Houssain, seeing that she was coming to him, had pulled his purse out of his bosom to make her a present; but while he was putting his hand into it, Morgiana, with a courage and resolution worthy of herself, plunged the poniard into his heart. Ali Baba and his son, shocked at this action, cried out aloud. "Unhappy wretch!" exclaimed Ali Baba, "what have you done to ruin me and my family?" "It was to preserve, not to ruin you," answered Morgiana; "for see here," continued she (opening the pretended Khaujeh Houssain's garment, and showing the dagger), "what an enemy you had entertained! Look well at him, and you will find him to be both the fictitious oil-merchant, and the captain of the gang of forty robbers. Remember, too, that he would eat no salt with you; and what would you have more to persuade you of his wicked design? Before I saw him, I suspected him as soon as you told me you had such a guest. I knew him, and you now find that my suspicion was not groundless."

Ali Baba, who immediately felt the new obligation he had to Morgiana for saving his life a second time, embraced her: "Morgiana," said he, "I gave you your liberty, and then promised you that my gratitude should not stop there, but that I would soon give you higher proofs of its sincerity, which I now do by making you my daughter-in-law." Then addressing himself to his son, he said: "I believe you, son, to be so dutiful a child, that you will not refuse Morgiana for your wife. You see that Khaujeh Houssain sought your friendship with a treacherous design to take away my life; and, if he had succeeded, there is no doubt but he would have sacrificed you also to his revenge. Consider, that by marrying Morgiana you marry the preserver of my family and your own."

The son, far from showing any dislike, readily consented to the marriage; not only because he would not disobey his father, but also because it was agreeable to his inclination.

After this, they thought of burying the captain of the robbers with his comrades, and did it so privately that nobody discovered their bones till many years after, when no one had any concern in the publication of this remarkable history.

A few days afterward, Ali Baba celebrated the nuptials of his son and Morgiana with great solemnity, a sumptuous feast, and the usual dancing and spectacles; and had the satisfaction to see that his friends and neighbours, whom he invited, had no knowledge of the true motives of the marriage; but that those who were not unacquainted with Morgiana's good qualities commended his generosity and goodness of heart.

Ali Baba forbore, after this marriage, from going again to the robbers' cave, as he had done, for fear of being surprised, from the time he had brought away his brother Cassim's mangled remains. He had kept away after the death of the thirty-seven robbers and their captain, supposing the other two, whom he could get no account of, might be alive.

At the year's end, when he found that they had not made any attempt to disturb him, he had the curiosity to make another journey, taking the necessary precautions for his safety. He mounted his horse, and when he came to the cave, and saw no footsteps of men or beasts, looked upon it as a good sign. He alighted, tied his horse to a tree, then approaching the entrance and pronouncing the words, *Open, Sesame!* the door opened. He entered the cavern, and by the condition he found things in, judged that nobody had been there since the false Khaujeh Houssain, when he had fetched the goods for his shop; that the gang of forty robbers was completely destroyed, and no longer doubted that he was the only person in the world who had the secret of opening the cave, so that all the treasure was at his sole disposal. Having brought with him a wallet, he put into it as much gold as his horse would carry, and returned to town.

Afterward Ali Baba carried his son to the cave, and taught him the secret, which they handed down to their posterity, who, using their good fortune with moderation, lived in great honour and splendour.

THE HISTORY OF CODADAD AND HIS BROTHERS

THERE formerly reigned in the city of Harran a most magnificent and potent sultan, who loved his subjects, and was equally beloved by them. He was endued with all virtues, and wanted nothing to complete his happiness but an heir. He continually prayed to Heaven for a child; and one night in his sleep, a prophet appeared to him and said: "Your prayers are heard; you have obtained what you have desired; rise as soon as you awake, go to your prayers, and make two genuflexions; then walk into the garden of your palace, call your gardener, and bid him bring you a pomegranate; eat as many of the seeds as you please, and your wishes shall be accomplished."

The sultan calling to mind his dream when he awoke, returned thanks to Heaven, got up, prayed, made two genuflexions, and then went into his garden, where he took fifty pomegranate seeds, which he counted, and ate. Some time afterward forty-nine of his wives presented him with sons, each one as vigorous as a young palm-tree, but Pirouzè, the fiftieth wife, remained childless. The sultan, therefore, took an aversion to this lady and would have had her put to death had not his vizier prevented him, advising rather that she be sent to Samaria, to her brother, Sultan Samer, with orders that she be well treated.

Not long after Pirouzè had been retired to her brother's country, a most beautiful prince was born to her. The prince of Samaria wrote immediately to the sultan of Harran, to acquaint him with the birth of a son, and to congratulate him on the occasion. The sultan was much rejoiced at this intelligence, and answered Prince Samer as follows: "Cousin, all my other wives have each presented me with a prince. I desire you to educate the child of Pirouzè, to give him the name of Codadad, and to send him to me when I may apply for him."

The prince of Samaria spared nothing that might improve the education of his nephew. He taught him to ride, draw the bow, and all other accomplishments becoming the son of a sovereign; so that Codadad, at eighteen years of age, was looked upon as a prodigy. The young prince, being inspired with a courage worthy his birth, said one day to his mother: "Madam, I begin to grow weary of Samaria; I feel a passion for glory; give me leave to seek it amidst the perils of war. My father the sultan of Harran has many enemies. Why does he not call me to his assistance? Must I spend my life in sloth, when all my brothers have the happiness to be fighting by his side?" "My son," answered Pirouzè, "I am no less impatient to have your name become famous; I could wish you had already signalised yourself against your father's enemies; but we must wait till he requires it." "No, madam," replied Codadad, "I have already waited too long. I burn to see the sultan, and am tempted to offer him my service, as a young stranger: no doubt but he will accept of it, and I will not discover myself till I have performed some glorious actions." Pirouzè approved of his generous resolutions, and Codadad departed from Samaria, as if he had been going to the chase, without acquainting Prince Samer, lest he should thwart his design.

He was mounted on a white charger, who had a bit and shoes of gold, his housing was of blue satin embroidered with pearls; the hilt of his cimeter was of one single diamond, and the scabbard of sandalwood, adorned with emeralds and rubies, and on his shoulder he carried his bow and quiver. In this equipage, which greatly set off his handsome person, he arrived at the city of Harran, and soon found means to offer his service to the sultan; who being charmed with his beauty, and perhaps indeed by natural sympathy, gave him a favourable reception, and asked his name and quality. "Sir," answered Codadad, "I am son to an emir of Grand Cairo; an inclination to travel has made me quit my country, and understanding that you were engaged in war, I am come to your court to offer your majesty my service." The sultan, upon hearing this, shewed him extraordinary kindness, and gave him a command in his army.

The young prince soon gained the esteem of the officers, and was admired by the soldiers. Having no less wit than courage, he so far advanced himself in the sultan's esteem, as to become his favourite. All the ministers and other courtiers daily resorted to Codadad, and were so eager to purchase his friendship, that they neglected the sultan's sons. The princes could not but resent this conduct, and all conceived an implacable hatred against him; but the sultan's affection daily increasing, he was never weary of giving him fresh testimonies of his regard. He always would have him near his person; and to shew his high opinion of his wisdom and prudence, committed to his care the other princes, though he was of the same age as they; so that Codadad was made governor of his brothers.

This only served to heighten their hatred. "Is it come to this," said they, "that the sultan, not satisfied with loving a stranger more than us, will have him to be our governor, and not allow us to act without his leave? This is not to be endured. We must rid ourselves of this foreigner." "Let us go together," said one of them, "and despatch him." "No, no," answered another; "we had better be cautious how we sacrifice ourselves. His death would render us odious to the sultan. Let us destroy him by some stratagem. We will ask his permission to hunt, and, when at a distance from the palace, proceed to some other city and stay there some time. The sultan will wonder at our absence, and perceiving we do not return, perhaps put the stranger to death, or at least will banish him from court, for suffering us to leave the palace."

All the princes applauded this artifice. They went together to Codadad, and desired him to allow them to take the diversion of hunting, promising to return the same day. Pirouzè's son was taken in the snare, and granted the permission his brothers desired. They set out, but never returned. They had been three days absent, when the sultan asked Codadad where the princes were, for it was long since he had seen them. "Sir," answered Codadad, after making a profound reverence, "they have been hunting these three days, but they promised me they would return sooner." The sultan grew uneasy, and his uneasiness increased when he perceived the princes did not return the next day. He could not check his anger: "Indiscreet stranger," said he to Codadad, "why did you let my sons go without bearing them company? Go, seek them immediately, and bring them to me, or your life shall be forfeited."

These words chilled with alarm Pirouzè's unfortunate son. He armed himself, departed from the city, and like a shepherd who had lost his flock, searched the country for his brothers, inquiring at every village whether they had been seen; but hearing no news of them, abandoned himself to the most lively grief. He was inconsolable for having given the princes permission to hunt, or for not having borne them company.

After some days spent in fruitless search, he came to a plain of prodigious extent, in the midst whereof was a palace built of black marble. He drew near, and at one of the windows beheld a most beautiful lady; but set off with no other ornament than her own charms; for her hair was dishevelled, her garments torn, and on her countenance appeared all the marks of affliction. As soon as she saw Codadad, and judged he might hear her, she directed her discourse to him, saying: "Young man, depart from this fatal place, or you will soon fall into the hands of the monster that inhabits it: a black, who feeds only on human blood, resides in this palace; he seizes all persons whom their ill fate conducts to this plain, and shuts them up in his dungeons, whence they are never released, but to be devoured by him."

"Madam," answered Codadad, "tell me who you are, and be not concerned for myself." "I am a lady of quality of Grand Cairo," replied the captive; "I was passing by this castle yesterday, on my way to Bagdad, and met with the black, who killed all my attendants, and brought me hither. I beg of you," she cried, "to make your escape: the black will soon return; he is gone out to pursue some travellers he espied at a distance on the plain. Lose no time, but fly."

She had scarcely done speaking before the black appeared. He was of monstrous bulk, and of a dreadful aspect, mounted on a large Tartar horse, and bore a heavy cimeter, that none but himself could wield. The prince seeing him, was amazed at his gigantic stature, directed his prayers to Heaven to assist him, then drew his own cimeter, and firmly awaited his approach. The monster, despising so inconsiderable an enemy, called to him to submit without fighting. Codadad by his conduct shewed that he was resolved to defend his life; for rushing upon the black, he wounded him on the knee. The monster, feeling himself wounded, uttered such a dreadful yell as made all the plain resound. He grew furious and foamed with rage, and raising himself on his stirrups, made at Codadad with his dreadful

cimeter. The blow was so violent, that it would have put an
end to the young prince, had not he avoided it by a sudden
spring. The cimeter made a horrible hissing in the air: but,
before the black could have time to make a second blow, Codadad
struck him on his right arm with such force that he cut it off.
The dreadful cimeter fell with the hand that held it, and the black,
yielding under the violence of the stroke, lost his stirrups, and
made the earth shake with the weight of his fall. The prince
alighted at the same time, and cut off his enemy's head. Just
then the lady, who had been a spectator of the combat, and was
still offering up her earnest prayers to Heaven for the young hero,
uttered a shriek of joy, and said to Codadad: "Prince and
Deliverer, finish the work you have begun; the black has the
keys of this castle, take them and deliver me out of prison."

The prince searched the wretch as he lay stretched on the
ground, and found several keys. He opened the first door, and
entered a court, where he saw the lady coming to meet him; she
would have cast herself at his feet, the better to express her
gratitude, but he would not permit her. She commended his
valour, and extolled him above all the heroes in the world. He
returned her compliments; and she appeared still more lovely
to him near, than she had done at a distance. I know not
whether she felt more joy at being delivered from the desperate
danger she had been in, than he for having done so considerable a
service to so beautiful a person.

Their conversation was interrupted by dismal cries and
groans. "What do I hear?" said Codadad; "whence come
these miserable lamentations, which pierce my ears?" "My
lord," said the lady, pointing to a little door in the court, "they
come from thence. There are I know not how many wretched
persons whom fate has thrown into the hands of the black.

They are all chained, and the monster drew out one every day to devour."

"It is an addition to my joy," answered the young prince, "to understand that my victory will save the lives of those unfortunate beings. Come with me, madam, to partake in the satisfaction of giving them their liberty." Having so said, they advanced toward the door of the dungeon, where Codadad, pitying them, and impatient to put an end to their sufferings, presently put one of the keys into the lock. The noise made all the unfortunate captives, who concluded it was the black coming, according to custom, to seize one of them to devour, redouble their cries and groans.

In the meantime, the prince had opened the door; he went down a steep staircase into a deep vault, which received some feeble light from a little window, and in which there were above a hundred persons, bound to stakes. "Unfortunate travellers," said he to them, "who only expected the moment of an approaching death, give thanks to Heaven which has this day delivered you by my means. I have slain the black by whom you were to be devoured, and am come to knock off your chains." The prisoners hearing these words, gave a shout of mingled joy and surprise. Codadad and the lady began to unbind them; and as soon as any of them were loose, they helped to take off the fetters from the rest; so that in a short time they were all at liberty.

They then kneeled down, and having returned thanks to Codadad for what he had done for them, went out of the dungeon; but when they were come into the court, how was the prince surprised to see among the prisoners those he was in search of, and almost without hopes to find! "Princes," cried he, "is it you whom I behold? May I flatter myself that it is in my power to restore you to the sultan your father, who is inconsolable for the loss of you? Are you all here alive? Alas! the death of one of you will suffice to damp the joy I feel for having delivered you."

The forty-nine princes all made themselves known to Codadad, who embraced them one after another, and told them how uneasy their father was on account of their absence. They gave their deliverer all the commendations he deserved, as did the other prisoners, who could not find words expressive enough to declare their gratitude. Codadad, with them, searched the whole castle, where was immense wealth: curious silks, gold brocades, Persian carpets, China satins, and an infinite quantity of other goods, which the black had taken from the caravans he had plundered, a considerable part whereof belonged to the prisoners Codadad had then liberated. Every man knew and claimed his property. The prince restored them their own, and divided the rest of the merchandise among them. Then he said to them: "How will you carry away your goods? We are here in a desert place, and there is no likelihood of your getting horses." "My lord," answered one of the prisoners, "the black robbed us of our camels, as well as of our goods, and perhaps they may be in the stables of this castle." "That is not unlikely," replied Codadad; "let us examine." Accordingly they went to the stables, where they not only found the camels, but also the horses belonging to the sultan of Harran's sons. All the merchants, overjoyed that they had recovered their goods and camels, together with their liberty, thought of nothing but prosecuting their journey; but first repeated their thanks to their deliverer.

When they were gone, Codadad, directing his discourse to the lady, said: "What place, madam, do you desire to go to? I intend to bear you company to the spot you shall choose for your retreat, and I question not but that all these princes will do the same." The sultan of Harran's sons protested to the lady, that they would not leave her till she was restored to her friends.

"Princes," said she, "I am of a country too remote from here; and, besides that, it would be abusing your generosity to oblige you to travel so far. I must confess that I have left my native country for ever. I told you that I was a lady of Grand Cairo; but since you have shewn me so much favour, I should be much in the wrong in concealing the truth from you: I am a sultan's daughter. A usurper has possessed himself of my father's throne, after having murdered him, and I have been forced to fly to save my life."

Codadad and his brothers requested the princess to tell them her story, and after thanking them for their repeated protestations of readiness to serve her, she could not refuse to satisfy their curiosity, and began the recital of her adventures in the following manner.

"There was in a certain island," said the princess, "a great city called Deryabar, governed by a magnificent and virtuous sultan, who had no children, which was the only blessing wanting to make him happy. He continually addressed his prayers to Heaven, but Heaven only partially granted his requests, for the queen his wife, after a long expectation, brought forth a daughter.

"I am that unfortunate princess; my father was rather grieved than pleased at my birth; but he submitted to the will of God, and caused me to be educated with all possible care, being resolved, since he had no son, to teach me the art of ruling, that I might supply his place after his death.

"There was, at the court of Deryabar, an orphan youth of good birth whom the sultan, my father, had befriended and educated according to his rank. He was very handsome, and, not wanting ability, found means to please my father, who conceived a great friendship for him. All the courtiers perceived it, and guessed that the young man might in the end be my husband. In this idea, and looking on him already as heir to the crown, they made their court to him, and every one endeavoured to gain his favour. He soon saw into their designs, and forgetting the distance there was between our conditions, flattered himself with the hopes that my father was fond enough of him to prefer him before all the princes in the world. He went farther; for the sultan not offering me to him as soon as he could have wished, he had the boldness to ask me of him. Whatever punishment his insolence deserved, my father was satisfied with telling him he had other thoughts in relation to me. The youth was incensed at this refusal; he resented the contempt, as if he had asked some maid of ordinary extraction, or as if his birth had been equal to mine. Nor did he stop here, but resolved to be revenged on the sultan, and with unparalleled ingratitude conspired against him. In short, he murdered him, and caused himself to be proclaimed sovereign of Deryabar. The grand vizier, however, while the usurper was butchering my father came to carry me away from the palace, and secured me in a friend's house, till a vessel he had provided was ready to sail. I then left the island, attended only by a governess and that generous minister, who chose rather to follow his master's daughter than to submit to a tyrant.

"The grand vizier designed to carry me to the courts of the neighbouring sultans, to implore their assistance, and excite them to revenge my father's death; but Heaven did not concur in a resolution we thought so just. When we had been but a few days at sea, there arose such a furious storm, that our vessel, carried away by the violence of the winds and waves, was dashed in pieces against a rock. My governess, the grand vizier, and all that attended me, were swallowed up by the sea. I lost my senses; and whether I was thrown upon the coast, or whether Heaven wrought a miracle for my deliverance, I found myself on shore when my senses returned.

"In my despair and horror I was on the point of casting myself into the sea again; when I heard behind me a great noise of men and horses. I looked about to see what it might be, and espied several armed horsemen, among whom was one mounted on an Arabian charger. He had on a garment embroidered with silver, a girdle set with precious stones, and a crown of gold on his head. Though his habit had not convinced me that he was chief of the company, I should have judged it by the air of grandeur which appeared in his person. He was a young man extraordinarily well shaped, and perfectly beautiful. Surprised to see a young lady alone in that place, he sent some of his officers to ask who I was. I answered only by weeping. The shore being covered with the wreck of our ship, they concluded that I was certainly some person who had escaped from the vessel. This conjecture excited the curiosity of the officers, who began to ask me a thousand questions, with assurances that their master was a generous prince, and that I should receive protection at his court.

"The sultan, impatient to know who I was, grew weary of waiting the return of his officers, and drew near to me. He gazed on me very earnestly, and observing that I did not cease weeping, without being able to return an answer to their questions, he forbade them troubling me any more; and directing his discourse to me: 'Madam,' said he, 'I conjure you to moderate your excessive affliction. I dare assure you that, if your misfortunes are capable of receiving any relief, you shall find it in my dominions. You shall live with the queen my mother, who will endeavour by her kindness to ease your affliction. I know not yet who you are, but I find I already take an interest in your welfare.'

"I thanked the young sultan for his goodness to me, accepted his obliging offer; and to convince him that I was not unworthy of them, told him my condition. When I had done speaking, the prince assured me that he was deeply concerned at my misfortunes. He then conducted me to his palace, and presented me to the queen his mother, to whom I was obliged again to repeat my misfortunes. The queen seemed very sensible of my trouble, and conceived extreme affection for me. On the other hand, the sultan her son fell desperately in love with me, and soon offered me his hand and his crown. I was so taken up with the thoughts of my calamities, that the prince, though so lovely a person, did not make so great an impression on me as he might have done at another time. However, gratitude prevailing, I did not refuse to make him happy, and our nuptials were concluded with all imaginable splendour.

"While the people were taken up with the celebration of their sovereign's nuptials, a neighbouring prince, his enemy, made a descent by night on the island with a great number of troops and surprised and cut to pieces my husband's subjects. We escaped very narrowly, for he had already entered the palace with some of his followers; but we found means to slip away and to get to the sea-coast, where we threw ourselves into a fishing-boat which we had the good fortune to meet with. Two days we were driven about by the winds, without knowing what would become of us. The third day we espied a vessel making toward us under sail. We rejoiced at first, believing it had been a merchant-ship which might take us aboard; but what was our consternation, when, as it drew near, we saw ten or twelve armed pirates appear on the deck. Having boarded, five or six of them leaped into our boat, seized us, bound the prince, and conveyed us into their ship, where they immediately took off my veil. My youth and features touched them, and they all declared how much they were charmed at the sight of me. Instead of casting lots, each of them claimed the preference, and me as his right. The dispute grew warm, they came to blows, and fought like madmen. The deck was soon covered with dead bodies, and they were all killed but one, who, being left sole possessor of me, said: 'You are mine. I will carry you to Grand Cairo, to deliver you to a friend of mine, to whom I have promised a beautiful slave. But who,' added he, looking upon the sultan, my husband, 'is that man? What relation does he bear to you? Are you allied by blood or love?' 'Sir,' answered I, 'he is my husband.' 'If so,' replied the pirate, 'in pity I must rid myself of him: it would be too great an affliction to him to see you disposed of to another.' Having spoken these words, he took up the unhappy prince, who was bound, and threw him into the sea, notwithstanding all my endeavours to prevent him.

"I shrieked in a dreadful manner at the sight of what he had done, and had certainly cast myself into the sea also, but that the pirate held me. He saw my design, and therefore bound me with cords to the main-mast, then hoisting sail, made toward the land, and got ashore. He unbound me and led me to a little town, where he bought camels, tents, and slaves, and then set out for Grand Cairo, designing, as he still said, to present me to his friend, according to his promise.

"We had been several days upon the road, when, as we were crossing this plain yesterday, we descried the black who inhabited this castle. At a distance we took him for a tower.

As it drew near we saw ten or twelve armed pirates appear on the deck.

and when near us, could scarcely believe him to be a man. He drew his huge cimeter, and summoned the pirate to yield himself prisoner, with all his slaves and the lady he was conducting. You know the end of this dreadful adventure and can foresee what would have been my fate had you, generous prince, not come to my deliverance."

As soon as the princess had finished the recital of her adventures, Codadad declared to her that he was deeply concerned at her misfortunes. "But, madam," added he, "it shall be your own fault if you do not live at ease for the future. The sultan of Harran's sons offer you a safe retreat in the court of their father; be pleased to accept of it, and if you do not disdain the affection of your deliverer, permit me to assure you of it, and to espouse you before all these princes; let them be witnesses to our contract." The princess consented, and the marriage was concluded that very day in the castle, where they found all sorts of provisions, with an abundance of delicious wine and other liquors.

They all sat down at table; and after having eaten and drunk plentifully, took with them the rest of the provisions, and set out for the sultan of Harran's court. They travelled several days, encamping in the pleasantest places they could find, and were within one day's journey of Harran, when Codadad, directing his discourse to all his company, said: "Princes, I have too long concealed from you who I am. Behold your brother Codadad! I, as well as you, received my being from the sultan of Harran, the prince of Samaria brought me up, and the Princess Pirouzè is my mother. Madam," added he, addressing himself to the princess of Deryabar, "do you also forgive me for having concealed my birth from you? Perhaps, by discovering it sooner, I might have prevented some disagreeable reflections, which may have been occasioned by a match you may have thought unequal." "No, sir," answered the princess "the opinion I at first conceived of you heightened every moment and you did not stand in need of the extraction you now discover to make me happy."

The princes congratulated Codadad on his birth, and expressed much satisfaction at being made acquainted with it. But in reality, instead of rejoicing, their hatred of so amiable a brother was increased. They met together at night, and forgetting that had it not been for the brave son of Pirouzè they must have been devoured by the black, agreed among themselves to murder him. "We have no other course to choose," said one of them, "for the moment our father shall come to understand that this stranger, of whom he is already so fond, is our brother, he will declare him his heir, and we shall all be obliged to obey and fall down before him." He added much more, which made such an impression on their unnatural minds, that they immediately repaired to Codadad, then asleep, stabbed him repeatedly, and leaving him for dead in the arms of the princess of Deryabar, proceeded on their journey to the city of Harran, where they arrived the next day.

The sultan their father conceived the greater joy at their return, because he had despaired of ever seeing them again: he asked what had been the occasion of their stay. But they took care not to acquaint him with it, making no mention either of the black or of Codadad; and only said, that being curious to see different countries, they had spent some time in the neighbouring cities.

In the meantime Codadad lay in his tent weltering in his blood and little differing from a dead man, with the princess his wife, who seemed to be in not much better condition than himself. She rent the air with her dismal shrieks, tore her hair, and bathing her husband's body with her tears, "Alas! Codadad, my dear Codadad," cried she, "is it you whom I behold just departing this life? Can I believe these are your brothers who have treated you so unmercifully, those brothers whom thy valour had saved? O Heaven! which has condemned me to lead a life of calamities, if you will not permit me to have a consort, why did you permit me to find one? Behold, you have now robbed me of two, just as I began to be attached to them."

By these and other moving expressions the afflicted princess of Deryabar vented her sorrow, fixing her eyes on the unfortunate Codadad, who could not hear her; but he was not dead, and his consort, observing that he still breathed, ran to a large town she espied in the plain, to inquire for a surgeon. She was directed to one, who went immediately with her; but when they came to the tent, they could not find Codadad, which made them conclude he had been dragged away by some wild beast to be devoured. The princess renewed her complaints and lamentations in a most affecting manner. The surgeon was moved, and being unwilling to leave her in so distressed a condition, proposed to her to return to the town, offering her his house and service.

She suffered herself to be prevailed upon. The surgeon conducted her to his house, and without knowing, as yet, who she was, treated her with all imaginable courtesy and respect. He used all his endeavours to comfort her, but it was vain to think of removing her sorrow. "Madam," said he to her one day, "be pleased to recount to me your misfortunes; tell me your country and your condition. Perhaps I may give you some good advice, when I am acquainted with all the circumstances of your calamity."

The surgeon's words were so efficacious, that they wrought on the princess, who recounted to him all her adventures; and

when she had done, the surgeon directed his discourse to her:
"Madam," said he, "you ought not thus to give way to your
sorrow; you ought rather to arm yourself with resolution, and
perform what the duty of a wife requires of you. You are bound
to avenge your husband. If you please, I will wait on you as
your attendant. Let us go to the sultan of Harran's court;
he is a good and a just prince. You need only represent to him
in lively colours, how Prince Codadad has been treated by his
brothers. I am persuaded he will do you justice." "I submit
to your reasoning," answered the princess; "it is my duty to endeavour to avenge Codadad; and since you are so generous as to
offer to attend me, I am ready to set out." No sooner had she
fixed this resolution, than the surgeon ordered two camels to be
made ready, on which the princess and he mounted, and repaired
to Harran.

They alighted at the first caravanserai they found, and
inquired of the host the news at court. "Deryabar," said he,
"is in very great perplexity. The sultan had a son, who lived
long with him as a stranger, and none can tell what is become of
the young prince. One of the sultan's wives, named Pirouzè,
is his mother; she has made all possible inquiry, but to no purpose. The sultan has forty-nine other sons, all by different
mothers, but not one of them has virtue enough to comfort him
for the death of Codadad; I say, his death, because it is impossible he should be still alive, since no intelligence has been heard
of him, notwithstanding so much search has been made."

The surgeon, having heard this account from the host, concluded that the best course the princess of Deryabar could take
was to wait upon Pirouzè; but that step required much precaution: for it was to be feared that if the sultan of Harran's sons
should happen to hear of the arrival of their sister-in-law and

her design, they might cause her to be conveyed away before she could discover herself. The surgeon weighed all these circumstances, and therefore, that he might manage matters with discretion, desired the princess to remain in the caravanserai, whilst he repaired to the palace, to observe which might be the safest way to conduct her to Pirouzè.

He went accordingly into the city, and was walking toward the palace, when he beheld a lady mounted on a mule richly accoutred. She was followed by several ladies mounted also on mules, with a great number of guards and black slaves. All the people formed a lane to see her pass along, and saluted her by prostrating themselves on the ground. The surgeon paid her the same respect, and then asked a calendar, who happened to stand by him, whether that lady was one of the sultan's wives. "Yes, brother," answered the calendar, "she is, and the most honoured and beloved by the people, because she is the mother of Prince Codadad, of whom you must have heard."

The surgeon asked no more questions, but followed Pirouzè to a mosque, into which she went to distribute alms, and assist at the public prayers which the sultan had ordered to be offered up for the safe return of Codadad. The surgeon broke through the throng and advanced to Pirouzè's guards. He waited the conclusion of the prayers, and when the princess went out, stepped up to one of her slaves, and whispered him in the ear: "Brother, I have a secret of moment to impart to the Princess Pirouzè: may not I be introduced into her apartment?" "If that secret," answered the slave, "relates to Prince Codadad I dare promise you shall have audience of her; but if it concern not him, it is needless for you to be introduced; for her thoughts are all engrossed by her son." "It is only about that dear son," replied the surgeon, "that I wish to speak to her." "If so," said the slave, "you need but follow us to the palace, and you shall soon have the opportunity."

Accordingly, as soon as Pirouzè was returned to her apartment, the slave acquainted her that a person unknown had some important information to communicate to her, and that it related to Prince Codadad. No sooner had he uttered these words, than Pirouzè expressed her impatience to see the stranger. The slave immediately conducted him into the princess's closet who ordered all her women to withdraw, except two, from whom she concealed nothing. As soon as she saw the surgeon, she asked him eagerly what news he had to tell her of Codadad. "Madam," answered the surgeon, after having prostrated himself on the ground, "I have a long account to give you, and such as will surprise you." He then related all the particulars of what had passed between Codadad and his brothers, which she listened to with eager attention; but when he came to speak of the murder, the tender mother fainted away on her sofa, as if she had herself been stabbed like her son. Her two women soon brought her to herself and the surgeon continued his relation; and when he had concluded, Pirouzè said to him: "Go back to the princess of Deryabar, and assure her from me that the sultan shall soon own her for his daughter-in-law; and as for yourself, your services shall be rewarded as liberally as they deserve."

When the surgeon was gone, Pirouzè remained on the sofa in such a state of affliction as may easily be imagined; and yielding to her tenderness at the recollection of Codadad, "O my son!" said she, "I must never then expect to see you more! Unfortunate Codadad, why did you leave me?" While she uttered these words, she wept bitterly, and her two attendants, moved by her grief, mingled their tears with hers.

CODADAD AND HIS BROTHERS

Whilst they were all three in this manner vying in affliction, the sultan came into the closet, and seeing them in this condition, asked Pìrouzè whether she had received any bad news concerning Codadad. "Alas! sir," said she, "all is over, my son has lost his life, and to add to my sorrow, I cannot pay him the funeral rites; for, in all probability, wild beasts have devoured him." She then told him all she had heard from the surgeon, and did not fail to enlarge on the inhuman manner in which Codadad had been murdered by his brothers.

The sultan did not give Pìrouzè time to finish her relation, but transported with anger, and giving way to his passion, "Madam," said he to the princess, "those perfidious wretches who cause you to shed these tears, and are the occasion of mortal grief to their father, shall soon feel the punishment due to their guilt." The sultan, having spoken these words, with indignation in his countenance, went directly to the presence-chamber, where all his courtiers attended, and such of the people as had petitions to present to him. They were alarmed to see him in passion, and thought his anger had been kindled against them. He ascended the throne, and causing his grand vizier to approach, "Hassan," said he, "go immediately, take a thousand of my guards, and seize all the princes, my sons; shut them up in the tower used as a prison for murderers, and let this be done in a moment." All who were present trembled at this extraordinary command; and the grand vizier, without uttering a word, laid his hand on his head, to express his obedience, and hastened from the hall to execute his orders. In the meantime the sultan dismissed those who attended for audience, and declared he would not hear of any business for a month to come. He was still in the hall when the vizier returned. "Are all my sons," demanded he, "in the tower?" "They are, sir," answered the vizier; "I

[283]

have obeyed your orders." "This is not all," replied the sultan, "I have farther commands for you"; and so saying he went out of the hall of audience, and returned to Pirouzè's apartment, the vizier following him. He asked the princess where Codadad's widow had taken up her lodging. Pirouzè's women told him, for the surgeon had not forgotten that in his relation. The sultan then turning to his minister, "Go," said he, "to this caravanserai, and conduct a young princess who lodges there, with all the respect due to her quality, to my palace."

The vizier was not long in performing what he was ordered. He mounted on horseback with all the emirs and courtiers, and repaired to the caravanserai, where the princess of Deryabar was lodged, whom he acquainted with his orders; and presented her, from the sultan, with a fine white mule, whose saddle and bridle were adorned with gold, rubies, and diamonds. She mounted, and proceeded to the palace. The surgeon attended her, mounted on a beautiful Tartar horse which the vizier had provided for him. All the people were at their windows, or in the streets, to see the cavalcade; and it being given out that the princess, whom they conducted in such state to court, was Codadad's wife, the city resounded with acclamations, the air rung with shouts of joy, which would have been turned into lamentations had that prince's fatal adventure been known, so much was he beloved by all.

The princess of Deryabar found the sultan at the palace gate waiting to receive her: he took her by the hand and led her to Pirouzè's apartment, where a very moving scene took place. Codadad's wife found her affliction redouble at the sight of her husband's father and mother; as, on the other hand, those parents could not look on their son's wife without being much affected. She cast herself at the sultan's feet, and having bathed them with tears, was so overcome with grief that she was not able to speak. Pirouzè was in no better state, and the sultan, moved by these affecting objects, gave way to his own feelings and wept. At length the princess of Deryabar, being somewhat recovered, recounted the adventure of the castle and Codadad's disaster. Then she demanded justice for the treachery of the princes. "Yes, madam," said the sultan, "those ungrateful wretches shall perish; but Codadad's death must be first made public, that the punishment of his brothers may not cause my subjects to rebel; and though we have not my son's body, we will not omit paying him the last duties." This said, he directed his discourse to the vizier, and ordered him to cause to be erected a dome of white marble, in a delightful plain, in the midst of which the city of Harran stands. Then he appointed the princess of Deryabar a suitable apartment in his palace, acknowledging her for his daughter-in-law

Hassan caused the work to be carried on with such diligence, and employed so many workmen, that the dome was soon finished. Within it was erected a tomb, which was covered with gold brocade. When all was completed, the sultan ordered prayers to be said, and appointed a day for the obsequies of his son.

On that day all the inhabitants of the city went out upon the plain to see the ceremony performed. The gate of the dome was then closed, and all the people returned to the city. Next day there were public prayers in all the mosques, and the same was continued for eight days successively. On the ninth the king resolved to cause the princes his sons to be beheaded. The people, incensed at their cruelty toward Codadad, impatiently expected to see them executed. The scaffolds were erecting, but the execution was respited, because, on a sudden, intelligence was brought that the neighbouring princes who had before made war on the sultan of Harran, were advancing with more numerous forces than on the first invasion, and were then not far from the city. This news gave new cause to lament the loss of Codadad, who had signalised himself in the former war against the same enemies. The sultan, nothing dismayed, formed a considerable army, and being too brave to await the enemies' attack within his walls, marched out to meet them. They, on their side, being informed that the sultan of Harran was marching to engage them, halted in the plain, and formed their army.

As soon as the sultan discovered them, he also drew up his forces, and ranged them in order of battle. The signal was given, and he attacked them with extraordinary vigour; nor was the opposition inferior. Much blood was shed on both sides, and the victory long remained dubious; but at length it seemed to incline to the sultan of Harran's enemies, who, being more numerous, were upon the point of surrounding him, when a great body of cavalry appeared on the plain, and approached the two armies. The sight of this fresh party daunted both sides, neither knowing what to think of them; but their doubts were soon cleared; for they fell upon the flank of the sultan of Harran's enemies with such a furious charge, that they soon broke and routed them. Nor did they stop here; they pursued them, and cut most of them in pieces.

The sultan of Harran, who had attentively observed all that passed, admired the bravery of this strange body of cavalry, whose unexpected arrival had given the victory to his army. But, above all, he was charmed with their chief, whom he had seen fighting with a more than ordinary valour. He longed to know the name of the generous hero. Impatient to see and thank him, he advanced toward him, but perceived he was coming to prevent him. The two princes drew near, and the sultan of Harran, discovering Codadad in the brave warrior who had just defeated his enemies, became motionless with joy and surprise. "Father," said Codadad to him, "you have sufficient cause to be astonished at the sudden appearance of a man whom perhaps you concluded to be dead. I should have been so, had not Heaven preserved me still to serve you against your enemies." "O my son," cried the sultan, "is it possible that you are restored to me? Alas! I despaired of seeing you more." So saying, he stretched out his arms to the young prince, who flew to such a tender embrace.

"I know all, my son," said the sultan again, after having long held him in his arms. "I know what return your brothers have made you for delivering them out of the hands of the black; but you shall be revenged to-morrow Let us now go to the palace where your mother, who has shed so many tears on your account, expects to rejoice with us on the defeat of our enemies. What a joy will it be to her to be informed that my victory is your work!" "Sir," said Codadad, "give me leave to ask how you could know the adventure of the castle? Have any of my brothers, repenting, owned it to you?" "No," answered the sultan; "the princess of Deryabar has given us an account of everything, for she is in my palace, and came thither to demand justice against your brothers." Codadad was transported with joy, to learn that the princess his wife was at the court. "Let us go, sir," cried he to his father in rapture, "let us go to my mother, who waits for us. I am impatient to dry her tears, as well as those of the princess of Deryabar."

The sultan immediately returned to the city with his army, and re-entered his palace victorious, amidst the acclamations of the people, who followed him in crowds, praying to Heaven to prolong his life, and extolling Codadad to the skies. They found Pirouzè and her daughter-in-law waiting to congratulate the sultan; but words cannot express the transports of joy they felt when they saw the young prince with him: their embraces were mingled with tears of a very different kind from those they had before shed for him. When they had sufficiently yielded to all the emotions that the ties of blood and love inspired, they asked Codadad by what miracle he came to be still alive.

He answered that a peasant mounted on a mule happening accidentally to come into the tent where he lay senseless, and perceiving him alone and stabbed in several places, had made him fast on his mule, and carried him to his house, where he applied to his wounds certain herbs, which recovered him. "When I found myself well," added he, "I returned thanks to the peasant, and gave him all the diamonds I had. I then made for the city of Harran; but being informed by the way that some neighbouring princes had gathered forces, and were on their march against the sultan's subjects, I made myself known to the villagers, and stirred them up to undertake his defence. I armed a great number of young men, and heading them, happened to arrive at the time when the two armies were engaged."

When he had done speaking, the sultan said: "Let us return thanks to God for having preserved Codadad; but it is requisite that the traitors who would have destroyed him should perish." "Sir," answered the generous prince, "though they are wicked and ungrateful, consider they are your own flesh and blood: they are my brothers; I forgive their offence, and beg you to pardon them." This generosity drew tears from the sultan, who caused the people to be assembled, and declared Codadad his heir. He then ordered the princes, who were prisoners, to be brought out loaded with irons. Pirouzè's son struck off their chains, and embraced them all successively with as much sincerity and affection as he had done in the black's castle. The people were charmed with Codadad's generosity, and loaded him with applause. The surgeon was next nobly rewarded in requital of the services he had done the princess of Deryabar and the court of Harran remained thereafter in perfect joy and felicity.

THE STORY OF SINBAD THE VOYAGER

IN the reign of the Caliph Haroun-al-Raschid, there lived at Bagdad a poor porter called Hindbad. One day, when the weather was excessively hot, he was employed to carry a heavy burden from one end of the town to the other. Having still a great way to go, he came into a street where a refreshing breeze blew on his face, and the pavement was sprinkled with rose water. As he could not desire a better place to rest, he took off his load, and sat upon it, near a large mansion.

He was much pleased that he stopped in this place; for the agreeable smell of wood of aloes, and of pastils, that came from the house, mixing with the scent of the rose-water, completely perfumed the air, Besides, he heard from within a concert of instrumental music, accompanied with the harmonious notes of nightingales. This charming melody, and the smell of savoury dishes, made the porter conclude there was a feast within. His business seldom leading him that way, he knew not to whom the mansion belonged; but to satisfy his curiosity he went to some of the servants, whom he saw standing at the gate in magnificent apparel, and asked the name of the proprietor. "How," replied one of them, "do you live in Bagdad, and know not that this is the house of Sinbad the sailor, that famous voyager, who has sailed round the world?" The porter, who had heard of this Sinbad's riches, lifted up his eyes to Heaven, and said, loud enough to be heard: "Almighty creator of all things, consider the difference between Sinbad and me! I am every day exposed to fatigues and calamities, and can scarcely get barley-bread for myself and my family, whilst happy Sinbad expends immense riches and leads a life of pleasure. What has he done to obtain a lot so agreeable? And what have I done to deserve one so wretched?"

Whilst the porter was thus indulging his melancholy, a servant came out of the house, and taking him by the arm, bade him follow him, for Sinbad, his master, wanted to speak to him.

The servants brought him into a great hall, where a number of people sat round a table, covered with all sorts of savoury dishes. At the upper end sat a venerable gentleman, with a long white beard, and behind him stood a number of officers and domestics, all ready to attend his pleasure. This personage was Sinbad. The porter, whose fear was increased at the sight of so many people, and of a banquet so sumptuous, saluted the company trembling. Sinbad bade him draw near, and seating him at his right hand, served him himself, and gave him a cup of excellent wine.

When the repast was over, Sinbad addressed his conversation to Hindbad, and inquired his name and employment. "My lord," answered he, "my name is Hindbad." "I am very glad to see you," replied Sinbad; "but I wish to hear from your own mouth what it was you lately said in the street." Sinbad had himself heard the porter complain through the window, and this it was that induced him to have him brought in.

At this request, Hindbad hung down his head in confusion, and replied: "My lord, I confess that my fatigue put me out of humour, and occasioned me to utter some indiscreet words, which I beg you to pardon." "Do not think I am so unjust," resumed Sinbad, "as to resent such a complaint, but I must rectify your error concerning myself. You think, no doubt, that I have acquired, without labour and trouble, the ease which I now enjoy. But do not mistake; I did not attain to this happy condition, without enduring for several years more trouble of body and mind than can well be imagined. Yes, gentlemen," he added, speaking to the whole company, "I can assure you my troubles were so extraordinary, that they were calculated to discourage the most covetous from undertaking such voyages as I did, to acquire riches. Perhaps you have never heard a distinct account of my wonderful adventures; and since I have this opportunity, I will give you a faithful account of them, not doubting but it will be acceptable."

THE FIRST VOYAGE

"I inherited from my father considerable property, the greater part of which I squandered in my youth in dissipation; but I perceived my error, and reflected that riches were perishable, and quickly consumed by such ill managers as myself. I further considered, that by my irregular way of living I wretchedly misspent my time; which is, of all things, the most valuable. Struck with these reflections, I collected the remains of my fortune, and sold all my effects by public auction. I then entered into a contract with some merchants, who traded by sea. I took the advice of such as I thought most capable, and resolving to improve what money I had, I embarked with several merchants on board a ship which we had jointly fitted out.

"We set sail, and steered our course toward the Indies through the Persian Gulf, which is formed by the coasts of Arabia Felix on the right, and by those of Persia on the left.

SINBAD THE VOYAGER

At first I was troubled with sea-sickness, but speedily recovered my health, and was not afterward subject to that complaint.

"In our voyage we touched at several islands, where we sold or exchanged our goods. One day, whilst under sail, we were becalmed near a small island, but little elevated above the level of the water, and resembling a green meadow. The captain ordered his sails to be furled, and permitted such persons as were so inclined to land; of which number I was one.

"But while we were enjoying ourselves in eating and drinking, and recovering ourselves from the fatigue of the sea, the island on a sudden trembled, and shook us terribly.

"The motion was perceived on board the ship, and we were called upon to re-embark speedily, or we should all be lost; for what we took for an island proved to be the back of a sea monster. The nimblest got into the sloop, others betook themselves to swimming; but for myself, I was still upon the back of the creature when he dived into the sea, and I had time only to catch hold of a piece of wood that we had brought out of the ship. Meanwhile, the captain, having received those on board who were in the sloop, and taken up some of those that swam, resolved to improve the favourable gale that had just risen, and hoisting his sails, pursued his voyage, so that it was impossible for me to recover the ship.

"Thus was I exposed to the mercy of the waves all the rest of the day and the following night. By this time I found my strength gone, and despaired of saving my life, when happily a wave threw me against an island. The bank was high and rugged; so that I could scarcely have got up, had it not been for some roots of trees, which chance placed within reach. Having gained the land, I lay down upon the ground half dead, until the sun appeared. Then, though I was very feeble, both from hard labour and want of food, I crept along to find some herbs fit to eat, and had the good luck not only to procure some, but likewise to discover a spring of excellent water, which contributed much to recover me. After this I advanced farther into the island, and at last reached a fine plain, where at a great distance I perceived some horses feeding. I went toward them, and as I approached heard the voice of a man, who immediately appeared, and asked me who I was. I related to him my adventure, after which, taking me by the hand, he led me into a cave, where there were several other people, no less amazed to see me than I was to see them.

"I partook of some provisions which they offered me. I then asked them what they did in such a desert place, to which they answered, that they were grooms belonging to the Maharâja, sovereign of the island, and that every year, at the same season they brought thither the king's horses for pasturage. They added, that they were to return home on the morrow, and had I been one day later, I must have perished, because the inhabited part of the island was at a great distance, and it would have been impossible for me to have got thither without a guide.

"Next morning they returned to the capital of the island, took me with them, and presented me to the Maha-râja. He asked me who I was, and by what adventure I had come into his dominions. After I had satisfied him, he told me he was much concerned for my misfortune, and at the same time ordered that I should want nothing; which commands his officers were so generous as to see exactly fulfilled.

"Being a merchant, I frequented men of my own profession, and particularly inquired for those who were strangers, that perchance I might hear news from Bagdad, or find an opportunity to return. They put a thousand questions respecting my country; and I, being willing to inform myself as to their laws and customs, asked them concerning everything which I thought worth knowing.

"There belongs to this king an island named Cassel. They assured me that every night a noise of drums was heard there, whence the mariners fancied that it was the residence of Degial. I determined to visit this wonderful place, and in my way thither saw fishes of one hundred and two hundred cubits long, that occasion more fear than hurt, for they are so timorous, that they will fly upon the rattling of two sticks or boards. I saw likewise other fish about a cubit in length, that had heads like owls.

"As I was one day at the port after my return, a ship arrived, and as soon as she cast anchor, they began to unload her, and the merchants on board ordered their goods to be carried into the custom-house. As I cast my eye upon some bales, and looked to the name, I found my own, and perceived the bales to be the same that I had embarked at Bussorah. I also knew the captain; but being persuaded that he believed me to be drowned, I went, and asked him whose bales these were. He replied that they belonged to a merchant of Bagdad, called Sinbad, who came to sea with him; but had unfortunately perished on the voyage, and that he had resolved to trade with the bales, until he met with some of his family, to whom he might return the profit. 'I am that Sinbad,' said I, 'whom you thought to be dead, and those bales are mine.'

"When the captain heard me speak thus, 'Heavens!' he exclaimed, 'whom can we trust in these times? There is no faith left among men. I saw Sinbad perish with my own eyes, as did also the passengers on board, and yet you tell me you are that Sinbad. What impudence is this? You tell a horrible falsehood, in order to possess yourself of what does not belong to you.' 'Have patience,' replied I; 'do me the favour to hear what I have to say.' Then I told him how I had escaped, and by what adventure I met with the grooms of the Maha-raja, who had brought me to his court.

"The captain was at length persuaded that I was no cheat; for there came people from his ship who knew me, and expressed much joy at seeing me alive. At last he recollected me himself, and embracing me, 'Heaven be praised,' said he, 'for your happy escape. I cannot express the joy it affords me; there are your goods, take and do with them as you please.' I thanked him, acknowledged his probity, and offered him part of my goods as a present, which he generously refused.

"I took out what was most valuable in my bales, and presented them to the Maha-raja, who, knowing my misfortune, asked me how I came by such rarities. I acquainted him with the circumstance of their recovery. He was pleased at my good luck, accepted my present, and in return gave me one much more considerable. Upon this, I took leave of him, and went aboard the same ship, after I had exchanged my goods for the commodities of that country. I carried with me wood of aloes, sandal, camphire, nutmegs, cloves, pepper, and ginger. We passed by several islands, and at last arrived at Bussorah, from whence I came to this city, with the value of one hundred thousand sequins. My family and I received one another with sincere affection. I bought slaves and a landed estate, and built a magnificent house. Thus I settled myself, resolving to forget the miseries I had suffered, and to enjoy the pleasures of life."

Sinbad stopped here, and ordered the musicians to proceed with their concert, which the story had interrupted. The company continued enjoying themselves till the evening, when

SINBAD THE VOYAGER

Sinbad sent for a purse of a hundred sequins, and giving it to the porter, said: "Take this, Hindbad, return to your home, and come back to-morrow to hear more of my adventures." The porter went away, astonished at the honour done, and the present made him. The account of this adventure proved very agreeable to his wife and children, who did not fail to return thanks to God or what providence had sent them by the hand of Sinbad.

Hindbad put on his best apparel next day, and returned to the bountiful traveller, who welcomed him heartily. When all the guests had arrived, dinner was served. When it was ended, Sinbad, addressing himself to the company, said, "Gentlemen, be pleased to listen to the adventures of my second voyage; they deserve your attention even more than those of the first." Upon this every one held his peace, and Sinbad proceeded.

THE SECOND VOYAGE

"I designed, after my first voyage, to spend the rest of my days at Bagdad, but it was not long ere I grew weary of an indolent life. My inclination to trade revived. I bought goods proper for the commerce I intended, and put to sea a second time with merchants of known probity. We embarked on board a good ship, and after recommending ourselves to God, set sail. We traded from island to island, and exchanged commodities with great profit. One day we landed on an island covered with several sorts of fruit-trees, but we could see neither man nor animal. We went to take a little fresh air in the meadows, along the streams that watered them. Whilst some diverted themselves with gathering flowers, and others fruits, I took my wine and provisions, and sat down near a stream betwixt two high trees which formed a thick shade. I made a good meal, and afterward fell asleep. I cannot tell how long I slept, but when I awoke the ship was gone.

"I got up and looked around me, but could not see one of the merchants who landed with me. I perceived the ship under sail, but at such a distance, that I lost sight of her in a short time.

"In this sad condition, I was ready to die with grief. I cried out in agony, and threw myself upon the ground, where I lay some time in despair. I upbraided myself a hundred times for not being content with the produce of my first voyage, that might have sufficed me all my life. But all this was in vain, and my repentance came too late.

"At last I resigned myself to the will of God. Not knowing what to do, I climbed up to the top of a lofty tree, from whence I looked about on all sides, to see if I could discover anything that could give me hopes. When I gazed toward the sea I could see nothing but sky and water; but looking over the land I beheld something white; and coming down, I took what provision I had left, and went toward it, the distance being so great that I could not distinguish what it was.

"As I approached, I thought it to be a white dome, of a prodigious height and extent; and when I came up to it, I touched it, and found it to be very smooth. I went round to see if it was open on any side, but saw that it was not, and that there was no climbing up to the top, as it was so smooth. It was at least fifty paces round.

"By this time the sun was about to set, and all of a sudden the sky became as dark as if it had been covered with a thick cloud. I was much astonished at this sudden darkness, but much more when I found it occasioned by a bird of a monstrous size, that came flying toward me. I remembered that I had often heard mariners speak of a miraculous bird called the roc, and conceived that the great dome which I so much admired must be its egg. As I perceived the roc coming, I crept close to the egg, so that I had before me one of the bird's legs, which was as big as the trunk of a tree. I tied myself strongly to it with my turban, in hopes that next morning she would carry me with her out of this desert island. After having passed the night in this condition, the bird flew away as soon as it was daylight, and carried me so high, that I could not discern the earth; she afterward descended with so much rapidity that I lost my senses. But when I found myself on the ground, I speedily untied the knot, and had scarcely done so, when the roc, having taken up a serpent of a monstrous length in her bill, flew away.

"The spot where she left me was encompassed on all sides by mountains, that seemed to reach above the clouds, and so steep that there was no possibility of getting out of the valley. This was a new perplexity: so that when I compared this place with the desert island from which the roc had brought me I found that I had gained nothing by the change.

"As I walked through this valley, I perceived it was strewed with diamonds, some of which were of a surprising bigness. I took pleasure in looking upon them; but shortly saw at a distance such objects as greatly diminished my satisfaction, namely, a great number of serpents, so monstrous, that the least of them was capable of swallowing an elephant. They retired in the daytime to their dens, where they hid themselves from the roc, their enemy, and came out only in the night.

"I spent the day in walking about in the valley, resting myself at times in such places as I thought most convenient. When night came on, I went into a cave, where I thought I might repose

in safety. I secured the entrance with a great stone to preserve
me from the serpents; but not so far as to exclude the light. I
supped on part of my provisions, but the serpents, which began
hissing round me, put me into such extreme fear, that I could
not sleep. When day appeared, the serpents retired, and I came
out of the cave trembling. I can justly say, that I walked upon
diamonds, without feeling any inclination to touch them. At
last I sat down, and notwithstanding my apprehensions, not having closed my eyes during the night, fell asleep, after having
eaten a little more of my provision. But I had scarcely shut my
eyes, when something that fell by me with a great noise awaked
me. This was a large piece of raw meat; and at the same time
I saw several others fall down from the rocks in different places.

"I had always regarded as fabulous what I had heard sailors
and others relate of the valley of diamonds, and of the stratagems
employed by merchants to obtain jewels from thence; but now I
found that they had stated nothing but truth. For the fact is,
that the merchants come to the neighbourhood of this valley
when the eagles have young ones; and, throwing great joints of
meat into the valley, the diamonds upon whose points they fall
stick to them; the eagles, which are stronger in this country than
anywhere else, pounce with great force upon those pieces of
meat, and carry them to their nests on the rocks to feed their
young: the merchants at this time run to the nests, drive off the
eagles by their shouts, and take away the diamonds that stick to
the meat.

"Until I perceived the device I had concluded it to be impossible for me to leave this abyss, which I regarded as my grave;
but now I changed my opinion, and began to think upon the
means of my deliverance. I began to collect the largest diamonds
I could find, and put them into the leather bag in which I used

The spot where she left me was encompassed on all sides by mountains that seemed to reach above the clouds, and so steep that there was no possibility of getting out of the valley.

to carry my provisions. I afterward took the largest of the pieces of meat, tied it close round me with the cloth of my turban, and then laid myself upon the ground with my face downward, the bag of diamonds being made fast to my girdle.

"I had scarcely placed myself in this posture when the eagles came. Each of them seized a piece of meat, and one of the strongest having taken me up, with the piece of meat to which I was fastened, carried me to his nest on the top of the mountain. The merchants immediately began their shouting to frighten the eagles; and when they had obliged them to quit their prey, one of them came to the nest where I was. He was much alarmed when he saw me; but recovering himself, instead of inquiring how I came thither, began to quarrel with me, and asked, why I stole his goods. 'You will treat me,' replied I, 'with more civility when you know me better. Do not be uneasy, I have diamonds enough for you and myself, more than all the other merchants together. What ever they have, they owe to chance, but I selected for myself in the bottom of the valley those which you see in this bag.' I had scarcely done speaking, when the other merchants came crowding about us, much astonished to see me; but they were much more surprised when I told them my story.

"They conducted me to their encampment, and there having opened my bag, they were surprised at the largeness of my diamonds, and confessed that in all the courts which they had visited they had never seen any of such size and perfection. I prayed the merchant who owned the nest to which I had been carried (for every merchant had his own), to take as many for his share as he pleased. He contented himself with one, and that the least of them; and when I pressed him to take more, 'No,' said he, 'I am very well satisfied with this, which is valuable enough to save me the trouble of making any more voyages, and will raise as great a fortune as I desire.'

"I spent the night with the merchants, to whom I related my story a second time, for the satisfaction of those who had not heard it. I could not moderate my joy when I found myself delivered from the danger I have mentioned. I thought myself in a dream, and could scarcely believe myself out of danger.

"The merchants had thrown their pieces of meat into the valley for several days, and each of them being satisfied with the diamonds that had fallen to his lot, we left the place the next morning and travelled near high mountains, where there were serpents of a prodigious length, which we had the good fortune to escape. We took shipping at the first port we reached, and touched at the isle of Roha, where the trees grow that yield camphire. This tree is so large, and its branches so thick, that one hundred men may easily sit under its shade. The juice of which the camphire is made exudes from a hole bored in the upper part of the tree, is received in a vessel, where it thickens to a consistency, and becomes what we call camphire; after the juice is thus drawn out, the tree withers and dies.

"In this island is also found the rhinoceros, an animal less than the elephant, but larger than the buffalo. It has a horn upon its nose, about a cubit in length; this horn is solid, and cleft through the middle. The rhinoceros fights with the elephant, runs his horn into his belly, and carries him off upon his head; but the blood and the fat of the elephant running into his eyes, and making him blind, he falls to the ground; and then, strange to relate! the roc comes and carries them both away in her claws, for food for her young ones.

"In this island I exchanged some of my diamonds for merchandise. From hence we went to other ports, and at last, having touched at several trading towns of the continent, we landed at Bussorah, from whence I proceeded to Bagdad. There I immediately gave large presents to the poor, and lived honourably upon the vast riches I had gained with so much fatigue."

Thus Sinbad ended his relation, gave Hindbad another hundred sequins, and invited him to come the next day to hear the account of the third voyage.

THE THIRD VOYAGE

"I soon lost the remembrance of the perils I had encountered in my two former voyages," said Sinbad, "and being in the flower of my age, I grew weary of living without business, and went from Bagdad to Bussorah with the richest commodities of the country. There I embarked again with some merchants. We made a long voyage and touched at several ports, where we carried on a considerable trade. One day, being out in the main ocean, we were overtaken by a dreadful tempest, which drove us from our course. The tempest continued several days, and brought us before the port of an island, which the captain was very unwilling to enter, but we were obliged to cast anchor. When we had furled our sails, the captain told us that this, and some other neighbouring islands, were inhabited by hairy savages, who would speedily attack us; and, though they were but dwarfs, yet we must make no resistance, for they were more in number than the locusts; and if we happened to kill one of them they would all fall upon us and destroy us.

"We soon found that what he had told us was but too true; an innumerable multitude of frightful savages, about two feet high, covered all over with red hair, came swimming towards us, and encompassed our ship. They spoke to us as they came near, but we understood not their language and they climbed up the sides of the ship with such agility as surprised us. They took down our sails, cut the cables, and hauling to the shore, made us all get out, and afterward carried the ship into another island, from whence they had come.

"We went forward into the island, where we gathered some fruits and herbs to prolong our lives as long as we could; but we expected nothing but death. As we advanced, we perceived at a distance a vast pile of buildings, and made toward it. We found it to be a palace, elegantly built, and very lofty, with a gate of ebony, which we forced open. We entered the court, where we saw before us a large apartment, with a porch, having on one side a heap of human bones, and on the other a vast number of roasting spits. We trembled at this spectacle, and being fatigued with travelling, fell to the ground, seized with deadly apprehension, and lay a long time motionless.

"The sun set, the gate of the apartment opened with a loud crash, and there came out the horrible figure of a black man, as tall as a lofty palm-tree. He had but one eye, and that in the middle of his forehead, where it looked as red as a burning coal. His fore-teeth were very long and sharp, and stood out of his mouth, which was as deep as that of a horse. His upper lip hung down upon his breast. His ears resembled those of an elephant, and covered his shoulders; and his nails were as long and crooked as the talons of the greatest birds. At the sight of so frightful a giant we became insensible, and lay like dead men.

"At last we came to ourselves, and saw him sitting in the porch looking at us. When he had considered us well, he advanced toward us, and laying his hand upon me, took me up by the nape of my neck, and turned me round as a butcher would do a sheep's head. After having examined me, and perceiving me to be so lean that I had nothing but skin and bone, he let me go. He took up all the rest one by one, and viewed them in the same manner. The captain being the fattest, he held him with one hand, as I would do a sparrow, and thrust a spit through him; he then kindled a great fire, roasted, and ate him in his apartment for his supper. Having finished his repast, he returned to his porch, where he lay and fell asleep, snoring louder than thunder. He slept thus till morning. As to ourselves, it was not possible for us to enjoy any rest, so that we passed the night in the most painful apprehension that can be imagined. When day appeared the giant awoke, got up, went out, and left us in the palace.

"When we thought him at a distance, we broke the melancholy silence we had preserved the whole of the night, and filled the palace with our lamentations and groans.

"We spent the day in traversing the island, supporting ourselves with fruits and herbs as we had done the day before. In the evening we sought for some place of shelter, but found none; so that we were forced, whether we would or not, to go back to the palace.

"The giant failed not to return, and supped once more upon one of our companions, after which he slept and snored till day, and then went out and left us as before. Our situation appeared to us so dreadful that several of my comrades designed to throw themselves into the sea, rather than die so painful a death, upon which one of the company answered that it would be much more reasonable to devise some method to rid ourselves of the monster.

"Having thought of a project for this purpose, I communicated it to my comrades, who approved it. 'Brethren,' said I, 'you know there is much timber floating upon the coast; if you will be advised by me, let us make several rafts capable of bearing

us. In the meantime, we will carry out the design I proposed
to you for our deliverance from the giant, and if it succeed, we
may remain here patiently awaiting the arrival of some ship;
but if it happen to miscarry, we will take to our rafts and put
to sea.' My advice was approved, and we made rafts capable
of carrying three persons on each.

"We returned to the palace toward the evening, and the
giant arrived shortly after. We were forced to submit to seeing
another of our comrades roasted, but at last we revenged ourselves on the brutish giant in the following manner. After he
had finished his supper he lay down on his back and fell asleep.
As soon as we heard him snore, according to his custom, nine of
the boldest among us, and myself, took each of us a spit, and
putting the points of them into the fire till they were burning hot,
we thrust them into his eye all at once and blinded him. The
pain made him break out into a frightful yell: he started up, and
stretched out his hands, in order to sacrifice some of us to his
rage: but we ran to such places as he could not reach; and after
having sought for us in vain, he groped for the gate and went out,
howling in agony.

"We quitted the palace after the giant and came to the shore,
where we had left our rafts, and put them immediately to sea.
We waited till day, in order to get upon them in case the giant
should come toward us with any guide of his own species; but
we hoped if he did not appear by sunrise, and gave over his
howling, which we still heard, that he would prove to be dead;
and if that happened, we resolved to stay in that island, and not
to risk our lives upon the rafts. But day had scarcely appeared
when we perceived our cruel enemy, accompanied with two others
almost of the same size, leading him; and a great number more
coming before him at a quick pace.

SINBAD THE VOYAGER

"We did not hesitate to take to our rafts, and put to sea with all the speed we could. The giants, who perceived this, took up great stones, and running to the shore, entered the water up to the middle, and threw so exactly that they sunk all the rafts but that I was upon; and all my companions, except the two with me, were drowned. We rowed with all our might, and escaped the giants, but when we got out to sea we were exposed to the mercy of the waves and winds, and spent that night and the following day under the most painful uncertainty as to our fate; but next mornng we had the good fortune to be thrown upon an island, where we landed with much joy. We found excellent fruit, which afforded us great relief and recruited our strength.

"At night we went to sleep on the sea shore; but were awakened by the noise of a serpent of surprising length and thickness, whose scales made a rustling noise as he wound himself along. It swallowed up one of my comrades, notwithstanding his loud cries, and the efforts he made to extricate himself from it; dashing him several times against the ground, it crushed him, and we could hear it gnaw and tear the poor wretch's bones, though we had fled to a considerable distance.

"As we walked about, when day returned, we saw a tall tree, upon which we designed to pass the following night, for our security; and having satisfied our hunger with fruit, we mounted it before the dusk had fallen. Shortly after, the serpent came hissing to the foot of the tree; raised itself up against the trunk of it, and meeting with my comrade, who sat lower than I, swallowed him at once, and went off.

I remained upon the tree till it was day, and then came down, more like a dead man than one alive, expecting the same fate as my two companions. This filled me with horror, and I advanced some steps to throw myself into the sea; but I withstood this dictate of despair, and submitted myself to the will of God.

"In the meantime I collected a great quantity of small wood, brambles, and dry thorns, and making them up into faggots, made a wide circle with them round the tree, and also tied some of them to the branches over my head. Having done this, when the evening came I shut myself up within this circle, feeling that I had neglected nothing which could preserve me from the cruel destiny with which I was threatened. The serpent failed not to come at the usual hour, and went round the tree, seeking for an opportunity to devour me, but was prevented by the rampart I had made; so that he lay till day, like a cat watching in vain for a mouse that has fortunately reached a place of safety. When day appeared he retired, but I dared not to leave my fort until the sun arose.

"I felt so much fatigued by the labour to which it had put me, and suffered so much from the serpent's poisonous breath, that death seemed more eligible to me than the horrors of such a state. I came down from the tree, and was going to throw myself into the sea, when God took compassion on me and I perceived a ship at a considerable distance. I called as loud as I could, and taking the linen from my turban, displayed it, that they might observe me. This had the desired effect; the crew perceived me, and the captain sent his boat for me. As soon as I came on board, the merchants and seamen flocked about me, to know how I came into that desert island; and after I had related to them all that had befallen me, the oldest among them said that they had often heard of the giants that dwelt in that island, that they were cannibals; and as to the serpents, they added, that there were abundance of them that hid themselves by day, and came abroad by night. After having testified their joy at

*Having finished his repast, he returned to his porch, where he
lay and fell asleep, snoring louder than thunder.*

my escaping so many dangers, they brought me the best of their provisions; and the captain, seeing that I was in rags, was so generous as to give me one of his own suits. We continued at sea for some time, touched at several islands, and at last landed at that of Salabat, where sandal wood is obtained, which is of great use in medicine. We entered the port, and came to anchor. The merchants began to unload their goods, in order to sell or exchange them. In the meantime, the captain came to me and said: 'Brother, I have here some goods that belonged to a merchant, who sailed some time on board this ship, and he being dead, I design to dispose of them for the benefit of his heirs.' The bales he spoke of lay on the deck, and showing them to me, he said: 'There are the goods; I hope you will take care to sell them, and you shall have factorage.' I thanked him for thus affording me an opportunity of employing myself, because I hated to be idle.

"The clerk of the ship took an account of all the bales, with the names of the merchants to whom they belonged, and when he asked the captain in whose name he should enter those he had given me the charge of, 'Enter them,' said the captain, 'in the name of Sinbad.' I could not hear myself named without some emotion; and looking steadfastly on the captain, I knew him to be the person who, in my second voyage, had left me in the island where I fell asleep.

"I was not surprised that he, believing me to be dead, did not recognise me. 'Captain,' said I, 'was the merchant's name, to whom those bales belonged, Sinbad?' 'Yes,' replied he, 'that was his name; he came from Bagdad, and embarked on board my ship at Bussorah.' 'You believe him, then, to be dead?' said I. 'Certainly,' answered he. 'No, captain,' resumed I; 'look at me, and you may know that I am Sinbad.'

"The captain, having considered me attentively, recognised me. 'God be praised,' said he, embracing me, 'I rejoice that fortune has rectified my fault. There are your goods, which I always took care to preserve.' I took them from him, and made him the acknowledgments to which he was entitled.

"From the isle of Salabat, we went to another, where I furnished myself with cloves, cinnamon, and other spices. As we sailed from this island, we saw a tortoise twenty cubits in length and breadth. We observed also an amphibious animal like a cow, which gave milk; its skin is so hard, that they usually make bucklers of it.

"In short, after a long voyage I arrived at Bussorah, and from thence returned to Bagdad, with so much wealth that I knew not its extent. I gave a great deal to the poor, and bought another considerable estate in addition to what I had already."

Thus Sinbad finished the history of his third voyage; gave another hundred sequins to Hindbad, and invited him to dinner again the next day to hear the story of his fourth series of adventures.

THE FOURTH VOYAGE

"The pleasures which I enjoyed after my third voyage had not charms sufficient to divert me from another. My passion for trade, and my love of novelty, again prevailed. I therefore settled my affairs, and having provided a stock of goods fit for the traffic I designed to engage in, I set out on my journey. I took the route of Persia, travelled over several provinces, and then arrived at a port, where I embarked. We hoisted our sails, and touched at several ports of the continent, and then put out to sea; when we were overtaken by such a sudden gust of wind, as obliged the captain to lower his yards, and take all other necessary precautions to prevent the danger that threatened us. But all was in vain; our endeavours had no effect, the sails were split in a thousand pieces, and the ship was stranded; several of the merchants and seamen were drowned, and the cargo was lost.

"I had the good fortune, with several of the merchants and mariners, to get upon some planks, and we were carried by the current to an island which lay before us. There we found fruit and spring water, which preserved our lives. We stayed all night near the place where we had been cast ashore and next morning, as soon as the sun was up, advancing into the island, saw some houses, which we approached. As soon as we drew near, we were encompassed by a great number of negroes, who seized us and carried us to their respective habitations.

"I, and five of my comrades, were carried to one place; here they made us sit down, and gave us a certain herb, which they made signs to us to eat. My comrades, not taking notice that the blacks ate none of it themselves, thought only of satisfying their hunger, and ate with greediness. But I, suspecting some trick, would not so much as taste it, which happened well for me; for in a little time after, I perceived my companions had lost their senses, and that when they spoke to me, they knew not what they said.

"The negroes fed us afterward with rice, prepared with oil of cocoa-nuts; and my comrades, who had lost their reason, ate of it greedily. I also partook of it, but very sparingly. They gave us that herb at first on purpose to deprive us of our senses, that we might not be aware of the sad destiny prepared for us; and they supplied us with rice to fatten us; for, being cannibals, their design was to eat us as soon as we grew fat. This accordingly happened, for they devoured my comrades, who were not sensible of their condition; but my senses being entire, you may easily guess that instead of growing fat I grew leaner every day. The fear of death under which I laboured caused me to fall into a languishing distemper, which proved my safety; for the negroes, having eaten my companions, seeing me to be withered, and sick, deferred my death.

"Meanwhile I had much liberty, so that scarcely any notice was taken of what I did, and this gave me an opportunity one day to get at a distance from the houses and to make my escape. An old man, who saw me and suspected my design, called to me as loud as he could to return; but I redoubled my speed, and quickly got out of sight. At that time there was none but the old man about the houses, the rest being abroad, and not to return till night, which was usual with them. Therefore, being sure that they could not arrive in time enough to pursue me, I went on till night, when I stopped to rest a little, and to eat some of the provisions I had secured; but I speedily set forward again, and travelled seven days, avoiding those places which seemed to be inhabited, and lived for the most part upon cocoa-nuts, which served me both for meat and drink. On the eighth day I came near the sea, and saw some white people like myself, gathering pepper, of which there was great plenty in that place. This I took to be a good omen, and went to them without any scruple. They came to meet me as soon as they saw me, and asked me in Arabic who I was, and whence I came. I was overjoyed to hear them speak in my own language, and satisfied their curiosity by giving them an account of my shipwreck, and how I fell into the hands of the negroes. 'Those negroes,' replied they, 'eat men, and by what miracle did you escape their cruelty?' I related to them the circumstances I have just mentioned, at which they were wonderfully surprised.

"I stayed with them till they had gathered their quantity of pepper, and then sailed with them to the island from whence they had come. They presented me to their king, who was a good prince. He had the patience to hear the relation of my adventures; and he afterward gave me clothes, and commanded care to be taken of me.

"The island was very well peopled, plentiful in everything, and the capital a place of great trade. This agreeable retreat was very comfortable to me, after my misfortunes, and the kindness of this generous prince completed my satisfaction. In a word, there was not a person more in favour with him than myself; and consequently every man in court and city sought to oblige me; so that in a very little time I was looked upon rather as a native than a stranger.

"I observed one thing which to me appeared very extraordinary. All the people, the king himself not excepted, rode their horses without bridle or stirrups. This made me one day take the liberty to ask the king how it came to pass. His Majesty answered, that I talked to him of things which nobody knew the use of in his dominions.

"I went immediately to a workman, and gave him a model for making the stock of a saddle. When that was done, I covered it myself with velvet and leather, and embroidered it with gold. I afterward went to a smith, who made me a bit, according to the pattern I showed him, and also some stirrups. When I had all things completed, I presented them to the king, and put them upon one of his horses. His Majesty mounted immediately, and was so pleased with them, that he testified his satisfaction by large presents.

"As I paid my court very constantly to the king, he said to me one day: 'Sinbad, I love thee and I have one thing to demand of thee, which thou must grant.' 'Sir,' answered I, 'there is nothing but I will do, as a mark of my obedience to your Majesty.' 'I have a mind thou shouldst marry,' replied he, 'that so thou mayest stay in my dominions, and think no more of thy own country.' I durst not resist the prince's will, and he gave me one of the ladies of his court, noble, beautiful, and rich. The ceremonies of marriage being over, I went and dwelt with my wife, and for some time we lived together in perfect harmony. I was not, however, satisfied with my banishment, therefore designed to make my escape the first opportunity, and to return to Bagdad.

"At this time the wife of one of my neighbours fell sick, and died. I went to see and comfort him in his affliction, and finding him absorbed in sorrow, I said to him as soon as I saw him: 'God preserve you and grant you a long life.' 'Alas!' replied he, 'how do you think I should obtain the favour you wish me? I have not above an hour to live.' 'Pray,' said I, 'do not entertain such a melancholy thought; I hope I shall enjoy your company many years.' 'I wish you,' he replied, 'a long life; but my days are at an end, for I must be buried this day with my wife. This is a law which our ancestors established in this island, and it is always observed. The living husband is interred with the dead wife, and the living wife with the dead husband. Nothing can save me; every one must submit to this law.'

"While he was giving me an account of this barbarous custom, the very relation of which chilled my blood, his kindred, friends, and neighbours came in a body to assist at the funeral. They dressed the corpse of the woman in her richest apparel, and all her jewels, as if it had been her wedding day; then they

placed her in an open coffin, and began their march to the place
of burial, the husband walking at the head of the company.
They proceeded to a high mountain, and when they had reached
the place of their destination, they took up a large stone, which
covered the mouth of a deep pit, and let down the corpse with all
its apparel and jewels. Then the husband embracing his
kindred and friends, suffered himself, without resistance, to be put
into another open coffin with a pot of water, and seven small
loaves, and was let down in the same manner. The ceremony
being over, the aperture was again covered with the stone, and the
company returned.

"It is needless for me to tell you that I was a melancholy
spectator of this funeral, while the rest were scarcely moved, the
custom was to them so familiar. I could not forbear communicating to the king my sentiment respecting the practice: 'Sir,' I
said, 'I cannot but feel astonished at the strange usage observed
in this country, of burying the living with the dead. I have been
a great traveller, and seen many countries, but never heard of so
cruel a law.' 'What do you mean, Sinbad?' replied the king:
'it is a common law. I shall be interred with the queen, my
wife, if she die first.' 'But, sir,' said I, 'may I presume to ask
your Majesty, if strangers be obliged to observe this law?'
'Without doubt,' returned the king; 'they are not exempted,
if they be married in this island.'

"I returned home much depressed by this answer; for the
fear of my wife's dying first and that I should be interred alive
with her, occasioned me very uneasy reflections. But there was
no remedy; I must have patience, and submit to the will of God.
I trembled, however, at every little indisposition of my wife, and,
alas! in a little time my fears were realised, for she fell sick and
died.

"The king and all his court expressed their wish to honour the funeral with their presence, and the most considerable people of the city did the same. When all was ready for the ceremony, the corpse was put into a coffin with all her jewels and her most magnificent apparel. The procession began, and as second actor in this doleful tragedy, I went next the corpse, with my eyes full of tears, bewailing my deplorable fate. Before we reached the mountain, I made an attempt to affect the minds of the spectators: I addressed myself to the king first, and then to all those that were round me; bowing before them to the earth, and kissing the border of their garments, I prayed them to have compassion upon me. 'Consider,' said I, 'that I am a stranger, and ought not to be subject to this rigorous law, and that I have another wife and children in my own country.' Although I spoke in the most pathetic manner, no one was moved by my address; on the contrary, they ridiculed my dread of death as cowardly, made haste to let my wife's corpse into the pit, and lowered me down the next moment in an open coffin with a vessel full of water and seven loaves.

"As I approached the bottom, I discovered by the aid of the little light that came from above the nature of this subterranean place; it seemed an endless cavern, and might be about fifty fathoms deep.

"Instead of losing my courage and calling death to my assistance in that miserable condition, however, I felt still an inclination to live, and to do all I could to prolong my days. I went groping about, for the bread and water that was in my coffin, and took some of it. Though the darkness of the cave was so great that I could not distinguish day and night, yet I always found my coffin again, and the cave seemed to be more spacious than it had appeared to be at first. I lived for some days upon my bread and water, which being all spent, I at last prepared for death.

"I was offering up my last devotions when I heard something tread, and breathing or panting as it walked. I advanced toward that side from whence I heard the noise, and on my approach the creature puffed and blew harder, as if running away from me. I followed the noise, and the thing seemed to stop sometimes, but always fled and blew as I approached. I pursued it for a considerable time, till at last I perceived a light, resembling a star; I went on, sometimes lost sight of it, but always found it again, and at last discovered that it came through a hole in the rock, large enough to admit a man.

"Upon this, I stopped some time to rest, being much fatigued with the rapidity of my progress: afterward coming up to the hole, I got through, and found myself upon the seashore. I leave you to guess the excess of my joy: it was such that I could scarcely persuade myself that the whole was not a dream.

"But when I was recovered from my surprise, and convinced of the reality of my escape, I perceived what I had followed to be a creature which came out of the sea, and was accustomed to enter the cavern when the tides were high.

"I examined the mountain, and found it to be situated betwixt the sea and the town, but without any passage to or communication with the latter; the rocks on the sea side being high and perpendicularly steep. I prostrated myself on the shore to thank God for this mercy, and afterward entered the cave again to fetch bread and water, which I ate by daylight with a better appetite than I had done since my interment in the dark cavern.

"I returned thither a second time, and groped among the coffins for all the diamonds, rubies, pearls, gold bracelets, and rich stuffs I could find; these I brought to the shore, and tying them up neatly into bales, I laid them together upon the beach, waiting till some ship might appear.

"After two or three days, I perceived a ship just come out of the harbour, making for the place where I was. I made a sign with the linen of my turban, and called to the crew as loud as I could. They heard me, and sent a boat to bring me on board, when they asked by what misfortune I came thither; I told them that I had suffered shipwreck two days before, and made shift to get ashore with the goods they saw. It was fortunate for me that these people did not consider the place where I was, nor inquire into the probability of what I told them; but without hesitation took me on board. When I came to the ship, the captain was so well pleased to have saved me, and so much taken up with his own affairs, that he also took the story of my pretended shipwreck upon trust, and generously refused some jewels which I offered him.

"We passed by several islands, and among others that called the isle of Bells, about ten days' sail from Serendib, and six from that of Kela, where we landed. This island produces lead mines, Indian canes, and excellent camphire.

"The King of the isle of Kela is very rich and powerful, and the isle of Bells, which is about two days' journey in extent, is also subject to him. The inhabitants are so barbarous that they still eat human flesh. After we had finished our traffic in that island, we put to sea again, and touched at several other ports; at last I arrived happily at Bagdad with infinite riches. Out of gratitude to God for His mercies, I contributed liberally toward the support of several mosques, and the subsistence of the poor, and gave myself up to the society of my kindred and friends, enjoying myself with them in festivities and amusements."

Here Sinbad finished the relation of his fourth voyage. He

made a new present of one hundred sequins to Hindbad, whom he requested to return with the rest next day at the same hour to dine with him, and hear the story of his fifth voyage. Hindbad and the other guests took their leave and retired. Next morning when they all met, they sat down at table, and when dinner was over, Sinbad began the relation of his fifth voyage as follows:

THE FIFTH VOYAGE

"All the troubles and calamities I had undergone," said he, "could not cure me of my inclination to make new voyages. I therefore bought goods, departed with them for the best seaport; and that I might not be obliged to depend upon a captain, but have a ship at my own command, I remained there till one was built on purpose. When the ship was ready, I went on board with my goods: but not having enough to load her, I agreed to take with me several merchants of different nations with their merchandise.

"We sailed with the first fair wind, and after a long navigation, the first place we touched at was a desert island, where we found an egg of a roc, equal in size to that I formerly mentioned. There was a young roc in it just ready to be hatched, and its bill had begun to appear. The merchants whom I had taken on board, and who landed with me, broke the egg with hatchets, pulled out the young roc, piecemeal, and roasted it. I had earnestly entreated them not to meddle with the egg, but they would not listen to me.

"Scarcely had they finished their repast, when there appeared in the air at a considerable distance from us two great clouds. The captain whom I had hired to navigate my ship, said they were the male and female roc that belonged to the young one and pressed us to re-embark with all speed, to prevent the misfortune which he saw would otherwise befall us. We hastened on board, and set sail with all possible expedition.

"In the meantime, the two rocs approached with a frightful noise, which they redoubled when they saw the egg broken, and their young one gone. They flew back in the direction they had come, and disappeared for some time, while we made all the sail we could to endeavour to prevent that which unhappily befell us.

"They soon returned, and we observed that each of them carried between its talons rocks of a monstrous size. When they came directly over my ship, they hovered, and one of them let fall a stone, but by the dexterity of the steersman it missed us. The other roc, to our misfortune, threw his burden so exactly upon the middle of the ship, as to split it into a thousand pieces. The mariners and passengers were all crushed to death, or sank. I myself was of the number of the latter; but as I came up again, I fortunately caught hold of a piece of the wreck, and swimming sometimes with one hand, and sometimes with the other, I came to an island, and got safely ashore.

"I sat down upon the grass, to recover myself from my fatigue, after which I went into the island to explore it. I found trees everywhere, some of them bearing green, and others ripe fruits, and streams of fresh pure water. I ate of the fruits, which I found excellent; and drank of the water, which was very good.

"When I was a little advanced into the island, I saw an old man, who appeared very weak and infirm. He was sitting on the bank of a stream, and at first I took him to be one who had been shipwrecked like myself. I went toward him and saluted him, but he only slightly bowed his head. I asked him why he sat so still, but instead of answering me, he made a sign for me to take him upon my back, and carry him over the brook, signifying that it was to gather fruit.

"I believed him really to stand in need of my assistance, took him upon my back, and having carried him over, bade him get down, and for that end stooped, that he might get off with ease; but instead of doing so (which I laugh at every time I think of it) the old man, who to me appeared quite decrepit, clasped his legs nimbly about my neck. He sat astride upon my shoulders, and held my throat so tight, that I thought he would have strangled me, the apprehension of which made me swoon and fall down.

"Notwithstanding my fainting, the ill-natured old fellow kept fast about my neck, but opened his legs a little to give me time to recover my breath. When I had done so, he thrust one of his feet against my stomach, and struck me so rudely on the side with the other that he forced me to rise up against my will. Having arisen, he made me walk under the trees, and forced me now and then to stop, to gather and eat fruit. He never left me all day, and when I lay down to rest at night, laid himself down with me, holding always fast about my neck. Every morning he pushed me to make me awake, and afterward obliged me to get up and walk, and pressed me with his feet.

"One day I found in my way several dry calabashes that had fallen from a tree. I took a large one, and after cleaning it, pressed into it some juice of grapes, which abounded in the island; having filled the calabash, I put it by in a convenient place, and going thither again some days after, I tasted it, and found the wine so good, that it soon made me forget my sorrow, gave me new vigour, and so exhilarated my spirits, that I began to sing and dance as I walked along.

"The old man, perceiving the effect which this liquor had upon me, and that I carried him with more ease than before, made me a sign to give him some of it. I handed him the calabash, and the liquor pleasing his palate, he drank it all off. There being a considerable quantity of it, he became intoxicated, and the fumes getting up into his head, he began to sing after his manner, and to dance, thus loosening his legs from about me by degrees. Finding that he did not press me as before, I threw him upon the ground, where he lay without motion; I then took up a great stone, and crushed him.

"I was extremely glad to be thus freed forever from this troublesome fellow. I now walked toward the beach, where I met the crew of a ship that had cast anchor, to take in water. They were surprised to see me, but more so at hearing the particulars of my adventures. 'You fell,' said they, 'into the hands of the Old Man of the Sea, and are the first who ever escaped strangling by his malicious tricks. He never quits those he has once made himself master of till he has destroyed them, and he has made this island notorious by the number of men he has slain.'

"After having informed me of these things, they carried me with them to the ship, and the captain received me with great kindness, when they told him what had befallen me. He put out again to sea, and after some days' sail, we arrived at the harbour of a great city.

"One of the merchants who had taken me into his friendship invited me to go along with him, and carried me to a place appointed for the accommodation of foreign merchants. He gave me a large bag, and having recommended me to some people of the town, who used to gather cocoa-nuts, desired them to take me with them. 'Go,' said he, 'follow them, and act as you see them do, but do not separate from them, otherwise you may endanger your life.' Having thus spoken, he gave me provisions for the journey, and I went with them.

"We came to a thick forest of cocoa-trees, very lofty, with trunks so smooth that it was not possible to climb to the branches that bore the fruit. When we entered the forest we saw a great number of apes of several sizes, who fled as soon as they perceived us, and climbed up to the top of the trees with surprising swiftness.

"The merchants with whom I was, gathered stones and threw them at the apes on the trees. I did the same, and the apes out of revenge threw cocoa-nuts at us so fast, and with such gestures, as sufficiently testified their anger and resentment. We gathered up the cocoa-nuts, and from time to time threw stones to provoke the apes; so that by this stratagem we filled our bags with cocoa-nuts, which it had been impossible otherwise to have done.

"When we had gathered our number, we returned to the city, where the merchant who had sent me to the forest gave me the value of the cocoas I brought: 'Go on,' said he, 'and do the like every day, until you have got money enough to carry you home.' I thanked him for his advice, and gradually collected as many cocoa-nuts as produced me a considerable sum.

"The vessel in which I had come sailed with some merchants who loaded her with cocoa-nuts. I embarked in her all the nuts I had, and when she was ready to sail took leave of the merchant who had been so kind to me.

"We sailed toward the islands, where pepper grows in great plenty. From thence we went to the isle of Comari, where the best species of wood of aloes grows. I exchanged my cocoa in those two islands for pepper and wood of aloes, and went with other merchants a pearl-fishing. I hired divers, who brought me up some that were very large and pure. I embarked in a vessel that happily arrived at Bussorah; from thence I returned to Bagdad, where I made vast sums from my pepper, wood of aloes, and pearls. I gave the tenth of my gains in alms, as I had done upon my return from my other voyages, and endeavoured to dissipate my fatigues by amusements of different kinds."

When Sinbad had finished his story, he ordered one hundred sequins to be given to Hindbad, who retired with the other guests; but next morning the same company returned to dine; when Sinbad requested their attention, and gave the following account of his sixth voyage:

THE SIXTH VOYAGE

"You long without doubt to know," said he, "how, after having been shipwrecked five times, and escaped so many dangers, I could resolve again to tempt fortune, and expose myself to new hardships. I am, myself, astonished at my conduct when I reflect upon it, and must certainly have been actuated by my destiny. But be that as it may, after a year's rest I prepared for a sixth voyage, notwithstanding the entreaties of my kindred, who did all in their power to dissuade me.

"Instead of taking my way by the Persian Gulf, I travelled once more through several provinces of Persia and the Indies, and arrived at a seaport, where I embarked in a ship, the captain of which was bound on a long voyage. It was long indeed, for the captain and pilot lost their course. They, however, at last discovered where they were, but we had no reason to rejoice at the circumstance. Suddenly we saw the captain quit his post, uttering loud lamentations. He threw off his turban, pulled his beard, and beat his head like a madman. We asked

him the reason, and he answered, that he was in the most dangerous place in all the ocean. 'A rapid current carries the ship
along with it,' said he, 'and we shall all perish in less than a
quarter of an hour. Pray to God to deliver us from this peril;
we cannot escape, if He do not take pity on us.' At these words
he ordered the sails to be lowered; but all the ropes broke, and
the ship was carried by the current to the foot of an inaccessible
mountain, where she struck and went to pieces, yet in such a
manner that we saved our lives, our provisions, and the best of
our goods.

"This being over, the captain said to us: 'God has done what
pleased Him. Each of us may dig his grave, and bid the world
adieu; for we are all in so fatal a place, that none shipwrecked
here ever returned to their homes.' His discourse afflicted us sensibly, and we embraced each other, bewailing our deplorable lot.

"The mountain at the foot of which we were wrecked formed
part of the coast of a very large island. It was covered with
wrecks, with human bones, and with a vast quantity of goods
and riches. In all other places, rivers run from their channels
into the sea, but here a river of fresh water runs out of the sea
into a dark cavern, whose entrance is very high and spacious.
What is most remarkable in this place is, that the stones of the
mountain are of crystal, rubies, or other precious stones. Here
is also a sort of fountain of pitch or bitumen, that runs into the
sea, which the fish swallow, and turn into ambergris: and this
the waves throw up on the beach in great quantities. Trees also
grow here, most of which are wood of aloes, equal in goodness to
those of Comari.

"To finish the description of this place, which may well be
called a gulf, since nothing ever returns from it, it is not possible
for ships to get off when once they approach within a certain

distance. If they be driven thither by a wind from the sea, the wind and the current impel them; and if they come into it when a land-wind blows, the height of the mountain stops the wind, and occasions a calm, so that the force of the current carries them ashore: and what completes the misfortune is, that there is no possibility of ascending the mountain, or of escaping by sea.

"We continued upon the shore in a state of despair, and expected death every day. At first we divided our provisions as equally as we could, and thus every one lived a longer or shorter time, according to his temperance, and the use he made of his provisions.

"I survived all my companions, yet when I buried the last, I had so little provision remaining that I thought I could not long endure and I dug a grave, resolving to lie down in it because there was no one left to inter me.

"But it pleased God once more to take compassion on me, and put it in my mind to go to the bank of the river which ran into the great cavern. Considering its probable course with great attention, I said to myself: 'This river, which runs thus under ground, must somewhere have an issue. If I make a raft, and leave myself to the current, it will convey me to some inhabited country, or I shall perish. If I be drowned, I lose nothing, but only change one kind of death for another.'

"I immediately went to work upon large pieces of timber and cables, for I had choice of them, and tied them together so strongly that I soon made a very solid raft. When I had finished, I loaded it with rubies, emeralds, ambergris, rock-crystal, and bales of rich stuffs. Having balanced my cargo exactly, and fastened it well to the raft, I went on board with two oars that I had made, and leaving it to the course of the river, resigned myself to the will of God.

SINBAD THE VOYAGER

"As soon as I entered the cavern I lost all light, and the stream carried me I knew not whither. Thus I floated some days in perfect darkness, and once found the arch so low, that it very nearly touched my head, which made me cautious afterward to avoid the like danger. All this while I ate nothing but what was just necessary to support nature; yet, notwithstanding my frugality, all my provisions were spent. Then a pleasing stupor seized upon me. I cannot tell how long it continued; but when I revived, I was surprised to find myself in an extensive plain on the brink of a river, where my raft was tied, amidst a great number of negroes. I got up as soon as I saw them, and saluted them. They spoke to me, but I did not understand their language. I was so transported with joy, that I knew not whether I was asleep or awake; but being persuaded that I was not asleep, I recited aloud the following words in Arabic: 'Call upon the Almighty, He will help thee; thou needest not perplex thyself about anything else: shut thy eyes, and while thou art asleep, God will change thy bad fortune into good.'

"One of the blacks, who understood Arabic, hearing me speak thus, came toward me and said: 'Brother, be not surprised to see us; we are inhabitants of this country, and came hither to-day to water our fields. We observed something floating upon the water, and, perceiving your raft, one of us swam into the river and brought it hither, where we fastened it, as you see, until you should awake. Pray tell us your history, for it must be extraordinary; how did you venture yourself into this river, and whence did you come?' I begged of them first to give me something to eat, and then I would satisfy their curiosity. They gave me several sorts of food, and when I had satisfied my hunger, I related all that had befallen me, which they listened to with attentive surprise. As soon as I had finished, they told me, by the person who spoke Arabic and interpreted to them what I said, that it was one of the most wonderful stories they had ever heard, and that I must go along with them, and tell it to their king myself; it being too extraordinary to be related by any other than the person to whom the events had happened.

"They immediately sent for a horse, which was brought in a little time; and having helped me to mount, some of them walked before to shew the way, while the rest took my raft and cargo and followed.

"We marched till we came to the capital of Serendib, for it was in that island I had landed. The blacks presented me to their king; I approached his throne, and saluted him as I used to do the Kings of the Indies; that is to say, I prostrated myself at his feet. The prince ordered me to rise, received me with an obliging air, and made me sit down near him.

"I related to the king all that I have told you, and his majesty was so surprised and pleased, that he commanded my adventures to be written in letters of gold, and laid up in the archives of his kingdom. At last my raft was brought in, and the bales opened in his presence: he admired the quantity of wood of aloes and ambergris; but, above all, the rubies and emeralds, for he had none in his treasury that equalled them.

"Observing that he looked on my jewels with pleasure, I fell prostrate at his feet, and took the liberty to say to him: 'Sir, not only my person is at your majesty's service, but the cargo of the raft, and I would beg of you to dispose of it as your own.' He answered me with a smile: 'Sinbad, I will take care not to covet anything of yours, or to take anything from you that God has given you; far from lessening your wealth, I design to augment it, and will not let you quit my dominions without marks of my liberality.' He then charged one of his officers to take care of me, and ordered people to serve me at his own expense. The officer was very faithful in the execution of his commission, and caused all the goods to be carried to the lodgings provided for me.

"I went every day at a set hour to make my court to the king, and spent the rest of my time in viewing the city, and what was most worthy of notice.

"The capital of Serendib stands at the end of a fine valley, in the middle of the island, encompassed by mountains the highest in the world. Rubies and several sorts of minerals abound, and the rocks are for the most part composed of a metalline stone made use of to cut and polish other precious stones. All kinds of rare plants and trees grow there, especially cedars and cocoanut. There is also a pearl-fishing in the mouth of its principal river; and in some of its valleys are found diamonds. I made, by way of devotion, a pilgrimage to the place where Adam was confined after his banishment from Paradise, and had the curiosity to go to the top of the mountain.

"When I returned to the city, I prayed the king to allow me to return to my own country, and he granted me permission in the most honourable manner. He would needs force a rich present upon me; and when I went to take my leave of him, he gave me one much more considerable, and at the same time charged me with a letter for the Commander of the Faithful, our sovereign, saying to me: 'I pray you give this present from me, and this letter, to the Caliph, and assure him of my friendship.' I took the present and letter and promised his majesty punctually to execute the commission with which he was pleased to honour me.

"The letter from the King of Serendib was written on the skin of a certain animal of great value, because of its being so scarce, and of a yellowish colour. The characters of this letter were of azure, and the contents as follows:

"'The King of the Indies, before whom march one hundred elephants, who lives in a palace that shines with one hundred thousand rubies, and who has in his treasury twenty thousand crowns enriched with diamonds, to Caliph Haroun-al-Raschid:—

"'Though the present we send you be inconsiderable, receive it, however, as a brother, in consideration of the hearty friendship which we bear for you, and of which we are willing to give you proof. We desire the same part in your friendship, considering that we believe it to be our merit, being of the same dignity with yourself. We conjure you this in quality of a brother. Adieu.'

"The present consisted, first, of one single ruby made into a cup, about half a foot high, an inch thick, and filled with round pearls of half a drachm each. 2. The skin of a serpent, whose scales were as large as an ordinary piece of gold, and had the virtue to preserve from sickness those who lay upon it. 3. Fifty thousand drachms of the best wood of aloes, with thirty grains of camphire as big as pistachios. And, 4. A female slave of ravishing beauty, whose apparel was all covered over with jewels.

"The ship set sail, and after a very successful navigation we landed at Bussorah, and from thence I went to Bagdad, where the first thing I did was to acquit myself of my commission.

"I took the king of Serendib's letter and went to present myself at the gate of the Commander of the Faithful, followed by the beautiful slave, and such of my own family as carried the gifts. I stated the reason of my coming, and was immediately conducted to the throne of the caliph. I made my reverence, and, after a short speech, gave him the letter and present. When he had read what the king of Serendib wrote to him, he asked me if the prince were really so rich and potent as he represented himself in his letter. I prostrated myself a second time, and rising again, said: 'Commander of the Faithful, I can assure your majesty he doth not exceed the truth. Nothing is more worthy of admiration than the magnificence of his palace. When the prince appears in public he has a throne fixed on the back of an elephant, and marches betwixt two ranks of his ministers, favourites, and other people of his court; before him, upon the same elephant, an officer carries a golden lance in his hand; and behind the throne there is another, who stands upright, with a column of gold, on the top of which is an emerald half a foot long and an inch thick; before him march a guard of one thousand men, clad in cloth of gold and silk, and mounted on elephants richly caparisoned.

"While the king is on his march, the officer who is before him on the same elephant cries from time to time, with a loud voice: 'Behold the great monarch, the potent and redoubtable Sultan of the Indies, whose palace is covered with one hundred thousand rubies, and who possesses twenty thousand crowns of diamonds. Behold the monarch greater than Solomon, and the powerful Maha-raja.' After he has pronounced those words, the officer behind the throne cries in his turn: 'This monarch, so great and so powerful, must die, must die, must die.' And the officer before replies: 'Praise be to him who liveth for ever.'

"Furthermore, the King of Serendib is so just that there are no judges in his dominions. His people have no need of them. They understand and observe justice rigidly of themselves.'

"The caliph was much pleased with my account. 'The wisdom of that king,' said he, 'appears in his letter, and after what you tell me, I must confess, that his wisdom is worthy of his people, and his people deserve so wise a prince.' Having spoken thus, he dismissed me, and sent me home with a rich present.

Sinbad left off, and his company retired, Hindbad having first received one hundred sequins; and next day they returned to hear the relation of his seventh and last voyage.

THE SEVENTH AND LAST VOYAGE

"Being returned from my sixth voyage," said Sinbad, "I absolutely laid aside all thoughts of travelling; for, besides that my age now required rest, I was resolved no more to expose myself to such risks as I had encountered; so that I thought of nothing but to pass the rest of my days in tranquillity. One day, however, as I was treating my friends, one of my servants came and told me that an officer of the caliph's inquired for me. I rose from table, and went to him. 'The caliph,' said he, 'has sent me to tell you that he must speak with you.' I followed the officer to the palace, where, being presented to the caliph, I saluted him by prostrating myself at his feet. 'Sinbad,' said he to me, 'I stand in need of your service; you must carry my answer and present to the King of Serendib. It is but just I should return his civility.'

"This command of the caliph was to me like a clap of thunder. 'Commander of the Faithful,' I replied, 'I am ready to do whatever your majesty shall think fit to command; but I beseech you most humbly to consider what I have undergone. I have also made a vow never to go out of Bagdad.' Hence I took occasion to give him a full and particular account of all my adventures, which he had the patience to hear out.

SINBAD THE VOYAGER

"As soon as I had finished, 'I confess,' said he, 'that the things you tell me are very extraordinary, yet you must for my sake undertake this voyage which I propose to you. You will only have to go to the isle of Serendib, and deliver the commission which I give you, for you know it would not comport with my dignity to be indebted to the king of that island.' Perceiving that the caliph insisted upon my compliance, I submitted, and told him that I was willing to obey. He was very well pleased, and ordered me one thousand sequins for the expenses of my journey.

"I prepared for my departure in a few days, and as soon as the caliph's letter and present were delivered to me, I went to Bussorah, where I embarked, and had a very happy voyage. Having arrived at the isle of Serendib, I acquainted the king's ministers with my commission, and prayed them to get me speedy audience. They did so, and I was conducted to the palace, where I saluted the king by prostration, according to custom. That prince knew me immediately, and testified very great joy at seeing me. 'Sinbad,' said he, 'you are welcome; I have many times thought of you since you departed; I bless the day on which we see one another once more.' I made my compliments to him, and after having thanked him for his kindness, delivered the caliph's letter and present, which he received with all imaginable satisfaction.

"The caliph's present was a complete suit of cloth of gold, valued at one thousand sequins; fifty robes of rich stuff, a hundred of white cloth, the finest of Cairo, Suez, and Alexandria; a vessel of agate broader than deep, an inch thick, and half a foot wide, the bottom of which represented in bas-relief a man with one knee on the ground, who held a bow and an arrow, ready to discharge at a lion. He sent him also a rich tablet, which, accord-

ing to tradition, belonged to the great Solomon. The caliph's
letter was as follows:

"'Greeting, in the name of the sovereign guide of the right
way, from the dependant on God, Haroun-al-Raschid, whom
God hath set in the place of vicegerent to his prophet, after
his ancestors of happy memory, to the potent and esteemed
Raja of Serendib:—

"'We received your letter with joy, and send you this from our
imperial residence, the garden of superior wits. We hope when
you look upon it, you will perceive our good intention and be
pleased with it. Adieu.'

"The King of Serendib was highly gratified that the caliph
answered his friendship. A little time after this audience, I
solicited leave to depart, and had much difficulty to obtain it.
I procured it, however, at last, and the king, when he dismissed
me, made me a very considerable present. I embarked immediately to return to Bagdad, but had not the good fortune to
arrive there so speedily as I had hoped. God ordered it otherwise.

"Three or four days after my departure, we were attacked
by corsairs, who easily seized upon our ship, because it was no
vessel of force. Some of the crew offered resistance, which cost
them their lives. But for myself and the rest, who were not so
imprudent, the corsairs saved us on purpose to make slaves of us.

"We were all stripped, and instead of our own clothes, they
gave us sorry rags, and carried us into a remote island, where
they sold us.

"I fell into the hands of a rich merchant, who, as soon as he
bought me, carried me to his house, treated me well, and clad

me handsomely for a slave. Some days after, not knowing who I was, he asked me if I understood any trade. I answered, that I was no mechanic, but a merchant, and that the corsairs who sold me, had robbed me of all I possessed. 'But tell me,' replied he, 'can you shoot with a bow?' I answered, that the bow was one of my exercises in my youth. He gave me a bow and arrows, and, taking me behind him upon an elephant, carried me to a thick forest some leagues from the town. We penetrated a great way into the wood, and he bade me alight; then, shewing me a great tree, 'Climb up that,' said he, 'and shoot at the elephants as you see them pass by, for there is a prodigious number of them in this forest, and if any of them fall, come and give me notice.' Having spoken this, he left me victuals, and returned to the town, and I continued upon the tree all night.

"I saw no elephant during the night, but next morning, as soon as the sun was up, I perceived a great number. I shot several arrows among them, and at last one of the elephants fell, when the rest retired immediately, and left me at liberty to go and acquaint my patron with my booty. When I had informed him, he gave me a good meal, commended my dexterity, and caressed me highly. We went afterwards together to the forest, where we dug a hole for the elephant; my patron designing to return when it had fallen to pieces and take its teeth to trade with.

"I continued this employment for two months, and killed an elephant every day, getting sometimes upon one tree, and sometimes upon another. One morning, as I looked for the elephants, I perceived with extreme amazement that, instead of passing by me across the forest as usual, they stopped, and came to me with a horrible noise, in such number that the plain was covered, and shook under them. They encompassed the tree in which I was concealed, with their trunks extended, and all fixed their eyes upon me. At this alarming spectacle I continued immovable, and was so much terrified, that my bow and arrows fell out of my hand.

"My fears were not without cause; for after the elephants had stared upon me some time, one of the largest of them put his trunk round the foot of the tree, plucked it up, and threw it on the ground. I fell with the tree; and the elephant, taking me up with his trunk, laid me on his back, where I sat more like one dead than alive, with my quiver on my shoulder. He put himself afterward at the head of the rest, who followed him in troops, carried me a considerable way, then laid me down on the ground, and retired with all his companions. After having lain some time, and seeing the elephants gone, I got up, and found I was upon a long and broad hill, almost covered with the bones and teeth of elephants. I confess to you, that this object furnished me with abundance of reflections. I admired the instinct of those animals; I doubted not but that was their burying-place, and that they carried me thither on purpose to tell me that I should forbear to persecute them, since I did it only for their teeth. I did not stay on the hill, but turned toward the city, and, after having travelled a day and a night, I came to my patron.

"As soon as he saw me, 'Ah, poor Sinbad,' exclaimed he, 'I was in great trouble to know what was become of you. I have been at the forest, where I found a tree newly pulled up, and a bow and arrows on the ground, and I despaired of ever seeing you more. Pray tell me what befell you, and by what good chance you are still alive.' I satisfied his curiosity, and going both of us next morning to the hill, he found to his great joy that what I had told him was true. We loaded the elephant which had carried us with as many teeth as he could bear; and when we were returned, 'Brother,' said my patron, 'for I will treat you no more as my slave, after having made such a discovery as will enrich me, God bless you with all happiness and prosperity. I declare before Him, that I give you your liberty. I concealed from you what I am now going to tell you.

"'The elephants of our forest have every year killed a great many slaves, whom we sent to seek ivory. God has delivered you from their fury, and has bestowed that favour upon you only. It is a sign that He loves you, and has some use for your service in the world. You have procured me incredible wealth. Formerly we could not procure ivory but by exposing the lives of our slaves, and now our whole city is enriched by your means. I could engage all our inhabitants to contribute toward making your fortune, but I will have the glory of doing it myself.'

"To this obliging declaration I replied: 'Patron, God preserve you. Your giving me my liberty is enough to discharge what you owe me, and I desire no other reward for the service I had the good fortune to do to you, and your city, but leave to return to my own country.' 'Very well,' said he, 'the monsoon will in a little time bring ships for ivory. I will then send you home, and give you wherewith to bear your charges.' I thanked him again for my liberty and his good intentions toward me. I stayed with him expecting the monsoon; and during that time, we made so many journeys to the hill that we filled all our warehouses with ivory. The other merchants, who traded in it, did the same, for it could not be long concealed from them.

"The ships arrived at last, and my patron, himself having made choice of the ship wherein I was to embark, loaded half of it with ivory on my account, laid in provisions in abundance for my passage, and besides obliged me to accept a present of some curiosities of the country of great value. After I had returned him a thousand thanks for all his favours, I went aboard. We set sail, and as the adventure which procured me this liberty was very extraordinary, I had it continually in my thoughts.

"We stopped at some islands to take in fresh provisions. Our vessel being come to a port on the main land in the Indies, we touched there, and not being willing to venture by sea to Bussorah, I landed my proportion of the ivory, resolving to proceed on my journey by land. I made vast sums by my ivory, bought several rarities for presents, and when my equipage was ready, set out in company with a large caravan of merchants. I was a long time on the way, and suffered much, but endured all with patience, when I considered that I had nothing to fear from the seas, from pirates, from serpents, or from the other perils to which I had been exposed.

"All these fatigues ended at last, and I arrived safe at Bagdad. I went immediately to wait upon the caliph, and gave him an account of my embassy. That prince said he had been uneasy as I was so long in returning, but that he always hoped God would preserve me. When I told him the adventure of the elephants, he seemed much surprised, and would never have given any credit to it had he not known my veracity. He deemed this story, and the other relations I had given him, to be so curious, that he ordered one of his secretaries to write them in characters of gold, and lay them up in his treasury. I retired well satisfied with the honours I received, and the presents which he gave me; and ever since I have devoted myself wholly to my family, kindred and friends."

Sinbad here finished the relation of his seventh and last voyage, and then, addressing himself to Hindbad, "Well, friend," said he, "did you ever hear of any person that suffered so much as I have done, or of any mortal that has gone through so many vicissitudes? Is it not reasonable that, after all this, I should enjoy a quiet and pleasant life?" As he said this, Hindbad drew near to him, and kissing his hand, said, "I must acknowledge sir, that you have gone through many imminent dangers; my troubles are not comparable to yours; if they afflict me for a time, I comfort myself with the thoughts of the profit I get by them. You not only deserve a quiet life, but are worthy of all the riches you enjoy, because you make of them such a good and generous use. May you therefore continue to live in happiness till the day of your death!" Sinbad then gave him one hundred sequins more, received him into the number of his friends and desired him to quit his porter's employment, and come and dine every day with him, that he might have ample reason to remember Sinbad the voyager and his adventures.